Reign
of the
Rat

Gil Smolin

ad lib
BOOKS LLC
www.adlibbooks.com

Published by:

ad lib
BOOKS LLC

Ad Lib Books, LLC
217 E. Foxwood Dr.
Raymore, MO 64083
www.adlibbooks.com

ISBN:0-9752976-2-7

Library of Congress Control Number: 2005922051

Books published by Ad Lib Books are available at special quantity discounts for sales promotions, premiums or fund raising. For information, please call or write:
Special Markets Department, Ad Lib Books, LLC
217 E. Foxwood Dr
Raymore, MO 64083
816-331-6160

Printed in the United States of America
First printing: May 2005

This book is dedicated to the real heroines,
Julie and Erica Smolin.

ACKNOWLEDGEMENTS

Ed Stackler and Carol Gaskin taught me about writing and more importantly about sharing and friendship. The wisdom and advice of Matt Bialer and his staff, Cheryl Capitani and Anna Bierhaus, kept me on the right path through challenging times. Jack Whitcher, my close friend, planted the idea for a plot that grew into a novel. The words of Fari Amini still guide my hand. Mary Theobald and Julie Henry's wise counsel directed me into the publishing world. My dear wife, Julie, taught me that a full life is lived by extending the boundaries and that learning is living. My young daughter, Erica, wishes to see the movie and I hope I can accommodate her.

prologue

The scorching desert breeze wafted across the Upper Sinai *wadi* and swept up into the hills, bringing with it the stench of decaying flesh. The smell nauseated Brother Jeremiah, who sat on the front steps of the venerable gray stone monastery on the mount.

He looked to the east. There, shimmering on the horizon in the midst of an infinite sea of undulating sand dunes, rose Jerusalem. Usually the city looked like a refuge in the desert, but lately the acrid smoke from the burning corpses blurred Brother Jeremiah's vision.

Wincing from the stinging fumes, the friar shifted his portly frame and cupped his hands in prayer. The winds were a cruel reminder of the blight visiting the land, a curse from heaven. But why was God so afflicting his chosen people? Perhaps, as had been prophesied so many years before, Armageddon had come at last.

Amen, Holy Father, amen. Rising from the steps, Brother Jeremiah retrieved the cedar bucket he had filled with fresh water and trudged down the hot, stony path, carefully finding his footing on the smooth cobblestones until he reached the outskirts of Jerusalem. Even on the city's level streets, his worn sandals slipped on the dusty pebbles. As he shuffled on the precarious stones, he recited his devotions and caressed the ancient crucifix around his neck. The metal amulet had been blessed by the Pope four hundred years earlier and presented to his order, the Order of St. Lazarus, when they were charged with caring for the sick. The holy object was meant to protect the brothers and he and the others believed that it had. So far, not one of them had fallen ill.

He patrolled the narrow alleyways, hoping to offer succor to his flock, but the people huddled in their homes, paralyzed with terror and grief. The good friar found only vermin-eaten bodies scattered on the otherwise deserted streets, an all too common sight.

Breathing heavily, he put down the pail and stood in the street, a lone, bent figure. With a swipe of his hand, he scattered a bevy of feasting rats, then moved the decaying body they had blanketed from the middle of the road to a sheltered spot against a stone building. There was so little he could do.

Brother Jeremiah placed a cloth over his nose, then continued to wander the streets, looking for someone who needed water. Whenever he heard the cries of women and children, or the violent coughing that, along with the fever, retching and bloody diarrhea, ushered in the final stages of the disease, he approached that house, but was always refused entry. No one dared to let anyone in.

When the last drops from his watering bucket soaked into the soil of his mountaintop flower garden, Brother Jeremiah stood up, ignoring the pain in his knees, and surveyed the two scraggly peach-colored roses. The sandy soil had resisted his efforts for the past seventeen years, but the fragrant flowers, however meager, brought to the otherwise barren place a hint of beauty and life.

He dusted off his hands and hurried toward the two makeshift tents a few hundred yards down the hill. Brother Jeremiah entered the first rectangular tent and scanned the rows of cots occupied by those in his care who now lay dying from the new scourge. A frenzied scream pierced the underlying chorus of wretched groans. One of the brothers had placed an incandescent iron rod on the grotesquely swollen lymph node of their newest patient. The burning of the pus-filled glands, as recommended by the local physicians, did not seem to prevent the ultimate outcome, the Black Death.

Swatting at the marauding flies, Brother Jeremiah approached an emaciated man wracked with violent coughing and chills. To try to calm the man, he grasped one of the two withered stumps that had once been arms.

The patient smiled weakly in gratitude.

Brother Jeremiah recognized the signs of death. When the man vomited, splattering most of the bed with green bile tinged with blood, Brother Jeremiah was neither surprised nor repulsed. He laid his cool hand over the man's eyes, made the sign of the cross and said, *"Per istam sanctam unctionem..."*

Touching the man's ears, nostrils, lips, hands, feet and chest, he repeated the anointing words of the last rites over each. When he accidentally pressed on the man's chest, one of the many large pustules covering the man's body ruptured, oozing foul-smelling green pus. Before he could stop himself, Brother Jeremiah recoiled. God must be testing his faith.

When he returned an hour later, the poor soul was no longer breathing. Brother Jeremiah bent to pull the sheet over the dead man's face, as he had done for a hundred others that week. When he did, he noticed something — something strange and amazing. The man's rashes had totally disappeared. The man was being cleansed of his lifelong affliction. God, in His infinite mercy, had performed a miracle.

Brother Jeremiah crossed himself and kissed the talisman. God had given him a sign of hope.

It was the Year of our Lord 1354 and the Black Plague was destroying civilization.

chapter one

SEPTEMBER 2004
BAGLUN, NEPAL

He had no time to rest, but Bhai, drenched by the incessant rain, stood barefoot in the muddy and infested water, gazing across the endless terraced fields of rice until they disappeared into the mist. Closing his eyes, he lifted his chin and allowed the prickling drops to massage the muscles of his young face. For the past five weeks, the warm rain of the summer monsoon had veiled the punishing sun. When he opened his eyes it was all still there; the vivid green terai of the Nepalese foothills, the only place he had ever known.

The rice stalks had to be picked; his family's survival depended on it. His parents, sister and older brother all had to work in the fields in order to make a living. In the best of seasons, they would reap barely enough food to survive the winter. Buddha and Shiva had not been kind the previous spring.

Bhai sighed. He would never be able to leave the village, like the schoolmaster's son, to go to Tribhuvan University in Kathmandu. Even the village leader's daughter had gone off to school. A girl. And Bhai's grades were better than either of theirs. He pushed the bothersome thoughts out of his mind. The rice had to be picked. Ignoring the throbbing ache in his lower back that radiated down his leg, Bhai bent over and began pulling the stalks.

A sudden knifelike pain sheared through him, and gasping, he fell to his knees, the muddy water splattering his face. The long monsoon and harvest season were destroying his body as never before. Would both body and mind rot in the never-ending fieldwork?

Despite his youth, the aching grew steadily worse and he couldn't imagine how he would continue this work for many more years. He would have to speak to his father about his back. Maybe he could get permission to see the Vedic medicine man when the traveling healer returned to Baglun. Villagers said the practitioner had cured the old beggar woman of her deafness.

Bhai remained on his knees, the only comfortable position left to him and continued picking the stalks. Crawling along, he peered over at the adjoining row and saw his father grimace, then look away. Illness could not and would not be tolerated during the harvest season.

Pulling out a handful of rice, Bhai noticed a deep cut on his middle finger. He turned his hand to examine the cut more closely and was surprised to see that two of his fingernails were gone. He patted the muddy ground, looking for them, and then realized the futility of his search. Many years ago he had heard a tale from his grandfather about rotting hands, when bad times tormented the valley, but he couldn't remember what it meant.

Refusing to surrender to despair, Bhai reached for more rice stalks. He would try to keep his hands as dry as possible when he was out of the fields and wait for the farm work to end with the arrival of the winter cold.

chapter two

Michael Cohen entered Wheeler Hall, a turn-of-the century brown brick building with depressingly small windows and a creaky oak floor. He wore his signature uniform: black t-shirt, black shorts and sandals. His wardrobe and long black hair provoked the students to whisper, only half jokingly, about the sexy professor and his decidedly less-than-sexy subject. That label was going to change today.

When the crop of new fall students settled into their seats, Michael announced, "Today we meet a disease that has brought suffering to mankind for thousands of years, since the dawn of recorded history."

He knew how to work an audience. It was one of his strengths — one he had almost forgotten. It was the one–on–one situations that were difficult for him.

Lately, he'd noticed his passion for teaching and his rebellious drive had started to fade; his lectures had begun to sound like dry renditions of old dissertations. Sometimes Michael wondered if he was wasting his time. While he explored the depths of science, the administration was slowly choking off his oxygen, sapping his fervor. Budgetary cuts to the University. Prioritization. Pragmatism. He'd heard it all. He had worked so hard for the department — over a hundred scientific papers, ten years of continuous federal funding and the discoveries in Norway, Eritrea and Italy.

Michael moved behind the lectern, opened his briefcase on the adjacent table and surveyed its contents. He had to be careful not to overdo his demonstration. It could be dangerous. But it was time to bring a message home to the arthritic hierarchy and these assembled students with their innocent, scrubbed faces.

His voice carried to the top of the lecture hall. "Not knowing is true knowledge. Presuming to know is a disease. First realize you are sick; then you can move toward health. So wrote Lao-tzu, two thousand five hundred years ago, at a time when Confucius, Buddha and the Tao flourished like lotus blossoms afloat on the cesspool of humanity."

He paused to see if the students were with him. They were. The word *cesspool* always got to them.

"The philosophies of these great men have not grown outdated," he continued. "People and their basic natures do not change with the roll of centuries. Technology can only take us so far. To move forward, we must first realize where we have been. To find cures for modern diseases, we have to understand the scourges of the past."

All eyes followed him as he strode to the top of the classroom, locked the door, then stood looking out over the sloping seats of the cavernous lecture hall as if he had just scaled Kilimanjaro.

"Ignorant of the past and its lessons, how dare we attempt to move forward?"

He felt his students' gazes and wondered what this latest group thought of him. He had once enjoyed a reputation as a young zealot who loved working in the field almost as much as he loved holding forth flamboyantly for Berkeley's best and brightest.

Not so for the last year or more. But today, he was going to stir their passion for research into the origins of disease by offering a lesson they, and he, wouldn't soon forget.

Returning to his desk, Michael's voice boomed over the students' heads. "Today, we investigate one of the most devastating diseases to ever afflict humankind. The Black Death. Many of you think you're immune to this horrifying disease, that it's extinct, that it poses no threat in your clean modern world. Right?"

The smirk on the face of an unshaven student with a twisted Oakland A's cap supplied the answer.

"Wrong." Michael pointed a finger at the cocky youth. "Dead wrong."

The student's look changed to a fixed glare.

Sweeping an arm to include his entire audience, Michael said, "It could happen again in the foreseeable future if bacterial resistance continues at the present rate. We've already identified staphylococcal germs that are resistant to all antibiotics. Patients infected with this germ are developing pneumonia and dying, *today*."

The rumble in the lecture hall told him they were ready.

"Open your notebooks."

The soft noise of hundreds of books springing open sounded like the flutter of so many butterfly wings, reminding him of a dig he'd worked on in the rainforest of Brazil.

Then silence fell. He had them. It felt like the days when he had first started teaching, when standing before a room full of young minds gave him an adrenaline rush. Once again, the familiar heat suffused his body, spread out from his solar plexus, shot through his groin. This was the old feeling, that nearly sexual burst of energy generated from love of his work — energy and heat he would transmit to his students. He remembered why he had once loved teaching, seeing the young faces of his students catch the fever of discovery.

Michael surveyed the contents of his briefcase again: a bone fragment, copies of ancient documents and two plastic blood agar plates. Like an alchemist's arcane tools, these things represented the best educational method he could think of employing to resurrect the old diseases that the archeobiologists studied. He paused for an instant to finger the bone fragment of a plague victim from the eighth century A.D. Most scientists thought his field was a dead science; the recovery and study of bacteria, viruses and parasites from past human life was not exactly the exciting stuff that spawned blockbuster movies. But archeobiology was *not* a dead science and he wanted the students and his boss, Roy Woods, to understand that. Never again would a group of his students walk away from one of his lectures unmoved, coolly closing their notebooks and making lunch dates.

They already knew the technical, scientific terms and statistics of the old diseases. He wanted them to go beyond objective knowledge and facts; he wanted them to know what life was like before antibiotics, disinfectants and vaccinations.

"Let's go back in time," he announced, twirling a hand. "Let's travel back to the Dark Ages — a time of ignorance, prejudice and disease. Infectious illnesses ran rampant then. Among them, one of the worst diseases ever to visit our planet — the Black Plague."

Michael emerged from behind the lectern. "The Black Plague, a heinous monster conjured up in the uncharted reaches of civilization — the Gobi Desert in the 1320s and brought unseen into society upon the backs of wild rats, who transferred the disease to their city cousins. In 1334, an epidemic that would eventually kill off two-thirds of China's people struck Hopei Province — five million people dead."

Michael strolled into the aisles, his voice rising.

"Carried along the trade routes, the Black Death worked its way west. At first, the plague attacked only the weak, the infirm. Eventually, the disease visited even the healthy and the strong. All were humbled before its onslaught. Kings and peasants alike shared the same horrid fate. The Black Death ravaged the clean and the filthy, the rich and the poor. It was a truly egalitarian monster."

Before Michael, the students sat in silent, rapt attention.

"As always, people looked for scapegoats. They attacked lepers and Jews, who were accused of polluting society and blamed for incurring God's vengeance."

Michael paced as he spoke, making eye contact with his students one at a time. "The Black Death was an incredibly contagious disease. It seemed you only needed to see a person who had the plague, and within three days you would be dead. Those infected developed an overwhelming pneumonia with high fever, vomiting, bloody sputum and severe chills. The pneumonic form of the disease involved the lungs and killed virtually everyone who contracted it. In the bubonic form, painful, large pus-filled lymph nodes covered the body."

A burly muscular jock-type in the front row shuddered visibly, as did several of the women.

"Most of the people in Europe died. But in time, the bacteria found its survivors too resistant or too scattered geographically to continue its reign of terror. Like a forest fire that burns itself into extinction, the Black Death smoldered and skulked away after liquidating *millions* of Europeans.

Michael paused dramatically. "So what caused the plague?" he asked. "Does anyone have any idea?"

A few hands shot up.

"Yes?" Michael said, pointing to a bearded student.

"The cause was multifactorial, Professor Cohen. One must include the overcrowding, extreme poverty, abundance of rats and— "

"Thank you for your insight," Michael said. "Those were all facilitators, but I'm on another track."

A disappointed look appeared on the student's face.

Strolling back to the table, Michael reached into his briefcase and extracted the two plastic blood agar plates. Carrying the Petri dishes, he walked slowly up the center aisle of the auditorium. An eerie, breathless silence pervaded the room. Every eye followed him.

"This, folks, is what caused the Black Plague," Michael stated loudly. "On these plates is the microorganism that killed those hundreds of millions of people. One quarter of the world's population. Not poverty, not filth. *Pasturella pestes,* now called *Yersinia pestes.* That's what caused the pestilence. Fleas feeding on the blood of infected rats spread this germ to humans when they bit them."

Michael raised the Petri dishes and several students recoiled.

"The germs in this dish came from a frozen corpse I found in Greenland during a dig last year. The body was that of a man who lived in the fourteenth century, according to the carbon dating. I cultured these germs from his intestines. In this dish are germs that were alive six hundred fifty years ago, wiping out villages and destroying civilizations."

"And yes, they're still alive."

Out of the corner of his eye, Michael caught the fearful expression of the student with the A's cap.

"These organisms, by aerosol, can still spread the plague. After coming in contact with these germs, breathing them, one would soon experience severe abdominal cramping, bloody diarrhea, pneumonia, rashes and black scabs all over the body. And finally, an excruciatingly painful death."

With these words, Michael removed the covers of the Petri dishes, exposing the red agar within, spotted with smooth, round white colonies of growing organisms. Innocent-looking carriers of death.

"Released into this room, these germs would spread all over you like an invisible swarm of bees."

Taking a deep breath, Michael lifted the plates over his head. Around him, several students gasped.

Michael hurled the plates through the air. When the dishes shattered on the steps, red globs splattered at the students' feet.

Like a wildfire in a strong wind, panic swept through the room. In front of Michael, a trembling young lady sat silently, her mouth agape, a look of glazed horror on her face. Next to her, a blond girl screamed. Behind Michael, a group of clamorous boys rushed to the locked door.

At the top of his voice, Michael yelled, "Stop!" The stampeding herd froze. "There's no danger. It's okay."

The students hesitated, then stopped to listen.

"No danger at all. Please. Sit down."

Warily returning to their seats, the students watched every step they took, avoiding the area around the broken Petri dishes.

"The plates only contained a harmless type of staphylococcus, a germ that grows on your skin. It may cause a zit or two, nothing more."

"Jesus Christ," the blond shouted.

The bearded boy said, "Are you crazy?"

Michael held up his hands in a gesture of surrender. "I wanted you all to feel a little of the fear and anguish that existed during the plague years. Rats thrived and people were scared to death, just like you. Some fled aimlessly. Others screamed, cried and panicked, like you did. People don't change. You reacted just like the people in the fourteenth century. You were there.

"I may have gone — probably did go — a little too far to show you that. For that, I apologize, but you did get the point."

Michael sat on the table next to the lectern. "The past has a lot to tell us. Archeobiology is alive. It's vibrant. It can teach us a great deal about our history. At the same time, it can teach us about ourselves." Michael nodded with satisfaction as he surveyed his students. A few were still angry, but he had their attention. "Together, hand-in-hand, we're going to venture into dark and terrifying places."

He was alive, soaring, his body infused with energy.

"And now, class, let us visit the time when the rats ruled the world."

chapter three

Alice Morgan-Wright squinted as the glaring late-afternoon sun angled in through the two picture windows of the World Health Organization laboratory. Even after a full year, the view amazed her. Below her lay Pokhara, Nepal, a city in a valley sheltered by the Himalayan Mountains. Ringed by the tallest mountains on earth, Alice had a feeling of isolation — but also of being protected from the madness of the outside world.

Off in the distance, perhaps fifteen miles away, the rocky snow-capped peaks soared into the clouds. Mount Annapurna, the 26,500-foot high monster, dominated the view. Nearer, covering the valley, rice fields blanketed the flatlands as well as the terraced slopes on either side of the valley. The water in the fields glowed in the bright sun like long rows of golden fluorescent bulbs.

She scanned the sky, searching. Almost every day she saw the hawk, his great wings carrying him high above the world. Again today she saw movement, just a speck at first, a lone figure circling upward on a thermal draft. Did he have a destination in mind? Or, like her, did he stay above the tumult, going where the currents carried him... watching, surveying the land?

She had fancied hawks her guardian spirits, ever since that day when the hot Tanzanian sun beat down on her face, and the native boy worked himself in and out of her unwilling body. The hawk had circled above them, no idle observer, calling to her, beckoning her to fly away from the contamination below.

Alice shook herself and turned from the window. She didn't want to think about the past. She leaned over the cluttered laboratory bench to examine the glass slides from the eyelid scrapings.

Being in Nepal was no accident, no whim, she reminded herself. She was where she belonged, like her father before her, helping the less fortunate. The Morgan-Wright tradition of service. Was it compassion or escaping mother's humdrum society life that drove her?

Solitude allowed Alice to pursue her work without emotional baggage weighing her down and without her mother's constant judgement. Even the low-tech lab pleased her. Not that the World Health Organization, the WHO, was happy with the set-up. No, they wanted state-of-the-art. They wanted the facility to look good.

For the most part, she ignored what they wanted. She didn't need the expensive fluorescent or electron microscopes that the WHO kept trying to convince her to requisition. She needed more technicians to read the chlamydial eye cultures and scrapings from the amiomycin- and placebo-treated groups, not more equipment.

The lab contained all that was necessary for her to produce extensive trachoma treatment results. The new antibiotic they were testing might cure the widespread and hard-to-cure chlamydia infections. Loss of vision and infant mortality from trachoma-induced pneumonia could some day be a thing of the past.

Alice studied the last of the slides. Koirala entered, his tall, slender body exhibiting its customary, almost feminine grace. Maybe his elegant bearing was a sign of class. After all, he was the Nepalese prime minister's nephew, from a wealthy family. Most importantly, he was a darn good technician. He'd been with her from the beginning of the amiomycin study. The two of them made an excellent team.

The lazy ceiling fan, a relic of a past era, lifted a few of Alice's notebook pages with a gentle riffling sound. Koirala hurried over to collect the pages, placing the book atop the table amongst the three black microscopes, the culture-viewing box, slides, notebooks and labeled brown solution bottles.

He leaned against the non-functioning air conditioner perched uselessly in one of the windows next to the two freestanding carbon dioxide incubators, two refrigerators and freezer.

"Anything new on the eyelid cultures?" Alice asked. She dabbed at the sticky hairs at the back of her neck that had come loose from her shiny blond knot of hair.

"No, Madam Doctor, today I am only finding the usual flora. No pathogens. I will check the throat cultures now. Dr. Wilson instructed us to re-check those cultures on a six-hour schedule."

Most of the natives here, like Koirala, spoke better Queen's English than she did. Her own British accent was diluted, mutated from spending four years at Sarah Lawrence College in the United

States. People said she sounded like a hybrid Ameri-Brit. That suited her fine. She felt more anonymous without the accent of her childhood announcing her as a moneyed, upper crust Englishwoman. Now, she thought, she sounded more like a member of the international medical research world. The true British accent sounded somehow stilted to her ears.

"I will be missing Dr. Wilson," Koirala said.

Until recently, Alice had a young British woman with a Ph.D. in epidemiology, Jennifer Wilson, assisting her.

Coming out of her reverie, Alice added, "She didn't want to go, but she had to get back to London. Her father's not well."

"Something bad?"

"Just old age. He wants her to take over the running of the Wilson Foundation."

"A great honor for someone so young. When does she start?"

"After she sees a strange case in Baglun, she'll be off to England and the job," Alice said.

Pointing to the incubator, she asked, "How many chlamydial eye cultures are cooking?"

"We are culturing everyone in the study area having red eyes, discharge and symptoms of infection, Madam Doctor. Dr. Wilson collected over one hundred and ninety samples before she left. About ninety are, as you say, cooking."

"What we really need to do is routine conjunctival scrapings on everyone, not just those who are symptomatic. And we should do it every four to six months. Don't you agree?"

Koirala sighed genteelly. "Yes, Madam. But to do it we will need two or three more technicians, especially if we look for the chlamydia bacteria in the babies with pneumonia."

"The WHO's pockets are full. They keep wanting us to spend more money. I'm going to strongly recommend we get more technicians. That's just one of the changes I'm going to suggest."

"Suggest, Madam?" Koirala asked with a slight smile.

"Oh, I may be a little more forceful than that." Alice grinned. Her technicians knew she could be demanding in her dealings with her bosses in Geneva. She hoped the staff respected her for her determination and unwillingness to settle for mediocrity.

From somewhere in the distance came the floating sounds of long

Tibetan trumpets accompanied by the parallel harmonies of chanting Buddhist monks. The sound and the view out the window called to her again as she caught a glimpse of a second hawk rising to meet the first.

"I need a break," she told Koirala. "I'm going over to the ridge. Call me if you find anything on the throat cultures."

Outside in the orange glow of the impending sunset, Alice strode past the row of bicycles in the rusted rack, then took the flat dirt trail that led to the ledge, several hundred feet away. She kicked up a swirl of dust with her hiking shoes, while around her mosquitoes swarmed and buzzed. After a year in Nepal, she had grown used to them. They rarely bit her.

Alice would miss her energetic, if idealistic colleague, despite Jennifer's domineering personality. Alice smiled to herself. Until Jennifer had arrived, she'd become accustomed to the almost musical flow of her native technician's speech. Hearing Jennifer's true-blue, aristocratic British accent opened up a wellspring of memories… memories of her mother, her family and Michael Cohen. Those memories, she was better off without.

Reaching the cliff's edge, Alice stopped to stretch her long legs and admire the glowing rays amidst the billowy cumulus clouds as the sun set behind the snowcapped Fishtail Mountain. Picking up a couple of pebbles, she rolled them in her hand, then tossed them into the wind.

When she re-entered the lab to help Koirala, he waved her over.

"Madam Doctor, there is something strange with these throat cultures."

"How's that?"

"We are entering our autumn flu season, and the number of children sick with URIs is always increasing at this time."

"The reports from the field indicate that. The rate is no different from the last few years."

Koirala nodded. "In the past we usually see many germs in these sick people."

"Of course. If it's bacterial, you would expect that."

"Now I am seeing less, Madam Doctor."

Alice shrugged. "Must mean it's viral."

"Fewer germs in everyone," Koirala insisted. "Not only the ones with colds."

"That *is* odd. Is this a significant number of cases you're talking about?"

"As I am saying, it is everyone in the study. In the few cultures I checked today, the lower count seems more pronounced."

Alice frowned at the dozens of piles of culture plates. "That means both the treated and placebo groups are involved."

"I believe that is so," Koirala said. "What does it mean?"

"Fewer germs?" Alice shook her head, mystified. "I can't think of any scientific, plausible explanation for it. It doesn't make sense." She walked over to Koirala and rested her arm on his shoulder. "Let's see the data."

chapter four

Bhai stood at the side of the rutted, dirt road, staring at his feet. Was this karmic retribution? Four toenails gone, disappearing silently like autumn leaves. Since he had to continue to stand in water all day for the next two months, he would certainly lose more of his nails. He was beginning to look like an old man, but more troubling was the fact that his water-wrinkled hands and feet looked strange, different. Was it the color of his limbs?

Splashing along in the mud on the shoulder of the road, Bhai caught up with his father, a broken, gray-haired man who was walking in front of his family, leading them back to their one-room hut.

Bhai bowed and asked permission to speak. His father nodded his assent. "I am having many problems with my back and my hands and feet," he said, extending his hands before his father.

After a cursory glance, his father said, "Yes."

"I was hoping to see the Vedic doctor in Baglun."

"We must work every day until all is finished."

"I can go with the schoolmaster Saturday morning and be home by afternoon."

"Is this agreeable with the schoolmaster?"

"Yes, sir."

Bhai's father nodded briefly and walked on.

Leaving the jeep, Bhai entered the world of new smells and noises that was the central market of Baglun. The odor of saffron and other spices permeated the air, perfuming the more familiar fecal smell. The crowds of people pressed in on him — women dressed in bright saris and men in tight gray pants, jackets and multicolored skull-hugging hats. Pigs and chickens roamed the streets, scooting amongst the people.

Bhai pushed his way toward the square, looking for the itinerant

Indian Vedic doctor. He had little time. The schoolmaster had to return within the hour.

He hurried past the never-ending row of vending stalls filled with herbs, chicken and pig parts, potatoes, cauliflower, mustard greens and rice and saw a crowd forming near the statue of Ganesh. In the center of the standing throng, below the smiling elephant god, sat the Ayurvedic physician in a lotus position, lecturing to the people.

"Good karma can be yours by prayer, sacrifice and good deeds. That is the way. Bad karma may be punished in life by the Vedic gods. The god Rudra can cause you pain; the god Agni, fever."

Displaying two thick hardcover books, he continued. "The canals that are moving out from the navel carry the rasos, the vital juices, to all parts of your body. When one of the winds in your body fails, bad juices form. These bad juices, doshas, cause the illnesses that I can cure."

He waved the dusty textbooks in the air. "These books, the *Rasa Vaisesika* and the *Atharvaveda,* hold the answers to all diseases. I have studied these and many other books for many years with the great gurus in Madurai and Madras. I can heal any of your ailments. Free of cost. It is my karmic duty."

One gentleman bowed, then sat facing the physician.

"I am having severe stomach pains. Here and here," he said, pointing.

The doctor placed his hand on the man's wrist and closed his eyes. After a minute, he said, "Good." He then put his hand on the man's stomach and slowly rotated it clockwise, then counterclockwise, three times. While doing so, he watched the man's face.

"Undigested nutrients. You are forming these. What you need is this herb." He removed a small tin can from his cloth bag and handed it to the man. "Five rupees. The cost of these unusual herbs from a special and distant place."

The man removed several coins from his pocket and handed them to the doctor.

"It is most important that you drink horse's urine. This *mutra* will be most helpful. Take this much every day for a month," he instructed, holding his thumb and index finger one inch apart.

When the man began to rise, Bhai slipped into the spot in front of the Ayurvedic healer. He heard several people curse.

The doctor smiled.

"I am losing my nails," Bhai said, extending his hand.

"That is an easy problem to solve. There is an obstruction of the body channels. All the doshas are involved — *vata, pitta* and *kapha*. But it is mainly the vata. You will need to eat lentils with your rice three times a day and drink goat's milk at least twice a week. In addition, these herbs will be most useful."

Pulling another small tin from his bag, he handed it to Bhai. "Five rupees."

"I do not have that. I only have twenty-five paisa."

A grimace flashed across the doctor's face. "Let the herbs be a gift," he whispered, snatching the coin from Bhai's hand. When he did so, Bhai felt a subtle pain.

The Vedic doctor gasped and dropped the money. Gaping down at his hand, Bhai saw the ends of two of his fingers had torn and blood oozed from the ragged wounds.

chapter five

What's Roy Woods up to? Was it the lecture?

Kicking off his Birkenstocks, slightly damp from his trek across the Berkeley campus, Michael ran his bare feet through Roy's plush, dark-green carpet, a mini-escape from a restrictive concrete world that threatened to wear down his free spirit.

Roy always delivered good news immediately, in person. The fact that he'd summoned Michael to the archeology department two days after the staff meeting suggested bad news.

Michael studied Roy's office, a cartographer's delight. The musty, overcrowded room was appointed with maps of ancient Greece and Egypt, cross-sections of medieval ships and curling photographs of colleagues on digs. A globe of the pre-Columbian view of the world stood in one corner, and shards of ancient pottery bearing chicken-scratch diagrams lay scattered like a puzzle on the table. The workplace of an archeologist.

Roy burst in looking like the absent-minded professor he was — clothes disheveled and mismatched, gray hair growing wildly in every direction and popping out of his ears like white cocoons, and a perpetually-startled expression.

"This has been one heck of a day," he said, tossing a handful of papers onto his desk. "And now this meeting. I don't know what to say, Michael. That lecture."

"Roy, it might have been *outré,* but I needed to make the subject live, the students—"

"That was not for the students. You did it to rekindle your own enthusiasm."

A saddened look crossed Roy's face. "And to make matters worse, I'm sorry to say, the archeology staff has turned down your request for funding of your new project."

"What?" Michael had expected a setback — another budget cut, sure, but this was a full-fledged disaster. "Because of the lecture?"

Roy shrugged wearily. "That didn't help, but Mother has to take into consideration the big picture."

Roy's referring to the University as "mother" always irritated Michael. "And what big picture is that?"

"The financial, as well as the scientific end of things. That's our responsibility."

"I'm this close to proving the dedifferential theory." Michael held his thumb and index finger millimeters apart. "Another year or two in the field and the lab..."

"Even if you succeed, then what? It's not even a marketable item."

"Marketable?" Michael said, his voice rising. "What does that have to do with anything? I'm talking about pure science — a major, basic discovery."

"I understand that." Roy's soothing tone didn't disguise his impatience. "But we have to face the fact that archeobiology is not a profit-making field and it never will be. There's just so much money your department can drain from the budgetary pool."

Michael threw up his hands. "You always knew that. Recovering the 1918 flu virus from frozen corpses in Norway wasn't marketable, either."

"The Longyearbyen project came at a time when we had plenty of funds and it was good PR. Now we have to be more circumspect."

"What's more important than explaining the evolution of diseases, the rise and fall of epidemics, the continual struggle between man and the surrounding microbial world?"

"We have to make hard choices." Roy preoccupied himself with the mess on the table. "There's not enough money in our budget for long shots."

Michael sighed with frustration. He had a good track record. In the past, most of his long shots had become reality with hard work and time. But he knew he should save his breath.

"It's a bullshit decision," he said.

"There's no lack of respect or support for your work. It's only a matter of financial priorities."

"Roy, administrative double-talk is beneath you."

Roy faced Michael's accusatory glare. "Dean Walker feels you should take on the Pfizer study. You're perfect for it. It'll bring in a huge donation, and the royalties might be invaluable for our department."

"You can't be serious," Michael said. "It's hack work."

Roy's lips tightened. "Maybe it is hack work, but if you don't do it, there's no chance you'll ever get your grant approved, and you'll never get the associate director's position, no matter how productive you are."

"I'm not the administrative type. I don't want any titles. Save them for someone who cares. I came here to do creative work, to teach and work in the lab. Unhindered. That was our understanding. Check our agreement, Roy."

Roy folded his arms across his chest.

"You're suffocating me." Michael pointed to Roy's desk drawer. "Check my contract. Marketability was mentioned nowhere. If it were, I'd have taken the Farberg job and made four times what I get here."

"The financial climate has changed."

Michael absently eyed a 1920s photograph of Howard Carter at the tomb of King Tutankhamen. He felt a pang of empathy for the boy-king. He, too, was being mummified by shortsighted administrators and bean-counting auditors. He had open-ended offers sitting on his desk from Hopkins, Yale and Harvard. He would have to rethink those opportunities. Despite his love for the Bay Area, his need to find meaningful answers to science's riddles took precedence over everything else.

Roy rested a hand on Michael's shoulder. "You came here as a rising star, a man destined to make a mark on the world. I was elated that you accepted our offer."

"And now?"

"And now, you tell me." Swinging an arm, Roy inadvertently swept several of the papers from his desk. "The situation is simple. If you want to keep moving up the food chain, you have to make pragmatic choices."

True, Michael was going nowhere in the academic rat race, but that didn't concern him; his work did.

"So mediocrity wins," he concluded.

"You have invitations to speak all over the globe," Roy answered. "Dr. Michalaki Cohen, the *wunderkind*. Make the most of it." His tone softened. "Help the department and we'll help you. Do the Pfizer work."

chapter six

The road was rutted and slippery, and her bicycle skidded sideways whenever she changed speeds. Standing up and pumping the pedals in order to move, Jennifer Wilson struggled on her trip from the Baglun bus station to the small village four miles away. After this "house call" it was back to London and her position with her family's foundation. Her tour of duty with the World Health Organization was finished.

When the rain began to fall again, the mud became like glue, clinging to the bicycle tires. Jennifer got off and slogged alongside the bike in the raging downpour that all but obliterated visibility for more than a few inches. Periodically, she paused to peel away the strands of her drenched blond hair that stuck to her forehead, and wring the excess rainwater from her khaki shirt.

Jennifer could see a smattering of huts looming in the distance. According to the directions, this should be the village.

Leaving the bicycle at the side of the road, Jennifer sloshed through the tall grass, past the rice fields toward the row of thatch-roofed stone houses.

She spied a lone figure performing a *puja* in front of a stone lingam situated at the nearest house.

"I'm looking for the village leader," Jennifer shouted above the noise of the pounding rain.

The man quickly completed his ritual offering, pointed to a large hut, then hurried off toward the rice fields.

"Hello, are you there?" Jennifer called near the entrance to the shack.

After a moment of silence, a tall, dark-skinned man with flowing yellow-white hair emerged, wearing a white t-shirt and a faded lungi. He glared at Jennifer as if she were a demon that had been conjured up by his enemies.

Jennifer clasped her hands in a salutatory manner and bowed.

"*Namaste.* I'm Dr. Wilson. The World Health Organization sent me to check on your health problems—"

"We are having no health problem."

"We had a report of fingers falling off..."

The man waved imperiously. "Bad nails, rashes. It is only a fungal infection. Nothing more. It happens every year at this time."

"Fingers falling off?"

"That is a fantasy. Thank you, madam, but we are having no need for outside help."

"It seems as if I made an unnecessary trip," Jennifer said politely, eyeing the rigid face of the village leader. She hesitated. "Are you certain that—"

"We are fine here. Thank you."

The village chief seemed unusually inhospitable. Not offering a visitor tea or a place to rest after a long trek in the rain? Something had to be amiss.

Jennifer turned to leave the village.

"Wait." A small man splashed his way across the path toward Jennifer, speaking rapidly in a shrill voice. "I am Mr. Uphad, the schoolteacher. I put the call in to Pokhara."

The village chief hurried past Jennifer to block the teacher. "Mr. Uphad is making a mistake," he said, pivoting to face her. "We do not need outside ... interference."

Jennifer met the pleading eyes of the teacher, who stepped determinedly from behind the chief.

"With your permission, Chief, I'd like to talk to Mr. Uphad."

The village leader glared at the schoolteacher. "I am thinking this will come to no good."

"I insist on talking with the doctor," squeaked Mr. Uphad.

"Of course, you can talk to anyone. I am only hoping that you think carefully about what you are planning to say, Mr. Uphad." The chief spun around and disappeared inside his hut, leaving Jennifer and Mr. Uphad standing alone in the pouring rain.

"Please understand," said Mr. Uphad apologetically. "It is crucial to the village that the harvesting not be interrupted. This must be the chief's primary concern."

The schoolteacher ushered Jennifer along the road, gingerly placing each foot into the muddy quagmire, watching protectively as she followed.

"However, we do have a problem," he continued. "Some sixteen people have developed deformities of their hands or feet. Twelve of these people have begun to lose their parts of their fingers or toes."

"Lose their fingers? How?"

"Picking rice causes sores on the hands. They won't heal. The fingers become infected, then easily tear or rip."

Jennifer's mind began whirling. *Leprosy?*

"Some of these people are also getting quite sick," the teacher added.

"Can you describe their symptoms?"

"Severe breathing problems, possibly pneumonia, fever, stomach cramps, bloody diarrhea, rashes."

Nope, not leprosy. That has a slow onset with none of the respiratory or other symptoms. Sounds more like... "When did all this start?" Jennifer asked, alarms going off in her head.

"Bhai, the boy, was the first. He lost some of his nails, maybe ten days ago."

"This whole business sounds quite contagious," Jennifer said, trying to sound casual. "Can I see this Bhai?"

The schoolteacher nodded as they passed through the village. After a few minutes of mud-laden tromping, they arrived at a particularly small stone hovel with a palm-thatched roof. Entering, Jennifer saw a bone-thin boy of about fourteen sleeping on the wet dirt floor in the corner. The water level in the shed was only slightly lower than outside as rain dripped through the sieve-like roof.

The teacher approached the boy and whispered, "Bhai, Bhai. It is me, Mr. Uphad." There was no response. Shaking the boy vigorously, the teacher awakened him.

Bhai yawned, stretched, and gazed about, wide-eyed. "Mr. Uphad? Are you there?"

"Yes, I'm right here. This lady is a British doctor."

"Lady? It's so dim. I cannot see you clearly."

The schoolteacher raised his eyebrows at Jennifer, clearly startled.

"It's raining," Jennifer said gently. "So you might ..."

Sitting upright, the boy stared straight at the two people standing five feet in front of him. "I can't see well." He rubbed his eyes, then swung his hand back and forth a few inches from his face. The tips of several fingers were missing.

"It's all blurry," he cried. "I can't see."

"He was losing his sight," Jennifer said over the telephone to Brian Mackenzie, head of the Peace Corps in Nepal. Sitting in the public telephone booth in Baglun, Jennifer dropped her voice, but continued insistently. "None of the others have lost their vision yet, but otherwise they are all following the same course. It's a blasted epidemic."

"Did you call Alice?"

"She's in the field. Won't be back for two days."

"I'll warn Alice. You get out of there," Brian ordered. "We need to start taking quarantine precautions."

"We need a WHO team. Right now."

"I'll contact both the WHO and Peace Corps. We've got to warn our field workers."

"Tell them Alice would be a natural to lead the team. She's a world-class microbiologist and only a few miles down the road in Pokhara," Jennifer said. She sighed. Here was something she could really get involved in, and she had to return to bloody England. "I wish I could stay."

"Alice?" Brian said. "Yeah, she would be great. I'll call Anton Koenig in Geneva. He's the WHO person who'd be in charge of something like this. I'll see if we can get her. And that Cohen fellow, the plague guy in the States. He worked with us in the Bangalore yersinia outbreak."

"Isn't Etienne Roche closer though, setting up a microbiology lab somewhere near Madras?" Jennifer asked.

"Etienne? I'll check my directory. Anyway, leave it to me, Jen. I'll round up a team. In the meantime, get the hell out of there!"

chapter seven

Sipping his pulpy orange juice at a wooden table by the large picture window in the Caffé Trieste in San Francisco, Michael replayed the scene of two days previous in Roy's office. How could they ask him to give up his work? Inhaling deeply, he absorbed the smell of fresh-brewed coffee that saturated the air around him. The cappuccino machine behind the counter hissed loudly, obscuring for a moment the Caruso aria playing on the jukebox in the corner.

Was the lack of funds his real problem or was it something much deeper, much scarier? Was he losing interest in his field? Outside, the sun beat down on narrow Grant Street, in the North Beach section of the city, with its funky used-clothing shops, coffeehouses, Italian restaurants, bakeries and delicatessens. Places that usually made Michael feel at peace and at home. But not today.

With his funding dwindling or cut off, he wouldn't be able to finish his work in Kaffa. Well, if they wouldn't give him the grant, he'd have to go to the places that would. Industry had been hounding him, offering unlimited salary, laboratory funding and space and an assortment of perks. Maybe he was foolish to opt for the noble path of teaching and doing unfettered research.

Standing to get a refill, Michael tossed off his bombardier jacket, then heard the clattering of dishes on the rickety tables behind him. When he turned, he found himself looking into the glistening eyes of Vera Sarkov, a former girlfriend, one of the four-month romances that had dotted his life but left him feeling empty.

Vera was thick-bodied in an athletic way and sturdy as a boulder. Shapely to be sure, but he liked her because she listened with her heart. Michael always thought it a necessity in her profession. The best physicians were good listeners.

"What's coming down, Mickey?"

Michael always wondered if she had learned her English from the American movies she was allowed to see in Russia during her medical school years. She reached around him for a cup of coffee, exposing her cleavage. Vera never changed.

"How's it going in your stuffy archeology department?" she asked.

"I gave a controversial lecture with bad results. I guess I didn't think it out."

"In Berkeley, where 'anything goes' it's hard to imagine."

"And Roy Woods keeps telling me archeobiology is a dying, non-money-making field that no one cares about it. It's just not sexy enough. He cut my funds again."

Vera rolled her eyes sympathetically. "All technocrats are the same. Like in Russia, they are stupid. As you like to say, 'No vision.'" She gestured toward her table. "Join me?"

Michael followed her and sat as she unbuttoned the rest of the white hospital jacket that covered her red silk shirt.

"Sounds tough," she said. "You still sitting every day?"

"Meditating? I stopped. But I did get away for my birthday, hiking in the Marin headlands. I wanted to be alone, to think about what's going on in my life."

"I think you're alone too much. That's the problem. What did you come up with?"

"No solutions, but it was relaxing. Peaceful. The sound of the Pacific Ocean pounding on the rocky shore, it was a perfect getaway."

"So what are you going to do?"

"I'm still getting great offers. Maybe I should leave Berkeley and go where I can do my work."

"The students will miss you. I'll miss you." Vera leaned forward, further extricating herself from her tight shirt.

Looking away from the tempting reminder of Vera's bounteous figure, Michael asked, "Anything new at the General?"

Vera retreated back into her jacket. "I'm stuck in the ER for the next six months. The two days on, two off routine."

"Sounds like a drag."

"You know, Mickey, why don't we get together and have a good little heart-to-heart? It's been a while. How about you and me have lunch on Friday?"

Michael hesitated.

"It's lunch. We'll only be talking... in public." Vera winked.

"Come on."

"Friday?" He smiled despite himself. "Okay. Thanks. I'll try to drop over."

"That's my *boychik*."

From her hard blue plastic seat in the emergency room at Mission General Hospital in San Francisco, Jennifer Wilson watched the frenetic activity around her. She had been waiting restlessly for almost three hours in the icy cold room. Twisting, turning, bending over, pacing, she tried to find a magical position that would alleviate her cramps.

Feeling quite ill, she'd had to make an unplanned stopover on the West Coast. Her return to London would have to be delayed.

To her left, a barefoot African-American man in a torn black t-shirt snored, the reek of cheap wine wafting toward her with every noisy out-breath. To her right, an ashen-faced Asian man in a gray suit removed a yellow-stained handkerchief from his attaché case and coughed into it.

Like sharks in a feeding frenzy, white-clad nurses and orderlies whisked about the room, snatching patients. Jennifer smelled the typical eau d'ER, nervous perspiration mixed with disinfectant. Or was the almost sweet scent of sickness coming from her own pores?

"Hector Lopez," the nurse behind the Plexiglas reception window shouted. "Lopez?"

Come on, call my name.

Daddy could get her preferential medical service, of course, but she hesitated to call him. It was the middle of the night in London. She simply had to sit and wait.

The first gut-wrenching wave of nausea had swept over her the previous night as she'd brushed her teeth in the foul-smelling communal bathroom in a shabby Kathmandu hotel. She'd blamed the food. Even after two years abroad, her clean British intestines weren't accustomed to the flora and fauna growing in the filthy environs of the developing world. She always carried home some new intestinal guests from her travels. She shouldn't have eaten lunch in that grungy café in Baglun; the vegetables were not served hot.

But this time, her gastric problem felt different. Worse. The bloody diarrhea and severe cramps had grown increasingly intense, when normally they would have passed by now.

Jennifer was frightened.

Half an hour later, the nurse behind the Plexiglas window called her name. She heard her and tried to respond, but the best she could do was wave her hand. Her mind started to blank out, and again she tried to call out. This time a guttural, "Here," escaped her dry lips.

The tidy Asian man next to her called out to the orderlies, directing them to Jennifer. She felt them lift her, then drag her down a gurney-cluttered corridor to a room. They slid her into a molded chair and left. A cold sweat swept over her, leaving another wave of nausea in its wake. She leaned her head forward toward her knees and tried to take slow, deep breaths. She knew the routine. It just wasn't helping. She started shivering; first her torso, then her legs. She looked around the tiny cubicle for a vomit bag and saw only a small white trash can to the left of her chair. She scooted it nearer with her foot.

A bleary-eyed nurse came in just as Jennifer bent over the can. The woman waited, pretending to scan the blank chart. When the heaving eased, she said, "Dr. Wilson? I'm Ms. Nagarian. I need to take your history and get some vitals."

The swarthy-skinned woman approached and sat. "When did this start?"

Jennifer tried to answer, but coughed instead, hacking up mucus. The nurse's eyes widened, and she slid her chair back to the curtained entrance to the room.

"When did—"

"I need a warm blanket. Please," Jennifer stammered. "The chills are getting worse." Even her voice shook. Hugging herself, she wished she had on her sweatshirt. She focused on her feet in her Trek sandals; her toes were turning blue.

The nurse hesitated, then pushed the intercom button and called out, "Hot blanket to interview room five." Then, in a quieter tone, she added, "It'll be here right away, Doctor."

Jennifer knew that a mere blanket wasn't going to do much good. The shaking increased, making her muscles contract with such force that pain shot through her limbs. Clenching her jaw, she tried to stop her teeth from banging against one another. She regretted not wearing something warmer than just a shirt, cargo pants and sandals — her uniform for long flights. She'd left her luggage at the airport.

Maybe she needed to walk, get the circulation up and flowing again. The nurse stared at her while she stood up, intending to pace back and forth across the little room.

"What's wrong?" Nurse Nagarian asked.

Jennifer's legs felt unattached to her body, foreign. It took all of her concentration to hold onto the gurney for support as she searched for her feet.

To keep her mind focused when she spoke to the nurse, she fixed her eyes on a brown mole on the woman's nose. "Just got back from Asia...WHO duty."

The nurse stood and approached Jennifer. "Do you want to lie down?"

"Need to walk to keep warm," Jennifer managed, panting. "Was fine until this hit me last night. In Kathmandu."

The nurse banged the intercom button. "Get me that blanket. Stat."

Jennifer halted her progress alongside the gurney. The cramp hit like a lance driven into her stomach. A groan, originating somewhere deep inside her, started to grow. It rumbled out of her mouth as she doubled over and dropped to the cold white floor, trying to grasp the bed for support.

"Help me," she pleaded, but she couldn't seem to focus on the nurse. She coughed again, and her body slid to the floor.

She heard the nurse call, "Dr. Sarkov — interview room five. Sarkov, stat to room five."

On the solid surface of the floor, Jennifer lay twisting, trying to escape the pain. It followed her. Something blocked her throat, making it impossible to speak, almost impossible to breathe. She curled into a fetal position. Still no air.

She was suffocating. She knew the feeling. She remembered snorkeling in Indonesia, her capacity for holding her breath for over one minute taking her far beneath the surface. Daddy had been impressed. Past that one-minute marker, the instinctive urge to gulp in air had taken over and forced her to burst above the water. That same urge slammed through her now. Still no air made it past her mouth.

She attempted to clear her throat by coughing. Nothing happened. She coughed again, and a warm liquid flowed out of her mouth. Her eyes tried to focus on the small puddle forming on the linoleum floor in front of her; it was unmistakably red — blood red.

From what seemed a great distance she heard the nurse screaming, "Code blue room five. Dr. Sarkov, code blue room five."

"Dr. Sarkov doesn't come on duty for another two hours," a voice squawked over the loudspeaker.

"Then get me another doctor. Any doctor. Stat."

Jennifer Wilson knew what that code meant, and it wasn't good. She wanted to tell the nurse something, something important, but her throat was blocked. She rolled over to her side, and the blood ran out of her mouth and streamed across her cheek onto the floor. It felt warm, almost comforting. Gurgling, drowning, she tried to wipe some of it away from her mouth, but more only followed. It ran out of her nose and mouth, an endless stream flowing like lava. Again and again, Jennifer wiped the blood away from her face, desperately trying to breathe in the precious air.

The door burst open and Jennifer saw a balding, freckle-faced man in a white coat bend over her. The doctor's image wavered in and out of focus. There was something Jennifer wanted to tell him, but she couldn't.

"I left her on the floor for CPR," the nurse said.

"Throw the gurney mattress onto the floor and let's get her on it." Jennifer felt hands lifting her.

"Dr. Wilson, I'm Dr. Marcus. Bill Marcus, the resident on duty. Can you hear me? We're moving you into a treatment room. Can you hear me? Dr. Wilson?"

Where is Daddy?

Bill turned to the nurse. "Get me some oxygen in here."

Jennifer couldn't talk; the air left her, and she felt herself pulled below a dark surface, darker than the waters of the sea in Indonesia.

chapter eight

The day began no differently than most. All the technicians arrived promptly at eight and the professional staff drifted in at varying times thereafter. Rowan Morgan-Wright wondered if the difference was due to the manner of payment; the technicians were paid by the hour, while the professional staff earned fixed salaries. She always arrived on time.

Sitting at a lab bench cluttered with notepapers and bottles at the Institute of Tropical Medicine in London, she held up a row of test tubes. They all held clear, straw-colored solutions. No growth.

She pushed several brown bottles aside and placed the tubes back onto the bench top, closed her eyes and ran her fingers through the snarls in her frizzy hair. *Failed again. What could be wrong?* The fusarium organisms refused to attach to the dermal cells.

Her technician entered the small room. "Anything growing, Dr. Morgan-Wright?"

"The tubes are clear. I suspect not."

"What next?"

Rowan wished she knew. She had been certain of success this time. The articles in the *Journal of Dermatology* gave almost cookbook instructions and yet... She wondered if the authors would intentionally leave out a crucial step in order to sabotage the work of their competitors. The Americans were capable of that, especially the group in Chicago. Unethical, the whole lot.

Rowan answered, "We've seen the attachment in tissue culture, haven't we? We shall have to go back to that step and reevaluate..."

The intercom system rang out, "Dr. Morgan-Wright, telephone. Line three."

"Pull those fungal tissue cultures from the incubator, could you? I shall be right back."

Striding from the lab in her squeaky, patent leather shoes, she picked up the phone in the hallway and heard her sister Alice's voice.

"Rowan, how are things at the Institute?"

Rowan wondered how her sister always managed to call when her life was going badly. She would not tell Alice the truth. She didn't need any false sympathy at the moment.

"Everything is going swimmingly. How about you? How's the trachoma work? Amiomycin the answer?"

"We haven't broken the key."

Rowan felt relieved that she didn't have to cheer yet another of her sister's successes. Suffering with an older, taller, elegant and brilliant sister — their parents' favorite — had been a constant blight on her life.

"I'm calling for a different reason," Alice said urgently. "An outbreak of some unusual disease has just erupted in the area. I've been asked by the WHO to form a team to investigate."

Another feather in Alice's cap. "So?"

"I'd like you to be part of the team. With your knowledge of microbiology, computers and fieldwork, I think you'd be invaluable."

Rowan flushed, unabashedly pleased by her sister's praise. "It might be hard to leave. We're quite advanced in our work."

"Come on, Rowan. It would be great to work together. Etienne Roche is coming."

"I don't know ..."

"Please. We need you. *I* need you."

Rowan looked into her lab at the technician removing the tissue cultures from the incubator. All she saw was a dead-end. "It might be quite difficult to arrange, but you can count on me."

"Great. I'll need you ASAP."

"I'll speak with Buckley. I might be able to leave within a fortnight ...possibly sooner."

After replacing the phone, Rowan stood motionless, racking her brain. Try as she might, she couldn't remember any other time in their difficult past when her sister had asked her for help.

No Etienne Roche. Alice scanned the Kathmandu airport entranceway, but could make out only a sea of brown and black faces.

When she'd accepted the Baglun investigation, she had insisted that Etienne be part of the group. He knew Asia and the exotic diseases of the area, and they had worked well together in Tanzania on a WHO project.

She continued to search for him as crippled beggars tugged at her feet, taxi drivers yelled at her and porters pushed, hitting her with the luggage they carried. She forged through the throngs of sweaty people, toward the airline check-in counters, their prearranged meeting place. The flight to Pokhara would leave in twenty minutes and Etienne was nowhere to be found.

As a wave of claustrophobia gripped her, Alice decided to forget about meeting him at the counter and make her way to the gate. Even though she'd worked in the developing world for five years, the crowds occasionally got to her. Just then, she saw the back of a tall, dark-haired man walking in front of her.

"Etienne."

The man turned, a grin forming. Alice ran over, embraced him and gave him a kiss on his beard. He maintained the embrace and reciprocated with intense kisses on both of her cheeks.

"How's one of my favorite people?" Etienne said. "You look glowing. Field work seems to only enhance your beauty."

"I doubt that. But it's great to see you."

"Same here. When Mackenzie called about this emergency job I was elated that you were running this business."

He hadn't changed — still the good old doting Etienne, though she saw a frosting of gray in his hair and beard. They walked arm-in-arm, her long-legged strides matching his, reminiscing about their Peace Corps-WHO tour. After he had rescued her from the boys in Tanzania, he had stayed close by writing letters, acting like a loving guardian protecting his damaged ward.

Sometimes she wished he would behave more in character, like the forty-five-year-old WHO pediatrician colleague he was — married, with a wife and two kids.

The flight from Kathmandu to Pokhara was uneventful, a blessing on any flight on Royal Nepal Airlines. At the Pokhara airport, Alice and Etienne once again had to fight their way through hordes of people. The summer monsoon had tapered off, and the sun beat down mercilessly. Alice wiped away the sweat forming on her face, then fanned herself.

The crowds, poorer than those in Kathmandu, were dressed both in suits and dhotis. Beyond the airport, people in rags searched the garbage piles in the gutters for food. Pigs and wild dogs rummaged alongside them. The stench of feces filled the air. Mothers gripping emaciated children with runny noses extended skeletal hands for rupees.

Alice strolled along with Etienne in the dry, eighty-five-degree weather, tossing worn bills into the beggars' cups while they walked the gauntlet on their way to the city. As usual in the developing world, her height, light skin and European bearing attracted attention.

Alice never failed to marvel that the inhabitants of Pokhara seemed to spend their entire existence outdoors. As always, the streets were mobbed. She noticed that many people stared at Etienne. A six-foot-three-inch white man with gray eyes and graying hair, he had no problem standing out. In this setting he looked like a wandering ghost.

"How's Rowan?"

Alice shrugged. "We haven't seen each other for more than a year, and no matter how hard I've tried, we're still not close. I've asked her to join our team."

"That should give you an opportunity to improve the relationship."

Alice hoped so. She loved her jealous and unhappy sister.

Spying a barefoot, elderly man eating an orange on the rusty fender of a dilapidated black taxi, Alice motioned Etienne to follow her, but he ran ahead. Old-fashioned chivalry.

"Do you speak English?" he yelled.

The small man stared at him with bits of orange showing through his few remaining teeth, no doubt alarmed by the appearance of a towering, stern-featured giant.

"If you do, would you please take us to the center of town?" Etienne commanded.

"Our camp is situated on the outskirts," Alice corrected, amused. "I can direct him."

The man dropped his orange peel and picked up Etienne's valises. Etienne tapped the man's hand, then grabbed his luggage. "I'll handle the bags. You take care of the driving," he said, winking at Alice.

Alice always enjoyed the evening breeze as it swept through the open window and door-holes of the dining tent, cooling the room after the oppressive heat of the day. She surveyed the fifteen staff members of the emergency WHO-Peace Corps Team, seated around one of the two long wooden tables inside the tent. On the left side sat members of the technical staff, locals, mostly; on the other side sat the professional staff. Alice wondered why they always preferred to separate. Was it timidity, social stratification or comfort?

She glanced toward Etienne, who, like a needy Teddy Bear, grinned at her through his trimmed goatee. She checked her watch.

When Rowan finally sidled into the tent, she cleared her throat, waiting for the conversations to die down. "I'm sorry I couldn't be here sooner. I had a great deal of work, still unpacking."

A show of independence from her younger sister.

Etienne smiled.

Alice silently watched her sister kiss Etienne, a little too warmly, then find a seat. Rowan looked disheveled, as usual, but Alice had always envied her sister's lush, curly hair, a gift that Rowan characterized as "frizzy." Alice's own dark hair was broom-straw straight, and had to be corralled into a braid or chignon to stay out of her eyes. She sighed indulgently. Her sister could be so pretty if only she would stand up straight and buy some clothes that flattered her plump figure.

Alice stood to make the announcement most of the team members expected. "Over the past three days, eleven people have died from a bloody pneumonia and diarrhea. Some only twelve miles from Pokhara," she began. "The area from Baglun to Pokhara is going to be quarantined." She paused. "No one in, no one out, except for emergencies."

"What are we going to do with the sick people?" Etienne asked.

"The worst cases are being isolated and hospitalized at Green Pastures Hospital and in a wing of the local Pokhara Hospital."

"And where are the cultures and scrapings?"

"We've obtained lots of material from the raw ends of the fingers and toes," Alice told him. "The scrapings are being prepared now and the cultures are still cooking."

"How long do you suppose it will take to find the organism?" Rowan asked.

"Probably not long," Alice answered confidently. "We've got lots of material, including tissue."

Koirala looked up from the field lab's microscope to meet the
expectant faces. "Nothing."

"What do you mean nothing?" Rowan asked.

"There's sufficient tissue, but I am seeing no pathogens. Not a
one. The scrapings we took from the fingers and toes are being all
negative on the Gram stain."

"That's totally impossible," Alice insisted.

"I checked all the slides twice, Madam Doctor. I'm being quite
certain."

Etienne shook his head. "I'll get the cultures. They have to show
something."

He strode to the incubator and pulled out two trays piled high
with Petri dishes. Placing the trays on the lab bench, Etienne, Alice,
Rowan and Koirala sorted the agar plates into groupings. All the blood
agar plates were to be read by Alice, all the mannitol salt, chocolate,
Lowenstein-Jensen and other special media plates by Koirala, all of
the cooked meat and other broth solutions by Etienne and all the
Sabouraud's media by Rowan, the expert on fungal infections.

Alice and her three colleagues sat quietly on their stools, uncovering one plate at a time.

After lifting off the top of the first plate, Alice examined the dish
carefully under a low-power magnifier in order to identify the
different types of cellular colonies. She saw only two, both white-
colored. Using her small metal spatula, she removed some of the first
colony and spread it onto a glass slide. She labeled the slide, flamed
the spatula to kill the live germs, allowed it to cool, then removed a
small sampling of the other type of colony and repeated the scraping
procedure. After collecting six labeled slides, Alice passed them to
Koirala, who directed several of the Nepalese technicians to stain the
material for examination.

"In addition to the Gram stain, do the Wright's stain and the five-
minute Diffco on my slides," Alice instructed. "The silver stain and
KOH for the fungal—"

"Please, don't worry. I have the WHO protocol for staining,"
Koirala said, flashing his best half-moon smile.

Alice continued the process with the rest of the blood agar plates
until she had examined all of them and removed all the varieties of
colonies for testing by Koirala and his team. Then she moved over to

help Rowan finish with the last four of her Petri dishes.

"Not much growth," Rowan said. "We'll have to incubate these plates for a couple of weeks to make sure we don't miss anything, don't you think?"

Turning to Koirala, Alice asked, "Anything?"

"So far only normal flora. Some staph, diphtheroids, no pathogens."

"With all the disease, you'd think there would be some growth. What's happening with the viral cultures?" Alice asked Etienne.

He pulled a stack of plastic trays from the incubator. "I checked these a half hour ago."

"By yourself? So fast?"

"Wasn't much work. Koirala was right. There was no growth. The sheets of cells were unaffected ... unbroken." He frowned in puzzlement. "This is going to be more difficult than we thought. I'll have to call Mac in Kathmandu and tell him I'll be here longer than a couple of weeks."

"How can these people be dying from an infectious disease, and yet we see no viral, fungal or bacterial pathogens on culture?" Alice wondered aloud.

Koirala shook his head and shrugged. "What do we do now?"

Looking past Koirala, Alice saw the same question etched on the faces of all of her staff.

chapter nine

The vibration of his cell phone against his hip interrupted Michael's talk on cholera. Surreptitiously extracting the gadget from its belt-clip holder, he maintained eye contact with his audience. He didn't want to lose the connection. His students had forgiven his excesses and now laughed about "The Lecture." The students of Archeology 4.1 were now fully engaged in exploring the survival efforts of the people of Europe and Asia who had been attacked by deadly germs during the Middle Ages.

Michael checked the caller ID. Vera. Calling about their Friday lunch so soon? He would call her back.

The phone continued to buzz every fifteen seconds. On the third call, Michael dismissed the class and answered the page. Vera wouldn't disturb him at work unless it was important.

"Mickey, I need you immediately. Come to the General ER."

"What's wrong? Are you OK?"

"ASAP."

Weaving through the din and hyperkinetic activity of the Mission General Hospital ER, Michael asked the receptionist for Dr. Sarkov. She waved him away and yelled into the loudspeaker, "The Code Blue in treatment room two is now a Code Red."

A terminal infectious disease case. Wonder what's in season?

He waited in the eye of the storm, watching the swirling scene until Vera danced by.

"Mickey, thanks for coming," she said. "This morning has been hell. A nightmare. Come with me." She grabbed his arm before he could answer and pulled him down the gurney-crowded hall.

"A WHO epidemiologist, Jennifer Wilson, arrived this morning from Nepal," Vera explained as he trotted to keep up with her. "She had chills, fever of a hundred and four and ... "

Entering the treatment room, Michael saw three doctors and orderlies bent over a limp body lying on a bed. One of them looked up.

"Did CPR, Vera," said the man whose photo-ID tag identified him as Dr. Bill Marcus. "We're using the mask and pressure bag."

Michael stared at the frothy blood oozing out of the woman's nose and mouth.

"The aspirator never cleared her. Lungs solid shut, like a blood-logged sponge. She's suffocating."

"Start an IV," Vera ordered. "Connect an EKG and call the respiration therapist on duty."

Bill frowned. "It's a waste of time. It's hopeless."

Turning to Michael, Vera said, "We found out she's some British high muckamuck's daughter. He's been calling every five minutes since we notified him. He's taking a private jet from London. Be here tonight."

Fever, chills, bloody pneumonia? Michael walked over to the unconscious woman and rolled up her sleeves, exposing a morbilliform rash on both forearms. He remained silent for a moment, his heart pumping rapidly.

What the hell is going on?

It looked like … no, it couldn't be. A frightening coincidence. But all the signs were there.

He looked up at Vera. "I'm not sure this is possible, but whatever she's dying of looks a hell of a lot like the pneumonic plague."

"The *what?*" Vera exclaimed, wide-eyed.

"The Black Plague."

The laboratory was as warm and humid as a greenhouse. The windows overlooking Twenty-Third Street dripped with moisture. Michael wiped his sweaty forehead while he stood with Vera behind the Mission General Hospital laboratory technician, waiting for the material on the slides on the black marble table in front of them to stain.

When the timer went off, the technician rinsed the slides, heat-fixed some, and left the others to air-dry. Placing an oil drop atop the first slide, he put it under the microscope, turned to Michael and nodded.

Michael looked through the eyepieces and noted artifactual debris and red blood cells scattered throughout the slide. Scanning several microscopic fields at higher magnification, he saw something else that stood out as being highly unusual; there was almost no bacterium on the slide.

"Did you do viral and fungal cultures?" he asked.

"All negative." The technician added, "In my twelve years in the lab, I've never seen someone with a bloody pneumonia have a negative sputum culture. It's bizarre."

Next, Michael studied the slides taken from specimens of Jennifer's blood and stool. He examined slide after slide under low, high and oil magnification, but they, too, were devoid of pathogenic organisms. He sat back and rubbed his neck. "Damn, there's nothing."

If the disease was an infectious process — and Michael was certain that it was — it had to be caused by an unusual microorganism. But what?

Only the readout of the DNA analysis remained. Michael moved past the technician, slid his rolling chair along the laboratory bench and stopped in front of the DNA Analyzer. He punched the printout button, and the paper started to unroll like a ticker tape. Michael groaned.

"Is it the plague?" Vera asked warily.

"No."

"What is it then?"

Adrenaline charged through his body. He paused, trying to calm himself. He needed to make sense out of the readout.

After sitting silently for a few moments, staring at the coalescing drops on the window, he wiped his forehead. "This is impossible. There's nothing growing. Nothing at all."

chapter ten

It was too much to bear. He clutched the bittersweet letter he had received a mere two days ago saying that his daughter was in good health and looking forward to returning to London. The telephone call, a stranger telling him that Jennifer might not survive her bloody pneumonia... so cold and impersonal. His daughter, his legacy, the future of the Wilson Foundation being taken away.

Paralyzed with grief, Sir Hilary Wilson sat somberly on the quilt chest at the foot of his four-poster bed.

His personal secretary, Winston Reimer, knocked softly on the door, peeked in and then perched beside him. He was a skinny man, unable to sit still and he used his bony, spider-leg fingers to produce a staccato accompaniment to his words.

"We must leave shortly, sir." His fingers crept along his legs. "Your jet will be ready to depart within the hour. "

Sir Hilary thought Reimer looked like someone out of an earlier century, with his pressed black suit and hair parted in the middle of his scalp. One of the first to join Sir Hilary's team since he formed the philanthropic Wilson Foundation, Reimer had remained enthusiastic and faithful, carrying out all of Sir Hilary's needs without question. *Rare traits in anyone these days.*

Sir Hilary stuffed Jennifer's letter into his vest pocket. He was going to save his beloved child.

"Call Dr. Harkins immediately and find out who the best infectious disease experts in San Francisco are."

Moving out of the bedroom and into his office, Sir Hilary walked over to his seventeenth-century mahogany desk, where he scanned the row of photographs lining its perimeter. His eyes fell upon three pictures in particular. In one, he stood erect, looking proud and distinguished at the dedication of the medical school library in Oxford he had built to honor his mother. Another showed Jennifer sitting on his lap in front of a Hindu temple in Madurai, in southern India. After his wife had died during childbirth, he'd taken Jennifer with him on all his trips. His daughter had been nine the year they'd spent working in a Hyderabad hospital as part of a Christian mission for the Wilson Foundation.

Now she was dying. All the women in his life might be gone before the day was out.

The last photograph, taken just hours before Jennifer left Kathmandu for her two-year assignment in Pokhara caught the resolute set of her shoulders while she loaded a Jeep with medical supplies.

Sir Hilary picked up the pot of tea his butler had placed on the desk and poured a cupful.

Would she still be in good health if he had insisted she stay in London and cease her dangerous fieldwork? The question swirled behind his eyes, but no answer arrived to give him solace. He let the vision of Jennifer's leaving sweep over him as he closed his eyes to the photographs and the pain they now elicited.

Sir Hilary raised his delicate teacup and examined his hands. The arthritis, unusually severe for a man of fifty-six, made his hands looked like he remembered his grandmother's — crippled, distorted claws that frightened little children and gave them bad dreams.

"Excuse me, sir." Reimer materialized from the shadowy hallway. "I have the names you requested. A Dr. William Endicott at the University of California and a Dr. Michael Cohen at Berkeley."

"Place an emergency call to both of them at once. They have to help my girl survive."

Sipping the last of the Earl Grey tea, Sir Hilary toasted the line of photographs.

He was going to save his daughter.

The president and majority stockholder of Farberg Pharmaceuticals Limited, Erik Bittner received few visitors except for the staff who helped him run his estate and the Board members of Farberg. Sitting behind his oak refectory-style conference table, he now held court with six of the Board members. Only five-foot-five inches tall, Erik was, at close to three hundred pounds, a huge man. With his round, flushed face and perpetual grin he looked like the European version of the Happy Buddha.

After taking a sip of his coffee, Erik leaned back and stared at the dark beams on the ceiling. Strong, supporting, yet rarely noticed. He lowered his eyes, focusing on the group.

"The data sheets indicate that our losses will be rather large this year, greater than last," Erik said in his deceptively sweet voice.

"The sales from our antibiotics are sluggish. Competition is fierce," Max Karpman, the Chief Financial Officer, reported.

Erik nodded. Despite their business differences, his balding, hunched-over friend had served him well for a long time. "Competition has always been intense and we remained profitable," Erik noted. "For the last few years we've become lazy, lacking in initiative and creativity."

"We have great hopes for the amiomycin study in Nepal," the Chief Science Officer answered.

"Inconsequential. Who has trachoma? The poor. This study is a waste of our assets."

"The WHO and the individual countries will buy the drug if it is effective," Max pointed out.

"Nonsense. Get our researchers to find a new mood enhancer. Something like that." Erik shifted his obese frame in his seat.

"It's not our area of expertise," Max objected. "The company has been producing antibiotics for forty years. Incidentally, we just received an inquiry about research funding from the elusive *Herr Doktor Cohen.*"

"Is he doing anything profitable?"

"Mainly basic conceptual work."

"Make contact. In the meantime, get me a new mood enhancer."

"We know antibiotics."

"I wish you knew finances."

The CFO opened his mouth but did not speak.

"Leave the nonprofit work to the Red Cross." Erik pushed himself up from the chair and felt a pain flare along the nerves in his lower back. He could tolerate physical pain, but not incompetence. Farberg needed a shakeup.

"I'm exasperated by the losses on my investment," he said softly, "and by lame excuses. I want positive results."

Silently, the men watched Erik.

"And I want it before the next meeting... or we shall see a new set of faces sitting at this table."

chapter eleven

Slumped in their seats, the staff sat in a semicircle around Alice. No one spoke. Alice gazed out the window of their hurriedly assembled field lab, watching the puffy clouds, which seemed to erupt from the peaks of the Himalayan Mountains.

"It can't be," Etienne said. "No pathogens growing on any media?"

"What more can we do?" Koirala asked.

Alice closed her eyes, picturing the protocol for identifying an unknown organism. She had committed that page in *Bergey's Manual* to memory many years before in graduate school at Cambridge. The painful truth was that there was little left to do.

She popped her eyes open. "We have to start antibiotic therapy."

"And treat what?" Rowan asked.

"I know we don't have the organism yet, but we can't wait to find out what it is," Alice answered.

"If we start treatment, we will never find out what it is," Rowan snapped, standing up in agitation. "The antibiotic will ruin all of our future cultures and scrapings."

"I know what the textbooks say. But we have no other choice. People are dying."

"Alice is right," Etienne echoed. "We must act."

Rowan frowned, but didn't object. "How do you plan to treat this unknown organism?"

"With broad-spectrum antibiotics," Alice answered. "Shotgun therapy."

"That sounds perfect," Etienne said.

"We have to be certain that the something we do is correct," Rowan said. "What antibiotics are you going to use?"

Good, she's on board, Alice thought. "Ciprofloxacin."

"There's the fungus possibility," Rowan pointed out.

"What do we have available?" Alice asked Etienne.

He gestured at the boxes of supplies lining the makeshift shelving in their rudimentary lab, cobbled together from the facility used for the trachoma study in Pokhara. "We have amphotericin, but it's pretty toxic."

"Use it. Let's start with those two drugs and see the response," Alice advised.

"Have you read my 'Quantitative Resistance Theory'?" Rowan asked acidly.

"Of course," Alice replied. She hadn't really — well, she'd skimmed it — but that counted, didn't it? "But maybe you could summarize it for the benefit of the team."

"It was my doctoral thesis." Swinging her arms rhythmically, Rowan paced the floor. "The greater the effort to eliminate an organism, the greater the effort made by that organism to survive. Unless you totally wipe out the causative germ, you will eventually be faced with an even more deadly enemy."

Etienne grimaced. "Perhaps. Nevertheless, we have to treat this disease now."

"I understand," Rowan responded. "Let me clarify. Unless we *totally* eliminate this germ, we will be faced with a worse situation."

"Worse than this?" Koirala waved an arm toward the pile of unhelpful Petri dishes.

Rowan stopped walking and held up her hands like a traffic officer. "*Much* worse. The world already has a deadly staphylococcal germ that is resistant to all antibiotics. We're no longer talking pimples and sties; this form of staph can cause a deadly pneumonia. And its resistance is due to indiscriminate use of antibiotics — penicillin and the like."

"Bacterial resistance has always—" Etienne began.

"*All* types of organisms respond this way," Rowan interrupted vehemently. "Plants, even humans. It's universal."

"That's true" Alice concurred.

"Look, we let Saddam Hussein survive in 1991, and no one doubts that he became a more virulent enemy than before. And Kosovo. The surviving Albanians in Kosovo are much more dangerous than ever before. It's endless."

"That's been human nature since recorded history." Etienne shrugged, looking at Alice.

"That, my dear friend, is also bacterial nature since recorded history," Rowan stated flatly. "Your risky shotgun therapy had better work."

Alice pulled a crumpled piece of paper out of her pocket, unfolded it and ran her hand over it to press out the wrinkles. Working in the developing world could be rewarding, but also fatal. *The nightmare in Tanzania and now this.*

"There's more bad news," she whispered. "I received a fax from the WHO today informing me that Jennifer Wilson is in isolation in a hospital in the States. She's dying."

"Your tech? *Mon Dieu.*" Etienne gasped. "What happened?"

"A severe infection. A bloody pneumonia, not unlike some of the Baglun cases."

Rowan's face darkened. "What caused her infection?"

"The doctor didn't say. I requested that information."

Jennifer had gotten too close to the disease.

Alice stared out the window again at the spreading, dispersing Himalayan clouds. She pictured Jennifer walking through the airport, on the plane, in the streets of San Francisco, in the hospital… Her mind traveled to the horrific image of the Baglun outbreak spreading, dispersing, indiscriminately invading the United States.

The heavy rain made the farm work particularly grueling. The pulling of the rice stalks had been much more difficult than usual. By the time he returned to his home in the center of the city of Pokhara it was six in the evening and Shakar was sapped of energy. All he wanted to do was dry off, eat dinner and relax by listening to music on his small radio, a source of great pleasure for him. He felt especially tired after taking care of his visiting relatives from Baglun. Such a talkative and bothersome group of people.

When he entered the low thatched doorway of his hut, he was irked to find that his dry clothes had not been laid out on his seat. He took a deep breath, but didn't smell the usual aromatic spices associated with his rice dinner. Instead, a strange odor filled his house. Taking a few steps toward the kitchen area, he noticed the lack of food on the floor mat and the cold heating plate.

He heard faint noises coming from the second room. Removing

his squeaky sandals, he silently approached. What he saw when he pushed aside the hanging straw door made his heart quicken.

Inside the dim room, both his daughters lay sleeping on his floor mattress. His wife, kneeling beside them, sobbed quietly. She looked up when he entered, tears running down her face. Walking closer to the bed, Shakar saw that his daughters' pale faces were partially caked with a brown crust. Seeing the amber-colored bottle on the box that served as a bedstand, he walked over and picked it up. The label had several long, difficult words, but he recognized the doctor's name at the bottom. He put the bottle down and stared at his beloved children while his wife continued to weep next to them.

How could this be? They had both seemed fine when he'd left in the morning. They'd had colds for the past few days, but nothing unusual for this time of year. He turned toward his wife for an explanation, but she shook her head helplessly and remained silent.

Shakar's youngest daughter moaned, then coughed. Almost simultaneously his eldest daughter, Didi, began choking, her eyes opening wide with fear. She tried to cough, attempting to clear her airway, but no air would pass. Finally, Didi's coughing cleared the obstruction from her chest. When Shakar moved closer, he saw the bloody, pea-sized clot on her dress. Her chest rose and fell quickly as she gasped for breath. Looking back at Didi's face, Shakar gazed at a stream of blood oozing out of the corner of her mouth.

His wife began to cry.

There was nothing he could do. The blood wouldn't stop. He held Didi to his chest until his little angel lay dead in his arms. Shakar's other daughter joined her before sunrise.

chapter twelve

"What the hell are you saying?" Vera snapped, staring at the DNA Analyzer.

When Michael handed her the printout, Vera's face tensed. "Nothing? Our patient has a bloody pneumonia with no germs growing? Bullshit. Someone screwed up."

"I agree," Michael said. "There have to be germs."

"We try again?"

"With different and more media. This germ is probably contagious *and* fastidious. An unusual combination."

Clutching her chest, Vera asked, "How contagious?"

"Who knows? But we have to be careful. We'd better take prophylactic antibiotics."

"Have you ever heard of anything like this?"

"No. I think we need big-time lab help. CDC help. You told me you know someone there."

"My old Stanford medical school colleague, Dave Epstein. The crude bastard tried to screw every woman in the class." Picking up the speakerphone with an unsteady hand, she dialed the Centers for Disease Control.

"Dave, it's Vera Sarkov."

"Calling to say you miss me?" Dave chuckled. "Still working your pretty ass off at the University of California?"

Vera winked at Michael. *Told you so.* "Don't be an asshole, Dave," she said sharply. "We have a hell of a problem here. We need to talk — serious-like. Right now."

"What's up?"

"We have a bad case here. A woman with severe chills and fever is suffocating on her blood and dying. Blood is filling her lungs. The lab—"

"An AIDS patient?" Dave interrupted.

"Not even HIV-positive."

"Strange. What is it?"

"You're not going to believe it, but her cultures are all negative."

"No way. It's a virus or something like Legionnaire's disease. Get your lab people cooking and I'm sure you'll find something," Dave said.

"It's not Legionnaire's, Dave. We looked for *legionnella pneumophila*. There are no gram negative bacilli."

"Keep looking. I know..."

Michael interrupted. "We've done the testing. Even the DNA probe says there are no organisms, and it can't be wrong."

"Who's speaking?" Dave asked.

"Michael Cohen. I'm a professor at Berkeley. I work with germs from—"

"Archeology, right?"

"There are no cases like this in the literature," Michael continued. "It's a new strain or type of organism."

Dave exhaled heavily into the phone. "It's new?" There was a pause, then he added, "The people over at the National Center for HIV will know more about this shit than I do."

"I doubt if anyone knows about this shit," Michael said.

"What's the patient's history?" Dave asked.

"She's a Dr. Jennifer Bedford-Wilson. Was with the WHO and just got back from Asia," Vera answered.

"She related to the Bedford-Wilsons in England?" Dave asked.

"Daughter," Vera confirmed.

"Jeez."

Michael said, "This could become serious — another pneumonic plague, like the Black Plague. It has to be stopped in the prodromal stages."

Silence on the phone.

"Dave?" Vera asked.

"I'm thinking," Dave said. "Seal all the fucking rooms where she's been and put her in isolation. I'm going to call some of my people. We'll send a team out to check the lab material. Everyone who was in contact with her gets treated with broad-spectrum antibiotics. Stat."

After Vera hung up, Michael added, "Notify the hospital administration and get the Health Department in on it, too."

"What about us?"

"We'd better get some cipro into us right now. If this acts like the plague, her contacts will get infected. Us included."

Vera ran off to speak to the hospital administrator, while Michael sat with the technician at the microscope.

"Let me see the scrapings again," he said patiently. "There has to be something."

Scanning the slide under low power, Michael found the area with the most sputum material. Quickly switching to oil immersion, he systematically examined several fields. Nothing. There were rare Gram positive dots, artifacts, but nothing suggestive of bacterial, fungal or parasitic elements. What were they fighting?

Leaning on Reimer's arm, and with Dr. Endicott, an infectious disease expert, accompanying them, Sir Hilary trudged down the long deserted hallway of the so-called Gold Coast, an exclusive, high-priced ward of the University Hospital reserved for the wealthy. The news was bad. Jennifer was unresponsive to all the intravenous antibiotics that had been administered. Dr. Cohen had reported he had not yet been successful in finding the causative organism.

After the three men donned protective masks, caps, shoe covers, gowns and latex gloves, Sir Hilary took a deep breath and entered Jennifer's private room in the quarantined isolation area. He heard the whooshing noise of the respirator and the beeps of the cardiac monitor. Familiar, comforting sounds. He looked at his daughter lying in the bed, pale and still except for the barest movement of her chest.

When Sir Hilary approached, the nurse rose and slipped out of the room. Endicott checked the levels of glucose and electrolytes in the two IVs. Smelling urine, Sir Hilary examined the clear plastic bag on the floor. It was almost full. The around-the-clock nursing was costly and pitiful.

Jennifer gazed blankly at the ceiling, her rare blinks and artificially aided chest movement the only signs of life. Sir Hilary combed her ivory-colored hair with his fingers, then knelt beside her. She looked so delicate, so lovely, even with the blasted tubes and wires.

A flattened EEG, they had said. Essentially brain dead. Blasted nonsense. She was a fighter. She would recover.

Sir Hilary lifted her limp, cold hand and kissed it. Shutting his eyes, he rested his head against her arm. He would keep her alive no matter the cost.

"Don't get too close," Endicott said.

A sudden clang of alarm bells startled Sir Hilary. "What's going on here?" he shouted.

"Her heart has stopped," Endicott said.

Sir Hilary looked at the electrocardiogram pattern — only a horizontal line.

"Do something!" he shouted.

"I'm afraid it's hopeless."

"Don't you dare tell me that. Do something now!"

"It's not safe to do mouth-to-mouth."

"Reimer."

Sir Hilary's assistant ran to the bed, removed Jennifer's oxygen mask, and leaned forward, ready to exhale, as Dr. Endicott jerked him away.

"Please, she's still contagious." Endicott pressed the emergency buzzer that brought the nurse running into the room.

"Get me the defibrillator, the adrenaline vials and the rest of the cardiac arrest pack," Endicott ordered. "Hurry."

The nurse raced out of the room.

Sir Hilary stood like a statue, watching his daughter. He glanced at the monitor. The line was still flat. When he looked back at Jennifer, he thought he saw a faint but perceptible relaxation of her face. Was it his imagination? Could it be? Was she relieved to be leaving her dead shell?

"Oh, my darling girl." Sir Hilary collapsed into the bedside chair as two nurses and a resident ran into the room.

The day was a long and painful one for Sir Hilary. After desperate efforts, the doctors conceded to the obvious and removed Jennifer's body from the ward. She had wanted to be cremated and have the ashes strewn over Nepal. Following the autopsy, he would honor his daughter's wishes.

Sir Hilary sat at a desk in Endicott's office, aimlessly rearranging the papers on it. Michael Cohen stood nearby; he had come to offer condolences.

When Sir Hilary stopped fussing with the papers, Reimer, who had been sitting on the sofa nearby, asked, "Do you want some tea, sir?"

"My life seems so empty and meaningless. Maybe it always was."

Reimer sighed deeply. "Not at all, sir. Look at what you've accomplished, the Wilson Foundation, the good work... "

"Of one thing I am certain: Jennifer would want me to continue the work."

"Absolutely."

"It's a cruel loss," Michael sympathized, "and a perplexing one."

"Yes. You still don't know what killed her, do you? All your sophisticated equipment and nothing. Extraordinary."

"We did all we could," Endicott said.

The usual platitudes. "Apparently, it wasn't enough, was it?" Sir Hilary said.

He felt overwhelmed by a parade of confusing emotions, ranging from fury to a severe aching in his chest. He groaned, his eyes welling with tears. "I'm going to miss her terribly. She wanted to carry on the work of the foundation, get married, have a full life and now..."

"A dreadful loss," Reimer mumbled.

Sir Hilary felt his face flush. "Of course, if you had found the organism she might be alive today."

"Possibly," Michael responded. "She was severely ill when she arrived."

"Waiting for hours in the blasted emergency clinic and the inability of the lab to find the germ didn't help." Sir Hilary rose to his feet, pointing at the doctors like an Old Testament prophet. "I am not pleased by the treatment my daughter received here. Not at all."

"Sir Hilary, it's natural you would want someone to blame for such a tragedy, but that's an unfair assessment," Endicott protested patiently. "This germ must be extremely rare if our equipment couldn't detect it. She couldn't have received quicker or more adequate treatment at any other center. Our infectious disease department and Dr. Cohen are, rightfully, world-renowned. The CDC is equally baffled."

Sir Hilary found himself in the demeaning position of having difficulty controlling his emotions. "I suppose you're right," he acqui-

esced, stiffly retaking his seat. "Please forgive a devastated father for
being so intolerant and unfair."

He lowered his head, staring at his knees. *Sweet Jennifer. My joy
and hope. My future.* The pain was indescribable.

Michael thought about the ramifications of the Jennifer Wilson
case and Sir Hilary's unwarranted accusations as he parked his dented
old Jeep near the cable car depot at the foot of the Hyde Street Pier.
Strolling across the tracks, he entered the South End Rowing Club. In
the locker room he stripped off his clothes, pulled on his swim trunks
and cap, then jogged out to the beach. He needed to clear his mind
before watching the autopsy.

Michael dived into the blue-gray water and began to swim. Even
though it was September and San Francisco Bay was at its warmest, at
sixty-three degrees the water still felt numbingly frigid. If he surren-
dered to the cold, Michael knew an exhilarating experience would
ensue. And sure enough, the tingling continued as he carved one
smooth stroke after another.

How in the world did Jennifer contract such a virulent bug?

Ahead of him, a half-mile away, rose the Golden Gate Bridge, the
center of its span obscured by the low, late-summer fog drifting in off
the ocean. The bridge's supporting towers glowed a rusty red in the
brilliant sun.

Michael rhythmically stroked through the water, as his thoughts
wandered. *A wildfire form of pneumonia from Asia.* He couldn't get
the case off his mind. A new and virulent strain of microbe. It could be
a nightmare. Finding and tracing the origins of this organism, and
bringing it under control was the exact type of work he wanted to do,
and he felt that he was the best person to do it.

The smell of formaldehyde in the cool, barren corridor bit at
Michael's eyes and nose. Coughing, he removed a handkerchief from
his pocket and dabbed at the tears that poured down his cheek as they
approached the autopsy room. "Even in anatomy class I never got
used to this acrid smell," he complained.

Vera laughed huskily. "We have to get you down here more often,

Mickey. You'd be surprised. There's lots of archeobiological stuff happening all the time."

She pushed the doors open and a blast of cold air hit him. Rubbing his hands together, Michael followed Vera to a gray metal desk overflowing with manila folders. While she spoke to the nose- and ear-ringed male secretary crouched in a chair, Michael looked about. One wall held the three-tiered steel drawers containing the bodies. In front of each triad of slabs stood a plain steel table. Twenty yards away, technicians in long white coats, each next to a gurney with a corpse, were dissecting a body.

"Jennifer's in section B. Cook's over there. Let's go," Vera said, jerking her chin toward the gurneys. "I still say we should wait for the CDC team."

"By the time they come, there'll be too many postmortem changes. We'll save them tissue for culture."

Michael walked slowly, listening to the sound of his sandals hitting the cold tile floor. Vera hurried ahead, provocatively swinging her hips. *If only she didn't try so hard.* When they reached the gurneys, Vera said, "Dr. Cook?"

An obese man with a cherubic face filled with red, crisscrossing cobwebs, turned huffily, as if affronted at being interrupted.

"I'm Dr. Sarkov. I called. We're here to observe the autopsy of Dr. Jennifer Wilson."

"I'm busy on a pressing case. Leave your name and number and I'll call when I'm ready."

"We need the results right now." Vera puffed up and narrowed her eyes.

"It's urgent," Michael added.

Dr. Cook glared at Michael, then cleared his throat. "She's over in the contamination area. What the hell does she have? You guys never give us enough info."

"We don't know," Vera admitted.

"Then why the rush?"

"She had a bloody pneumonia."

"Infectious?"

"We're worried about spread," Michael replied.

Dr. Cook raised an eyebrow.

"This is Dr. Cohen," Vera said, answering the unspoken question.

Cook ripped off his gloves, yanked off his gown and threw them into a large bin. Then he waddled ahead of them down the aisle. "How dangerous can this be?"

"Biosafety class three," Michael said.

"Be more specific."

Michael took a deep breath. "Yersinia pestes."

Cook spun angrily. "Jesus Christ. You've gotta be kidding. There was nothing about that in the report."

"It looked like it clinically, but we didn't find any germs in the cultures or scrapings."

Cook tsked disapprovingly. "Did you do serological testing?"

"We did a DNA analysis and we did the latex agglutination test, checking for antibodies to the yersinia and we found nothing."

Looking repeatedly down at his notepad and then at the numbers on the vaults, Dr. Cook halted. "Sixty-one B. This is it. You guys get some masks, gowns and gloves while I get her moved to the negative airflow ventilation hoods."

Dr. Cook summoned two technicians to help him transport the body to the contamination room. When Michael and Vera joined him, Dr. Cook slit open the translucent plastic body bag, exposing Jennifer's corpse. "Dead for eight hours… and she doesn't look too bad. Almost no rigor mortis."

Circling the body, he dictated to his hand-held recorder. "Woman, about thirty or thirty-five, blond hair, brown eyes, body in good condition—"

"Can you get to the pathology?" Vera asked. "I have to get back to the ER."

Cook raised his head, his lips curling into a near sneer. "Since your time is *so* important and you're in *such* a hurry, I guess I'll just have to accommodate you." He paused, meeting Vera's uncompromising stare. "Fine. We'll get on to the abnormalities."

Michael had always been impressed with Vera's self-confidence. He assumed that her strength had been formed, at least partially, by the demands of surviving in Russia during its economic collapse. Vera and her family had lost everything, yet she'd managed to make her way to an American medical school, where she had excelled.

"Morbilliform rash on trunk and extensor surfaces of the arms." Turning the body to the side, Cook added, "Small petechial hemorrhages on back, just off spine, running from T-three to L-one and two."

Michael said, "That could be artifactual."

"Obviously." Dr. Cook sniffed haughtily. "Two three-millimeter depigmented spots on thigh, one two-millimeter brown area..."

He droned on. Michael drew closer to look at the skin lesions. They looked familiar, but where had he seen them before?

"I'm going to start the dissection," Cook announced. Selecting a large scalpel with a straight, pointed blade, he plunged it into the center of the abdomen, slicing away the yellowish skin and fatty layer. The layers peeled easily away, exposing the red-brown muscle beneath, which quickly parted under the knife to lay bare the internal organs.

While Cook continued to dictate, Michael noted the small petechial hemorrhages on the small intestines and the apparently normal red-brown liver. The spleen, too, looked surprisingly healthy, pink and of normal size. *If the spleen was normal, then why the hemorrhages?*

Cook yanked at the intestines, uncovering the kidneys. "This abdomen looks pretty normal. Did she have abdominal problems?"

"Cramps and diarrhea. Some blood."

"Her chart only says pneumonia. You guys never write enough," Cook grumbled. "We'll have to get biopsies of the intestines."

Removing a trephine from a black instrument case, Cook placed it on the liver's surface, then spun it clockwise into the tissue, removing a plug. He dropped the tissue into a clear jar filled with formaldehyde. Returning to the liver, he swabbed the surface and placed the cotton-tipped applicator into a test tube partially filled with a straw-colored solution. He repeated the process several times, including the tissue deep inside the cut out area.

"Can you check for buboes?" Michael asked.

"There aren't any pus-y lymph nodes. I already checked. No nodes, no black eschar."

Dr. Cook then punched out and cultured sections of the spleen, stomach and intestines. "We'll get more tissue if anything looks suspicious on those sections," he noted.

He cracked open the chest with rongeurs, a bone cutting forceps, and pulled the rib cage apart exposing the lungs and heart.

Michael took in a breath and stared at the tissue. He had never seen lungs that looked so engorged — like a deep-red sponge oozing blood.

"Man, this is a mess," Dr. Cook said.

When he sliced through the lung tissue, blood squirted from every layer. "No wonder this gal couldn't breathe. The air sacs are filled with blood."

Cutting open the trachea and bronchi revealed, in addition to the blood, thick yellow-green pus.

"You didn't find any germs in the sputum?"

"Clean," Vera said.

"Impossible. These lungs have to be loaded with germs. It's not an allergic reaction; in those cases the lungs are pink and the fluid clear and frothy. This is bacterial. I'll lay a few bucks on that."

Michael agreed. It *had* to be bacterial. So where were the little buggers hiding?

chapter thirteen

Alice's worst fears had come to pass. Just a few short days since the field team had assembled in Pokhara, they were facing a disaster. Rowan was right, of course; it had been risky to treat blindly with broad-spectrum antibiotics. But what choice had they had?

She absorbed the odor of the nervous sweat of her staff as they stood in the Green Pastures Hospital wing reserved for the acutely ill patients.

Alice and her team put on sterile gowns, hats, masks and gloves and walked down the center aisle looking like a team of Martian scientists from a grade-D movie. Beds filled with patients in various stages of the mysterious disease lined both sides of the aisle. If the afflicted hadn't been too sick to care, she was certain they would have found the team's appearance terrifying.

She gazed compassionately at the elderly man lying in the first bed, the ends of his arms mummified in large, snowball-shaped bandages. He had lost his hands; only stubs remained. Alice ran her hand over the dressing while Rowan spoke softly, trying not to be heard by any of the patients.

"Things do not look promising. Not only did the initial antibiotics not work, but the four subsequent ones seem to be just as ineffective. The problem is, what do we do now?"

"We had to treat," Alice said. "We had to do something."

Etienne gently squeezed Alice's forearm.

"Maybe I would have done the same," Rowan whispered. "But even if the quantitative resistance theory isn't in play, we are in trouble. Big trouble."

Etienne walked closer to a patient, gently lifted his arm, and examined the giant lymph node in his armpit. Squeezing it between his thumb and forefinger, he said, "It's fluctuant, soft like a cyst. Probably purulent."

When he returned to the group, they all moved away from the patients. He asked Koirala, "What's the latest field situation?"

Koirala shook his head gravely. "We have had many faxes. There are over four hundred people affected. Thirty-two dead. The entire area between Baglun and Pokhara is involved. We are having scattered reports of cases from the surrounding villages of Butawal and Jomsom... and from Kathmandu. These are not yet confirmed."

"The States?" Etienne asked.

"Nothing new," Alice said.

"So far." Rowan frowned. "We need help. Immediately."

"Yes, but what kind of help?" Etienne asked.

"An expert in this type of infectious epidemic."

"AIDS people?" Koirala asked.

"This is behaving more like the plagues of the Middle Ages," Rowan said. "Skin lesions, enlarged oozing bubo-like lymph nodes, bloody diarrhea, pneumonia. A highly contagious killer..."

"...like the Black Plague," Alice finished. *"Yersinia pestes."*

Rowan nodded curtly. "That's what I've been thinking."

An emaciated, coughing patient, led by a nurse, stumbled by on the way to the restroom.

"But we found no germs. The patients should be swarming with the bacillus," Alice objected.

"And they should have responded to the penicillin we gave them," added Etienne.

"That's why we need an authority on the subject." Rowan paused. "There's no one better suited than Michael Cohen. He's the plague expert."

At the sound of his name, Alice felt her pulse race. *Not Michael. Never Michael.* She tried to steady her voice. "We should get someone from the Peace Corps or the WHO. It's their project. There must be many—"

"We need the best," Rowan persisted. "You yourself told me Cohen was the best. Don't you recall?"

Etienne was nodding hopefully. "Maybe Koenig could call him."

Alice glared at Rowan. "He doesn't work well in a team setting."

"That makes no difference. We need him." Rowan pressed her lips together in a firm line.

Alice took a deep breath.

Lin Hwang inhaled deeply, identifying the familiar odors of the freshly cooked Chinese food that permeated the room. Dim sum at Yank Sing Restaurant in the Embarcadero Center on Sunday morning was his favorite outing — almost a tradition. The noisy, pushy crowd at the entrance and the bulky handheld pager given to him by the hostess didn't bother him today. Minor annoyances. He and his wife hadn't been out for ten days, and he was relishing every moment.

After a fifteen-minute wait his pager flashed red, and a waitress led him into the back room, past the moving carts filled with dishes of appetizers. Mr. Hwang seated his wife, then waved at the first passing waiter.

"Tea and water please."

His bronchitis had cleared after he'd received the antibiotic medication in the ER at San Francisco's Mission General Hospital. His eldest son, Edward, who said the doctoring at the university was best, had suggested the visit, insisting the "ghosts" know medicine. Mr. Hwang had his doubts, but when his coughing and breathing problems had persisted, despite the herbs, leeches and acupuncture, he'd relented and gone to "the General." Now his lungs were clear and his breathing normal. He might have to thank his son.

When the next cart piled with appetizers rolled by, he pointed at the dish with chicken feet. His doctor said too much fat was no good, but he deserved this treat. After devouring the two feet, he eyed the rice noodles in black sauce, another of his best-liked items. After slipping half of the order onto his wife's plate, he cut up his portion with the side of a fork. He scanned the crowded restaurant and nodded to a friend of his who practiced international law. This was not Hwang's interest; he preferred corporate law. There was more money to be made.

The tray with the braised Peking duck appeared from around the corner, and he motioned with his index finger.

"I'll have two plates," he said in Mandarin.

After the waiter left, Mr. Hwang cut up the duck pieces for his wife and passed the dish over to her. When he sliced his own portion, his wife coughed violently and eventually spat out a piece of partially chewed duck onto her dish.

Why was she embarrassing him by her strange behavior? She never behaved this way. While his wife peered at the piece of duck and searched around in the sauce, he looked about the room. His lawyer friend hadn't noticed.

Then his wife lifted up her fork with a sauce-covered object on it. He leaned forward to examine it. It was a whole fingernail. Someone had dropped a nail into his wife's duck sauce.

It was disgraceful. Inexcusable. Waving his hand for attention, he heard his wife gasp. She was pointing to his hand, where two of his fingernails were missing.

Alice toyed with an empty Petri dish in the blessedly deserted lab. Privacy was difficult to come by in Nepal.

"Alice."

Looking toward the door, Alice saw Rowan standing there, hesitant to enter.

"I believe it would be a good idea for us to speak, don't you think?" she said.

"About what?"

"Michael."

Alice's stomach protested by rumbling. Michael was the last thing she needed to discuss. She motioned for Rowan to come sit on the stool next to her.

"I know it would be quite difficult for you if he came, but I believe we need his expertise," Rowan said.

"Koenig could find any number of experts at the WHO."

"Quite so. However, when you mentioned the plague and the Middle Ages, I thought..."

Alice had wondered about Rowan's persistence on having Michael come, and the present conversation made her even more curious. "I prefer someone stable and honorable."

They sat in silence; then Alice wrapped her arms around Rowan's huddled body. "Don't worry. Even if Michael comes, I'll be fine. We'll all be fine."

Michael would never have the audacity to accept the assignment, she thought. He would have to face her, work *under* her. *The bastard wouldn't dare.*

chapter fourteen

"We need you," Anton Koenig said in his clipped, cultured accent. Even though he was phoning from WHO Headquarters in Geneva, his voice sounded clear. "Urgently."

The words resonated within Michael. *Someone* appreciated his work.

"To do what?" Michael asked.

"This new strain of germ, whatever it is, could be worse than the Black Plague," Anton answered. "Something to make AIDS and Ebola seem like child's play."

"It's already here," Michael said, "in San Francisco."

"How is that possible? We just heard about it from—"

"It was brought here by a worker from Asia."

"Yes, that could be. There's an outbreak in Nepal," Anton said. "You're the plague expert. We want you to go there, find out what this new variant is, and put an end to it."

"We?"

"The WHO, of course, and the CDC."

"Who's out there?" Spinning in his office chair, Michael slipped his feet into his sandals, ready to start packing.

"An emergency team, most of whom were already working in the area on a trachoma project. Dr. Cohen, before you make a decision, I want you to think about the danger involved. It won't be safe."

His work in Eritrea surrounded by warring factions hadn't been safe either, but it had to be done. The unknown germ in Nepal was most certainly the source of Jennifer Wilson's infection. The microbe had to be found.

"I know the risks," Michael answered, visualizing Jennifer's horrible death. But he was needed.

Roy would not be able to guarantee his job if he went because the faculty didn't sanction long, unexpected leaves.

This was a risk worth taking.

He didn't have to think twice. The world faced an extremely dangerous mystery germ. Helping to solve the puzzle was an obligation and an opportunity of a lifetime.

Michael stared out the airplane window at the scenery below during the entire bumpy three-hour flight from Delhi to Pokhara. Once the plane reached ten thousand feet, the smog had disappeared and the snowcapped, rugged mountains loomed in the deep blue sky. The terrain gradually changed from the brown, uninspiring flatland of the Kathmandu valley to the lush green, terraced hills of the terai, covered with palm trees, rice paddies and fields of yellow plants. Finally the rocky, jagged foothills of the palisading Himalayas erupted before him.

He admired the imposing mountains, thrilled to be far from the arthritic-brained administrators and outré politics of Berkeley. He replayed his telephone conversation with Sir Hilary Wilson the previous day. Michael had called to see how Sir Hilary was doing and to tell him that he had accepted the WHO job. He intended to find the causative agent that had killed Jennifer and was now killing dozens of people in Nepal. Sir Hilary had coolly thanked Michael for the call, then gotten choked up and rung off.

The plane descended, bounced roughly along the hazardously short runway, then taxied over countless potholes on its way to the small Pokhara terminal. Upon deplaning, Michael found the air crisp and invigorating. He would have to remember to take it easy for a day or two until he acclimated to the higher altitude. He was now in a valley nestled among the grand mountains, a part of the magnificent range. A wondrous new world.

At the entrance of the run-down, dome-shaped terminal, an exceptionally tall, long-faced, bearded man greeted him.

"I'm Etienne Roche," he said cheerfully, extending his hand. "It's wonderful that you could come so soon. We need a great deal of help."

They loaded the Land Rover with Michael's duffel and backpack and drove off.

"Things are bad," Etienne confessed, wasting no time. "Twelve new deaths in the last couple of days. Two young girls, sisters, died less than five hundred yards from our camp."

Michael grabbed for the passenger handhold as the car hit a huge bump, almost tossing him from the vehicle. "What were the symptoms?"

"Sorry about that. Bad roads here." Etienne grinned wryly. "The least of our problems. People are dying from a bloody pneumonia or diarrhea. Others die from blood loss, still others from electrolyte imbalance, some… who knows what? Could be brain involvement."

"I was told that all the cultures are negative. Have you repeated them?"

"Yes, but everyone's on antibiotics, so it is now somewhat useless. As expected, they were all negative again."

Michael squinted at the stark, humbling scenery. He put on his orange and black San Francisco Giants cap to reduce the glare and avoid sunburn. "What about the fungal cultures?"

Etienne shrugged. "Three weeks and no growth. Just a few Candida."

"Are the sick people immunosuppressed?"

"Malnutrition, childhood, old age — the usual causes, but not more than everyone else in this country."

"Who's running the group?"

Etienne paused, eyeing Michael quizzically. "It's a WHO-Peace Corps team."

"I'm sure it's a highly competent group. I'm looking forward to joining you." After lurching along in silence for a few minutes, Michael asked, "Is the air always so clean?"

Etienne laughed. "Hardly. The morning rains washed the dust out. Temporarily."

Ahead and to either side, the Himalayas rose in the bright sun, dominant against the cobalt sky. "What brings you to this part of the world, Dr. Roche?"

"Call me Etienne. Everyone else does. I've been working for the Peace Corps since my days at the Sorbonne," Etienne continued. "Almost twenty years."

"What does your family think?"

"My wife has accepted my choice. And she's too busy with her elderly father and our two girls to wonder what I'm up to."

Michael laughed, liking him instinctively. "So you're relatively free to travel."

"I've made it my life."

Alice sat at her lab bench and tried to read the latest batch of blood agar culture plates, but her mind kept wandering. She had a nightmare unfolding in Pokhara, more deaths, and now Michael Cohen was coming. No one knew more about epidemics and the plague than Michael, but how could she work with him — *direct* him, for God's sake?

She still didn't understand what had happened with him. For the first time since the trauma in Tanzania, she had allowed herself to become sexually involved with a man, and he had abruptly run away from the relationship. Abandoned her. And despite herself, she still loved him. He continued to create havoc with her heart.

When she'd first met Michael, she'd still felt fragile, the hurt and fury over her brutal attack unwilling to release their grip. But she was also curious and pleased by the opportunity to meet someone whose work she admired. Dr. Tony Buckley, director of the Institute of Tropical Medicine, had been called to London on business, so he'd asked her to fill in for him at a dinner with a colleague. Her companion was a major authority in archeobiology, the author of three respected textbooks and a number of groundbreaking scientific articles. A legend. Dr. Michael Cohen.

Arriving late due to the crowded Underground, Alice was flushed as she entered the Swan Hotel. When she stopped to catch her breath, she saw Michael sitting in an overstuffed antique Queen Anne chair in the lobby, while the steam heating unit belched forth obscene noises at irregular intervals.

Dressed in denim jeans and a leather jacket, he looked a bit wild and rebellious. His square jaw, prominent nose and fierce, piercing brown eyes did nothing to detract from that initial impression. He rose to meet her, and his eyes roamed the length of her body, then slowly lifted to meet hers. Alice's face flushed. The men she normally dated were usually a bit subtler. This man was anything but. Squaring her shoulders, she extended her hand.

"Dr. Cohen? I'm Alice Morgan-Wright."

"Call me Michael."

"Tony mentioned you like string quartets. I thought after dinner we might go to a performance at the Barbican Centre."

"Sounds good to me. I grew up listening to string music. My mother was a violinist. Traveled all over the world."

"Splendid. I reserved two tickets for a Viennese group. They have a good, young violinist."

"I look forward to it. Especially with such a beautiful and charming colleague."

Her heart picked up its pace at his compliment and she had to remind herself to breathe. Then she chastised herself for acting so silly. Surely he hadn't meant what he'd said. He was only being a gentleman.

They had dinner at a South Indian restaurant in Soho. The food was exquisite and the conversation easy. Afterward, strolling toward a cabstand, Alice turned to Michael, "Your Ph.D. dissertation about plasmids fascinates me. How did you come up with it?"

Michael laughed. "Do you really want to know or are you just making conversation?"

"I'm genuinely interested. Your theory intrigues me."

Michael laughed. "To tell you the truth, it wasn't my idea. A student mentioned it in one of her papers. I just followed the signpost."

"Amazing."

"One of my Harvard professors said that it's the slightly eccentric people on the frontiers of science who are doing all the productive research. You have to disregard the rules — abandon them, break away from the norm and let your mind run wild in order to see the unseeable, think the unthinkable. Then the world begins to open up its secrets. That's the place my student found her plasmids."

"Is that your world too?"

"Rarely. But when I do forget the rules, when I unleash my brain, when I follow any path no matter how dangerous, then I find the truth waiting, ready to welcome me." He met her eyes, trying to see if she understood.

"It sounds like an exhilarating place."

"Yeah, scary. Like the place I'm going now." Michael reached for her, sweeping her into a fervid embrace.

At his sudden movement, Alice recoiled in fear, thoughts of Tanzania racing through her mind. Michael instantly backed away.

"I'm sorry. I probably shouldn't have done that."

Alice struggled to regain her composure. "No... um... it's okay." She attempted a smile, failing miserably. "You just startled me is all." Feeling foolish, Alice looked at the ground, not wanting to face Michael.

Michael gently lifted her chin and searched her eyes, looking for a clue to her unusual reaction. They were purposely blank.

Alice jerked her head away and began walking. Michael rushed to catch up. "Hey, slow down a minute."

"I'll just catch a cab," she shot over her shoulder, quickening her pace, anxious to get away.

"Alice, wait. Please." She turned to face him.

"Look, I don't know what just happened here," he admitted as he finally caught up to her, "but I'd still like to go to that concert if you're willing to spend the rest of your evening with a complete jerk."

Alice tried to suppress a smile. "You're not a jerk," she decided. "I just overreacted."

"Wanna start over?"

"Yeah. I'd like that."

The two began seeing each other. Sensing that he had to tread carefully, Michael kept his distance for their first several dates. Until their trip to Salisbury, a perfunctory visit to the cathedral followed by a relaxing picnic.

Walking in the plush, foot-high grass of the municipal park, wind blowing in her face, Alice breathed in the perfume of the wild roses.

Michael flopped down and removed his sandals. "Why don't you take off your shoes?"

She wrinkled her nose. "I'm not a fan of squashed bugs on my feet."

"Don't you know? All bugs magically avoid bare feet. It's their pheromones. Once they smell feet coming their way, they run home and stay indoors. Believe me. Try it."

"I certainly hope my feet don't smell that bad," Alice laughed, then lowered herself next to Michael and removed her tennis shoes.

"Now stretch and wiggle your toes. It announces their presence to the entomological world."

Amused at Michael's impish look, Alice wondered, "Does anybody know how silly the great professor can be?"

"Silly only when enchanted. Bewitched, you might even say."

Michael slid toward Alice, then brushed his lips gently against her cheek. His kiss cooled her flushed face. She closed her eyes and lay back on the supporting grass. Michael rolled to his side as he followed her. Stroking his stubble with the back of her hand, she allowed his long black hair to fall upon her like a protecting veil.

He lowered his lips to hers. His kiss began gently, then became more urgent as his tongue forced her lips apart. His hand wandered up the side of her thigh.

Alice suddenly felt as if she couldn't breathe. No matter how hard she tried to brush them aside, thoughts of Tanzania invaded her mind. As Michael's hand wandered up the length of her body, fear slammed into her and she shoved him away, rolling out from beneath him. She tried to scramble to her feet, but Michael's hand grasped her wrist, pulling her back to the ground. "What the hell is going on?" he demanded, his eyes blazing.

"I… um… nothing's going on," she finally managed. "I'm just not ready yet."

She tried to stand again, but he yanked her back, dropping her on her behind. He sat across from her, his eyes boring into hers. "Talk to me."

"I can't."

"Come on, Al. Talk to me. If I don't know what's wrong, how can I fix it?"

"You can't fix this, Michael. Nobody can."

"Might help to talk about it."

Alice sighed, lay back on the grass, closed her eyes and began to tell him the story that she'd never shared with anyone:

Tanzania. If she could only forget that day, when she had walked through the dusty path, overgrown with thick woods and underbrush, toward the clear swirling stream, to go for a swim, her Friday morning ritual. At six a.m., everybody in camp was still asleep. At the stream, she perched on the rocky embankment, taking in the new morning, her feet dangling in the cold, vividly clear water. Then she removed her sand-colored shorts and shirt and dived in.

The encompassing, womblike ambience refreshed her. Fifteen minutes later, she climbed out of the invigorating stream and squeezed the water from her clinging hair. Spreading her arms, she allowed the breeze to embrace her body.

Startled by a crackling noise, she spied three of the local native teenage boys emerging from the woods, smirks on their young black faces. They had been watching her.

Her eyes met theirs and fear jolted her body. When they rushed toward her, she turned and dove back into the water. She kicked and pulled with her arms, trying desperately to swim away, but coarse hands wrapped around her ankles and held on tightly.

Gulping more water than air, she twisted and kicked, struggling to break free. One of the boys grabbed her head and held it under the water. Then, when she was weak and numb, they dragged her to the shore. Gasping for air, dizzy and spent, she felt strangely detached as one of the boys forced himself upon her. When the pain entered her body, she looked into the sky and saw a bird, a hawk, floating overhead, high above the filth below. If she could only fly away.

Her screams had aroused Etienne, but he arrived too late to prevent her rape by the first boy. But if he hadn't arrived, she knew that she might not be alive today.

For weeks afterward, Etienne had listened to her sympathetically as she replayed the events and her feelings over and over again. Her outrage and pain were only intensified when no sincere attempt was made to catch and convict the boys, despite Etienne's protestations. He had even threatened the village chief.

Alice had become so embittered with the callousness of the community that she didn't think she could ever work with those people again, or return to do any fieldwork. She wanted to get out of the developing world, put it all behind her and forget.

When she opened her eyes, she stared for a moment at the fire in Michael's eyes. He was fighting to keep his composure, but Alice suspected he was already plotting a trip to Tanzania to exact revenge. Then she looked beyond him to the clear blue sky. There were no hawks. She didn't need them now.

chapter fifteen

Pokhara consisted of street after street bordered by mud or stone houses, and countless alleyways lined with rows of vending stalls where everything from food to clothing was sold. Despite his many travels to out-of-the-way places, Michael found the village to be a marvelous and exotic sight.

At the edge of town, Etienne drove him past a huge stupa honoring the Buddha. One hundred and fifty feet tall, the mound-shaped temple had a white base, a golden dome and a steeple section out of which stared an enormous image of the Buddha's all-knowing, all-seeing eye. Dozens of people, most of them dressed in traditional black and maroon Tibetan garb, walked clockwise around the stupa, spinning the prayer wheels that were anchored every five feet along the stupa's wall. In one corner of the courtyard, emanating from a small stone temple building, Michael heard deep, hypnotic chants.

"The Buddhists feel that the music sweeps through your body, releasing you," Michael said to Etienne as they passed.

"*Oui, bien sur.* So it does," he answered.

On the outskirts of town, Etienne left the main dirt road, and spewing rocks behind the car, drove down a winding, rocky side road leading to a grass-covered knoll overlooking the valley. A hastily lettered sign read: POKHARA WHO-PEACE CORPS EMERGENCY CENTER.

Etienne turned into the driveway of the camp and drove to a cluster of small, gray stone cabins. "This place was used for a trachoma study. Temporarily it has been converted for the crisis work." He pointed to the first cabin near the road. "Your living quarters. You're assigned your own cabin."

Michael surveyed the compound. It consisted of a beige-colored stone laboratory building that looked much like a stucco suburban ranch-style home, a dozen small and spartan cabins that served as living quarters and a low-lying, sixty-foot-long tent.

They unloaded the Range Rover, and Etienne announced, "We're having a meeting in the dining tent at noon. Everyone wants to meet you."

"Great."

"As you have probably figured out, we are at a dead end, so we're pretty excited about getting your input."

Entering the darkened cabin with its low, head-bruising open doorway and small window, Michael dropped his knapsack onto the dirt floor, causing an eruption of dust around his feet. The room was sparsely furnished with a sagging bed, a misshapen chair and table and an open closet with four wire hangers. Michael lit the kerosene lamp, then ran his hand over the hammocklike bed. He tossed the mattress onto the floor and unpacked.

Michael went outside and took a deep breath, filling his lungs with the cool air. His anticipated shortness of breath was milder than he'd expected, and he had no altitude-induced headache. He was ready for anything.

He checked his watch. It was time for the meeting. Walking briskly toward the dining tent, he thought through the questions he had for the team, mentally rehearsing them. He pushed open the tent flaps.

There, standing less than ten feet from him, as stunningly beautiful as he remembered her but now soberly staring at him, was Alice Morgan-Wright.

He couldn't breathe.

Alice could feel her heart pounding. Michael was gaping at her, his face flushed, but she was determined not to reveal her emotions to him or the staff in the room. Briskly rubbing her unusually cold, damp hands together, Alice pointed to a seat next to where Michael stood. He didn't move.

She cleared her dry throat and took a deep breath, then addressed her colleagues. "Dr. Cohen has joined our team," she said crisply, avoiding Michael's stare. "As most of you know, he's an expert in infectious diseases, especially epidemics and is here in a consulting capacity." She waved a hand to encompass the room. "The team welcomes you. We'll try to make you feel at home."

Etienne leaned over to whisper in Alice's ear. "Are you okay?"

Rowan hurried over to greet Michael, and gave him a prolonged kiss on his cheek. "It is so wonderful to see you again. We were excited to hear that you could come."

In her peripheral vision, Alice could see Michael staring at her in disbelief. She gulped some water and cleared her throat again, studiously ignoring him. *The bastard.*

"About the two girls who died here in Pokhara two nights ago..."

Rowan backed away from Michael, who remained stationary, almost rigid.

Alice continued. "The initial laboratory tests have been negative, like our results in all of the other cases. To be safe, we will assume the worst-case scenario — that the disease has spread from Baglun to Pokhara."

Several of the native staff members squirmed in their seats.

"What are we going to do?" asked one of the Nepalese technicians.

"Rowan and I have reviewed the WHO and CDC quarantine procedures. Anyone who was in contact with those children must be isolated and given antibiotics, and anyone who comes down with hand or feet lesions, or an upper respiratory or intestinal infection, has to be isolated and treated. We will use sterile procedures when dealing with these patients — masks, gowns, the whole works."

"May I ask Dr. Cohen something?" Etienne inquired. "Are there any other cases in the States besides Jennifer Wilson?"

Michael's rigid posture relaxed, as if grateful to be asked to talk about science. "As of yesterday, there were no other official CDC-reported cases."

Etienne nodded. "Jennifer Wilson left here, flew twenty-five hours on a plane to San Francisco, met a great number of people, and as far as we know, there are no other cases of this disease?"

"You're wondering why not," Michael said. "Good question. Possibly, well nourished, well rested, immunocompetent people don't get the disease."

"Jennifer got it," Alice snapped.

"I might humbly suggest she was overworked, thin, maybe loaded with parasites," Michael surmised. "If we feed the infected people well and have them rest, they may become more resistant to the germ and..."

Alice held up her hand. "In the meantime, we have to prepare for the worst. Let's get things in motion. Rowan will be in charge of the quarantining procedure for Pokhara. Etienne will check out the contacts of the dead children. Does all this sound reasonable to you, Dr. Cohen?"

"Please, call me Michael," he announced, surprisingly loudly and unevenly.

Alice remembered his saying the same words the night they met in London. For the first time since the beginning of the meeting, Alice caught the eyes of her former lover, his long dark hair falling over his shoulders. She wasn't going to respond to him. She rotated her body to address the rest of the team. "We will meet every evening at six to discuss each day's developments. In one hour the professional staff will meet with Dr. Cohen in the lab to discuss the situation."

Immediately after the meeting, after everyone had left the room, Rowan approached her older sister.

"As difficult as it may be, one has to behave civilly. After all, we're going to be working with him," she said.

Alice cocked her head in surprise. "I behaved properly. Much better than he deserves."

"We need him. We all have to work together."

"We will."

"I know he was unkind to you, but I have always found him to be respectful."

Alice sat atop the table and watched her sister fidget with her hair. "I haven't."

"Michael can be considerate. I saw that in London. He just told me that he wouldn't have come if he'd known you were here."

"I have my doubts. He needs someone to torture." Alice studied her sister's sullen face. *If only she would wear a touch of make-up or tuck in her shirt.* Alice recognized Rowan's pre-outburst expression. *Not now, please.*

The dam burst. "He asked me first, you know. If I hadn't had a cold that night, you never would have met Michael, taken him to the concert. I would have escorted him. Dr. Buckley still wanted you for himself." Rowan's eyes flashed with jealous resentment.

Alice felt sideswiped. "You never told me that. But what possible difference does any of this make now? There was never anything between me and Tony, and whatever happened with Michael is over. This is ridiculous."

"I just thought you should know," Rowan said bitterly.

"Leave it alone, Rowan. This isn't the time." Alice hopped off the table, stalked out of the tent. She needed to talk to someone who understood.

She slumped into a chair in Etienne's cabin. "I didn't believe he would dare come. I should never have put his name on the list."

Etienne rested his hands on the back of her neck and massaged her tense shoulder muscles. "Rowan was so insistent. It would have been difficult to explain why you didn't..."

"He told Rowan he didn't know I would be here."

"I think he's telling the truth. Do you believe him?"

"I don't know."

"What he did in London was unconscionable, especially since he knew about Tanzania," Etienne said.

Alice nodded, but moved reflexively away from Etienne. She felt impure again and needed to be apart from him, from everyone, untouched. She closed her eyes. When the image of the Tanzanian forest flashed into her mind, she quickly opened them. She would not allow any more replays. "I don't think I can handle Michael and all the other problems too," she said tiredly.

"You can send him into the field or to Kathmandu on a fact-finding mission," Etienne said. "I'll help keep him busy, out of your way."

"And Rowan? She's been acting so strangely about him. What's she up to?"

Alice slumped onto her bed, the ache recurring. She allowed herself to reflect on her last two months with Michael during his summer sabbatical from Berkeley. He'd moved into her London apartment, and they'd spent every moment together. Day and night. Long talks, followed by long sex and then more talk. Alice cherished both. He met her friends, and sometimes they joined Rowan for a pint at a local pub.

After five weeks, Alice arranged for him to meet her mother at her family's estate near Oxford. Her mother had insisted. There would be a picnic, a small party, then a trip to Bath by themselves. Considering their accelerating closeness, it seemed the proper thing to do.

The night before their trip to her country home, Alice and Michael stayed in a small bed-and-breakfast hotel in Upper Slaughter. In bed, when he'd wrapped his strong arms around her, she'd felt as if he were trying to protect her from her frightening memories.

Lying in bed the next morning, Michael said, "Let's keep the visit to Oxford short."

Alice pulled away in surprise. "Short? My family is looking forward to our visit. I told them we'd be there for the day. They've invited guests."

"If we leave early, we'll have more time together in Bath — by ourselves. I have less than a week left."

"I want to be alone with you, too, but this family visit is important."

"I know, Al."

Michael nuzzled her neck for a moment, then kissed her.

When Alice saw a pained expression cross his face, she rolled out of his arms. "Don't you think it would be rude to run out on them?"

"Not if we tell them in advance," he answered. "Then they'd know it's not because of them."

She watched him closely. "What's really going on?"

Michael sat up and breathed deeply. "The truth is that I don't like these types of family visits. Never have."

"Your family never got together?"

"I can't remember a single Thanksgiving spent with my busy parents, let alone extended family."

"Then why did you say yes?"

He sighed. "I knew it was important to you. I think half a day at your mom's house is a reasonable compromise."

"This is not about my family, is it?"

Michael stood up, wandered to the window and looked out onto the green, rolling hills.

"For God's sake, what's going on?" Alice asked.

"It's hard to explain."

Alice felt the tears welling. "I would never force you to be with my family, or with me for that matter."

Michael returned to the bed, sat motionless for a moment, then gently pulled her hand to his mouth and kissed it. "Okay, let's go."

Alice drove between the vast, manicured lawns bordered by spires of English oak trees, and focused on the ever-enlarging white-stone manor house. After parking in the U-shaped drive, she grasped Michael's arm, guided him up the white marble steps, and rang.

Lady Morgan-Wright opened the huge wooden door and greeted them. The woman's svelte figure made her appear younger than her sixty years. "Alice, dear." They kissed cheeks, tastefully missing by inches.

Alice's mother trained her penetrating, metallic gray eyes on Michael. Alice knew her over-critical mother analyzed much but said little. *Caveat emptor.* "So nice of you to come, Dr. Cohen." She ushered them into the house. "We're out on the terrace having drinks and nibbles, my dears."

Alice watched her mother glide across the marble foyer, as graceful as any model. They passed through a formally-appointed drawing room, a cozy, book-lined study and out a set of French doors onto the terrace. There, around the lawn, Alice was greeted by the smiling faces of friends and family.

Rowan approached, her hair an untamed halo of dark ringlets.

"It's so wonderful that you could come," she said, extending her hand to Michael. "What every party needs is a dashing professor to enliven things."

"At parties, that's definitely not me," Michael replied, laughing.

Lady Morgan-Wright added, "Alice speaks so highly of you. And she is such a perfectionist."

"She hasn't seen all my flaws yet."

"Is this your first trip to Oxford, Dr. Cohen?" Lady Morgan-Wright continued.

"Yes, I—"

Michael's cell phone buzzed. He excused himself and walked away to the quiet and shade of an alder tree. After a few moments of hushed conversation, he sought out Alice.

"Al, that was Roy Woods. He's frantic. I have to get back immediately. There's going to be a surprise site visit by the NIH in two days. I've got to be there."

"Do you have to leave right now?"

"I'll have to get a flight out of London tomorrow morning. Early."

She should have seen the signs, the obvious precursors of things to come. Roy's message may have been a ruse, but what followed certainly wasn't.

The quick trip to London, off to the States and then nothing. No calls, no e-mails, no letters and no responses to her messages on his voicemail.

What had she done?

By the time his first letter arrived a few weeks later, she was so angry that she tore it up without reading it. Other letters followed. She read those, but couldn't respond.

One month later, he finally called.

"Al, thanks for taking my call. How're you doing?"

Alice remained silent.

"Sorry. I guess that's an insensitive question." Michael took a deep breath. "I want to try to explain what happened after Oxford. It may make it easier for both of us."

She was not going to make it easy for him.

"I've always had... let me say... difficulty with commitment. Many women friends, lovers, but no real intimacy. It felt right and I wasn't harming anyone — until you."

She should hang up.

"Like everything else in my life, I suppose *this* has to do with my folks. My dad lecturing on Greek literature all over the world, while mom toured seeking fame and God knows what else, both leaving me alone with a series of rotating nannies. Good ladies but not the real thing."

Excuses.

"I guess I felt abandoned and I've never been able to feel safe when involved..."

The latest psychobabble. Lame justifications for his behavior. The boys in Tanzania could probably come up with excuses, too.

In the last letter, he had written that he regretted what he did and was going to work at changing. But Alice knew he would never really be there for her.

She had opened up to him and he had betrayed her trust. She had put her fragile, damaged soul in his hands, and he had crushed it.

In Pokhara she had gotten on with her life. Just being in the developing world had been a difficult process after Tanzania. She'd finally reestablished her equilibrium. And now Michael was here.

Sitting in his cabin, Michael couldn't concentrate on anything that had been said at the meeting. All he could think of was Alice. How was it possible that no one had mentioned her name to him before he came? Staying would be intolerable for both of them and yet he couldn't leave.

Maybe it was destiny, his opportunity to face and overcome his "issue." He watched the clips playing in his mind, scenes from the special moments he had shared with her.

He recalled when he'd first met her. The contrast of her leonine hair sweeping over a velvety black shirt, and her bold teal eyes in her chiseled and tanned face, reminded him of a big cat, a cougar. Tall, slim, graceful… and dangerous?

How could she still be single? Michael felt excited and strangely intimidated by her.

She was beautiful.

Michael pulled at his hair, trying to tame it. A magical spell had been cast and he was an infatuated teenager, self-conscious about his appearance, his words, and the impression he would make on this stunning woman. Dormant feelings of passion surged through his body.

Awakening from his reverie, Michael decided to face Alice. It had to be done. He strode to the lab, each step creating a powdery storm on the path. He entered and found Alice looking at the culture plates.

"Al."

She didn't look up. "I didn't think you'd have the nerve to show your face. This is a most awkward circumstance. Do you have something you want to say to me? Our staff meeting is in twenty minutes."

"We've got to talk. If we're going to work together, we have to clear up our differences."

Alice looked up and folded her arms across her chest. "I believe that will be impossible."

"I know this is hard for you, but it's hard for me, too. Believe me," Michael said. "What I did was bad. Running away was—"

"Cruel and mean."

"I'm sorry." Michael sat at the lab bench. "I've thought a great deal about the reason for our breakup."

"I presume insanity played a major role."

"Your family wasn't the reason I left. Obviously you weren't. I wasn't ready for a... permanent relationship. I felt trapped."

If there was an anger pheromone, Michael was certain he was smelling it. He took a deep breath and forged ahead. "We've been tossed together again. We've got to put aside our difficulties, our past. We don't have a choice. A lot of people are depending on us."

"Then I hope you don't handle all of your problems by running away, because if you do, we're in big trouble."

The intensity of her anger didn't surprise Michael. Although he was the consultant brought in for advice, he realized he would have to be extra-sensitive to her role as leader of the group if this arrangement was going to work.

"You didn't call for a month," Alice blurted.

"I wrote—"

"The cowardly way."

"I explained the reasons why I—"

"'Woe is me' mush about your childhood." Alice stood abruptly. "You never even inquired about my feelings."

She snatched up her notebook and marched off toward her cabin.

chapter sixteen

Stockton Street in San Francisco, between Broadway and Pacific Streets, was always mobbed on Saturdays, even on rainy days. Today was sunny. Mr. Hwang had decided to accompany his wife while she did their weekly shopping. The outing would give him a chance to walk in the sunlight and see old friends.

Leafy bok choy, oranges, red and green grapes and an array of colorful and exotic fruits and vegetables overflowed from the stalls in front of the produce stores. Fresh fish on ice, live fish in tanks and bowls and braised Peking ducks hanging from hooks enhanced the distinct and complex odor in the crowded street. Jewelry shops with sparkly window displays, red and yellow Chinese signs, chattering lottery ticket sellers and colorful street-lamp banners added to the festive ambience.

Mr. Hwang walked in the street to avoid the milling crowds on the sidewalk. He led his wife to the Far East Fish Market. Good prices and fresh fish. Struggling through the throng of shoppers, he pushed his way into the store. The effort bothered him more than usual and he felt a dribble of perspiration creep down his brow. He grabbed a fistful of ice from a wooden table laden with rows of fat silver fish and held it against his forehead.

"What's wrong?" Mrs. Hwang asked.

"I'm hot."

"Hot? It's chilly in here."

The ice helped cool him down and he was ready to shop. Arrayed in front of him was today's catch of carp — the very thing he and his wife had come for. Reviewing the fish laid out on the ice, he spied a large, clear-eyed one. Perfect for dinner. Edward and his girlfriend were coming over. He pointed to it and his wife dutifully hurried over to claim their choice.

A hot wave washed over him once again. What was wrong? He never should have come shopping. Usually he left the chore to his wife, but he had been feeling nauseated and thought going out would help.

Finding it difficult to breathe, he headed out to the street. But the thought of fighting his way through the crowds overwhelmed him, so he staggered back into the store. While his wife was negotiating a price for the fish, Mr. Hwang's throat closed up.

He couldn't breathe. Leaning against the wall, he grabbed another handful of ice and placed it against his flushed cheeks. Despite the ice, the burning feeling was worsening.

He tried to forcibly inhale or exhale. With a surprising suddenness, a gush of blood spurted out of his mouth and sprayed the rows of fish. He heard shrieks and gasps all around him. At least he could breathe again. When he felt the room begin to spin, he searched the surrounding faces for his wife. She approached slowly with a fearful expression.

The second burst of blood was his last. Splattering his wife, he fell forward, grasping and tearing her dress and knocking her down with him onto the slimy, wooden floor.

"Keep me informed," Vera said to the head of the Department of Public Health. "It's crucial."

"You're not on my list. I can call your boss, Kennedy, and tell him—"

"What the hell can he do?" she shouted. "Call me. He's an administrator. Useless."

"I'm an administrator too," the curt voice responded.

Plopping into a squeaky rocking chair in the residents' room at the back of the ER, Vera grabbed her plastic cup, half-filled with cold, black coffee, and gulped down the contents.

"This is a goddamn emergency," she said slowly. "A possible outbreak of a deadly disease. We have to know if any suspicious cases appear anywhere in the Bay Area."

"As I said, I will call Kennedy if—"

"And I'll call the freaking mayor and tell him that some sphincter-squeezing bourgeois is planning to delay our ability to respond to a potential disaster — making the problem much vorse." Her accent always thickened when her temper rose.

The ensuing silence told Vera all.

"You call my goddamn number immediately if you hear of a case of a bloody pneumonia or diarrhea anywhere in this area." She slammed down the phone.

Bureaucrats are the same all over the world. Anal-retentive cowards. Crunching the plastic container in her fist, she tossed it in the general direction of the trashcan, adjusted her scrub suit and headed back to the ER.

"Rowan, what's the field workers' report?" Alice opened the next staff meeting, relieved to see Michael had taken a seat toward the back of the lab, out of her line of sight.

"The total as of tonight is over five hundred people with rashes, finger or toe injuries or suspicious symptoms," Rowan replied. "Sixty new cases of upper respiratory infection."

Etienne chimed in. "I've cultured their throats and quarantined them. It'll be Koirala's job to track the contacts of the URI patients."

Koirala raised his hand. "My team is reading the slides. At forty-eight hours we've not found any pathogens."

Michael approached the lab's center table. "Can we suspend school for a month in Baglun and Pokhara?"

Alice shrugged. "I don't really see the point of that."

"I believe Dr. Cohen's suggestion is sound," said Rowan.

Alice wondered if either she or Rowan could ever be objective about anything Michael might suggest. She turned to Koirala. "You know the area and the politics. Would that be possible?"

"I think we could do that," Koirala answered. "First we must call the district school administrator and be getting his permission."

"Etienne, why don't you call? Your WHO credentials and pediatric training will give you the clout we need. Don't be too heavy or scary. The quarantine has been frightening enough. We don't want to start a riot."

For a moment, the group was silent. Then Michael added, "We should probably have the population avoid large group gatherings: movies, festivals…"

"We have only one movie theater here and in Baglun and no local jaatras or festivals for three weeks," Koirala said. "Then the *Mani*

Rimdu. The sherpas will be upset if we cancel that."

"It might be wise to cancel it." Michael glanced at Alice. "Medically-speaking."

Alice felt her face flush. How dare Michael attempt to take charge? His arrogance was intolerable. Trying to control her anger, she said, "Koirala, you have my permission to cancel those activities."

Michael sat.

"The markets are crowded and that will be difficult to control," Etienne worried.

Alice nodded. "At this point, it would be premature to close down the city. Since I need you in the lab, I'll put Koirala in charge of crowd control." She faced Koirala. "You can assign the field workers to this job. Take as many as you need."

Koirala bowed. "Yes, Madam Doctor."

Michael arose hesitantly, then softly added, "I think we have to prepare ourselves for the worst. If this gets ahead of us, we'll have a catastrophe on our hands."

Is he being intentionally provocative?

"As I said an hour ago, of course we have to prepare for the worst," Alice snapped, measuring her words tightly. "We don't have much of a choice, do we?" Inhaling deeply to still her anger, she turned to Michael. "Dr. Cohen, will you kindly give us your suggestions about finding this elusive germ?"

While the staff surrounded him, Michael picked up the WHO laboratory protocol. Tapping the monograph, he took a deep breath. "This is a good protocol for finding the culprit. Yet in all these cultures we've found nothing."

"You're not saying there's no hope of finding the germ, are you?" Rowan asked.

"I'm definitely *not* saying that. In fact, there's plenty of hope because the damn germ is there, in every sick and dying patient. All we need to do is flush it out of hiding. The problem is *when*. Time is not working for us, not with the likelihood that the germ is doubling or tripling in number every eight hours."

Koirala looked stricken at the thought. "What else can we do that we haven't?"

"We need to attack the problem systematically."

The staff moved closer. Alice remained where she was. Let

Michael handle the science; he was good at that.

"Non-pathogens, then pathogens. First, we need to rule out a non-pathogen causing the disease. A germ that's always present, like the air around us, therefore seemingly invisible when you're looking for the causative organism."

Rowan frowned. "What do you mean?"

"I'm talking about unusual responders."

Alice saw the questioning faces. "You had better explain that."

"My point is, is it possible that all the people have this germ, but only the unusual responders are dying? We find no pathogen because it's the normal flora that's killing them."

"Interesting idea," Etienne said. "We never thought of that."

"For good reason. It's not likely. When it does happen, it's not so sudden and not in such great numbers. I mention it to be complete."

"Does my quantitative resistance theory come into play?" Rowan asked.

Michael sat quietly rubbing his hands together. Alice listened to the hissing of the incubator and the whirring of the fan.

Michael finally responded, "Could be. To tell for sure we need to get a history of antibiotic exposure in these people."

Etienne waved a hand. "Why use valuable time? Up here, it's unlikely they ever get *any* antibiotics."

"Nonetheless," Michael answered, "I think Rowan's theory is sound; so we have to rule out the possibility of normal flora mutating and becoming virulent because of previous exposure to antibiotics."

Rowan beamed.

"Past exposure doesn't have to be excessive," Michael continued. He gestured toward the stacks of culture plates. "For example, staphylococcus. Not thought of as a problem because it's ubiquitous and usually innocuous." Michael thought about his lecture fiasco. "But it can kill."

"Like what's happening here," Rowan said.

"Right. An innocuous germ turning into a killer when treated by too many ineffective antibiotics."

"So my theory may be at work," Rowan said.

"Yes. Amiomycin, for example…"

Koirala sprang from his seat. "What? The amiomycin can cause a common germ to kill?"

Michael paused in surprise. "I'm giving you a hypothetical example."

"You're saying our trachoma study is causing this?"

"No. I'm only saying that this type of situation could arise if..."

Koirala turned and glared at Alice. She remembered their discussion about the decreased number of bacteria in the sputum. *Could Michael be right? Could the amiomycin have caused a common bacterium to become virulent and kill all the other germs by competitive inhibition?* Alice felt her face tighten. *Not likely.*

"Our trachoma study was *not* responsible for this epidemic," she said defensively. "I totally reject that implication."

Michael quickly responded, "I also doubt it. I was just giving an example."

"Well, I resent your inference. We have controlled the use of the antibiotic by limiting it to a select group of patients."

Michael held up his hands. "I'm sure you're right. I apologize."

Alice's eyes remained fixed on Michael.

"Getting back to something Etienne said," he continued, breaking eye contact with her, "I beg to differ that people in this remote area would not have been exposed to antibiotics. They're unregulated and all over Nepal, just like aspirin in the States. The antibiotics that people buy off the shelves without any prescription could be responsible for our problem."

Etienne asked, "How can we test to see if a non-pathogen is causing the disease?"

"A simple process that's often overlooked. Record the number and types of germs, even non-pathogens, recovered from the sick patients on scrapings and cultures, then randomly sample a hundred healthy people and see if there's a statistical difference in any organism found in the two groups. We'll also have to test the non-pathogens for resistance to antibiotics. No resistance, no problem."

"I'll start on it today," Alice said, writing on her notepad.

"Next, we have to think about the known pathogens that cause extremity and skin problems, pneumonia and death. Did we check for necrotizing fasciitis?"

"Is that the flesh-eating bacteria reported in England?" Etienne asked.

"Yes."

"What causes it?"

"*Streptococcus pyogenes*, a hemolytic group A strep," Michael answered.

"The one that causes strep throat?" asked Koirala.

"Right. I don't know about Pokhara valley, but it's common everywhere else."

"We thought of that," Alice said. "We found beta hemolytic group A strep present in only one case. The rest were clean."

Michael sniffed the air. "I don't smell any unusual odors, but what about the usual gangrene formers like clostridia and pseudomonas?"

"No growth on anaerobic or aerobic plates," Koirala answered.

"Did you check for Legionnaire's disease?"

"No legionnella," Etienne said.

"Check for rickettsia. It causes skin lesions, pneumonia and can be fatal."

"There hasn't been any rickettsia in this area. No vectors, no ticks," Alice said.

"Could it also be that rickettsia doesn't like the altitude?" Rowan asked.

"Nope." Michael shook his head. "It causes Rocky Mountain spotted fever in the States. Order the immunofluorescent reagent stain for rickettsia and test the skin lesions. Do biopsies." He glanced out the window. "I've noticed cats all over the place. Did you check for cat scratch fever? Especially *bartonella henselae*. There was lots of it in the Middle Ages and it killed a lot of people."

"There are no feral colonies and no organisms," Alice said. "We looked."

Michael tapped his pen on the table.

"Madura foot has been around for thousands of years, especially in Asia and the tropics and subtropics. The afflicted get skin nodules, pustules—"

"Isn't that due to a fungus?" Etienne interrupted.

"Yes. Sporotrichosis and the chromoblastomycoses. The chromo family is really lethal."

Alice moved closer to the group. "All of our fungal cultures were negative."

"What stain did you use?" Michael asked.

"Sabouraud's."

He nodded. "You need to do potassium hydroxide stains of the skin scrapings, and if that doesn't show anything you'll have to biopsy the infected area and do Gomori methenamine silver stains."

"We don't have that stain," Alice answered, her voice rising.

"I suggest you get it. It's your best chance of recovering fungi. Scrape, biopsy and culture all the patients."

Alice stopped writing, then said, "I'll call Geneva and also get the techs moving."

"That's plenty for now." Michael stood. "The faster we all work, the better. If history taught me anything, it's that the death rate is going to climb, and rapidly."

Koirala, his face taut, turned to Alice. "Madam Doctor, could our trachoma study be doing this?"

She gazed at the young man reassuringly. "Absolutely not. Dr. Cohen misspoke when he suggested it. He was speaking hypothetically."

"What have I done?" Koirala slumped onto a stool and hung his head. "The people trusted me. I was their guide."

Alice rested her hand on his shoulder. "We didn't do this."

Koirala's body shuddered.

After glaring needles at Michael, Alice moved to the center of the group and announced, "Let's get to work. I'll meet with each of you individually to plan our next steps."

After the group left the lab, Alice walked back to Koirala and sat down next to him. "You've been a great help to your people and did nothing wrong. You didn't betray anyone's confidence. The epidemic started in Baglun, not here. When we break open the code and the data for our trachoma study, I'm positive we'll find no correlation between our drug and the disease."

"Are you certain?"

"I'm positive."

Michael hovered at the door, then entered after Koirala left. "Al, thanks for being open to my suggestions. Being a team is essential to—"

"Your comments about the amiomycin were cruel," she snapped. "But that's not new for you, is it?"

Michael didn't answer.

"You think about the science and not the fallout of what you say."

"That's totally untrue."

"As far as this project is concerned, we're all pulling together. We have to. But as far as I'm concerned, I don't forgive you or your behavior in the past or just now."

"I was giving a theoretical answer. I had no idea—"

"We've been working for two years trying to help these people, and for you to even hint we're responsible for this disaster is unkind and thoughtless."

Michael drew himself up to his full height. "I was insensitive to bring it up in front of the group, but we have to explore every option, no matter how unpleasant. We're trying to save lives, not egos."

"This is not about my ego," Alice shouted, then lowered her voice. "If you had any questions about our trachoma study you should have spoken to me, in private."

Michael took a deep breath. "Realistically one has to have some doubts... about..."

Alice gathered up her notes and stormed from the lab. *Who does he think he is? And — oh my God — what if he's right?*

chapter seventeen

Roused out of bed by a two a.m. phone call, a dazed Michael stumbled in total darkness from his cabin toward the laboratory telephone. Someone must be confused by the time zone or this must be one hell of an emergency. A sharp pain struck his knee, and his flashlight revealed a misplaced carton filled with laboratory supplies sitting on the dirt path. *Walking with your eyes barely open is hazardous.*

The voice on the phone was familiar.

"Dr. Cohen, please hold the line for Sir Hilary."

A middle of the night apology for rude, accusatory comments was unlikely.

"Sir Hilary here. Is this Dr. Cohen?"

"Please call me Michael," he said dully.

"I've obtained some interesting information and wanted to confirm it."

"At two in the morning?"

"Am I to understand it is your opinion the amiomycin study led to bacterial resistance and the conversion of a non-pathogenic germ to the virulent, resistant one?"

"How the heck did you hear about that?"

"People who work in developing nations live in a proverbial small world."

"As to your question, amiomycin is only one of a long list of possible causes of this disease. An unlikely one."

"If that is so, then the trachoma study could be the cause of my daughter's death."

Michael rubbed his temples with his free hand. "Your daughter died from a germ. One that I'll find. There's no one to blame for the presence of deadly germs in the world, unless you think there's a higher being pulling strings, trying to keep the population under control."

"As a religious man, I find that comment offensive."

"I've spent a lot of time thinking about this. It's my field. I'm sorry if the remark offended you."

"I would like to hear from you personally about your progress in discovering this germ."

A request that would not bring his daughter back to life and would only continue the agony.

"Within limits, I'll be happy to do that."

"The Wilson Foundation is financing a new wing in the Epidemiology Department at Oxford. They kindly agreed to name the building after Jennifer, a memorial honoring her dedication to the field."

A healthy outlet for the grieving father.

"I'm sure she would have been proud."

"I will be flying to Nepal to carry out my daughter's wish to have her ashes scattered over the subcontinent. I would like to visit Pokhara."

The last thing the group needed was Sir Hilary's interference or, even worse, for him to get the disease. "I'm afraid that's not possible. The area is quarantined to all but emergency traffic."

"We shall see."

Sitting on her lab bench, Alice swiveled around to face the group. "We've followed Dr. Cohen's suggestions. Let's see what we have. Rowan?"

Rowan scrolled through the data on her laptop. "The KOH preps and the Gomori stains revealed no unusual flora. Rare candida, nothing else. All the fungal and viral cultures remain negative. The IF reagent stain for rickettsia was negative."

Michael narrowed his eyes in thought. "There has to be something we're not thinking of."

"No pathogenic growth," Rowan continued. "We have found staph, but so far there's no difference in the affected and non-affected population. The staph is sensitive to erythromycin, vancomycin and bacitracin, as expected." Rowan waved her hand. "There it is. Rather depressing, isn't it?"

"Not as depressing as the field reports," Etienne responded.

"We've confirmed reports of patients sick or dying in every zone in Nepal. There are over a thousand cases."

"The germ has to be there," Alice insisted.

Michael and Koirala discussed the logistics involved in limiting person-to-person contact. Suddenly, one of the field workers dashed in, handed Koirala a message and hurried out.

After reading the note, Koirala collapsed in his seat.

"What's up?" Michael asked.

"It's my son, young Bahadur. His flu has suddenly become worse and he is being sent to Green Pastures Hospital. They suspect it might be the new germ." Koirala searched the faces of the assembled group. "I never imagined this would be happening to my family."

"We'll find the germ," Michael said.

"He is my eldest."

"When we find it, I promise you we'll stop the disease. Immediately. Your son, no one, need suffer."

"I am hoping the same, Dr. Michael." Koirala spoke in a low voice. "I shall never forgive the trachoma study."

Michael glanced at Alice. "The study didn't cause this," he said firmly. "Please understand that the antibiotic didn't..."

Koirala bowed his head.

Every bed was filled. Pokhara Hospital needed more room. Michael, Etienne, Rowan and Alice — fully capped, masked, gowned and gloved, walked from bed to bed. Michael stopped to examine an elderly man with unusual skin lesions, three elevated red masses on both arms.

"How long have you had these bumps?"

"I am having them only one week," the man said in a raspy voice.

"Are you taking the pills and shots?"

"Yes, Doctor."

"And the bumps are still growing?"

"Yes, Doctor."

"Anything else bothering you?"

"Only..." The man coughed nervously. "Only below. My stools it is being like water."

"Have you ever taken any antibiotics before?"

"I do not know, Doctor."

Michael released the man's hand and was about to walk away when he noticed an unusual change on the man's forearm. Areas of pigmentation and depigmentation with knobby underlying nerves were scattered on the skin.

Michael ran from bed to bed checking for skin lesions. Only one other patient had a similar change. What did it mean? Was this the clue he needed?

Turning to Alice, Michael asked, "Did you see the brown spots and ropy nerves on that patient?"

"Yes, what do you make of them?"

"I've seen lesions like this before," Michael answered. "In lepers."

Michael edged by a wandering cow in the hospital lobby. Rowan ran up to join him, her baggy khaki shirt stained with sweat.

"I have Harrison's internal medicine text in my cabin. There's a whole section on dermatology with two color plates of skin lesions. We can check out the man's skin changes."

"Let's give it a go. Are Alice and Etienne coming?"

"They're staying for a bit."

Rowan jumped into the Land Rover, followed by Michael. "Things have been frenetic, so I haven't had any time to talk to you, in private."

Michael glanced at her.

"It's quite a wonderful surprise to have you here."

Michael started up the engine. "I know some people who were less than happy to see me."

"Alice? Quite so. But for me it is rather a joy to see you again."

Michael smiled. "Thanks."

"I could never understand why she continued to speak so ill of you."

"I can."

"You are not self-centered or a coward. Rather, the opposite."

"She said that about me?"

"You have many admirable traits I find refreshing."

Michael patted Rowan's hand. "If my ego ever needs a boost, I know where to go."

"I hope you will."

Michael drove to her cabin where she led him to the curtained closet that held a precariously high tower of books. She tossed one book after the other off the teetering pile until she reached her goal. "Here. The latest edition."

Michael sat on her bed, opened the text to the index and searched for the skin section. Rowan sat down next to him. Locating the color plates, Michael scanned the photos. There was nothing remotely similar to the lesions he had seen on the patients. "Vitiligo and congenital melanosis come closest, but it's not those."

"The patients' lesions look infectious." Rowan moved closer.

"Those two men's lesions look like leprosy," Michael mused, "but that's a chronic, indolent disease, not acute in onset like this. And lepers don't get a bloody pneumonia or diarrhea."

Michael felt Rowan's arm brush his waist.

He needed to leave. "I'd better get back to the lab."

As he left Rowan's cabin, his mind turned to an unnerving event that had occurred in the smoky, crowded Wild Boar pub, a place he and Alice had frequented in the Kensington District of London. He had been drinking bitters and ale as he'd waited for Alice.

Michael had looked up to see Rowan. He'd met her once before and found it difficult to believe she and Alice were sisters. Two years younger, and four inches shorter, Rowan was a woman who with her dowdy clothes, unkempt hair and slumped posture, looked as if she wanted to be invisible.

After a few minutes of general conversation, a serious look had formed on Rowan's face. "Michael, you seem to be a kind man, and I don't want to see you hurt."

"What do you mean?"

Rowan took a slug of her Guinness. "It is rather difficult for me to say this about my own sister, who I love and cherish, but I've seen a great many hearts broken by her. Beautiful, brilliant, charming. It's easy for men to fall in love with her."

Michael sipped his drink and waited.

"It's always been easy for her to move on to the next man in the queue," Rowan went on. "It is quite true that for the last year or so she hasn't been dating at all, but prior to that…"

Staring at Rowan, Michael asked, "What's the bottom line?"

Rowan pursed her lips in a pout. "I just wanted you to know that Alice is probably only with you… sleeping with you, because of who you are in the academic world. She's using you like she did Dr. Buckley. You might do better to consider someone more serious. Believe me, she'll end the relationship as soon as…"

Michael flushed. "I'll judge your sister for myself." He gulped down his drink and banged the glass on the table.

Rowan's mouth dropped open. "This is not easy for me. I only wanted to warn you. I know how much you care for her."

Michael stared into the noisy crowd. He didn't want to hear her bitter words. He didn't even want to think about them. But he felt confident he understood people and could tell when they were using him. He'd picked up no such vibe from Alice. It didn't fit her personality and she didn't need him to advance, either socially or professionally. Clearly Rowan was lying.

Alice, joined by Etienne and Koirala, meandered over to the lab.

"Those skin lesions may be our best clue," Etienne remarked.

"Why is that?" Alice asked.

"I think Cohen recognized them."

"If he doesn't bolt when things get too complicated, he might be helpful."

Etienne put his arm around her. "Do you want me to send him to Kathmandu?"

"No need. I'm okay. It's a pain I can endure."

"He is most helpful in the lab," Koirala said. "He is examining all of our suspicious specimens."

"I didn't know that."

"Oh yes, Madam Doctor. He has me put aside all questionable slides and cultures and he is examining them after supper. Sometimes until midnight."

"Probably doesn't trust us to read the cultures ourselves," Alice snorted haughtily. She held open the door of the lab for her companions.

Koirala headed for the bench. "That pile is the one he will be examining tonight."

"If he doesn't run away. Apparently, he has a history of leaving if things don't go his way," Etienne said looking at Alice.

She wondered if Etienne's wife and daughters might accuse him of having the same problem.

"Did he get any leads from the cultures or scrapings?" she asked Koirala.

"He did not say. He did say he wished we had more technician help."

"Can you call your uncle and see if he can get us more workers?"

"The Prime Minister is always busy. I will try to speak to him tomorrow," Koirala promised. "Is there anything else you will be needing?"

"No, thanks."

"Then I will examine the remainder of the slides."

After Koirala went to the other end of the lab, Etienne whispered, "The way he smiles whenever he looks at you, I think he has a crush on you."

"And I on him, but not enough to let it go anywhere."

Etienne smiled gently. "You're a lucky woman to have so many good friends."

Alice grasped his hands in hers. "Especially ones like you."

After supper, on her way back to her cabin, Alice noticed the lights in the lab.

Michael?

As Koirala had predicted, Michael was there, hunched over the microscope examining slides. She cleared her throat, and he glanced up.

Rubbing his eyes, he yawned. "No damn luck. There's nothing on these cultures. Absolutely no pathogens and the non-pathogens are in equal number in the sick and healthy villagers."

"I didn't know you did this every night."

"There's a lot you don't know about me."

Michael turned back to the microscope, removed the slide and placed a culture plate under a magnifier. "The usual principles of microbiology aren't making sense, so I'm trying to think differently."

"How's that?"

"I have to find another trail, using different logic. But at the moment I can't see it."

Alice approached him. "You've always been good at deductive reasoning."

Michael buried his face in his hands and exhaled noisily. "I wonder if I'm wasting my time and everyone else's by being here."

Alice tensed.

"You don't want me here, and I've been of no help whatsoever. Everything I've tried has led to a frustrating dead end."

She felt her eyes narrow and her lips tighten. "Are you planning to run again?"

"Of course not. I'm just saying that so far I'm not doing anyone any good."

"You're too much," she snapped. "The world is your blasted plaything. People only walk-ons. Things don't go your way and you're gone. What a selfish attitude."

"That's totally untrue. I never said I planned to leave. Whatever I say you take the wrong way."

"And I thought you'd changed. Working in the lab by yourself. You're only here to save your reputation, not people. Aren't you?"

Michael's eyes widened with outrage. "Of course not."

"You're doing the cultures by yourself because you don't trust our work, do you?"

Alice flounced out of the lab. How could she have loved someone like him?

chapter eighteen

"No AIDS," the Chinese doctor at the San Francisco Powell Street Hospital announced, removing his mask. "All the autopsy and lab tests on your father were negative."

"Of course. My father wouldn't have AIDS," Edward Hwang answered sharply.

"The severity of his infection made us wonder. Such a severe, bloody pneumonia and enteritis."

"Ridiculous."

"Please, follow me," the doctor ordered. He lead Edward from the nursing station to a wooden bench in the hallway entrance and sat. Edward looked at the once pink, dirty walls and soiled linen on the gurneys in the hallway and shuddered.

"I have bad news," the doctor said. "Your mother is not doing well. She has also developed a pneumonia. We have her on antibiotics, but they don't seem to be helping... so far."

"Is she dying?"

The doctor looked out the doorway into the crowded street. "In the last four days, three people have arrived at our hospital with a severe pneumonia similar to your mother's and father's."

"How are they doing?"

"Despite all our medication, most have not done well."

"What the hell does that mean?"

"They... expired."

"So she's *dying?*" Edward couldn't believe his ears. The day before his father had seemed well, and his mother was going to cook a fish dinner.

"Why don't you get these people over to the University Hospital?" he demanded. "They need good medicine, not what you losers do here. If my mother hadn't insisted, I would have never come here."

The doctor winced. "We're doing all we can. The doctors at the university would not be able to do any better."

"Bull. I want my mother transferred immediately. Give me the papers to sign."

"She's too ill to travel. I do not advise it."

"I want my mother moved."

"Actually, it will not be necessary. Someone from the university is coming here today to check on our patients."

Loud noises caused Edward to turn and look toward the entrance, where two patients coughing violently were being helped into the hospital.

Vera stormed into the Powell Street Hospital, followed by the infectious disease resident, Bill Marcus. Pushing past the information desk, she stomped to the office of the Chief of Administration. After entering, she knocked.

"Mr. Hsieh."

The elderly Asian–American man dropped his Chinese newspaper and stared at the woman standing in front of him.

"I beg your pardon," he stammered.

"I wanted to see, first-hand, the incompetent who failed to report the four lethal cases of bloody pneumonia."

"To whom am I speaking?" The man pulled up and straightened the knot of his tie.

"The mayor's representative who's going to have your ass and close down this bug-infested hole."

The man stood, wide-eyed and gaping. "I was told that the sixteen cases were reported—"

"Sixteen? My God. Are there any survivors?"

"Seven are still alive."

"Are they in isolation?"

"Yes, sir, uh, ma'am."

"Take me to them. Right now."

"Yes sir," he repeated as he raced past Vera.

Groaning, Michael stared at the computer monitor as Rowan entered the latest data. Patients were dying. The germs were screaming out what they were, but he was missing the message. All the cultures were negative. *Damn.*

"Rowan?"

Michael looked up to see Alice standing behind him.

"Any new data?" she asked.

"Not a thing." Rowan shook her head. "I keep wondering whether I'm looking at the germ and not seeing it."

"Have you started the Ziehl-Neelsen stain for leprae?" Alice asked.

"I ordered the material from Mac. It'll be here in a couple of days."

"I think you need a break from those slides." Alice put her hand on her sister's shoulder. "I had the same problem. I would see a small positive staining, a straight line or a dot, and wonder if that was the germ... but then the cultures grew nothing."

Michael stared at Alice. "Say that again."

She eyed him quizzically. "I said that I saw some artifacts that could have been—"

"You saw Gram positive dots that didn't grow on the media?"

Alice stepped back. "I saw what could be Gram positive dots, but since—"

"I saw them too," Rowan said.

"Jennifer Wilson had them. I thought they were artifacts," Michael said, his voice rising.

"But the cultures are all negative," Rowan objected. "The DNA analysis—"

"Gram positive dots that don't grow on culture," Michael repeated. "Damn it. How could I be so stupid?"

"What doesn't grow on culture?" Rowan asked.

"Why didn't I think of it before?" Michael whacked his forehead with his palm. "Our little adversary doesn't grow on artificial media and doesn't respond to the usual antibiotics."

Alice cupped her mouth with her hand. "Mycobacterium?"

"Yes, mycobacterium."

"TB?" asked Rowan, looking confused.

"No. Leprosy. Lost nails and fingers, ropy nerves, pigmented spots, that's leprosy," Michael cried. "What threw me off the trail were the other symptoms and the acute course. This must be a totally new, virulent strain."

Spinning around, Michael replaced Rowan at the computer and banged on the keyboard. He needed to get information from Medline. He had to know more about his enemy.

"It's goddamn leprosy."

chapter nineteen

"It's me," Vera yelled into the phone as if the distance between the two necessitated the shouting.

"What's up?" Michael asked.

"Bad news. We have six cases of a bloody pneumonia just like Jennifer Wilson. Four died. I called ASAP."

"I was also going to call you today. We found the germ. It's the leprae bacillus."

"Jesus, leprosy? But that's a chronic disease."

"This is a hell of an acute variant. I called the WHO and told them about this virulent form. I'm about to call Dave at the CDC."

"I'll take care of him."

"Have you heard of any cases anywhere else in the States?"

"Nope."

"Tell Dave to trace all the passengers on Jennifer's flight from Thailand to the States. Start them prophylactically on dapsone immediately."

"I'll give the ER staff prophylactic meds too."

"Keep me informed about any new cases."

With adrenaline rushing through his body, Michael was ready for the counterattack against the microscopic killer.

"Etienne?" Michael called out as he stood outside his cabin. "I have to talk to you."

"Come in." Etienne pointed to his bed. "Please sit."

"I've been searching the Library of Congress for information that might lead to the answer to our problem," Michael announced. "I found our villain. Leprosy."

"Oh, *mon Dieu*." Etienne fell heavily into his chair.

"There's someone who's an expert on leprosy in this part of the world. I need to see him right away and I want you to come with me."

"Why me?"

"Because you worked with him."

Etienne frowned. "Who's that?"

"A monk in the Order of St. Lazarus. Brother Rose."

After a bumpy taxi ride over dusty dirt roads teeming with strolling pedestrians and weaving bicyclists, past street after street lined with multicolored vending stalls and small shops, Michael and Etienne arrived at the one-room train station, a ramshackle wooden structure that looked more like a shack than a depot.

There, Michael was told by an elderly, frail man, that they would have to wait for two hours for the next train for Muniguda. To pass the time, Michael and Etienne sat outside in the sun on a tottering bench, talking about the epidemic. The fecal stench surrounding the station assaulted him, but Michael knew that within fifteen or twenty minutes, he would become desensitized and the odor would disappear.

The few toothless beggars in the area watched them closely, but did not approach, apparently deciding to avoid a confrontation with the imposing-looking men.

"How well do you know Brother Rose?" Michael asked.

Etienne stroked his goatee and grinned at the memory. "We met when I was assigned the task of upgrading a microbiology laboratory in Visakhapatnam. We spoke often because he frequented the facility. A decent and dedicated man."

"Alice sent a fax to the good Brother. He's agreed to educate us about leprosy in Asia, then come back to Pokhara with us. Be part of our team."

Michael concentrated on preventing a hoard of mosquitoes, which was much more aggressive than any he had encountered before, from feasting on his exposed skin. The DEET solution he had smeared over his body was only effective in causing a burning irritation.

Eventually, the train rumbled into the station like a puffing jogger. It arrived only thirty minutes late, "a modern miracle," according to one of the other passengers.

Eyeing the accommodations, Michael said, "This is worse than I remember."

"And this is First Class."

Etienne closed his eyes and dozed. Michael opened the window. Neither the air-conditioner nor the fans were working, and it was hot. He settled into his hard wooden seat, trying to get comfortable. Across from him, an emaciated woman breast-fed her hungry, unclothed infant. She looked up at Michael with a proud, toothless smile. Next to the window a sad, shirtless boy picked his nose, ignoring the staccato arguing of his parents, who were sitting across from him.

Two noisy, jerky hours later, the train arrived in Muniguda. Michael and Etienne headed for the small, empty hovel that apparently served as the station house. Only a dozen or so deserted shanties disrupted the barrenness of the flat, brown countryside. Typical rural India.

"Etienne? Dr. Cohen?"

Turning, Michael saw a short man who looked to be in his mid-fifties. His face was ruddy and weathered, his hair so disheveled it might not have been combed for years. On his face, an untidy brown bird's nest of a beard grew wildly. The road map of wrinkles on his face indicated that he must smile a great deal. He wore a typical brown monk's habit.

"Brother Rose?" Michael asked.

The man's eyes crinkled in telltale fashion as he extended his hand. "I'm pleased to meet you. And Etienne, it's good to see you again."

Etienne and Brother Rose embraced.

After renting three rusty, three-speed bicycles, Michael, Etienne and Brother Rose set off through the flatlands on a narrow rutted dirt road. Lush green rice fields stretched out monotonously on either side of the road, extending to the horizon. Barely visible in the distance, groups of field workers bent to push the rice stalks underwater into the soil.

Beneath his loose-fitting habit, Brother Rose appeared lean and fit, well able to handle the two-wheeler. "Have you ever biked in rural India?" the friar asked merrily.

"I have not," Etienne responded.

"I did some cycling in Bangalore," said Michael, putting on his Giants cap.

"When you're on a bike in rural India, you suddenly become invisible to drivers. So it's really important that you stay out of the way of the cars. If you play chicken with one, you'll lose. Take my word for it."

Michael examined Brother Rose's face to see if he was joking. He wasn't.

"I'll lead the way to town," Brother Rose continued. "After many years in Muniguda, I'm slightly less invisible than you."

The first car that passed them came uncomfortably close, and Michael edged his bicycle almost to the dirt shoulder.

Brother Rose called, "The shoulders can be bad, too. Sometimes the gravel's wet or slippery, especially in the monsoon season, so be careful."

How easy it is to lose one's life here in the boondocks of India, Michael thought, recalling his Peace Corps tour. Life was so abundant, yet so fragile here. So easily replaced. If a car hit him, he would just be more food for the roving carnivores and ants.

"Where are you from, originally?" Etienne asked Brother Rose, snapping Michael out of his reverie.

"Jersey City. That accounts for my accent. My father was a truck driver, my mother a housewife. We were blue collar all the way. I suppose that's the reason for my accent."

"I always thought it was an interesting one," Etienne said with Gallic politeness.

"I had five brothers and sisters and we all went to parochial schools. I'm the only one who stayed with it. I went to seminary school in Boston," he chortled, "where my accent only got worse. Call me the blue-collar Brother."

"When the collar is turned, Brother, the color doesn't matter to people who…" Michael broke off as he hit a mudhole. He swerved toward the center of the road, jamming on his brakes. After skidding for a few feet, he came to a halt, falling like a ten-year-old.

"Are you okay?" Brother Rose cried.

Michael dusted himself off and jumped back on the bicycle. "I'm fine."

"Be careful. If a car had come, you coulda been creamed."

They continued on, with Michael keeping his eyes fixed on the graveled path.

"I joined the Order of St. Lazarus and was sent here when I was twenty-eight," Brother Rose resumed. "Like the other monks in this order, I've made it my life's work to care for these people with leprosy. That's been our mission for a thousand years."

"A truly noble cause," Etienne said.

Several cars whizzed by, missing the three of them by inches.

"This was my first assignment," Brother Rose continued. "I've been here for twenty-six years. I guess my next assignment will be in heaven." His expression grew wistful. "But these years here in Muniguda have been my heaven on earth. So many people I can help."

Brother Rose pointed down a dirt road leading out of the village. "We'll turn here. They told me to show you a typical village and typical cases. It's a mile up the road in a swampy area, so watch out for snakes and mudholes."

"A pretty remote place for a village," Michael remarked.

Brother Rose sighed. "The lepers are only allowed to form colonies in remote places. The villagers drive them away if they think they're too close to town. Several colonies in this area have already been burned down because they were too close for comfort."

While they pedaled, Michael noticed Brother Rose's crucifix bouncing against his habit, glowing in the sun.

"Where did you get that impressive cross?"

"It's an ancient piece that's been handed down for about twelve hundred years. It's always been in the possession of a member of my order. A Brother Jeremiah wore it during the Black Plague and survived to become head monk in our Jerusalem monastery. They say that whoever wears the crucifix will be protected."

"It has to be a great honor and responsibility to be given the cross," Michael said.

"It's humbling."

They cycled in silence until Brother Rose asked, "Do you have any concerns about shaking hands or touching people with leprosy?"

"I would feel comfortable with the physical contact," Etienne answered.

Brother Rose guffawed. "Good, because most of them love to be touched."

"How do you treat the lepers here? Dapsone? Multiple Dose Therapy?" Michael asked.

"Since the fourteenth century, a pressing from the seeds of an East

Indian tree has been popular among the people. It's called chaul-moogra oil. Many still use it. The government recommends using the MDT — dapsone, clofazimine and rifampicin. Little good it does us. We never get any of it in this region."

"Why not?" Michael asked.

"The corrupt health officials keep the money set aside for drugs or sell the drugs for profit."

"Assholes," Michael said.

Brother Rose didn't argue with his assessment.

"So these lepers get no medicine?" Etienne asked.

"They get nothing."

The area surrounding the village was a busy place, like any other rural community in the area. In the fields, dozens of workers were bent over, pulling up stalks of rice. The men were dressed only in loincloths and turbans, exposing most of their dark brown bodies to the blistering sun. The women wore colorful saris. When the three cyclists passed, most of the people working in the fields smiled and waved. The three of them returned the greetings.

The village consisted of twenty small huts. The walls and floors of the huts were made of mud and feces, a mixture called *tule,* according to Brother Rose. The roofs consisted of thatches of palm leaves. Cow-dung patties were stuck to all the walls. The barren, dusty scene reminded Michael of a backwater Mexican village.

The homes were lined up in two rough rows, with the area between forming the dirt road through the village. Everything was covered with a light brown dust, including the few skinny cows that wandered among the huts. Scrawny chickens ran aimlessly through the village, clucking wildly, while two goats tied to a post sat silently near the largest hut. An overriding fecal odor filled the air.

When Michael parked his bike, a dozen children suddenly appeared, scampering up to greet him, their white eyes standing out dramatically in their grinning Dravidian faces. The girls wore clean, pressed blue and white dresses, and the boys wore white short-sleeved shirts and dark blue pants. School uniforms, obviously.

Michael encouraged a girl to pull on his hair, which he'd bound in a ponytail. "It loosens my brains and makes me smarter." She and her friends giggled as they took turns tugging. Other kids laughed and yelled as they hugged Brother Rose. Picking up one of the smallest girls, he kissed her on the cheek.

"The children certainly appear healthy and full of vitality," Etienne observed. "Do they have leprosy?"

"No. Normally it takes years to get," Brother Rose said.

Outside another hut, Brother Rose introduced Michael and Etienne to the village chief. The handsome, white-haired man with the large white handlebar mustache looked like a stereotypical guru. Like the rest of the villagers, he was Dravidian, one of the black Caucasian race who inhabit southern India. Friendly people. Michael had enjoyed working with them during his Peace Corps days. The chief's feet were twisted and useless for walking. Using his crutches, he hobbled over to them, extending his nearly-fingerless hands in a greeting salute while Brother Rose grasped them. The old man bowed slightly to Michael and Etienne.

"He only speaks Hindi and a little Tamil," Brother Rose explained. "I can translate if you have anything to say."

"Excellent." Etienne nodded. "Tell him it is a great pleasure for us to be introduced into this most accepting community and..."

Chuckling, Brother Rose waved Etienne quiet, then spoke to the chief who smiled, exposing a few blackened teeth, and responded with a few words.

"I told him you're glad to be here and he asked us in for tea at six, when his wife returns from the field. As you can guess, he can't really make food on his own."

Pressing his hands together in a praying position, Brother Rose briefly touched his forehead and bowed to the chief. *"Namaste."*

The kindly old man returned the bow and hobbled back to his hut. As Michael watched the retreating figure, an emptiness swept through him. In this place, unchanged for centuries, time stood still. Michael felt overcome by a deep sadness.

Rowan glanced up when Alice entered her cabin. She disliked being disturbed during her private moments. And didn't her sister ever manage to look homely or messy? Here they were in the dust capital of the world, and Alice looked bloody lovely in her figure-enhancing cargo pants, her long black hair braided like a native's.

"The techs have collected another eighty scrapings and cultures from the villagers near our camp," Alice said wearily. "Could you get on them?"

Rowan slapped down her pen and pushed aside the paper on the tilted wooden desk. "I'm taking, if I may say so myself, a ruddy well-deserved ten-minute break."

"I'm sorry," Alice said, not sounding a bit sorry. "But with Michael and Etienne fetching help, we're short-handed. Koirala never complains, but I noticed that he and his helpers have been working past midnight every night and..."

"Quite. So now your sister is fair game. You can drive her ruthlessly."

"Please, Rowan." Alice sat heavily in the wooden armchair next to her sister's.

"I've been trying to write this blasted letter to Mother before she leaves on her winter cruises, not that you—"

"It's an emergency. It's overtime for all of us."

Rowan gave an exasperated sigh. "Please don't try to make me feel guilty. I did say I would help you and I meant it. But I didn't expect you to take advantage of my generosity."

Alice looked hard at Rowan. "I need your help in the lab."

"I'll be there shortly. I only need five minutes for the letter."

Alice pushed off the armrests and left quietly.

Another opportunity to boss her little sister around. Rowan didn't know why she had agreed to come. Alice would never treat her fairly. Being able to renew her relationship with Michael was an unexpected benefit, though.

Rowan picked up the paper and continued to write.

Brother Rose stood at the edge of the village looking out at the workers in the rice fields. Michael asked, "How did you come by your name, Brother?"

Brother Rose's face brightened. "Nothing deep. I was the gardener at the monastery, and I had good luck with roses; they interested me. If you let yourself go and look really carefully at the leaves, the swirl of the petals, it's like a whirlpool sucking you into the plant.

Sucking you into its beauty, its life." He paused. "Living with the lepers is like that for me. This is a whole new world they've let me enter. Filled with unexpected beauty and the energy of life."

Brother Rose's words struck Michael as both poignant and true. Being pulled into something. The project affected Michael that way. He felt needed again.

Michael watched while villagers paraded back into the colony, their workday in the rice fields or begging in town completed. He was stunned by the severity of the deformities he saw. The beggars were the worst of all; many had significant limb disfigurement, as though parts of their extremities had been melted away like paraffin in a candle. All of the beggars needed crutches. Those who were sighted led the blind into the village by having them hold on to the end of a stick. Almost all of the villagers were covered with splotchy red, brown and white discolorations on their skin, similar to the lesions Michael had seen in Pokhara, his first clue.

One elderly blind beggar had particularly grotesque changes on his face; massive brows, lumps over his cheeks and total loss of his nose, earlobes and hair. He looked like a walking cadaver.

While looking at the raw, rotting flesh and horrible deformities of the lepers, Michael held his breath. He didn't want to show any expression of discomfiture. However, the thought that a virulent, contagious form of this disease was spreading throughout Nepal, waiting to strike out at the world, made him shudder.

"They're so deformed," Etienne whispered.

Brother Rose clutched the amulet around his neck. "Only physically."

"It's terrible that they aren't getting the medicine," Etienne said.

"Many of these people are without hope. They've been considered sinners for two thousand years and sinners they'll remain." Brother Rose shook his head. "I wish I could also change that."

"Who is being treated in India?" Michael asked.

"The wealthy, the well-connected and those in the government."

"How are they doing?"

"Responding slowly. It can take a year or two of the triple therapy to cure someone. Dapsone alone doesn't work in our hands. We and Mother Teresa's group have recommended the use of triple therapy to the Indian government and the WHO."

After the last of the villagers passed, Michael and his companions walked toward the chief's hut.

"Which type of leprosy are you dealing with, the paucibacillary or the multibacillary?" Brother Rose asked.

"We don't know," Michael said. "The leprae bacillus doesn't grow on artificial media; that was our problem. We only began to stain the tissue with the Ziehl-Neelsen acid-fast stain just before we left. After the first two stains were positive for leprae, we were on our way here."

Etienne asked, "How do these drugs work?"

Michael knocked ants off a log at the side of the road and sat. The others did the same. "Dapsone works by interfering with the synthesis of folic acid in the bacteria, limiting its growth."

"If you use dapsone alone it takes much longer to see clinical improvement," Brother Rose added.

"Probably much too long with our deadly strain," Etienne said.

Michael nodded. "And clofazimine works on a different part of the germ; it interacts with the germ's DNA."

"The problem you'll have with that drug is that it has an even slower onset of action than the dapsone. The good news is that the two are synergistic," Brother Rose added. He suddenly jumped up and bowed to a stooped old woman crossing their path. After she'd bowed and passed, he whispered, "It's the chief's wife. We'll go and visit them shortly."

After he sat, Etienne asked, "And the third drug?"

"Rifampicin. It's the most potent killer of leprae bacilli available today. It gets to work right in the heart of the bacteria's nucleus. A single dose as low as six hundred milligrams will kill the great majority of leprosy germs."

"A perfect solution," Etienne said. "Why do you need all three?"

"Because it's not perfect," Michael answered. "Unfortunately, far from it. The bacterium is killed in a test-tube situation, but the actual speed of clinical recovery is not any better with rifampicin than with dapsone. The bacilli have a slow metabolism and growth, so slow they take up little antibiotic. The damn germ is almost impossible to attack and kill."

"But it's not invincible?" Etienne asked.

"Not at all." Brother Rose nodded with satisfaction. "But as

Michael noted, you need all three because they work on different parts of the germ. They complement each other."

"So if we now have a faster-growing mutant bug, shouldn't the triple therapy and the rifampicin work better?" Etienne asked.

"Theoretically," Michael said. "Yes."

Michael ducked his head to enter the chief's humble dwelling and followed Brother Rose and Etienne to a mat in the corner. There, Brother Rose bowed, then sat on the dirt floor. Etienne and Michael followed suit.

The chief's wife was nearly doubled over with scoliosis to the point of being unable to look at her guests. She removed a teapot from atop a burning cow dung patty, poured the tea into four wooden cups, then placed a cup in front of her husband and each of the guests. After an attempt at a bow, she slowly removed herself from the room.

The chief peered at Michael, lifted his cup with his bony atrophied wrists, and sipped the tea. The image made Michael think of someone holding a cup with two thick chopsticks. Not wanting to be rude, Michael took a sip from his own cup of tea. It was good, but scorchingly hot.

Brother Rose said something to the chief, who put his cup back onto the floor.

"I told him the tea was hot. He can't feel it. I didn't want him to burn his flesh," Brother Rose explained.

The chief looked at Michael again and said something.

"He wants to know why you're here. I told him you want to learn firsthand about Hansen's disease in Asia, and that you also plan to steal me away."

The chief spoke again.

"He said you could do worse."

Michael laughed, then said, "The chief has a good sense of humor."

"More than you think. He's put up with a lot, yet still has a good outlook."

The chief, who continued to stare at Michael, next said something in a serious tone. Michael felt the old man's eyes burning, riveting him in a sensation of otherworldliness.

"He thanks Shiva for bringing you both into the world of the untouchable," Brother Rose translated. "He also says that he has a special feeling about you, Michael. He can see it in your eyes, your being. He says you will make a difference. It's your karma, your destiny."

Michael bowed his head, then met the chief's urgent, but matter-of-fact gaze. He had a strange feeling about the chief's prophecy — as though the old man had seen directly to his soul.

Brother Rose whispered, "I think we'd better go. It won't be safe for us to travel in the dark. Kraits, cobras and other friendly night creatures are all over the place. And the villagers go to sleep at sundown. They can't afford any form of lighting."

Standing, Brother Rose bowed to their host. Michael and Etienne imitated his movements.

The fatherly-looking chief limped over to Michael and hugged him awkwardly. After a low, respectful bow, normally reserved for special people, the chief, with tears in his eyes whispered, *"Namaste."*

Michael could not speak.

chapter twenty

Rowan flooded the row of slides with the Ziehl-Neelsen stain, and then turned to pull a second set of slides from the box labeled: Pokhara Hospital Sputum Samples. She placed these slides in a row, equidistant from each other, and poured the stain from the bottle onto each of these. After shaking the solution off from the first row of slides, she slid one under the microscope. The tabletop beneath the slides was awash in a kaleidoscope of pinks and blues and every shade between, changing like a sunset each time more dye spilled onto the table.

Placing an oil droplet onto the slide, she focused in on the high-powered field of mucus, cells and debris. Moving the stage about, there was no mistaking the villain. Thin, red rod-shaped bacteria appeared everywhere. The patient's lungs were loaded with leprae bacillus. This was the sixteenth positive culture out of sixteen specimens.

How could they have missed this deadly killer?

If she ever had her own lab, she would make certain this would never happen. She would hire only the brightest microbiologists and buy the latest, most expensive equipment.

Rowan pushed the unexamined slides off to the side with her dye-stained hand and rested her head against the microscope. There was no need to check anymore. All the patients in the hospital had leprosy.

Rowan dragged herself into the next room where Alice was scraping colonies of organisms off the Lowenstein-Jensen media with a metal spatula.

"What's up?" Alice asked as Rowan collapsed onto a stool.

"Michael was right. They all have leprae."

"That's what I figured. I've already called the WHO. They're going to send us anti-leprosy medication ASAP."

"I was right in insisting that Michael come."

Alice looked up from the culture plates. "We would have eventually discovered the germ."

"Eventually is correct, after many more deaths."

"You don't give enough credit to our team's abilities to find—"

"And you don't give me credit either, do you?"

Alice stared for a few moments at her sister. "You were right. Outside assistance was helpful."

Rowan knew better than to say more. She had pushed her sister far enough.

Karma… destiny. When he awoke the next morning in his small mud hut in town, Michael found the chief's words and the image of his burning eyes still echoing in his mind, as if they'd been replaying all night. Maybe the old man was right; he might make a difference.

Michael felt he was where he belonged. He rolled off his floor mat, shook his long hair, then assumed the lotus position on his meditation pillow. For the next forty minutes he sat erect and perfectly still on the zafu. His mind wandered wildly for the first ten minutes and Michael gave it free rein. He observed his agitation. The Jennifer Wilson case, the terrible mutilation of the lepers, the nightmare in Nepal, Alice's hostility — all these thoughts fought for equal time.

Watching his musings come and go, Michael gave each one its due, but did not build on it. An idea formed. Michael saw it, and as though it was a small brush fire in a forest, he removed anything that would fuel it. Then, calmly, he let it die. The process continued until all the fires had burned themselves out.

There came the distant bleat of the odd goat, the calls of birds and the rustling of wind in the trees as he sat in his stillness. In this quiet place, Michael sensed that something was dreadfully wrong. Something ominous lay smoldering in the ashes, ready to flare up.

The three men sat in a squalid, rustic teahouse situated on the side of the main road near the Kathmandu airport.

"Brother Rose," Michael mused, "your dedication to the people in the valley is impressive."

"Indeed," said Etienne. "It's clear they love you dearly."

Brother Rose's ruddy face flushed even more pink. "Thank you both. These people have grown on me. They're family and the valley is like home. I miss them when I'm gone."

"I'm sorry we have to borrow you," Michael added, "but your expertise is vital."

"Aren't you a leprosy authority, too?"

"My specialty is the Black Death. I only know what little I do about leprosy because I believe the plague nearly killed it off."

Brother Rose's eyes widened. "Really? How?"

"The yersinia germ that caused the plague contains a plasmid that kills the leprosy organism. At least it did in the Middle Ages. Anyway, that's what I found."

"What's a plasmid?"

"It's a small extrachromosomal genetic element that confers certain properties to a bacteria."

Brother Rose chuckled. "That definition doesn't really help me at all."

"Sorry. A plasmid is a conductor that can orchestrate the cell to play different types of music. The one I'm interested in plays dirges and requiems."

Michael took a sip of his tea. He was relieved to find that it was somewhat hot, since the owner had served the little filled glasses with his fingers in the tea. "Plasmids can give their host cells new genetic properties. Basically, I think one yersinia germ gave the yersinia germ next to it the same ability to kill the leprae bacilli."

"Give me some examples of these so-called plasmids. Something I would know."

"How about staphylococcal plasmids? They carry a gene for penicillinase, making the staph germ resistant to penicillin."

Brother Rose nodded. "Germs resistant to penicillin. I've heard about that."

"Some plasmids produce substances called *colicins* or *bacteriocins*. These kill closely related strains of bacteria that don't carry the same plasmid. Most of these killer plasmids have been found in Gram-negative organisms — like the plague germ. Well, I think that in the fifteenth century, the plague released its killer plasmids, and the leprae it encountered were doomed."

"So why don't we use this plasmid of yours in Pokhara?" Etienne asked.

Michael shook his head wryly. "That would take some doing. We would have to find live, six-hundred-year-old plasmids."

"Why? Don't these plague germs and plasmids exist now?" Brother Rose asked.

"The germs exist, but I don't think the present-day plasmid has this capability. Anyway, it's all academic. The triple therapy is effective and available." Michael sipped his tea. "If we live through this, when grant money is more plentiful, I'm going to prove my premise and stand the archeobiology world on its freaking head."

"I'm sure you would enjoy that," Etienne said, chuckling.

Michael laughed too. "I'm also excited about the opportunity to cure this new leprosy disease."

"Helping others. Giving…" Brother Rose analyzed.

They remained silent for a few minutes. Etienne broke it. "The leprosy antibiotics will work, won't they?"

"The antibiotics are effective against regular leprosy," Michael said. "How the triple therapy will work against this virulent form is anyone's guess."

"What's your hunch?" asked Etienne.

"It should work better. The rapid growth of the bug should increase the incorporation of the antibiotic into the organism." Michael smiled. "However, we can always use a prayer or two."

"You can count on me for that," Brother Rose said.

A Jeep came screeching to a halt in front of the teahouse. Out jumped a six-foot-six-inch, two-hundred-fifty-pound red-faced man.

"Etienne, great to see you," he bellowed. Running up the steps two at a time, he clomped into the room, shaking the floor in the process.

Etienne said, "It is good to see you, too, Mac."

Brian MacKenzie reminded Michael of a red walrus, his wavy brick-red hair and beard giving him an untamable look.

He gave Etienne a bear hug, causing him to disappear somewhere inside Mac's huge arms. After releasing Etienne, he turned to Michael, who shied away.

"Michael, the boy wonder. Good to see you, you SOB. Returning to the Peace Corps?" Mac slapped Michael on the back. "I don't have any *khat* with me," he added with a wink.

Michael rolled his eyes. Unfortunately, Mac never changed.

"What's khat?" Brother Rose asked.

"An opiate grown in Yemen," Michael answered.

Mac turned to Brother Rose. "Hi, I'm Brian Mackenzie, Mac to friend and foe alike. I'm head man for the Peace Corps here in Nepal. You must be Rose."

"Brother Rose, from the Order of St. Lazarus."

"Yeah, the leprosy people. Good to meet you. Michael here says we're dealing with leprosy, and he says you're the man to advise us."

After giving Brother Rose what appeared to be a bone-crushing handshake, Mac jerked his thumb toward Etienne. "Frenchie here and I go back a long way. We had a ball in Yemen, trying to grow drought-resistant grains in a country that only grows opiates." Mac threw back his head and laughed at the sky. "They put up with us for two years, then tossed us."

Across the teahouse, Michael saw the owner and two Nepalese customers sitting at the counter, staring open-mouthed at Mac. They had also stared at Michael and Etienne, but their current expressions said it all: another Westerner, and they keep getting bigger.

Etienne asked, "How have things been in Pokhara for the last week?"

"Getting worse. During the eight days you were gone, things have gone to pot, pardon the expression."

"Did they get the anti-leprosy medicines?" Michael asked.

"We called Farberg Pharmaceuticals three days ago, as you asked, and the stuff should be here in a week."

"Totally unacceptable," Michael stated flatly. "Call Farberg again. I want the drugs in Pokhara by tomorrow. No excuses."

Mac looked hard at Michael.

"We need the drugs," Michael repeated, *"right now."*

Michael introduced Brother Rose to the rest of the staff sitting in the lab, minus Etienne and Koirala.

Alice greeted him warmly, then nodded to her sister.

"You were right, Michael," Rowan said. "Everything is positive. Sputum, blood, stools, skin biopsies, you name it. The patients are swimming in leprae bacilli."

"It's obviously multibacillary," Brother Rose said. "You'll need to give triple therapy."

"Could you type up your treatment schedule?" Alice asked. "I want to give it to all the health care workers and the entire staff."

Etienne rushed into the laboratory. "Sorry I'm late. Just finished my morning rounds of the children in isolation." His drooping face told all. He wiped his wet brow and goatee with his dusty handkerchief, then sat on the bench next to Alice. "Most of the children in the schools are positive for leprae. Eighteen have started to have a bloody diarrhea. Koirala is there with his son; he's very sick. *C'est tragique.*"

Alice ran her hand over Etienne's shoulder.

"We've no choice but to assume the entire population of the valley are primary contacts," Michael said. "We have to isolate the sick and start treatment on everybody. Triple therapy for everyone. Immediately."

"Thank you for your opinion, Dr. Cohen, but I'm still in charge of this project," Alice announced crisply.

Michael winced. Of course, Alice was right. Rowan glanced at him sympathetically. Everyone sat in silence until Michael said, "I was being presumptuous and overstepped my authority. Consider those comments my suggestions."

Alice inhaled deeply, then continued. "We haven't received any rifampicin and clofazimine. We got a little dapsone from the Nepalese government."

"Damn Mac, I told him it was urgent," Michael interrupted. "If it's okay with you, Alice, I'll call Farberg and have them send whatever we need. I have a connection to them. They tried to steal me from the University."

"Fine," Alice agreed. "Now, the quarantine. We have to expand it. No one should be allowed to leave the entire valley at this point. Absolutely no one. And we'll have to restrict entry to essential personnel."

"We'll have to call the WHO and have them send a team, fifteen or twenty locals, to help distribute the medication," Etienne added.

"And we must let the WHO know about the risk involved," Brother Rose warned.

"I'll do that," Alice said. "And I'll talk to the local officials, the airport people and our Embassy."

"Brother Rose is right," Etienne concurred. "We have to keep the number of people they consign to us to a minimum. The work is going to be extremely hazardous."

Rowan checked her notes. "I'll call Green Pastures Hospital here in Pokhara, Anandaban Leprosy Hospital in the Lalitpur District and Dr. Uphadya, the chief of Nepal's Leprosy Control Project. They should be told to start triple therapy as soon as possible."

"Good," Alice said. "Etienne, you and Rowan get the word out that I want everyone back to the dining hall. Everyone involved in the study including local officials." Alice looked at Michael. "We need to have an emergency meeting and begin instituting all of Dr. Cohen's suggestions."

Sitting on the dining table with his bare feet dangling, Michael gazed out at the standing-room-only crowd of brown, black and white faces. All trachoma project field workers, as well as all local hospital personnel, were invited. The overflow stood outside, crowded around the open windows and doors. Alice had asked Michael to talk to them about leprosy before they picked up the treatment protocol and their pills. Farberg had managed to accumulate and send enough drugs for the immediate staff. They said they were working on producing mass amounts.

"Leprosy. Hansen's disease." Michael glanced at Brother Rose. "The first definite recorded description of leprosy comes from the sixth century BC, from the Indian subcontinent."

A murmur arose in the crowd.

"That's right, it may have started here. Back then the disease was called *Kushta* or *Kushnati,* which means "eaten away.""

"Later, in the Greek and Roman worlds, for the first time lepers were shunned and segregated from society into colonies, a necessary and wise practice at the time. That separation, the leper colony, is unnecessary now because of antibiotics, but continues in most parts of the world due to bigotry and lack of information. Brother Rose knows this all too well."

Jumping off the table, Michael walked among the pressing crowd, speaking in his loudest lecture voice. "The temporary quarantine and isolation we're doing now is necessary to control this virulent strain.

Once the patients have therapeutic levels of the drugs in their blood-streams, they'll be able to resume normal activities. To congregate."

"How long will that take?" asked Koirala.

"Weeks."

"How is it spread?" a high-pitched voice from the audience asked.

Michael looked at the patchquilt of staring faces. "Aerosol. The leprosy bacteria spreads from lungs to lungs."

A rumbling of coughs filled the room.

"How many of us are going to get it?"

"I can't say. If we wear masks, gowns and gloves when we're in the hospital or even in the village, most of us should be fine."

"Is leprosy usually as severe as our cases?" a young man called. Michael recognized him as one of the health care workers he'd seen in the Pokhara hospital.

"Absolutely not. It's bad enough, but it's less contagious, more indolent and chronic. Bloody pneumonia and diarrhea are unheard of."

Alice interrupted. "Any more questions?"

Her words were met by silence. "If not, I want each staff member to take their allotment of pills. Take the three different types immediately. Afterward, we'll discuss the treatment protocol and how we plan to distribute the medicine to the villagers when it comes. We're going to end this epidemic as soon as the drug arrives."

Michael bowed his head and let the words penetrate.

chapter twenty-one

Sitting with the other Farberg board members in the overheated conference room in his Zurich home, Erik Bittner could smell the energy in the room. A useful CEO tool.

"I'm sure you know why I've called this emergency meeting," he began, shifting his bulk and tapping a fat finger on the polished conference table. "Can we supply the needs of the WHO?"

"We have shipped them a two-month supply for their staff," said the raven-bearded operating officer, Otto Kline.

"What about the rest of the valley?"

"We are increasing production in our two plants. It's a top priority."

"How many people are affected with this new strain of leprosy?"

"They said it could eventually be as high as thirty thousand."

Erik felt his eyes widen. "Will we have enough to handle two years of treatment for... several million people?"

"Millions?" one of the members questioned.

"The reports indicate the germ is rather contagious. We must be prepared for any emergency," Erik said in his honeyed voice. "Anything could happen."

"I doubt if we will have enough drug to care for that many people," Otto worried.

"Then I humbly suggest we initiate mass production of the anti-leprosy drugs."

"It's not so simple, Herr Bittner," Otto objected. "These drugs have always been money losers. Our factories are geared up to produce our more profitable broad-spectrum antibiotics."

"I've lost millions on the so-called profitable drugs. This outbreak offers us an opportunity to recoup our monies."

"It's time to change course," Max, the CFO, said predictably, always the yes-man.

Erik added, "There is no option. Our company has to produce

these drugs. No one else will." He looked sternly at his Board members. "Does everyone agree to the change in production?" He rose, not waiting for the toadies to nod their heads.

Studying the portraits of his ancestors hanging on the wall of his library, Erik knew that the epidemic would solve his immediate problems. He would not have to sell the family country estate near the Bodensee or their Zurich mansion. Indeed, he would not have to sell any of the Farberg properties. He would accomplish what his father never did; he would attain long-term financial solvency for the family.

Erik was startled when Max entered the study. An initial flush of anger at having his train of thought disturbed coursed through his body. "What is it?"

The Farberg CFO retreated a few steps. "I'm sorry to intrude. I only wanted to say I personally contacted the factory managers regarding your suggestions."

Erik finished drinking his coffee.

"They can readily convert production to the anti-leprosy drugs," Max continued.

Erik nodded. "That was good of you to arrange. We must provide the medication. Aside from the profit and humanitarian aspects, our reputation is at stake."

"Otto is too timid, not a man of action."

"A naturally-occurring mutant leprosy is thrown our way and Farberg has the only treatment? We have to take advantage of this rare opportunity."

Max poured fresh coffee from the brewing pot into Erik's cup. "I was thinking," he said. "If the delivery of the drug were somehow delayed..."

Erik's nostrils flared as he caught the scent of Max's strategy, but he spoke casually. "A greater spread of the disease would ensue and—"

"And there would be a significant increase in the need for the drug." After taking a deliberate sip, Erik mused, "More people would get sick. That would be a concern."

"Once the drug is administered they would be fine."

Erik slowly returned the coffee cup to the desk. There would be so little downside and such a great upside — saving their family estates and no embarrassing financial crisis.

Could he do it?

"I'm not prepared to give you the verbal order to have delays."

A skeptical look crossed Max's face.

"Do you understand?" Erik prodded.

"I was only thinking that if we were to…"

"I will leave this matter totally in your hands. Do what you believe is best."

Her life was a disaster. Vera leaned against the wall of the treatment room and wondered if she could survive another month in the ER.

"Sarkov. Phone. Line three," the intercom blared.

"It's Michael," said the distant voice the instant she picked up. "Got some news."

"If it's bad, just hang up and let me live in ignorance."

Michael laughed. "We spoke with several leprosy experts. The consensus is that triple therapy should work best. The WHO confirms that."

"Where are you getting your meds?"

"Farberg. A Swiss company. They said they would supply us with all we need. I suspect they barely have enough, so get your procurement office moving. I think there's going to be a run on the meds."

"Then what happens?"

"Word has it that the WHO is seeking other companies to make the drugs. But that'll take time — too much time."

"I'll have the Director of Health Services call today."

"How are things in the city?"

"Our leprosy is still limited to Chinatown."

"Don't be fooled. It can spread rapidly. Get details on all reports of pneumonia and skin rashes."

"I'm doing that."

"Any news about any other cities…"

"Nothing." What she didn't tell Michael was that she was getting precious little cooperation.

Erik hated inquisitions. He found the WHO's questioning of Farberg's ability to produce the anti-leprosy drugs insulting.

With Max trailing behind him, Erik entered the noisy auditorium from the side door. He lumbered toward the platform, keeping his eyes fixed on the table with his nameplate. After sitting, he scanned the hall, a semi-circular space filled with several hundred theater-style chairs. The first four rows held a dour looking audience. He couldn't find one friendly face.

When Anton Koenig, chairman of the WHO's Executive Board, entered with his entourage of four associates, silence filled the room. Anton, a forgettable man in a gray suit with a complexion and personality to match, nodded and sat down at the table next to Erik and Otto. Anton and Erik had long competed for funds and scientists. Erik expected little support from him.

Adjusting his thick glasses and the gooseneck microphone in front of him, Anton said, "Welcome to the afternoon plenary session of our special Executive Board meeting."

Erik could hear a muted voice coming from the translation headphones lying on his table. The garbled sounds made as much sense as the meeting.

"This session," Anton droned, "is to determine the capability of the Farberg firm to produce the drugs the WHO will need for this emergency."

Erik opened his briefcase and removed several folders.

"As we heard in this morning's session, in the worst case scenario, the drug may have to be administered to at least three to five million people for a minimal period of three years."

The veritable windfall for Erik and Farberg provoked a low buzz of commentary from the audience.

"To address this issue, we have asked Erik Bittner, the president of Farberg Pharmaceuticals, to present the case for his company." Anton turned. "Herr Bittner."

Standing, Erik pointed to the back of the room. At once the lights dimmed and a slide appeared on the screen behind him.

"As you can see from our numbers for the past five years, we have increased production of rifampicin, clofazimine and dapsone. As the demand increased, we were quite capable of matching the requests."

"The amount of drug we need is sixty times greater than your highest volume," Anton interjected.

"Next slide, please. As you can see, we responded immediately to the emergency. We have halted production of our other products and are in the process of making our factories completely available for these medications. On the last line, we have projected the number of pills we will be able to produce. Quite adequate for your needs."

A voice from the audience asked, "How quickly can you convert?"

Max's plan for delaying production might have to be put aside temporarily. Production must be rapid enough to win the WHO contract.

"We're doing so as we speak." Erik glanced at Max. "I'm keenly aware of the exigency of the situation. We're moving with haste. I've insisted upon it."

"The epidemic has spread from Nepal to India," a woman's voice said. "It could be a nightmare. The population, the crowded conditions, the poverty and malnutrition... truly all the ingredients for a nightmare."

"We're quite aware of the consequences if the drug is not delivered in a timely fashion."

"We have all your submitted papers. We will review them and get back to you promptly," Anton said.

Erik nodded into the darkened auditorium, and as he left the room he heard Anton say, "We will now hear about our other options."

chapter twenty-two

Dressed in white coats, the Asian-American doctors and administrators of the San Francisco Powell Street Hospital lined up on the stone steps in front of the brown brick building, addressing the thousands of people crushing in around them. Vera, sent by the university to oversee the situation, watched as the chief administrator spoke into a hand-held microphone.

"We're totally filled. Every bed. And we have no anti-leprosy medicine. Dr. Sarkov here, from UC Hospital..." he nodded to Vera, "has advised me that it would be best if all of you went home and stayed there. In isolation."

He repeated the announcement in Mandarin.

The shouting from the crowd made it difficult for Vera to hear any specific comments.

"Leprosy spreads in situations like this. Crowds are unsafe," the administrator said. "Avoid them. Go home."

A young man yelled, "What about the dying?"

Vera stepped forward and took the microphone. "Take the severely ill to the Mission General Hospital ER and we'll assign you to a hospital. Everyone else must go home and stay there. Immediately."

The administrator translated her words, and the shouting from the crowd intensified. When he finished, the administrator beckoned to his assistant. "Get the police," he whispered. "The riot police."

Vera shouted, "All of you, go home. When the city gets the medication, we'll make an announcement where and when you can get the pills. In the meantime, please leave."

The thousands of people remained where they were.

Walking into the lobby, the administrator said to Vera, "You see our problem; the people are totally irrational. Why are they staying here waiting for the medicine? This is ridiculous and futile."

"According to the CDC, we won't be getting any this week. I

agree, I don't see…"

Vera never finished the sentence as hordes of people rushed into the hospital, sweeping her against the wall. The administrator fell to the ground as the people trampled over him.

Vera remained motionless while the mayor of San Francisco, Lou Robbins, studied the plans written up by the city's Director of Health Services. Lou, an old hippie, once called Crazy Louie, had beaten a drug habit and been "clean" for thirty years. The only remnants of his 1960s commune days were his shoulder-length hair and mismatched socks.

"What's wrong with these plans?" he asked.

Vera found them unacceptable, but she did not speak, waiting for Dave Epstein, her CDC contact, to do the talking. Swiveling around in his leather chair, Lou stood and strolled amongst the six members of his staff.

"No city-wide quarantine? Is that what you say?" Lou asked his Health Director, Ed Vasquez.

Ed rubbed his scrubby goatee. "Not yet, sir. The epidemic is limited to Chinatown. The Hwang family, their personal contacts and a few others."

"Bull. Over a hundred cases have been reported, and the total number of infected is probably much higher," Vera said. "We had a panic at the Powell Street Hospital."

Ed waved her off. "We plan to check and treat all of the Powell Street Hospital personnel and all of the Hwangs' direct contacts, as well as Jennifer Wilson's — even the people on the plane with her from Hong Kong to San Francisco."

"And you say that's not good enough?"the mayor asked Vera and Dave.

"This goddamn epidemic is going to spread beyond Chinatown, and then we're screwed," Vera answered.

"We're treating all the new cases," argued the Director.

"Screw the medication." Dave stepped forward. "The only thing that's going to stop the spread in Frisco is a full-blown quarantine. The people of this city have to be told to stay at home until the disease is under control. Period. That's the official, sanctioned CDC position."

"That's pretty extreme." Lou walked behind his cherrywood desk and looked through the slats of the venetian blinds at the outside traffic. "A logistical nightmare."

"You have to get on it now," Vera demanded. "ASAP."

"Is this a CDC order?" Lou asked Dave.

"No order, but our strongest recommendation. It may be a PR or political nightmare, but it's a necessary one," Dave replied.

"My decision will have nothing to do with politics. It never has. Everyone knows that."

"If it doesn't, then why not shut down the damn city?" Dave countered.

"This is the real world, not some laboratory experiment." Lou's voice betrayed his irritation. "Ed says no. Why should I listen to you?"

Vera cut in. "Because you don't want to kill a hundred thousand citizens of San Francisco. That's why."

Turning to Ed, Lou threw up his hands. "Good reason. Any comments?"

"It's using dynamite to kill a cockroach."

"This is one bug that needs dynamite," Vera responded earnestly. "In Nepal, it spread like—"

"I know. I know. You told me ten times." Lou popped two antacid tablets into his mouth, then rubbed his face briskly. "I know my constituents. I know what we can do. We already had one bad riot. A citywide quarantine would cause worse panic. I think my Director's plan of limited quarantine makes the most sense."

"I'm sure I'm right," Ed insisted

"You'd better be, or I'll have your balls," Lou said. "Now let's hope and pray for the best."

"In Nepal—" Vera began.

"Screw Nepal. This is not Nepal. This is San Francisco, for God's sake." Lou took a deep breath. "I appreciate your opinion, Doctor, but we don't share it."

"I'll just have to get a court order forcing you to close down the fucking city," Dave shouted.

"You do that." Lou stood. "You and Big Brother. The Feds are always sticking their noses in the wrong places."

Dave shrugged. "Better have your black suit dry-cleaned, Lou.

Getting a court order will take time, and this bacillus doesn't need much of that to start killing people."

Vera left Dave in her office making phone calls and ducked into a small, unused consultation room to make a call of her own.

Her words came out in a tumble. "Mickey, something real bad is coming down here. We had a riot in Chinatown — police, dozens injured. As you thought, we now have over a hundred leprosy cases. And the mayor refuses to quarantine the goddamn city."

"Did you get any triple therapy?"

"Nope. We're waiting. We have some dapsone. Mostly expired stuff. That's what we're giving the infected cases."

She heard Michael swear under his breath. "Not good enough," he said aloud. "Get that triple therapy and treat all primary contacts, right now."

"That's why I called. Do you have any drug to spare?"

"C'mon, Vera, we're in the undeveloped world here. We have dapsone and precious little of that. I was about to call you to see if you could pull strings in the States to send us supplies in Nepal."

Michael felt growing alarm as he replayed his conversation with Vera. Jennifer Wilson had unleashed a deadly organism on the city of San Francisco. He pictured the leprosy spreading like the plague had six hundred years ago. Fortunately, that would never happen. The triple therapy would prevent that.

With Alice's approval, he had worked out a plan for the entire staff. Everyone in Pokhara and the surrounding area would be checked for signs of leprosy and their lesion sizes would be recorded. Those with active disease would be isolated and treated. Those free of lesions would be treated later, when adequate supplies of antibiotics became available. With the extra workers from the Nepalese government and the WHO, Michael hoped it would be doable.

Michael's own screening assignment was the poorest section of the village, comprised of tiny, one-room mud huts that frequently housed six or more people.

The streets were crowded with people doing business as he,

Brother Rose and his two Nepalese assistants pushed their way past vending carts loaded with cauliflower, herbs, spices, rice, and brightly colored saris. Emaciated cows, pigs, chickens and goats strolled aimlessly along streets and alleyways like carefree citizens of the community. Michael didn't like all this activity, a leprosy bacillus's dream environment.

Elbowing through the throngs, he pulled his mask over his nose and mouth and fought his way to the first hut on his list. Inside, he found a young mother breast-feeding a baby. Two more children, naked boys of about four and six years of age, sat listlessly nearby with streams of green mucus running from their nostrils into their mouths. The grim-faced, toothless father squatted silently on the dirt floor watching his family. Michael bowed and smiled while the assistants explained the purpose of their visit.

The father offered them some tea, which Michael politely accepted; to do otherwise would be insulting. He sat next to the father and examined the peripheral nerve trunks and abnormal pigmented spots on the man's arms, which had grown since the last time he'd seen him. Michael told the grimacing Brother Rose what to write on the yellow notepad. He then checked the children and mother, who had no lesions.

The team went to the next mud hut, a few feet away. Inside, a couple of wide-eyed teenaged parents sat with their infant on a mat, eating rice. When Michael examined their upper limbs, a look of anxiety crossed the parents' faces. They had numb areas on their arms, in addition to lash and brow loss, and small pink bumps on their skin. Michael took out his ruler and measured the size of the lesions. Aghast at what he was seeing, he tried to smile in order to mask his inner horror.

Outside, with an alarmed look on her face, one of the assistants asked, "What is wrong, Dr. Michael?"

"Almost all of these people are developing leprosy, and the changes are occurring unbelievably fast. I measured that mother's largest bump four days ago. It was only three by four millimeters. Now it's more than five by five. Growth like that is unheard of. Where is that goddamn medicine? If it doesn't come this week..."

He turned, and Michael saw the depressed look on Brother Rose's face. "Don't worry, Brother. When we get the meds from Farberg, we'll stop this."

Brother Rose nodded. "Any other possibility is too horrible to contemplate."

Michael had come to the same conclusion.

"It's unbelievable that so few are escaping the leprosy epidemic." Brother Rose coughed, momentarily lifting his mask. "The people in the hospital are terribly mutilated: blind, faceless, limbless. They're in worse shape than the lifelong lepers in Muniguda."

"And they have the milder form of the disease," Michael said, "as compared to them." He pointed toward the burial grounds on the outskirts of the village.

Brother Rose closed his eyes and muttered a quick prayer. "I wonder who is better off," he said solemnly, between coughs, "these people or the villagers in the ground over there."

"That cough. Are you okay?" Michael asked.

Brother Rose shrugged. "The dust. But Michael, the medications work so slowly in the mutibacillary cases. It may take months to see any effect. By that time, so many people will die. Too many."

"That's why we have to contain it to the valley," Michael said.

"There are WHO reports of disease in India."

"We still have to control this outbreak. We'll have to close the marketplaces and restrict everyone to their homes. The next few weeks are critical."

Michael couldn't tell him that despite that same precaution, the plague had stopped only after three-fourths of Europe's population was dead.

The medicine had to work.

Back at the lab, Michael heard Alice and Etienne arguing with the field workers. "What's wrong?" he asked.

"The workers say the villagers think the trachoma medication is causing the epidemic and they are refusing to take this or any antibiotic," answered Etienne.

"Jeez." Michael slumped on a lab stool. "It'll be a nightmare if they don't take the anti-leprosy medication."

"Exactly. That is what Etienne and I are worried about," Alice said. "You spoke irresponsibly about the amiomycin, and this is the result of your recklessness."

Michael had had enough of Alice's accusations, especially the ones that weren't true. And it was true that the amiomycin could have triggered the problem. He took a deep breath, trying to calm his anger. "Since I was the one who first raised the issue, I should be the one to speak to the villagers."

"They'll not listen," one of the Nepalese workers said. "They're furious. It won't be safe for any of us to visit the patients in the study."

"I went into town this morning to check for leprosy lesions and had no problems," Michael said.

"They are angriest with the trachoma people. It may not be as dangerous for you," another field worker said.

"All the more reason for me to go. Who'll come with me?"

"It'll be risky for anyone to speak to the people about the trachoma study at this point," Etienne said. "Even you."

"I'm going. Who's coming with me?"

The silence was broken by a solitary voice. "I'll come," said Koirala. "And I will translate your words."

After setting up the speaker system in the Land Rover in the village square, Michael stood next to the car with Koirala.

"Tell the people I want to talk to them about the trachoma medication," Michael said to Koirala, who immediately spoke into the microphone.

The villagers gathered around the car, grumbling skeptically.

"Now tell them the trachoma medication didn't cause this epidemic."

After Koirala spoke to the assembled throng, jeers greeted his remarks.

"Say that the epidemic started in Baglun and not among the people in the trachoma study. Therefore the trachoma medication isn't responsible."

After finishing the translation, Koirala ducked as a rock flew by his head.

"Damn. Stand back." Michael grabbed the microphone. "Listen, the medicine is safe. Totally safe."

Someone in the crowd shouted "pig liar" in English. Michael turned too late to avoid the onion that smacked against his head.

"Get in the car," Michael ordered Koirala.

Michael raised his hand. "Please, we're not harming anyone with our trachoma medicines. We want to help you. We only want..." A small stone glanced off his shoulder.

When the crowd drew closer, shaking fists and sticks, Koirala started up the engine and yelled, "We must be leaving, Doctor Michael."

At the roar of the engine, the villagers charged the Land Rover. The vehicle shot back in reverse, and Michael raced toward it. A second rock struck his forehead just as he jumped aboard. Koirala floored the gas pedal, leaving the crowd engulfed in dust. Michael wiped the blood away from his eyes.

Before the evening meeting, Michael walked out to the road and back, still shaken from the results of his screening of the villagers and his attack. The trachoma study was dead. And they would need to do a great deal of PR before the locals accepted any medications from anyone, even for the dreaded leprosy.

It was October, and the weather was decidedly cooler than it had been just a month earlier. The winter rainy season was approaching. He shivered at the stark realization that the flu season would increase people's susceptibility. Even worse, the *M. Leprae* grew best in cool temperatures. And worst of all, the likelihood of the germ developing resistance to the drugs would increase, a phenomenon called accelerated spread that happened in situations like this. The longer the hosts went without the drugs, the more lethal the germ would become. They needed the medications *now,* and he was going to get them.

chapter twenty-three

Summoned to take an urgent phone call, Michael hurried to the lab and punched in the code for the direct line to the Peace Corps headquarters in Kathmandu. Alice, Etienne and Brother Rose watched.

"Mac, this is Michael. Alice said you had pressing orders for me?"

"Marching orders," Mac said. "Koenig called. He wants you and Brother Rose to get your butts out of Pokhara immediately. Your consulting days are over. You found the germ; your work is done. The bug is too damned contagious."

"No way."

"What do you mean? Those are your orders. The disease is spreading all over Pokhara. We don't want you dead. Bad PR. I want the two of you out today, the sooner the better."

"Mac, I have a job to do. I'm staying."

"You did your job. You have nothing to gain by staying. When the drug gets there they'll stop it. They don't need you or Rose for that."

"Since you mentioned the damn drugs, we need them now. Not in a few days or next week, but now. No more bureaucratic bullshit."

"They're coming. A Sir Hilary Wilson bought a large quantity from Farberg and is personally delivering the drugs this week."

Damn. Sir Hilary had figured out a way to get to Pokhara.

Michael looked over to Alice, who was watching him with narrowed eyes, holding her breath. "The team needs my help. I'm not abandoning them."

"As your WHO liaison I'm ordering you to leave," Mac said.

"I appreciate your concern, Mac, but I'm staying until the epidemic is over. I will, however, get Brother Rose out."

After hanging up, Michael turned to his friend, feeling strangely elated at his decision. "He says—"

"I'm not going either," interrupted the monk. "I believe I was brought here for a reason. I know I can help."

Alice let out a deep breath. "Thank you, Brother." She turned to

Michael and nodded. "And thank you for staying."

Alice left the lab and began walking. Gazing across the lush, wet terraced fields of yellow mustard plants and dark green cauliflower leaves, all covered by the orange glow of the setting sun, Alice felt energized. Soon the deaths would end. And Michael wasn't running away. In fact, even ordered to leave, he was staying — not abandoning the team, not abandoning her. Maybe he *could* change and be depended on.

She ambled back to her cabin and saw him, standing on the path next to the dining tent. For an awkward moment they stared at each other; Alice broke the connection and looked off into the sky, then back to Michael.

"There's something I need to say to you." Alice kicked at the dusty road. "Since you arrived, I've been... hard on you."

"It's understandable."

They stood silently on the road until Alice gathered the strength to go on. "I also want you to know that I appreciate what you're doing. Your coming, and even more, your staying."

"It was an easy decision."

Alice let her eyes rest on the surrounding peaks. "Sometimes I think about getting away from here. Going back to England."

"There are no guarantees of safety anywhere."

Alice started toward her cabin, Michael following. "The drug will be here soon," she hoped.

"In the meantime," Michael said, "we have to keep everyone's spirits up and convince the people that it's safe to take the leprosy medicine."

"I'll make a point of showing them that the staff is taking the drugs, too."

"Great idea."

When she entered her cabin, Michael stopped at the entrance.

"There is a concern," Alice said, turning back to Michael.

"Only one?"

"Rowan's theory. Resistance."

"The triple therapy has been used for years with only a few cases of resistance." He made a show of crossing his fingers and smiled.

"No traffic out of San Francisco." Dave paced the creaky floor in

the conference room of City Hall, while his white shirt worked its way
out of his pants. The distribution of muscles and fat over his body
reflected his past weight-lifting and his present lack of it.

Vera wondered what she had once found attractive in this man.
Swinging his hands wildly, he repeated, "Nothing out. Whatever
essentials come in, stay in. Whoever comes in, stays in. Get it?"

Mayor Robbins stood facing the window, his hands clasped
behind his back, a look of unlikely calm on his face. The two dozen
administrators and staff in attendance, pads in hand, sat on metal
folding chairs, trying to absorb the news. They hurled a rapid burst of
questions at Dave.

"Why not quarantine Chinatown? That we can do," said a man in
a gray three-piece, pinstriped suit.

"That's not good enough," Dave answered.

The man grunted.

"Also, Dr. Sarkov tells me that there are at least two dozen
reported cases outside of Chinatown." Dave glanced at Vera. "That's
why."

"Most of the police and firemen live outside of the city. What do
we do with them?" asked the crew-cut, ruddy complexioned police
chief.

"Pick a minimal force to stay in the city. Keep the rest in reserve
for an emergency."

"Most of our food comes from outside the city, too. How do we
handle that?" asked the mayor.

"I'll leave that up to you."

"There are vital workers who live in the city and need to travel.
And truckers use our freeway to get from the Peninsula to the East
Bay," said a heavily freckled, angry-looking man.

Holding up his hand, Dave said, "Whoa. I'm not here to solve all
your fucking problems. You are."

"Mr. Mayor, did you approve this crazy scheme?" the man in the
suit asked.

Dave cut in. "Listen. It's a done deal. Closed for debate. The
governor is also on board. We quarantine the city in two days. Friday.
You'll have the weekend to test the closure."

"How long will this last?" the police chief asked.

Dave turned to Vera who said, "Until the medication starts to take effect. At least a few weeks... maybe a month or two."

"Jesus. This is a nightmare," shouted the man in the pinstriped suit.

"Right." The mayor loosened his tie. "Now earn your pay. You have four days to make it happen. There'll be no excuses."

After everyone but Vera filed out, Dave collapsed into one of the folding chairs. "These fucking chairs are terrible. No wonder everyone was so damn grouchy."

"You could have been more... respectful."

He eyed her with an expression Vera recognized as impersonal lust born of habit. "Talking about respect, how's the General Hospital treating my Stanford summa cum laude buddy?"

"Well enough," Vera said, stretching to give him an eat-your-heart-out eyeful.

"Want to tell me about it? How about dinner? You still like Chinese food?"

Vera stood to leave, finding sexual deprivation not such a bad option — infinitely preferable to a night of fighting off Dave.

"I have to get back to the ER."

chapter twenty-four

Michael stood at the side of the path and watched through his binoculars as two vans and two trucks rumbled down the road, churning up clouds of fine sand. The first full shipment of anti-leprosy drugs had arrived in Pokhara. The staff cheered, waving hats and scarves as the convoy from the airport turned up the steep, serpentine path to the camp.

"Thank God. The nightmare is almost over," Michael said to Alice.

Michael saw Sir Hilary jump out of the lead car, dust himself off, and walk toward them with reporters and a cameraman following close behind. He still wore a conspicuous black armband on his elegant linen Englishman-in-the-tropics suit. *At least he isn't wearing a pith helmet,* Michael thought.

The spidery-framed Reimer and a bruiser of a man, also got out of the car, but disappeared into the crowd.

Turning to the camera, one of the reporters spoke. "We're here in Pokhara, Nepal, the site of the deadly leprosy epidemic. Sir Hilary Wilson, head of the Wilson Foundation, is here with me. He's official-ly delivering the anti-leprosy medication to these brave workers."

A thin-lipped smile formed on Sir Hilary's face. "I'm pleased that our Foundation was given the opportunity to help the unfortunate, afflicted people of Nepal," he said in his nasal, aristocratic accent. "This wonderful emergency team, like the workers at Farberg, has been toiling tirelessly in an effort to stop this dreaded disease. We at the Wilson Foundation are only too pleased to be the nexus, the link if you will, between these two groups."

Michael stared at the public relations play being acted out before him.

"...a four-month supply of medicines, with more on its way to Kathmandu, India and the States," Sir Hilary continued. "The epidemic will soon be over. The cost to our foundation, although significant, is well worth every penny." He sighed piteously. "This is a bittersweet moment for me. My only daughter, Jen…" His voice broke, but he collected himself. "Jennifer, while working in this area, contracted leprosy and recently passed away." Sir Hilary's voice again wavered, and he clutched at a starched white handkerchief that materialized in one hand. "I can relate to the anguish that is being felt by the families who have lost close ones. We have…"

Reimer reappeared in the crowd and made a quick circling motion with a finger for Sir Hilary to wrap it up.

Wilson dabbed at his cheek. "I have a painful bond with these people."

The press coverage ended, and Rowan tugged at Michael's arm. "We made it," she shouted.

Alice wiped tears from her eyes. "We survived. Now it's time to help the others survive."

Michael nodded impatiently. There was still a great deal of work to do. He had to talk to the villagers and he needed Koirala.

Sir Hilary strode over, shaking hands with the lined-up staff like a visiting head of state. When he reached Alice and Rowan, Sir Hilary said, "The Drs. Morgan-Wright. I know your mother well. Enjoyed many a dinner party at your lovely estate in the Cotswolds."

The sisters smiled.

He grasped Michael's hand. "Dr. Cohen. I'm delighted to see you again. I'm looking forward to a tete-a-tete with you."

With the camera rolling, Michael smiled and said, "Thank you for your efforts, Sir Hilary. We now have a great deal of work to do, so I'm sure you'll understand that our talk may have to wait."

"I am a patient man. For the moment I shall simply get out of your way while you save lives." He backed away.

End of scene, Michael thought, looking at the camera as it followed Sir Hilary. *Exit stage left.*

Entering the technician's tent, Michael waved Koirala over. "Despite our lack of success last time, we've got to talk to the villagers about taking the drug. And of course see that your son is treated at once."

"I have been thinking about that, Dr. Michael," Koirala replied. "I am needing to talk to you."

They walked up the road leading to the cliff. Together they looked out at the valley and the distant village below.

"A seemingly peaceful place sitting among the mountains, don't you think, Dr. Michael?" Koirala mused wistfully. "At one time, we were a quiet village, but that seems so long ago."

"I'm sure it does."

"The wheel of life turns continuously, and all will be peaceful again when we... when the nightmare ends," Koirala said. He shook his head. "It was all seeming so wonderful. The world-famous WHO, here in our little valley, helping us rid ourselves from trachoma, a disease that has been with us, blinding us, for over two thousand years. Truly a miracle."

Michael furrowed his brows and studied the princely man. What was he getting at?

"We were being given amiomycin, a new wonder drug, one we now learn has a hidden, deadly side effect. My son, Bahadur, has passed on to a better life."

Michael gasped; he swallowed the lump that came to his throat. "I'm so sorry, Koirala. I didn't know. If only we had the treatment sooner. How sad and bitter this day must be for you." He paused, then added, "But be assured that this form of leprosy wasn't caused by the amiomycin. I was merely giving a speculative example."

Staring down at the village, Koirala persisted, "Because I am believing, despite your opinion to the opposite, that the amiomycin did cause this epidemic, I am extremely worried about the new medicines."

Michael nodded. "I understand. But germs can mutate without any help from antibiotics. They have been doing that throughout recorded history as far back as ancient Egypt."

"I must ask you an important question." Koirala fixed his aggrieved gaze upon Michael. "You must tell me the truth."

"Of course I will."

"Truly, did the amiomycin cause this?"

Michael took a deep breath. "I don't know. It's possible."

"Can you find out?"

"The trachoma study is ruined. It's over. There will be no more amiomycin administered."

"I must know the truth."

Michael was a scientist, a purist; he also wanted to know. Yet, if they proved an association between the two, the consequences could be devastating. Alice would be crushed. He had to consider the fallout.

"Please, Doctor Michael."

"I'll have to think it over," Michael said. "Now I have to ask you for another favor. I need your help convincing the villagers that the anti-leprosy medication is safe, so they'll all take it."

"Is it safe, Doctor Michael?"

"Completely. We have to convince them."

"Even though you are a stranger, I know you have a true heart — a Boddhisattva heart. But I'm worried. Can this medicine cause problems?"

Michael put his hands on Koirala's shoulders and met his eyes. "No. It can't."

Koirala closed his eyes and remained motionless for a few moments. Then he nodded. "I will trust in you and your words. I will go with you to speak to my people."

Michael held out his hand and Koirala shook it vigorously. But somewhere in the depths of Michael's mind a queasy feeling lurked. *Something is wrong.*

After placing a small wooden crate filled with forty-eight bottles of the anti-leprosy medication into the Land Rover, Koirala spoke to Michael. "The villagers are still not being receptive, Doctor Michael. I heard angry words. I think it best if the police come with us."

"No police."

"I think it is dangerous for us to go to the center of town."

"I agree. But I'm going." Michael leaped into the car and turned to Koirala. "Coming?"

The young man slid hesitantly into the passenger seat.

"Don't worry, my friend," Michael encouraged. "You'll be okay. Just stay in the car and translate into the loudspeaker while I talk."

Michael drove. Koirala removed his wooden bracelet and rubbed the beads between his fingers, mumbling prayers.

At the central village square, Michael waited in the car as the natives gathered around him. They didn't look any friendlier than they had the last time.

As planned, Koirala announced over the loudspeaker that the anti-leprosy medication had arrived and that those who wanted it should approach the car.

No one moved.

Michael jumped out of the auto and walked toward the enlarging crowd. Hostile shouts erupted and several people waved their fists.

"The people are very angry. Do not go too close," Koirala warned.

"Tell them I will take the medicine first."

After Koirala translated the words, the crowd quieted.

"Tell them they only need to take three pills. To show them how safe it is, I'll take nine pills, three times the number they're to take."

"Is that wise?"

"Not wise, but necessary."

Koirala spoke to the people, and Michael could feel the tension abate. "Get me some bottled water and three pills from each bottle."

Koirala held up the bottles so the people could see him remove the medicine. Then Michael swallowed all the pills, followed by a gulp of water.

"See? Harmless. I'm asking all of you to take only three."

Michael was surrounded by silence, until a young boy came closer. "I am Koirala's cousin. He said to trust you. I and my family and friends will take the pills."

Michael's throat tightened. "Thank you."

A line formed in front of the Land Rover, and Michael watched as Koirala recorded each person's name and handed him or her a paper cup of water and the three pills.

Dapsone, clofazimine and rifampicin at triple dosage. Michael expected he would feel quite nauseated for a few days, but it was worth it.

chapter twenty-five

The exuberant mood at the re-instituted evening staff meeting was contagious; even Michael felt at ease. Reports from the field indicated a halting of the progression of the disease. He didn't even mind Sir Hilary and the cadaverous Reimer snooping around the camp asking questions, taking photographs and checking out all the places Jennifer had stayed — treating her hut like a shrine by draping it with ropes of marigolds and fastening a small wooden plaque on the door.

Grabbing Rowan, Brother Rose gave her a sloppy kiss on her cheek. She blushed."Like St. George, we are going to slay the monster," he hollered.

At that, a loud cheer arose in the dining tent, with the new WHO and Nepalese arrivals hooting and yelling as much as the old-timers. Standing atop the table, Alice, her face radiant and flushed, called out, "A toast to hard work, luck and good medicine."

While everyone raised their glasses, Michael sat fascinated by the scene.

"I have a radio," one of the Nepalese shouted, beaming. "How about some music?"

Two minutes later, he returned with his portable short-wave set. Finding an old Motown song, he asked Rowan to dance. She looked over toward Michael, then followed the man onto the floor.

Alice extended her hands to Brother Rose. "Can you dance, Brother?"

"Are you kidding? Just watch me."

Michael sat back in his chair, contented, as most of the staff poured onto the makeshift dance floor. Watching Alice's lissome figure shimmy about the room with Brother Rose, he suddenly jumped up and jogged over to the dancing couple. He wanted her. After cutting in and without missing a step, Michael took Alice in his arms. Her eyes narrowed. Maybe she still didn't trust him and maybe it was too much to hope for, but he couldn't help feeling he and Alice had been given another chance. His eyes riveted on her attractive face, he twirled and spun her about the room. He was flying in space.

A perspiring, puffing Brother Rose leaned toward them. "If you were a woman, I'd ask you to dance," he said to Michael.

Michael stopped for a moment and laughingly embraced Brother Rose. As he did so, he saw Rowan stalking out of the tent.

When exhaustion hit and some of the happy, overworked staff filed slowly out of the dining tent into the cool night air, Michael wandered off alone. He gazed dreamily over the flickering lights of the village below and admired the moonlight casting its eerie light on the distant Himalayas. His assignment would soon be completed and he had promised Roy Woods that he would return to Berkeley. But *damn,* he was really going to miss Alice. He felt truly alive in her presence. Excited, nervous, passionate. Could they work things out? Could he?

Once Michael returned to the lab tent, the questions faded. He had to call UC Berkeley.

"Roy, I think we've licked the problem. The triple therapy arrived five days ago and we've started treating the villagers. I know it's too soon to say for sure, but it looks as if the disease is abating."

"I hope this means you're coming back."

"I wanted to talk to you about that."

"The regents are ecstatic about your success. Great PR. I saw the CNN coverage of Sir Hilary delivering the medication, and there you were. Exciting stuff."

Michael rolled his eyes and waited. The true excitement wasn't happening on television.

"However, the archeology staff sees things in a different light," Roy continued. "They're upset about filling in the extra time to teach your classes, no matter how important your mission and how famous you're becoming. I have a mini-rebellion on my hands."

"I'll have to stay until I'm sure everything's okay. It'll take me about a week to wrap things up."

"The interest in leprosy in the States is overwhelming now. The few cases in New York and Washington, D.C. had everyone jittery. I'm confident you'll get your grant to study the yersinia plasmid and leprosy now."

Michael wondered why Vera hadn't told him about the cases on the east coast.

"I was thinking the same."

"We'll look forward to seeing you shortly then?"

Michael walked slowly back to the dining hall. He couldn't stay in Nepal much longer.

"Michael?"

Alice stood before him, trying to catch her breath from the non-stop dancing, her blouse wet with perspiration, her chest rising and falling noticeably with each inspiration and expiration.

"Al."

He watched as she ran her hands through her loose ebony-colored hair, causing it to ride in the evening breeze. Without speaking, they looked at each other in the moonlight. Alice came closer; their hands, then bodies touched, the wind brushing her wet hair against his face. They remained entrenched in this close position. Had she forgiven him?

A gentle kiss on his cheek answered the question.

"What are you going to do, Brother?" Michael asked while saying his good-byes to the staff. His work done, he was to be among the first to leave Pokhara. Sir Hilary, Reimer and their associates had departed in the early hours of the morning on a private jet.

"Alice wants me to work with the lepers in the village; they're still shaken up. I decided to stay for another month or so. We may have stopped the disease, but I need to help these people deal with their losses."

"I understand," Michael said. "Please stay in touch. Let me know if there are any problems and I'll come running."

Brother Rose nodded. "After the month, I'll return to Muniguda. It's home."

"I'll miss you."

Brother Rose wrapped his arms about Michael and gently squeezed. "Life will be emptier without you, my friend. Please take care."

"And you take care of that cough."

Brother Rose turned and without looking back, left for the village.

Etienne walked over, kissed Michael on both cheeks, said, *"Bon chance,"* then sped off after Brother Rose.

Alice marched over from the lab. He saw a look of melancholy cross her face. "I suppose this time you do have to go."

More than anything, he wanted to say no. "I ran out in early semester," he explained to her yet again. "I have to get back or there'll be a lynching. Also, Roy said I'll probably get my grant to study the yersinia plasmid."

"I'm happy about the grant, but…"

Michael shrugged. "With everything under control, I'm not really needed here."

Her eyes teared. "How is it that we were brought together only to be separated again?"

Michael tried to control the sadness that was quickly enveloping him. The pain of leaving Alice was intolerable, worse than the anxiety of being close. "What are your plans?"

She shook herself, then spoke evenly. "It'll take time to close down the trachoma study — probably at least two months. Then I may go back to London to work at the Institute. They want me to continue my fieldwork elsewhere."

"I believe in fate, karma." In a hushed tone, Michael continued, "I'll try to get back during Christmas break."

"That would be wonderful."

The softness of her words touched Michael.

"Despite the Berkeley staff grumblings, I'm in a good position for a favor," he said. "I'll be back."

"If you can't make it then, could you come to London?"

"That I definitely can do… over Easter vacation."

Alice fell into his arms, and Michael, filled with a numbing sorrow, held her close. He silently thanked her for forgiving him. Finally, he reluctantly moved away and jumped into the Land Rover.

As the Nepalese driver pulled away, Michael looked back at the shrinking compound, wondering if he would indeed ever see any of these people again. Alice and Brother Rose — he was going to especially miss them. He was going to make a relationship with Alice work.

The driver slammed on the brakes, and Michael was thrust forward in his seat, narrowly missing the windshield.

"I'm sorry, Dr. Michael, but I'm taking a wrong turn," he said.

Turning the car around, he retraced their path. "I've been driving to the airport only a short time. I'll be getting it right one of these times."

Michael thought of those words, "Getting it right one of these times." His satisfaction was dissipating rapidly. Somewhere in the deep recesses of his brain, something gnawed at him like termites eating away at his peace of mind. Whatever was wrong was major.

Leaving Alice bothered him. Should he have stayed? Perhaps. But while he pondered that question, he sensed that brewing further below the surface was a far more insidious and deadly problem.

When they arrived at the airport, Michael didn't move. "Get it right eventually — by trial and error," he muttered. "Damn. Damn. *Damn.*"

The driver looked frightened. "I'm not understanding."

"Take me back," Michael said. "Right now. I'm not leaving. We're in big trouble."

chapter twenty-six

When Michael returned to the camp, a radiant Alice ran toward him. "You've decided to stay."

Michael hugged Alice and took a deep breath. "I had a terrifying thought."

"What?"

"The organism is being killed so quickly because it's metabolically active, like all virulent germs. It's rapidly incorporating the anti-leprosy drugs."

"But that's good, isn't it?"

"No, it's terrible. With this unusual growth rate, the goddamn germ will begin mutating at the same rapid rate."

"Mutating?"

"The germ is finding its way to resistance. It's probably mutating right now — at an unbelievably fast pace. In no time it's going to be far more resistant and dangerous than it already was." He paused, not letting her go. "Don't you see? It's creating a new, deadlier, *resistant* leprosy variant. Like the new resistant TB in Russia and Eastern Europe."

Alice pulled away and stared at Michael in dawning horror. "Rowan's theory."

"Exactly."

Michael pictured an endless row of slot machines, with the handles of each being pulled automatically, over and over again. Eventually, the jackpot would come up in one machine after the next — bacterial resistance.

"I pray I'm wrong, but if I'm right the bacteria could develop resistance within weeks or even days."

Alice stiffened. "You said it would take years. The leprae can't mutate that fast, can it?"

"If it does, it'll be a disaster beyond belief."

After the staff had gathered in the dining tent, Michael opened the emergency meeting. "I've spent almost twenty years studying how germs have behaved throughout history, looking at the big picture, the long-term outlook. Of one thing I'm certain; germs behave in an established, genetically determined fashion. Even this new variant."

Michael recognized the attentive and apprehensive look on Alice's face. "Even though this deadly leprosy germ is unusual, probably given life by a natural genetic alteration, it'll follow the pattern that all bacteria do. When attacked it'll mutate and eventually it'll produce resistant strains. *All bacteria do.*"

"That's my theory," Rowan said.

"Like I told Alice, the process with indolent germs, like the leprae bacilli, would normally take years — long after the germs are killed by the antibiotics. So usually there's no problem."

Michael paced the floor. "But since this new bacillus grows rapidly, kills rapidly, it also absorbs the antibiotics rapidly. That's why our leprosy patients are responding so quickly, much faster than leprosy patients afflicted with the regular leprae bacillus."

"That isn't good?" asked Brother Rose, frowning.

Michael grimaced. "I'm predicting that the germ will also develop resistance faster than normal. What usually takes years may take only weeks."

The staff sat dazed.

Rowan broke the silence. "You're describing my quantitative resistance theory. You're saying this virulent germ is going to respond aggressively to the triple therapy."

"This rapid mutation is all conjectural," objected Etienne. "It's only a theory, no?"

"I'm positive that our only hope is to kill *all* the germs before it becomes resistant," Michael replied. "And there's absolutely no downside to killing the organism as fast as possible. Doing less would be catastrophic."

Michael addressed Alice. "You and Rowan, you're both microbiologists. Have any ideas?"

Rowan spoke up first. "From a molecular biological perspective, we do not have the time to find the abnormal DNA segment and try to damage it. From my little reading on the subject, I quite agree, intense treatment is needed."

"Okay," Alice said. "Then we'll give everyone the maximum triple therapy. Toxic doses. Dapsone up to a hundred fifty milligrams daily, clofazimine up to a hundred milligrams daily and rifampicin six hundred milligrams monthly. Right now. People may become sick from the drugs, but we'll cut back only if serious side effects occur."

"We're fortunate that serious complications from the drugs are rare," Michael added.

"What are they? What should we be looking for?" Rowan asked in a raised voice.

"The biggest problems will be liver damage, severe allergic reactions like the pink bumps of erythema nodosum leprosum and severe GI symptoms. And a heavy dose of nausea." He recalled his own queasy stomach on the days following his dramatic demonstration.

"We don't have enough medication for the push you suggest," Etienne said.

"Immediate high doses are our only hope. The four month supply from Farberg will be good for at least three or four weeks at the levels Alice is talking about. We don't have a choice; we have to do it."

Alice added, "Somehow I'll get more medicine, but we can't worry about that now."

"I'm going to call the States and tell them to start the high doses, too," Michael said. "If we lose this battle, we're in for one hell of an onslaught. The germ will have breached the last barrier. There'll be no stopping it."

Michael saw Brother Rose lift his talisman from his robes and put it to his lips.

chapter twenty-seven

The pungent smell of antiseptics burned Vera's nose like chlorine from an indoor pool. She stood silently in a green mask and gown, watching the doctors and nurses work on the seriously ill patients — starting IVs, connecting monitors and positioning oxygen masks.

Bill Marcus lay covered with a small blanket, an intravenous drip flowing into his left wrist. An oxygen tent and a respirator helped him survive. A nurse in a mask, cap and gown leaned over him, applying a cool wet sponge to his upper body.

Over the last twelve hours, the doctors had doubled Bill's dose of the anti-leprosy therapy, but each hour his fever had risen. Now, the doctor told Vera, it stood at 104 degrees. Vera could picture the problem; blood-soaked lungs and hemorrhagic intestines, just like Jennifer's.

Observing her friend's wheezing, labored breathing, his cyanotic lips and nails, his pallor and the pulmonary monitor, Vera said to the nurse, "You'd better increase the oxygen support. He needs it."

Vera stared affectionately at the vivid freckles speckling his pale face and sensed, with a wave of grief, that he only had a few more hours to live.

After a few attempts at deep breaths, Bill removed his mask and tried to speak. He couldn't.

Replacing the mask, Vera felt the tears begin to run down her face. She grasped Bill's hand and sat on a chair next to his bed. "I won't leave. Like I told you the first day in the ER, we're a team. We're going to make it."

He smiled weakly.

Vera looked on helplessly. He coughed violently into the oxygen mask, filling it with blood. She watched as he gasped for air, but only the red fluid flowed through his nose and mouth. He ripped off the mask. Vera knew it was a futile gesture; his lungs were saturated. With panic in his eyes, Bill tried to breathe, but he was suffocating.

Vera grabbed him in her arms. *Screw the contagion.*

After a few seconds, Bill's body went limp. She released him and staring at the floor, Vera trudged down the seemingly endless corridor, her thoughts remaining with her friend. She'd miss him.

The buzzing of her cell phone startled her.

"Dr. Sarkov. A call from Atlanta. Hold please."

"Vera? Dave here."

She didn't want to talk to him at this solemn moment.

"Bad news."

Screw it. What she needed was good news.

"The meds are too damn slow. We're dealing with a voracious lion eating away its victim by gently tugging at its tail. It's frustrating."

Vera glanced back at Bill's room. "That's what's happening here, too."

"People are dying all over the east coast. My ass is on the line. What's happening in Frisco?"

"The drug isn't working any longer."

"We've nothing else," he shouted.

That horrible thought had been rumbling around in her head. She had to tell Michael about the lack of response and the spread.

Vera's lecture to the staff at San Francisco's Mission General Hospital was straightforward. All leprosy-suspected patients were to be placed in isolation, all contacts to be treated. The highest level of sterility and precautions were to be in effect.

Leaving the auditorium, heading toward the ER, Vera looked in to the leprosy isolation ward.

"Five children arrived with a bloody diarrhea; three of them have already died," the curly-haired doctor said. "The drugs are too slow-acting for the most acute cases."

Needing to escape the nightmare, Vera picked up the *San Francisco Chronicle* from the residents' table in the doctors' lounge. Reading the newspaper brought no solace. As Dave had said, the leprosy epidemic was spreading like tiny brushfires in the States. Total to date was sixteen cities. Worst hit were New York and Washington, D.C., each with a hundred dead. All cases were ultimately traceable to the plane Jennifer Wilson had been on. Tossing the paper onto the cluttered desk, she leaned back in her seat and closed her eyes. Images of the dying flamed through her mind. There was no escaping the daily news; the damn drugs were too slow or worse — ineffective.

chapter twenty-eight

Sitting in the lab at the computer, Rowan opened the information base for the trachoma study. She overlaid the therapy codes onto the patient information to see who had received active drug and who'd received placebo. After arranging the names in columns, she began the task of crosschecking the disposition and health of all those on the list.

Alice and Brother Rose came into the lab several times during the two-hour process to pick up supplies, glancing warily at the computer and Rowan, but not speaking.

Once she'd collected all the facts, Rowan punched up a statistical analysis program and printed out the numbers. At eleven p.m. she rubbed her eyes while the printer clacked loudly in the deserted lab. Looking about, she saw that the lab was not as deserted as she'd thought. Koirala sat on his knees in a yoga position in the corner of the room. She waved him over, then collected the papers from the printer.

As Koirala approached, Rowan scanned the final number:
P value 0.01.

She closed her eyes. It was as she'd suspected. The patients who had received the amiomycin were either dead or significantly sicker with leprosy than those who'd received the placebo.

The endemic, mild leprosy had mutated with the chronic administration of the trachoma antibiotic. In short, the amiomycin had caused the epidemic.

Rowan handed the paper to Koirala. He stared at the figures for a few moments. Then, with a cracking voice, he murmured, "Thank you," and left.

No one could have ever predicted that the amiomycin could do something like this. How was she going to tell Alice?

Michael looked up to see Rowan at the entrance to his cabin.

"May I come in?" she asked.

After an exhausting fourteen-hour day of distributing the high doses of drug to the villagers, Michael had been relaxing on the mattress he had tossed onto the floor. Dealing with one of Rowan's quirky spells was not high on his to-do list, but he waved her inside.

"Please," he said, pointing to the chair.

Rowan sat down next to him on the mattress. "I have some data that I need to show you."

Michael took the papers. "What's this?"

"It's self-explanatory."

Michael read through the data and the statistics. He took a deep breath and exhaled forcibly. "What do you plan to do with this information?"

"Tell Alice."

"What the hell will that accomplish?"

"She's the project director. She has to know. The world has to know. We can't repeat this mistake."

"It's not a mistake. It's a one-in-a-million unpredictable event."

"Alice has to be told."

Michael stood and handed the papers back to Rowan.

"Would you do it?" she asked.

"What? Why me?"

"I could never face her with this."

Michael groaned aloud. His relationship with Alice had finally revived, and now this? He couldn't do it, either. It would be too cruel.

"Why in the world did you do the study?" he demanded.

"I suspected you were right, which meant we'd have to warn others."

"I can't tell Alice. Not now."

"You must. I have to make this data public. Alice would be devastated if we didn't tell her first."

Alice picked at her masala dosa, idly worrying about the possibility of resistance occurring.

"Al, mind if I sit down?" Michael asked.

"Of course not." Alice patted the seat next to her. "How's the drug distribution going in your sector?"

"Fine. It's the responses to the therapy that are troubling."

Alice took a deep breath. Michael had changed — risking his life, staying when told to leave. She wanted to completely trust him, to let herself go and love him openly and deeply as she once did... but could she?

He looked so compassionate.

"I have to talk to you about something." Michael picked at the food on his plate.

The solemnity of his voice frightened Alice.

"Rowan handed me the results of her evaluation of the trachoma data."

Alice put down her teacup and stared at Michael's grave expression. "What's wrong?"

"From her statistics, well, it appears that the people taking the amiomycin were..." Alice felt her skin prickle. "...sicker, much sicker."

"Doesn't mean a thing." Alice felt herself swelling with rage. "The antibiotic could have simply lowered their resistance."

"I thought that, too, so I checked it out. I'm afraid not. The first signs of the virulent leprosy in Pokhara appeared in the people in the trachoma study."

"Lowered resistance," she said. "But what about that boy in Baglun? It started with him."

Michael tore a piece off of his masala dosa, then met her eyes sadly. "He and his family visited relatives in Pokhara — all of them were in the study. Shakar and the rest of his family were the first to die in Pokhara."

Alice let her silverware clatter on her plate. "I should have known. You took the data from Rowan so you could personally denigrate my trachoma work."

Michael's jaw dropped. "Why would I do that?"

"Were we getting too close again? Is that it?"

"I'm sorry about this. Please, Al. We have to deal with the facts no matter how painful."

"How could I have trusted you again? You must think I'm pretty gullible."

"Believe me, I didn't want this to be made public, but we... you... have to know the truth. We can't let others use this drug and make the same—"

"Mistake. Stupid me. Giving chronic antibiotic therapy."

"Not at all. It was working. You helped the trachoma. Leprosy is treated with chronic medications too. There are lots of situations where long-term antibiotics are needed."

"Thanks. Skewer me, then try to act innocent."

"Al, no one blames you. The science was perfect. This problem was completely unforeseen."

"Is this your patronizing phase? Poor, dull Alice."

Michael pushed his plate away and stood. "I'm sorry," he said quietly. "Truly sorry." He slipped out of the tent.

Alice wandered around the perimeter of the camp, kicking at the ground. How could she ever live with the thought that she had caused this nightmare?

Yes, nobody could blame her. The WHO people had organized and approved the project. She had been brought aboard after the study was set up. An innocent trying to help suffering people. But no matter what excuse her brain came up with, the ache in her chest wouldn't leave.

She entered Rowan's cabin and saw her sister reading in bed.

"Alice you look awful. What's wrong?"

"Michael just told me the news."

Dropping her book, Rowan jumped out of bed and directed her sister to a chair.

"You can't blame yourself. No one could have expected a connection. I certainly didn't when I asked to check the data."

"I know you meant well."

"He insisted on seeing the data. I never suspected he would be so callous as to confront you with it."

"Whenever I begin to trust him, he does something horrible."

Rowan put her arms around Alice. "Knowing what you've done must be torture for you."

Michael wandered down the path in the late-afternoon sun. Rounding a curve, he saw Alice sitting by a lone ginkgo tree under the protection of the fan-shaped leaves. She must still be angry. Understandably so. He backed away quietly, as she turned and asked, "What brings you out here?"

Michael didn't want another confrontation, but her voice sounded conciliatory. "This is my favorite spot when I need a break."

Alice nodded. "This golden sunset over the Annapurna range occurs every night and I rarely notice it anymore. Here we are in the most majestic splendor our world has to offer, and I don't even see it."

Michael stopped retreating. "The leprosy, these deaths, it's blinding us."

"We take far too much for granted."

Michael gazed down at Alice.

"I apologize for my outburst," she said. "It wasn't warranted. You and Rowan were right to look for the cause of the epidemic."

Michael picked at the bark of the tree.

"I can't tell you how painful it is to be responsible for this outbreak," she whispered.

Michael sat and put his arms around her. She trembled. He held her tighter and kissed the tear flowing down her cheek. "You didn't do anything wrong. You followed the WHO protocol. If you hadn't done the trachoma study someone else would have. This was destined to happen."

"Thanks for saying that," Alice mumbled. "Unfortunately, words won't bring back all those who have died."

Michael took her hand in his and kissed it. "I know, Al. I know."

Rowan sat in her darkened cabin, writing a letter to her mother. The rickety chair and table gave her little comfort or support. She moved the paper into the sliver of sunlight crossing the table, and stared at the blank sheet. She needed to tell someone, but how could she explain the difficult situation between her and Alice? How could she tell anyone about the pleasure she felt at Alice's debacle? Her overbearing, successful sister was feeling the pain of failure. It was about time.

She sat musing, when Michael knocked on her cabin wall, startling her from her dream world. "Rowan. We need to go to the burial site."

"We? Why us?" As much as she relished the thought of an outing with Michael, Rowan dreaded the thought of seeing all the bodies burning even more. Smelling the fumes when the wind shifted to the south was bad enough.

"Everyone else is busy..."

"So it's us."

"Right."

When they left the cabin, Rowan said, "You've been a bit distant since you've been here."

"Really? I guess I've got a lot on my mind."

"We used to talk in London."

Sort of. He used to ask her about Alice. He'd wanted to know everything about the woman he loved.

"Maybe when this settles down, we can sit down and have a heart-to-heart again," he said unenthusiastically.

"I miss the time we used to spend together."

He didn't answer.

Michael drove to the burial grounds outside Pokhara. They had to deliver food and supplies to the team of Nepalese workers who had been hired for the job of disposing of the dead bodies as rapidly as possible. Like most of the other staff members, he had avoided the area. Not only was it painful to view the deformed bodies of the leprosy victims; the danger of contagion was heightened at the burial site. But they were shorthanded. Now everyone had to do more.

Approaching the site, they were assaulted by the distinctive reek of burning flesh. Michael pulled his double mask higher over his face, but could do nothing to stop the burning sensation in his eyes. The masks, hospital gown and gloves made him perspire and otherwise gave him little comfort.

Rowan closed her eyes. "This is my first trip out here. The smell is disgusting."

"We'll drop everything off and get out of here as fast as possible."

"Thank you, Michael."

Through the smoke drifting over the landscape, Michael could see the piles of bodies looming in the distance, like a horrific mirage. They got closer, and the gruesome details revealed themselves;

corpses heaped into six large mounds, each mound containing hundreds of bodies — and all were on fire. Through the flames, Michael could make out hands, feet and heads.

When Rowan opened her eyes, she gasped at the view, paled and turned away. "It's ghastly." She collapsed against the car, burying her face in her hands.

Pulling up next to the site, Michael looked down into the massive open ditches alongside the pyres, each filled with hundreds of deformed bodies. Masked workers struggled to pull dead bodies off the two large trucks parked next to the gravesite; others tossed bodies into the ditches or onto the pyres, and still others maintained the fires by pouring gasoline on the massive burning piles.

Rowan began to weep. Trembling, she whispered, "There are so many. How is anyone going to survive this?"

Michael pressed her shoulder. "I think you'd better stay in the car. I'll see if I can get one of the workers to help me unload."

He called to one of the Nepalese, and the two of them unloaded the food and the masks, gowns and gloves from the jeep. Before leaving, Michael turned back to gaze at the burning bodies, intending to offer a prayer and pay his respects. He couldn't face the horror; he had to look away.

His mind filled with a vision of angry flames and acrid smoke, burial sites just like the one in Pokhara, occurring all over the world.

chapter twenty-nine

With a translator and Brother Rose accompanying him, Michael visited the Tibetan relocation camp situated on the outskirts of Pokhara. They saw no outdoor activity. The team had ordered all fieldwork stopped and all villagers confined to their homes, except for emergencies.

With its rows of small metal-domed cabins built by the government almost fifty years earlier after the Chinese invasion of Tibet, the camp looked like a town of abandoned barracks.

Michael entered the first cabin and came upon a young couple, the wife cradling a baby in her arms.

The parents' ruddy, round faces and sparkling eyes looked healthy and unchanged. This was promising.

Michael greeted the couple. Carefully pushing aside three sacks filled with mustard greens, he squatted next to the man, who had a long, wispy black mustache and black hair that grew to his waist. The man slid off his black and maroon robe, exposing his upper body. Michael scanned the man's arm for the telltale bumps and measured the six or seven lesions he found on each arm. He checked his chart again, then again.

There was no doubt about it. Despite the high doses of anti-leprosy medication, the lesions were larger. Michael's stomach churned. He must not show his anxiety. Frightening them would only make matters worse.

The woman removed her hand from her apron, exposing her fingers. Michael lifted her wrist slowly, and turned it in order to examine her. Her fingers were rotting away.

When they left the cabin, Brother Rose was beside himself. "They all have more lesions," he said. "It's awful."

Michael nodded grimly, his heart heavy. "It looks bad. The leprosy seems to be breaking through the antibiotic therapy."

"Not 'seems to be', it is."

Michael gestured to the rows of cabins. "Let's wait to hear the other field reports. These may be isolated results."

"God willing," pleaded Brother Rose, his voice shaky. "But we have no fallback position. If this doesn't work we have nothing to stop the leprosy." He wiped a line of perspiration from his brow, his sleeve falling back.

Michael gasped. Grabbing Brother Rose's hand, he demanded, "What's that?" A pigmented area spread across Brother Rose's forearm.

Brother Rose coughed, then looked ruefully at his skin lesion. "I saw it only the other day."

"Is this your only spot?"

"Yes, Michael," Brother Rose said, lowering his eyes.

"Damn it, Brother. Why didn't you tell me? You need rest to get your resistance up to fight this."

"I assumed it would be no problem since we had the drugs. I never thought—"

"Starting today you're in isolation. Rowan will take your place in the field with me. We're not going to lose you."

After being patched through to San Francisco, Michael told Vera the devastating news. "The field reports from Baglun and Kathmandu are all the same. The germ's developing resistance to the triple therapy. And the new symptoms seem worse."

"I know. We're seeing it too, Mickey."

"Your only hope is to bomb everyone exposed to Jennifer Wilson with the anti-leprosy drugs before resistance breaks out in the States. It's time for drastic measures."

Vera said, "It's too late for that. The lab people tell us the bacilli are resistant to everything. Even the triple therapy is totally ineffective."

Michael felt a rising wave of panic. He pushed it aside. "Then there's no option left but total isolation," he responded evenly. "You've got to keep all the sick separated, and keep the healthy people at home. It may be the only way to stop the spread."

"We've quarantined the city, but it's going to be hard to get buy in on isolation. Dave did appoint me as the official CDC representative for the Bay Area. That will give me a little more clout."

"You have no choice."

"The Surgeon General called the President. I think they're going to declare a State of Emergency for the whole east coast corridor from Boston to Washington, D.C. All the major cities are involved."

"Anywhere else?"

"Dave said there's scattered cases in a half dozen Midwest States."

"No matter how difficult, the Feds have to keep people at home. That's what worked in the Middle Ages with the plague."

"Jesus, Mickey," Vera snapped, "that only worked after seventy-five million people died."

"I know." Michael couldn't see any other solution. "Take care of yourself."

Michael squeezed his eyes shut. This time he pictured the freshly scrubbed faces of his students at Berkeley turning to wasted death masks as the outbreak ate its way across the United States.

He was going to stop the damn germ. It was his karma, he could feel it. But how?

Michael searched the mountain vista, as if the indifferent snowy peaks held the clue. The sun sat low in the sky and swaths of blue, red and orange painted the horizon. What would survive after the leprosy epidemic had run its course? These majestic mountains, surely. He envisioned silent cities, a world of empty buildings crumbling with time like the ones described in the poem Ozymandias.

To clear his mind, Michael started his walking meditation, watching through partially closed eyes as each foot fell on the dusty road. A ditch ran alongside the road, filled with excrement and garbage, but he tried to concentrate solely on his feet, blocking out everything else. He felt like Sisyphus, the Greek mythology figure, pushing a huge boulder upward, forever upward. The heel, the arch, the toes, the road. The earth, the breath.

After twenty minutes, now feeling calm and hopeful, he hastened to the emergency hospital to see Brother Rose before darkness fell. For his march through the swampy lowland toward the newly established emergency hospital tent located on the outskirts of Pokhara,

Michael wore his hiking shoes. Poisonous kraits were abundant in the area.

Pushing aside the door flaps of the long tent, he looked down the four long rows of beds. Standing nearest to him was a group of blind men waiting to be taken to the outhouse. Just beyond them he encountered the WHO Indian doctor in charge. Dr. Singh smiled a greeting.

"*Namaste*. How's the manpower situation?" Michael asked.

"It has been understandably difficult to get volunteers. The government will be sending some soldiers shortly."

"How's Brother Rose doing?"

"Ah yes, I wanted to speak to you about him."

Dr. Singh led him toward the back of the tent, which was filled to capacity with people in various stages of the disease. Passing a tall but bent man, Michael saw, even with the man's mask on, the grotesque red and brown lumps all over his face. The man was staring into space, his pupils white. But it was the deformities of the next man's extremities that were the most difficult to see. His hands and feet were rotting away, muscle strands and bones openly exposed.

And these were the milder cases. The patients dying with the bloody pneumonia and diarrhea were in the hospitals.

"I am thinking that Brother Rose may do better away from here."

"Is he dying?"

"Oh no. His disease is mild. Too mild to be isolated. I think it best if he returns to your camp. The chances for survival will be greater in his cabin."

Brushing against a man dripping blood from his hands, Michael winced as he was sprayed.

"As you can see, this is a dangerous place to be."

Michael wiped the blood from his hands onto his pants leg.

"He only needs to wear the mask and he can return to work — light work," Dr. Singh continued.

Arriving at Brother Rose's bed, Michael saw he was asleep.

"Brother Rose," Singh called.

"Don't wake him."

Brother Rose stretched. "Don't worry, Michael, I was only resting. Thinking."

"I came to visit, but I guess it turns out I'm here to take you back to camp. Dr. Singh says you'll be better off with us."

Brother Rose clutched his amulet and pressed it against his chest, then made a blessing motion that encompassed the tent. "Michael, we've got to do something for these people."

"I know," Michael answered. "We will."

chapter thirty

"Resistant?" Erik shouted. "What are you telling me?"

"Our reports from the States, India and Nepal are all the same," Max said.

Erik tossed the papers onto his desk then tramped over to the bar. "That's the absolute worst possible news you could have brought me."

"It was always a possibility that the germ could mutate to a resistant form."

"Not within a month." Erik slammed his fist on the bar, rattling the glasses. "Our microbiologists said it would take years, maybe never."

"They were wrong. This germ is new, unknown. No one could predict..."

Erik waved the glass in his hand. "You're saying we can't stop the blasted disease? Our medicine is useless?"

Max kept his distance, close to the study door. "At the moment there doesn't seem—"

"Tens of millions will die."

The CFO nodded miserably.

"I had Otto into convert all of our factories to producing the drugs. What have I done? We'll be bankrupt."

With a swipe of his hand, Erik batted two glasses off the bar. They smashed on the floor. He remained motionless for a few moments looking at the pieces. Then he spoke. "What is broken is broken." He pointed to the unbroken glasses. "We must save what remains."

The plane descended into Zurich Kloten Airport, and Sir Hilary watched the mountains surrounding the city rise up to meet it. *Jennifer loved the mountains*. Despite the passage of six weeks, his pain had not eased. Whenever he entered Jennifer's room or saw her photograph the agony was rekindled. He knew people thought he was exploiting his grief to promote his foundation, but his emotional outbursts were sincere. So far nothing had been able to mitigate his suffering. Maybe this would.

Reimer collected their luggage and they made their way through customs. Sir Hilary found the Farberg driver waiting for him by the curbside. He admired efficiency.

On the drive to Farberg corporate headquarters, he sat silently in the back seat of the black E series Mercedes-Benz, considering the scenery. A heavy fog hung over the countryside, all but obscuring the Uetliberg Mountains. But the whitewashed houses and cobblestone streets of Switzerland were tidy and quaint, making Sir Hilary think of the Swiss mania for secrecy and control. It made perfect sense that Farberg was a Swiss corporation.

Farberg's headquarters were housed in an undistinguished two-story brown brick building. Sir Hilary suspected they wanted to maintain their anonymity. He respected that. Inside, he and Reimer marched up to the smiling receptionist.

"Sir Hilary Wilson is here to see Erik Bittner," Reimer said bowing slightly.

"Welcome," the attractive red-headed woman said. "Herr Bittner is expecting you." She motioned them to a door at the end of the hall.

"Wait here," Sir Hilary ordered Reimer.

Upon entering, Sir Hilary saw Erik, a graying man the size of an elephant, spread behind his huge wooden desk, lost in thought, drumming his stubby fingers on his old-fashioned blotter.

"Ah, Sir Hilary, please be seated," said the obese man, looking up with a polite nod. "Tea or sherry?"

"Not at the moment," Sir Hilary answered coolly.

Erik raised an eyebrow. "Let me take this opportunity to say how impressed we were by your purchase of our antibiotics. It was an extremely generous act." He smiled earnestly. "Unfortunately, we've been informed that the leprae has mutated to a resistant form. The drugs will no longer work."

Sir Hilary frowned. "That's related to the reason for my visit."

"I was wondering why you wanted this urgent appointment."

"I'm not certain if you are aware of my personal misfortune."

Erik absently straightened the folders on his desk. "You're

referring to your daughter?"

"My beloved Jennifer, my only child, was murdered by this new leprae germ."

Erik's eyes widened. "Murdered?"

"She was part of your amiomycin-trachoma study team, the one that has now been proven to have caused this virulent strain."

"Ah," he replied sympathetically. "The data on that issue is still unconfirmed."

"The data is irrefutable. Your ill-considered study killed my daughter."

Erik cleared his throat uncomfortably. "Sir Hilary, I wish I could offer you some consolation, but I beg to differ. The trachoma study was under the auspices of the WHO. We only supplied the amiomycin."

Sir Hilary continued his rehearsed speech as if Erik hadn't spoken. "The torment I've suffered is the responsibility of your company. The heaviness, the ache, the emptiness in my life is because of you, Herr Bittner."

"We followed standard medical practices. We performed Phase One trials under the guidance of the WHO, and their safety monitoring committee checked—"

"I shall never forgive you for what you have stolen from me. I have filed a wrongful death lawsuit against your firm in the amount of two hundred million dollars. My lawyers will present you with the papers this afternoon."

Erik lumbered to his feet. "That's ridiculous."

"It would give me the greatest of pleasure to witness the demise of your firm." Sir Hilary strolled toward the door. "I needed to tell you this in person. I owed this to my daughter."

Erik waddled out of his office, Sir Hilary's comments dominating his thoughts. The old fool would never win the case. Farberg had carried out the entire project under the auspices of the WHO, carefully monitoring each step. But they didn't need the headache or the bad publicity, not to mention the extra cost of squelching the lawsuit.

At the solid metal door to the conference room, Erik slipped a card into a slot. The automated door opened, clicking behind him after he passed into the paneled room that smelled of stale cigar smoke.

He had arrived first. Wearing dark suits and somber expressions, the six Farberg board members filed into the boardroom for the emergency meeting and took their respective seats around the long, polished wooden table.

Erik sat at the head of the table, beneath an oil portrait of the white-haired Karl Farberg — his uncle. Erik's expression mirrored the cold eyes of his ancestor as he watched the procession with contempt. *Cloned, stringless puppets. They couldn't come up with any solutions if their lives depended upon it.*

"Our memos from the WHO regarding the resistance of the leprae bacillus are in your packet," Erik said, pointedly eyeing Chief Operating Officer Otto Kline. "Our profits from the three anti-leprosy medications will end immediately."

A murmuring arose among the board members.

"What is the WHO going to do?" Otto asked.

"We'll get to that in a moment." Erik cleared his throat loudly. "Gentlemen, I believe we are still well-placed to stop this unfortunate situation."

"How is that possible?" Otto asked. "At your insistence we converted all our efforts to making these useless drugs."

"The rapid development of bacterial resistance was a highly unlikely event. Now we move on." Erik turned toward the others. "We need to assist the WHO in ending this disaster as soon as possible, and improve our financial situation at the same time."

"I don't see any obvious solution to your... riddle," Otto said.

"The solution is to speed up our vaccine work. Our scientists have worked for ten years on the project. It's time to see the results of their efforts."

"We have accomplished a great deal," responded the science officer. A small man with huge, black glasses that magnified his eyes, he spoke in a high cartoonish voice. "But as I told Herr Bittner yesterday, we have a long way to go. The vaccine does impart immunity in ninety-five to ninety-eight percent of armadillos after a series of three injections."

"Armadillos?" a board member asked.

"They are the best experimental animals for testing the leprae bacillus," the scientist answered. "We are still doing Phase Two testing. It will be two years or more before it will be ready for human use."

"Under normal conditions," Erik said. "We must speed up the process."

"A reasonable, double-masked human trial would take at least that long," Otto answered.

"We don't have that long. Too many people will be dead by then. We must get a special dispensation by the WHO to start human treatment sooner."

"Didn't the Wellcome Drug Company in England test a vaccine many years ago?" Otto asked.

"In the early eighties," the scientist squeaked out. "It wasn't successful. This is potentially much more effective."

"Correct. Ending the leprosy epidemic is our immediate concern," Erik said.

"Herr Bittner, I repeat, it will take years to successfully develop—"

"We simply don't have the time, Otto. We have to hire the best scientists in the field and be willing to spend money, much more money."

"But can we afford to hire these scientists?" Otto asked.

"We can't afford not to. In addition, Anton and the others at the WHO have kindly offered to subsidize the vaccine project. We shall take them up on their offer."

"Money isn't the issue. Trials take time," the science officer insisted. "We will not be able to stop this epidemic with any vaccine, no matter how efficacious, for a long, long time."

The board members sat silently staring at Erik.

"The leprosy disaster, the resistance, is quite regrettable," Erik said calmly. "Now that it has occurred, we will direct our efforts toward stamping out the dreaded disease." Staring at the company science officer, he added, "We will expand and speed up our vaccine research and return to the production of our other antibiotic drugs."

Garbage cans overflowed onto the New York City streets. Piles of waste lay at the curbs. The debris blew aimlessly in the breeze, filling the smog-filled air with the putrid smell of exposed garbage. A few people hurried past the rubbish, wearing the city mandated surgical-type masks. The Mayor of New York looked out of his window at the filthy, deserted streets, and at the rare taxicab passing by, causing the garbage to scatter.

"The sanitation workers' strike is killing us," he said, closing the window.

"They're a hell of a lot smarter than most, Mr. Mayor," replied Vera who'd been sent to New York to help them deal with their leprosy outbreak.

The mayor pulled off his tie. "What now?"

"As the city's CDC representative, I have to insist on total quarantine," Vera said. "Not just the city, but all the boroughs, especially Brooklyn. They have the most cases."

"It's a nightmare."

"Everyone stays home, emergencies the only exception — like fire, police, that sort of stuff."

"You don't know New Yorkers. They'll never do it."

"Then we'll call out the National Guard."

"What about feeding the people?"

"Do what they're doing in Boston and Phillie. People who need food call a central number, and someone delivers the basics to the door. No people-to-people contact."

"How can I run a city that way?"

"A State of Emergency has been declared. You have no choice but to keep human contact to a minimum. That's how the disease spreads."

"What the damn CDC wants is impossible," the mayor insisted. "It's enough to drive me back to drinking."

Vera pulled her fingers through her unwashed hair. She remained quiet, for she had no encouraging words. Michael had told her that it was only going to get worse. He expected the entire country to be affected — severely.

Erik waited as Anton, a monochrome of gray as usual, opened the emergency meeting of the WHO by pounding his gavel against the lectern. "Gentlemen, gentlemen... and ladies, please." The audience ignored the mousy man's pleas. He pounded again.

After a few minutes, the din abated.

"We are here to discuss the leprosy crisis," he announced. "Lights."

When the room darkened, Anton continued. "On the first slide, I have noted the areas of serious involvement in shades of red. The darker the red, the worse the situation, such as India, Nepal and China. As you can see, essentially every country in the world is involved to some degree or another, and the situation is worsening."

Anton left the slide on the screen. The reds faded to pastels as he signaled for the lights to come back up. "We must come up with a solution to this world-wide problem, a policy the WHO can recommend to governments. First we will hear from Mr. Epstein, the U.S. representative."

He looked back to the panel of six experts sitting behind him and nodded to Dave Epstein, who then spoke into his microphone.

"Things in the U.S. are bad — real bad. The Northeast, Far West, Southeast. You name it, they're all involved. But we've dealt with epidemics from resistant microbes before, and we did damn well."

"What do you recommend then?" Anton asked.

"We're telling our people that isolation is everything. Sick are to be hospitalized in isolation wards. Person-to-person contact has to be zero. Do this and the germ will run its course — just like Ebola."

A heavyset man with rimless glasses that floated at the end of his bulbous, vein-laden nose raised his hand. "In my many years as staff epidemiologist here at the WHO, I have always looked for the carrier, the vector. Find the vector is my credo," he pronounced. "We have found the vector. It's us. Humans." Removing a handkerchief from his pocket, he blew into it. "Therefore, I agree with Herr Epstein that human isolation is the only answer."

"How many can we expect will die before the leprosy runs its course?" Anton asked.

"It's difficult to say. I can extrapolate of course..." answered the epidemiologist.

"Your best guess." Anton waved a hand vaguely.

The professor cleared his throat before saying, "Fifty million. Possibly a hundred."

A collective gasp arose in the audience.

"Worldwide," he clarified.

"That need not happen," Erik called from his chair on the stage.

"Your medication is useless," Anton answered.

"I'm not referring to the usual leprosy medication. We're working on a vaccine," Erik announced. "A potent vaccine that may save most of those lives. With your support, we can have it available within a year."

"That's all well and good, Herr Bittner, and we will get to your proposal in due course," answered Anton sternly. "But we desperately need something *now.*"

chapter thirty-one

Michael trudged out to the road, the soil like quicksand, sucking at his feet. He had to think. How could he stop this disaster? Could the yersinia plasmid work? It was such a long shot.

In the distance he spotted Alice, sitting slumped on a flat rock, dangling her feet and staring out at the terai. The yellow blanket of mustard plants was gone, and only an expanse of dark green covered the tiered fields.

She made room for him next to her, then said, "My father used to say that after all his traveling, the one thing that remained constant was that even the most beautiful places in the world look empty when you're struggling inside."

"He sounds like a wise man. You must miss him."

"More every year. He had a way of helping me sort things out. I think he would know how to get us out of this disaster."

The familiar crushing pain encompassed Michael. "It's hard to go through life without parents."

Alice nodded sadly. "It's been a long time since he passed away, but the world still seems an emptier place without him."

Michael leaned back on his elbows and looked off into the sky. "I remember my freshman year at Harvard. I was only fifteen — one of the youngest students in the school's history. That in itself was enough to make me feel like a pariah, socially isolated."

Turning away from the panorama, Alice stared at him. "That must have been difficult."

Michael nodded. "Yeah. As I said, I already felt like a semi-orphan; my parents were away so much. Family gatherings were always hard for me because my parents would breeze in, tell their happy exotic stories, and then leave me again with our nanny, du jour, or whichever relatives were keeping me at the time."

He didn't stop to allow Alice time to comment. "That year they'd come to visit me just before the Christmas break, because they were

going to be traveling for the holidays — without me, of course."
Michael sighed. "They took me out to dinner. I remember waving as
they drove away, feeling like I was one more errand they could tick
off their holiday list. See Michael, our son. Check. Let's see, what's
next? Buy Christmas and Hanukah cards. Check."

Alice inclined her head sympathetically as he continued.

"Then I got a phone call that changed everything. It's still so
clear. It was early the next morning. I was sleeping in the dorm. A
classmate woke me, and I jogged down the freezing hallway to the
phone in my green and white striped underwear. My favorite.

"It was my Aunt Cattie. I knew immediately something was
wrong. I asked what, and she began to cry hysterically. I was so
scared.

"'Micah,' she said, 'your mother and father had... a terrible auto
accident. It was bad... Icy roads...'"

Michael felt his throat tighten at the memory. "Tears started
running down my face. I couldn't stop. I stood shivering in the
hallway, crying. They were both gone, just like that. They were never
there for me and suddenly they would never be there. They were
dead."

He paused, but Alice didn't speak, waiting for him to continue.
He met her eyes briefly, but had to look away. "I dropped the receiver
and collapsed to the floor. How could they do that to me? I kept
crying and crying, right in front of my friends. The little lost kid. All
alone. Saying 'No, no, it can't be' over and over. I'll never forget that
feeling. One final and permanent abandonment."

Alice moved closer and wrapped an arm around his shoulders.
She kissed him softly on the cheek.

"I didn't go to the funeral — one more family gathering. I don't
even know how I made it through school, but I did... with pretty good
grades. I guess I just shut my feelings off by delving into the world of
books. Maybe that explains why I'm sometimes all head and little
heart." Michael swallowed hard and looked off toward the jagged
rocks. "I'm truly sorry about leaving you, Al. Sometimes it's too
painful to be around a loving family." He took a deep breath, then let
it out slowly. "And I'm sorry I haven't been much help here... yet."

Alice laced her fingers through his.

"Somehow, we'll end it," Michael said.

She rested her head on his shoulder.

They sat silently for a few minutes before he spoke. "I've been thinking of ways around the resistance."

She lifted her head abruptly and stared at him anxiously. "Like what?"

"My plasmid theory, for one."

"How do we use that?"

"I'm working on it. Hopefully I'll have an idea of what to do by morning."

She nestled back on his shoulder. "We don't have much time. But you're not alone, Michael. We're in this together."

She turned her face to his and he ran a finger down her cheek. He leaned in and brushed her lips with his. She responded eagerly, as if she were seeking comfort. For the fewest of moments, Michael let his mind escape the catastrophe that loomed all around them.

Michael sat in the lab staring at the computer. He ripped the sheet from the printer listing the latest number of leprosy cases reported by the WHO. He stared at the figures, amazed and appalled. In Nepal alone there were 80,000 cases. India: 46,000. United States: 31,200. He wrote down the totals, then did the same with the reports from the previous two-week periods. Recording the number of inhabitants of each country from Internet data, he estimated the at-risk population, then calculated the rates of spread for each week over the last month. Finally he plotted the curve on graph paper.

A precipitously rising curve. Unless something or someone intervened, the line reflecting the spread would continue on the same path until...

Michael released the paper. He never thought it possible that he would see it in his lifetime. If his rough figures were correct, the phenomenon of exponential or super-spread was going to occur — within *months*. Not only thousands would be dying each month, but tens and eventually hundreds of thousands... possibly millions.

The Black Plague Returns.

In the fading late afternoon glow, Michael dragged himself to his cabin. Reclining on his mattress on the floor, the past days' events and the possibility of accelerated spread crystallized in his mind. He took a deep breath and closed his eyes. There in the darkness flashed the image of Alice's exquisite face being eaten away by leprosy. The disease took the form of a ravenous scavenger, ripping and tearing away her flesh, covering her in blood. Then the behemoth ran wild, spreading out to engulf cities, then regions and then entire continents. He had to stop it.

He saw a dark avenging angel rise up from a grave, soar into the sky and sweep across the world, searching for and then devouring the hungry leprosy.

When he awoke in the morning, he lay still. He didn't want to move until he'd replayed the dream in his head. He knew what he had to do. Michael had studied and intimately knew the identity of this dark angel. It was the Black Plague — and it was time for it to rise again.

When Etienne, Brother Rose, Rowan and Alice arrived at Michael's cabin, he was sitting at his desk poring over the final details of his new strategy. He ushered them in with a wave.

Alice perched on the rickety bed frame. With folded arms and a grim face, Rowan leaned against the cabin wall. The men sat cross-legged on the mattress.

"We've run out of options and we're running out of precious time," Michael said. "I never imagined this germ would be as devastating as it is."

"And as resistant as it is," Alice added.

"At one time or other, I've talked with all of you about my theory that yersinia, the black plague organism, contains a plasmid — a factor that destroys the leprae bacillus." Michael glanced at Brother Rose, who nodded.

"I'm absolutely certain of it. That's the easy part. Making practical use of this information is the problem."

"You said it would take millions of dollars and years to prove," Brother Rose reminded him.

Michael gave a tight grin. "And the way things are going, we'll all be dead before I even get started."

"So what are you suggesting?" asked Etienne.

"There's a possibility that using my theory, we can find a cure in a relatively short time. It may not be much of a chance, but it may be all we've got."

"With the plasmid?" Alice asked.

"Right. We're much more likely to find the plasmid that kills the leprosy bacillus in yersinia of the Middle Ages, back when leprosy was plentiful, than in yersinia from the present, six hundred fifty years later. See, the leprosy-killing plasmid hasn't been needed at all during that time. Like old soldiers, unnecessary plasmids just fade away."

"So what are you saying?" Rowan asked, still frowning.

"Just this. As impossible as it may seem, we have to find live medieval yersinia germs from a body with some evidence of leprosy."

Wide-eyed, Brother Rose asked, "Are you kidding? You can find a live six-hundred-fifty-year-old germ?"

"I didn't say it would be easy."

"It will have to be in a cold place. The colder the better," Alice said.

"I was part of the team that found the viable 1918 flu virus in the tundra of northern Norway," Michael added. "A very cold place. So it's doable."

"Why do we need a corpse with leprosy?" Brother Rose asked.

"I believe the plague organism will follow Sutton's Principle."

"And that is…?" The monk raised his eyebrows.

Michael grinned. "Willie Sutton, a bank robber, was asked why he robbed banks. He said, 'Because that's where the money is.' I believe the plague organism thrived in the presence of the leprae germs. So a person with leprosy who has the plague organisms will most likely have the factor."

"I'm gobsmacked," Rowan said. "That's what I call a long shot."

"If you do kill off the leprosy, doesn't the patient develop the plague? Isn't it just as bad?" Brother Rose asked.

Michael shook his head. "We have loads of antibiotics that we know will destroy the plague germ. All we have to do is wait for the plague to eliminate the resistant leprosy germs, then give the patient the proper antibiotic. Afterwards, with time, we can purify the plasmid so even the plague or resistance won't be a problem."

Etienne threw up his hands. "Michael, this sounds bizarre."

"It's our only hope. And we can do it," Michael said. "We must do it, before we reach the next stage."

"What next stage?" Brother Rose and Alice spoke in unison.

"One that was reached only once in human history — during the Middle Ages when the Black Plague struck."

Alice stiffened. "Exponential spread?"

"Right." Michael noted Brother Rose's questioning look. "When the number of germs and infected people reach a critical mass, an exponential increase in the spread of the disease will occur. A ten or even hundredfold increase."

Brother Rose crossed himself. "A bacterial Armageddon."

"How far are we from that happening?" asked Rowan.

Michael inhaled with stubborn disbelief. "I've gone over the numbers, and I keep coming up with the same answer — within weeks. A couple of months at the most."

Brother Rose clutched his cross.

"Mon Dieu," whispered Etienne.

"When the super-spread phenomenon kicks in, the survival of our species will be at stake."

"Super-spread is still only a theory," Alice said.

Michael smiled wryly. "Denial is a powerful force. I've been there. But it'll happen unless we act immediately. We've got to go find that plasmid."

"We?" Rowan asked.

Michael turned to Alice. "I need a microbiologist. Will you come with me?"

"To the Arctic to look for a mummified leper?"

"We can head for Longyearbyen. It's where we found the flu virus, so I know the territory."

"That makes sense," Brother Rose said hopefully.

"Norway had a seventy-five percent mortality rate from the plague, unusually high for a sparsely populated area that far north. None of the other Scandinavian countries had anything like it. The organism in Norway probably was a particularly virulent form of yersinia."

Michael surveyed his team members. Etienne was nodding. Alice looked skeptical and Rowan's frown had deepened.

"Longyearbyen is about as cold as you can get." Michael went on. "They had several leprosy colonies in the area, and the plague definitely killed off those people."

"I can't leave Pokhara for a wild goose chase," Alice said. "I'm assigned here. And how will we get out? The valley is quarantined."

Michael shrugged. "We have to go. I'll speak to Dave at the CDC and Koenig at the WHO. Roy Woods will back my theory. They won't stop us. It's their only chance to end the disaster."

Alice's face was etched with conflict.

Michael banged the table that doubled as his desk. "It may be a wild goose chase, but it's the only damn chase in town. We don't have anything else that will stop the leprosy."

Alice spoke. "This is my project, Michael. I'm responsible for the people here. The amiomycin may have caused this. I can't go." She paused. "Leaving would be abandoning everyone."

"Brother Rose and Rowan can run things until we get back," Michael said patiently. "We'll need a third scientist. That means you, Etienne."

"I will gladly go." The Frenchman stroked his goatee. "I, too, have Arctic experience, from my days in Russia."

Alice questioned, "It takes lots of money to organize digs—"

"No problem. The WHO, World Bank or IMF will give us the funds," Michael countered.

"Don't forget the lab work."

"I'll get the CDC to do it."

"It's crazy." Alice gazed out the window, as if the answer was in the sky.

"Our plans should be secret," Michael resumed. "No need to raise false hope with the public. Only the five of us need know, plus our WHO and CDC contacts. It'll go more smoothly that way." He turned to Alice. "Please, Al, I need your help."

Alice met his eyes indecisively.

"I vote go," Brother Rose offered. "I believe you and Michael can do it... with lots of prayers."

"Thanks, Brother," Michael said.

"And please, Michael, take my amulet for good luck. I want a part of me and my order to be with you." Brother Rose removed the elaborately carved iron cross from around his neck and held it out to Michael. "It will protect you from the disease and lead you to the right path."

Michael felt a wave of shock and humility. "I can't accept that,

Brother. Didn't you tell me it's been passed down for centuries? I'm sure it means a great deal to you."

"That's exactly why I want you to have it."

"Has it ever been in the possession of someone outside the Order of St. Lazarus?"

"No."

"Then I can't take it."

Brother Rose smiled gently. "It has protected whoever has worn it."

"Then you're going to need it more than me," Michael answered. "You already have leprosy, and you're here in the midst of an epidemic."

"Please, Michael, take my gift. It's also a way for me to be with you. Please."

Michael stared at the ancient crucifix in Brother Rose's extended hand, then rose and grasped it in both hands. He gazed at the talisman reverently, then feeling an inner permission, placed the chain around his neck. It felt surprisingly heavy.

"Thank you, Brother. I'll be honored to wear it." He shook Brother Rose's hand vigorously.

Alice shook her head. "Okay. It's totally nuts, but you have me. I'll go."

Later that night, gathered around the lab computer, Michael, Alice and Etienne planned their expedition. Michael logged onto the Internet, searching for Norwegian history.

After reviewing the data, they agreed on Friesland as the area in which to dig, a region on the colder eastern side of Svalbard Island, only a day and a half's snowmobile ride northeast from Longyearbyen.

Alice read aloud from the screen, *"A major leprosy epidemic struck in the early thirteen hundreds, affecting most of the population of Svalbard. One hundred years later, the Black Plague spread from England, killing half of the island's population.* Now comes the best part. Another article I found states that leprosy essentially disappeared from Norway during the fourteenth century."

"Sounds perfect," Michael said. Beginning to feel hopeful again, he clutched the talisman.

"Getting out of Nepal's no problem," Anton said. "But Norway won't let you in unless you go through an isolation period. The Norwegians were adamant."

Michael stared at the phone. "What the hell does that entail?"

"You must have everything checked for leprae. Scrapings from your sputum, feces, urine, skin — you name it. After one or two days in isolation, if your scrapings are negative they'll let you in. You'll have to stay a total of five days while they make certain nothing is growing."

"Where can we do the testing?"

"Great Britain agreed to allow you to go through the process near Gatwick. A private WHO plane will take the three of you there. Our men will take you off the plane to a special housing facility."

"I hope everyone understands we don't have much time. Every day is crucial."

"We're aware of the time issue. Don't push it. It's five days minimum. The Brits weren't too excited about the idea until they were pressured by the CDC and some of your influential friends."

"Influential friends? Like who?"

"Like Sir Hilary Wilson."

The trip to Norway was becoming common knowledge — exactly what they didn't need. "How the hell did *he* find out?"

"I don't know. But Sir Hilary and Farberg have offered to help us in any way they can. They can finance—"

"We don't need them."

"Fine." Anton sounded pleased. "We'll keep this a WHO-CDC effort."

"How much support can we expect from the WHO?" Michael asked.

Anton hesitated. "Keep in mind that our resources are being stretched by the epidemic."

"What about supplies? Transportation?"

"We'll check on the gear used in the flu dig," Anton said. "And we can handle the airfare for the three members of your team."

"That's it?"

"I hate to say this, Michael, but your project is an extreme long shot. We can't expend significant amounts of resources on this effort of yours."

Bureaucrats again. "Fine. We'll do it ourselves. When do we leave Pokhara?"

chapter thirty-two

The poking, prodding, annoyance and boredom of their screening procedure in London behind them, Alice, Michael and Etienne had a five-day wait before the flight to Norway. Alice needed it. She wanted to be alone with Michael in her flat. They'd had so little opportunity for privacy in Pokhara.

After a prolonged debate with the WHO team, a compromise was reached. Two days in the special housing then they could leave. Without being asked, Etienne had gallantly checked into an inexpensive hotel in Russell Square.

Alice's apartment was in a narrow building with intricate black grillwork, on a street that Alice thought looked like something out of *Mary Poppins*. Across the way was a small park, where quaint wooden benches sat at intervals along winding paths lined with oak and maple trees, now shedding their browned foliage.

Alice felt more comfortable here in her cramped apartment than at her family estate. She sighed with contentment at the familiar foyer and adjoining rooms. The large crystal chandelier, ornate ceiling trimming, pastel-colored wallpaper and prerequisite oil paintings of foxhunting scenes still seemed as Victorian and comforting as ever. She found it difficult to fully embrace the feeling of being home, however, knowing what lay ahead of them. She wasn't as confident as Michael about their mission. She tried to imagine and savor the feeling of beating the odds and then coming home to stay.

She fetched two glasses of wine, then collapsed onto a cushy sofa next to Michael. "Sitting here makes the last couple of months seem like a terribly bad dream, doesn't it? Here we are, secure and hale in a safe place, not a care in the world, no aggro, just a workin' bloke an' 'is bit o' fluff sittin' 'ome, watchin' the tellie."

Michael chuckled and ran his lips through her hair. Alice felt the warmth of his breath and trembled, anticipating his next move.

She closed her eyes and deposited a trail of kisses down Michael's neck. She felt as if she were gliding high in the sky, far from the filth below. Tugging at his hand, she looked up at him just as he whispered, "I want you."

She glided her hands along his neck, reaching into his long hair, caressing it.

When they came together in a kiss, Alice felt his fingers tracing a gentle path from her temples to the corners of her mouth. His lips glided over her flushed cheeks, bringing coolness in their path. Michael wrapped his arm around her, pulling her in.

Collapsing into his embrace, she felt weaker and stronger at the same time, secure and protected. She allowed her lips to roam over his mouth, delicately tasting him, smelling him, rekindling her memories of their past. She stroked the side of his face, from the grating, unshaven cheek to the smoothness of his mane. She pushed him to the floor, and as they slid, Alice on top, they snatched at each other's clothes like children opening gifts. They rolled on the carpet, shedding clothing until they lay naked against one another amid a pile of garments.

Alice felt the strength of his body against hers. Michael looked up at her and whispered, "I love you."

How long she had waited to hear him say those words.

Alice lay against Michael's body in her cozy bed, exhilarated, warm and at peace, until the jangle of the telephone startled them both. Michael groaned as Alice pulled away.

"Are you there?" a voice shouted.

Alice mumbled, "Alice Morgan-Wright."

"Yes, sorry to ring so unexpectedly, but we were not aware of your exact itinerary, and Sir Hilary did so want me to confirm an appointment time with you and Dr. Cohen before you left London."

"An appointment with Sir Hilary?" Alice said, rising on one elbow. "How did you know where to find us?" She turned toward Michael, who shot up in bed.

"Sir Hilary presumed you might be at home."

"What does he want?"

"I am sure I do not know, madam. I am his valet. He wishes that I confirm an appointment with him today. Are you free?"

Alice and Michael stared at each other.

"Are you free?" the valet repeated.

Michael shrugged, then nodded yes.

"This evening would be fine," Alice said.

"Excellent. Will seven be agreeable? The address is 121 Wilbraham Court. It would be most appreciated if you could be prompt."

Alice winced at the loud click of the phone, then turned to face Michael. "Are you sure you want to do this?"

"No. But I think we need to thank him for clearing our way through customs here in London."

A knock on the door of Sir Hilary's townhouse summoned a grim-faced man in a black tuxedo. "Dr. Alice Morgan-Wright and Dr. Michael Cohen, I presume? Please come in and be seated. I will inform Sir Hilary of your arrival."

The butler disappeared into the back of the house. Michael found himself in a dim entrance foyer appointed with British furnishings from the Georgian period, the centrally placed oversized receptionist's desk deserted. Michael joined Alice on a stiff leather bench next to a brass coat rack and looked at the predictably-placed oil portraits of the Wilson ancestors. He thought the Wilsons a particularly unattractive family, thick-featured and sour. *How could Sir Hilary have fathered a blond wisp like Jennifer?* he wondered.

The butler returned shortly to escort them through a narrow corridor into a small office with a low, beamed ceiling and walnut paneling. The scattered Tiffany lamps were dimly lit. Mustiness permeated the overly-warm room, which felt to Michael like a funeral parlor.

Sir Hilary and Reimer wore dark, conservative suits, white shirts and plaid ties. The sepulchral-looking Reimer sat on a sofa, running his stick-fingered hands continuously over the armrest. Sir Hilary sat behind a massive oak desk, looking stately but sallow in the gloom.

Sir Hilary pushed himself up and extended a misshapen hand to Alice. "I'm delighted to see you both again," he began. "Would you care for a cup of tea?"

They both declined, and the butler disappeared. Sir Hilary invited them to sit. "Sorry for the lighting, but I have an aversion for bright lights and glare since Jennifer's... passing." He paused. "What is the latest news from Pokhara?"

"It's been quite an ordeal," Alice answered.

"This leprosy germ is behaving unusually, wouldn't you say?" asked Sir Hilary. "The resistance was quite a surprise to everyone."

"What's also somewhat surprising," Michael said, "is that you found us at Alice's house."

Sir Hilary smiled and directed his remarks to Alice. "An educated guess. As you may know, I arranged for your clearance through London. I simply assumed you'd stay there when you escaped the special facility. Your mother was kind enough to supply me with your number."

"I'm not sure I understand your stake in helping us." Michael made no attempt to be subtle, which earned him a sharp look from Alice.

Sir Hilary seemed taken aback. "Stake? I simply want to help. It's what I've spent my life doing with my foundation."

Michael looked to Alice, who was ignoring him. He decided to say nothing more and let Sir Hilary explain himself.

"You're on a mission of some sort," Sir Hilary said. "Am I correct?"

"We are," Michael answered.

"I simply thought if we assisted you in your endeavor, it might expedite your work."

Before Michael could respond Alice cut in. "How thoughtful," she responded in her best upper-class accent. "What kind of assistance?"

Sir Hilary looked relieved to have found a receptive party. "It depends on your needs. We can help in any number of ways. Tell me what you want."

Michael was unable to hold his tongue. "We appreciate the offer," he said, "but we're well underway."

Alice shifted in her seat. "Actually we're still in the early stages of our expedition."

Sir Hilary leaned forward at her mention of an *expedition*.

Michael smiled and placed his hand on hers. "We'll talk it over and let you know."

Alice pulled her hand away.

Sir Hilary made a show of extracting a large piece of paper from the pile on his desk and donning a pair of pince-nez glasses. "Michael, you have written that the plague germ, yersinia, may destroy or at least inhibit the leprosy germ. From your Ph.D. thesis, Harvard 1995, if I'm not mistaken." He looked up, his glasses reflecting the lamplight. "It is an unusual and rather extraordinary hypothesis, and I can't help but wonder if you two aren't off to find your plasmid and prove the theory."

Alice finally looked at Michael, this time in surprise.

"I imagine when one is in a desperate situation," Sir Hilary went on, "one must investigate every option, even if it requires that you take a trip to Norway. Longyearbyen, Norway."

Michael felt his eyes narrow and the tiny hairs on the back of his neck begin to rise. "How did you hear about that?"

"My dear Michael, the entire world is tuned in to Pokhara nowadays. And as your leprae has demonstrated, we live in a small world."

"I wondered how you found out about our itinerary."

"Does it matter?" Sir Hilary removed the glasses. "What is important is that I am quite flexible. I am more than willing to support your efforts."

"We'll have to think about your kind proposal," Michael answered.

"I was telling Mr. Reimer," Sir Hilary continued, "I feel a certain kinship with you both. You remind me of my parents. People who believed it was their job to save the world."

"They sound like noble people," Alice said. "And we do appreciate your offer. I wonder, though, how *exactly* would you support our work?"

Sir Hilary's tone became clipped and businesslike. "You and Michael would, in effect, work for the Wilson Foundation. I would underwrite the whole project. First class all the way. We can help set up a large support structure, superb laboratories—"

"We already have the support of the CDC and the WHO," Michael interrupted.

"My understanding is that they're offering little more than moral support and airfare." Sir Hilary waved a peremptory hand. "How can I convince you to be part of the Wilson Foundation team?"

"I don't think that's possible," Michael answered.

Sir Hilary raised an eyebrow. "It seems that our Michael isn't much of a team player."

"It's not that. I'm already committed to the CDC and the WHO. At this point, I can't change teams."

Sir Hilary leaned back in his chair. "In that case, I would be willing to donate a million U.S. dollars from the Wilson Foundation toward your work to be used at your discretion."

Alice looked at Michael, clearly impressed.

"And in return?" Michael asked evenly.

"The pleasure of stopping the epidemic that killed my Jennifer."

"How do you propose we get these funds?" Michael asked

"I'll stay completely out of your way. You purchase all the equipment, supplies and help you need, and then you send me the bills. The Wilson Foundation will pay for all of the expenses."

"Your offer is extremely generous. I think that arrangement will work," Michael said. "Thanks."

"It will be a great pleasure and honor to have us working as a team."

"The expedition will still have to be under the auspices of the CDC and the WHO," Michael asserted definitively.

"Absolutely." Sir Hilary rose. "What are your plans for your respite in London?"

"Getting in shape for our Arctic adventure," Michael said.

"Might I suggest a few days of karate. It toughens one mentally and physically. Helps one remain focused. Jennifer studied it during our time in Japan."

"I always had an interest in it."

"I can make the arrangements." Sir Hilary extended his hand. "I shall stay in touch. Good luck, Alice. Michael."

"Thanks." Michael heard alarm bells going off in some far recess of his consciousness. Luck was something they were going to need, even more than money.

chapter thirty-three

Michael, Etienne and Alice passed uneventfully through customs at the Oslo International Airport, an unexpected pleasure considering the reputation of the Norwegians for being strict and bureaucratic. Sir Hilary at work?

When Michael emerged through the customs door, a bald, round-faced cherubic-looking man shouted, "Over here."

"Lars. Great to see you." Michael's colleague hadn't changed in the four years since their dig in Longyearbyen. He wore his constant smile and a glow in his eye, along with a dark business suit, wrinkled white shirt and an askew tie. He still didn't look like the chief of the prestigious, uptight archeology department at the University of Oslo.

"You look terrific," Michael said vigorously shaking Lars's hand. "Come, I want you to meet some people, Dr. Alice Morgan-Wright... and Etienne Roche," Michael said. "Alice, this is Lars Christensen. An old friend."

"Not too old to appreciate a beautiful woman. It is a pleasure to meet you." Lars bowed, a wide grin on his face. "Oh, she is as lovely as you said, Michael. You are a lucky fellow."

"Thanks. I'm lucky too," Alice said, and winked playfully.

"Lars and I worked together for six months carving ice," Michael offered.

Lars laughed. "It wasn't all fun — a minus-twenty-degrees wind-chill, not to mention the bears."

"But you succeeded," Etienne said.

"Yes. We found the flu virus."

Inside the main terminal the newspaper vendors were yelling out the headlines.

"What's all the shouting about?" Michael asked.

Lars looked surprised. "You haven't heard about the latest leprosy outbreak here in Europe?"

"Europe? Where?"

"In Germany."

Michael rushed to the newsstand, where Lars translated the front-page story, *"Leprosy Epidemic Strikes Europe. German Health Officials Concerned. After an emergency session, the Municipal Council of Bendsheim yesterday announced a limited outbreak of leprosy at the Christoffel Blinden Mission Headquarters."*

"More than two dozen cases have been reported, and the firm's office building has been quarantined. Council members suspect that health care workers who recently returned from a tour of duty in Asia had contracted the disease and are spreading the germ. All those in contact with employees in the building have been isolated. The mayor states that residents of the city should—"

"Why they allowed those workers to come into Germany without a short quarantine period is beyond any logic," Michael muttered in frustration.

"Stupide." Etienne concurred.

Alice shook her head. "The sooner we dig the better."

Running her roughened hands through her hair, Vera noted that it felt oilier and dirtier than usual. She rubbed her bleary eyes, longing to keep them closed for a month. And her damn cold wouldn't go away. She needed a shower and some rest. But when? It had been eleven days since she'd arrived in New York, and just as long since she had taken a break. There were so many people to take care of, and they were so short-handed. Dave, that ass, was off in Geneva at some meeting, and she'd allowed him to coerce her into going to New York as his representative. She sat in the Bellevue ER thinking that she should be home.

She still couldn't believe Bill was gone. Four of the UC staff were home dying of leprosy, and the rest were overworked and exhausted. There were no other residents or faculty who could help. She needed to get back.

On top of all that, the isolation was no longer working in New York, despite the calling in of the National Guard to enforce the quarantine. The number of people coming into the Bellevue ER with leprosy was increasing, a scary development since there was no treatment.

Vera pushed up from her office chair and dragged herself to the staff lounge. She needed more coffee. She had to stay alert, but knew she couldn't continue on three hours of sleep per night.

"Dr. Sarkov, phone call," blasted out of the loudspeaker.

Vera moaned. She had been busting her hump for almost two weeks. This was one of the few times she had tried to rest. Screw the ER. She needed a break.

"Dr. Sarkov. Please go to the resident phone. Stat."

"What now?"

Struggling to her feet, she staggered down the corridor to the telephone. She knew it had to be bad.

"There's an emergency at Kings County Hospital. You have to leave immediately," an anonymous voice ordered.

"Can't the Guard handle it?"

"They wanted you. The mayor has a limo outside."

Vera dozed in the car. When they neared the hospital on Clarkson Avenue, she opened her eyes to see toothless vagrants sitting on stoops in front of the old brownstones, staring into space. One gray-haired black man dressed in a heavily soiled parka and torn denims, bent over, stuffing pages from a newspaper into his remnant of a shoe. Around the homeless, a breeze filled the air with debris. Vera realized these people now had no place to go. Sadly, they would become animal vectors spreading the disease.

On the next block, a couple of masked soldiers confronted a number of derelicts, moving them on.

When the driver rounded the corner, Kings County Hospital rose before her, a massive tomb-like structure. Built in a gothic style at the turn of the century, it was made of gray stone, and at regular intervals, grimacing gargoyles lurked along the rooftop. Bottles, balled-up papers and gnarled dogwood trees littered the tawny-colored lawns. Many of the hospital windows were cracked, and brown tangles of dead ivy peeled off the building like skin from a molting snake.

The car screeched to a stop at the ER entrance and Vera rushed inside.

The voices coming from the waiting room were loud. Unusually loud. When she entered, she saw forty or fifty patients shouting and physically fighting with the staff and orderlies — pushing, shoving and cursing one another.

Seeing Vera and the mayor's assistant, the senior resident yelled, "Dr. Sarkov will tell you the facts. Listen to her. Please. She's from the CDC. From the government."

Most of the patients stopped clamoring to listen.

"What's the problem?" Vera asked.

The senior resident said, "These people want the leprosy antibiotics. We told them that they're no longer effective, so we didn't get any more. We're out. But they don't believe us."

"That's bullshit," screamed an Asian American man, whose face was deformed by lesions that were eating away at his nose. "You just don't want to treat us. You're writing us off."

The resident yelled, "That's nonsense."

A significant number of the complainants were Asian American, African American or emaciated AIDS patients. Vera sensed that they were all sensitive to any possible discrimination.

"Please everyone, listen," she shouted. "The antibiotics are useless. Since the anti-leprosy drugs aren't effective, the company stopped shipping them. Not only are they not effective, they are actually making the epidemic worse."

"We want to see the medicine cabinets," the Asian American patient with the misshapen face shouted. "We heard you have the drugs stored away, saving them for yourselves."

"We'll be happy to take a couple of you around so you can see that we don't have any—"

"Bull. You're hiding it," screamed a skinny patient.

With that, the patients broke through the line of staff and orderlies and raced to the treatment rooms, with the staff chasing after them, grabbing them, pulling them.

Vera called after them. "This is stupid. Stop." She dashed behind the reception desk, watching helplessly as the panicked patients stampeded through the rooms. One patient broke a set of ventricular fibrillators, knocked over the anesthesiologist's monitor, and rifled through the medicine cabinets, hurling bottles of injectable medications onto the floor, smashing them in the process.

Vera watched as the hysteria spread to other patients who were sitting in the treatment rooms. Those who were able began to run madly down the hallway. The frenzied mob tore up everything in sight. Bottles were heaved against the walls, bedding torn, papers ripped up and hundreds of thousands of dollars worth of equipment tossed to the ground.

As far as Vera could tell, some of the patients seemed satisfied with destroying things, releasing their frustration and fear. Others were angry enough to be dangerous to the staff.

She had to stop the mayhem, but how? She couldn't move. It wasn't safe. An emaciated man thrashed at one of the nurses, who tried to restrain him. The police. They needed the police. Turning to the secretary, Vera ordered her to place the 911 call.

Suddenly, one of the patients charged Vera, knocking her back against a chair and to the ground. He tore at her scrub suit, ripping one button after another free, exposing her bra. She punched at her assailant's face, and the mayor's assistant ran to her aid, kicking the patient in the ribs, causing him to crumble off to the side. Pulling Vera up, he supported her to the exit. She glanced back at the mayhem. She should have seen this coming.

Once outside, she could hear the approaching police sirens. Vera felt chills running through her body. She took deep breaths, trying to recover her composure.

When the policemen finally came running up, Vera gasped, "It's total chaos in there. The patients have panicked. They're breaking everything."

"These patients lepers?" the police sergeant asked.

"What difference does that make?" Vera shot back.

"Are they?"

"Most of them have the disease."

"Then I can't send my men in."

"What the fuck are you talking about? Put on masks and help us. You'll be as safe in there as anyvere."

The sergeant folded his arms and stared at Vera.

Vera turned to the mayor's assistant. "Get the mayor on your cell phone."

He dialed, and the sergeant's face reddened as if it were going to explode.

Vera moved closer to the policeman and read his nametag. "I'm going to have your ass, Sergeant McGruder." She drew herself up to her full height.

McGruder unfolded his arms and struck his palm with his fist.

Taking a deep breath, he gestured to the six policemen standing nearby, then barked, "Where are the fucking masks?"

"The resident will get them for you and your men."

The resident ran off. Vera recalled similar riots that had erupted in Russia when the resistant strain of TB broke out five years ago.

After dinner, Michael motioned for the team to follow him outside. The absence of any winter sun made it feel dank, dreary and cold. The intense breeze chilled Michael even further. His boots crunched in the snow as he, Alice, Etienne and Lars, bundled in parkas and huddled together, trodded along the narrow shop-lined streets, following the signs to the center of Oslo.

"As I told you on the phone, we have to find lepers who died from the Black Plague," Michael said to Lars. "We need a viable germ... and the equipment we used for the Longyearbyen dig."

"I believe it is stored in Bergen at the local Museum of Archeology," Lars answered, his breath forming an icy cloud.

"Believe?" Michael said. "I thought you had it ready. Can we get it?"

Lars frowned. "I will check. But first you will need a permit."

"We have to start digging as soon as possible. Every day we delay, more people die," Alice pleaded.

Lars shook his head doubtfully. "It took five months for me to get the permit for our flu project, and that had our government pre-approval."

"I'll get the CDC and the WHO to pressure your government to let us to start digging immediately."

"No, Michael. It won't work. The government will take many months to consider any such plan. You are in the land of the bureaucrats. They will not be cooperative about letting you dig up bodies, especially since we are only dealing with a theory. That is our way."

"Damn it. We don't have enough time for your way," Michael insisted. "We'll have to bypass asking the government for approval."

Lars looked horrified. "You cannot dig without a permit."

"I'll make one up; it'll look better than an authentic one."

"Oh, no. No. If we get caught, my reputation, my position—"

"Jesus. Half the world could be dead by then. There's no other option," Michael yelled, then fell silent. "Sorry, Lars. But that's the truth."

The wind swept the group into a small coffeehouse, where they sipped hot chocolate.

Lars whispered, "If there will be a fake permit, then we have to carry out this project as unobtrusively and discreetly as possible."

"We don't have time for that either," Michael answered in a low voice. "Let's approach this scientifically."

"I don't see—"

"Let's assume the digging has to be done on a large scale, and in a seemingly legal way, permit or not, so people aren't suspicious," Michael said.

"We need an excuse to dig..." Alice tapered off in mid-sentence and stared at Lars.

"Oh, no." He shook his head miserably, his cherubic cheeks turning a vivid pink. "I would be roasted alive. I can't do this, even for you, my dear friend."

Alice said, "A department of archeology project. What a fabulous cover for digging."

"It's perfect." Michael pronounced. "We have to do it."

Lars squeezed his eyes shut like an adorable piglet. "The absolute earliest I can get this false document is two days." His eyes popped open. "Tonight I go to church."

Vera stood in front of the Brooklyn Veteran's Hospital. "There's no reason for us to be here," she said irritably. "I repeat: this is a *very* bad idea."

The mayor, accompanied by three assistants and four newspersons, one with a camera, strode into the building.

"I'm here to comfort the sick. It's my duty," the mayor announced in a stentorian fashion to no one in particular.

A burly African American doctor in a white coat met them at the entrance. He smiled at Vera. He must have recognized her from her pictures in the *New York Post*. Front page, no less. She was now the official Big Apple leprosy maven, a job she had repeatedly tried to resign from as she anxiously awaited the arrival of her replacement, Dave.

"Everyone in masks, gowns and gloves," the doctor said.

Trooping over to the reception desk to collect the items, the mayor and his entourage followed the orders.

"Where do you want to go?" the doctor asked Vera.

"It's his show." She jerked her chin toward the mayor. "I'm totally against this visit."

"I'll leave that to you, doc," the mayor said. "The general leprosy ward would be a good place to start."

"I might suggest the two-bedded wing where there is less... confusion."

"Confusion?"

"Let's say it's better suited for your needs. More controllable, easier on the eyes." The doctor inclined his head toward the camera.

"I can handle the confusion. This disease doesn't intimidate me," the mayor said loudly. "I want the people of this great city to see that I'm not going to back down from facing our crisis head-on. The general ward is what I want to see."

Shaking his head, the doctor looked at Vera, then led the group down a corridor toward an L-shaped nursing station. Two wide-eyed nurses watched while the entourage marched by, illuminated in bright lights, the camera rolling.

Several feet from the swinging doors that led to the ward, the doctor stopped. "Are you sure—"

"Let's go," the mayor said, turning to the camera. "I want to let my constituents know that neither the city administration nor I will abandon them."

The doors swung open, and Vera could hear the noise from the ward. Shouts, cries and a generalized moaning emanated from within. The foul odor of rotting flesh hit Vera, causing her to stagger. The room smelled like a lavatory where no one had flushed for a week. She moved forward with her best no-nonsense sway.

As if choreographed by a horror-film director, the chaotic assembly of deformed patients in the crowded room turned toward the visitors. The mayor reflexively put his hand over his mouth. A man with a collapsed nose and massive bumps on his face staggered toward the group, extending his rotting hand toward the mayor, who promptly vomited into his mask. Cameras rolling, he ran from the room, ripped off his mask and wiped the emesis from his face.

Vera asked the reporters, "Did you get that?"

chapter thirty-four

On the first part of the train trip from Oslo to Bergen, Michael stared out the window at the sunless sky and the desolate, gloomy landscape of glaciers and mountains. But when the train passed over the Hardanger Plateau and the Ice Cap, he was awed by the majestic gorges and waterfalls. In the dim northern light, the snow-covered scenery looked deceptively inviting. The perfect place to find a frozen body. He felt fortunate to have Alice and Etienne working with him. They were a good team. He bent over and kissed the forehead of his sleeping lover.

After nearly eight hours, the train started its descent into the valley where Bergen was located. The city lights brightened the encompassing darkness. Snow-covered A-frame houses appeared in greater numbers, and eventually the clapboard and stone walls that surround parts of the city also became visible. In the distance Michael could make out Vagen harbor, full of docked fishing boats. The white-capped North Sea crashed against the boats, battering the shore.

Michael, Alice and Etienne disembarked at five p.m., backpacks and suitcases in tow, and hiked toward the center of town. The air was frigid.

Michael had made reservations at the Norge Hotel, but before they checked in, he decided to visit the Leprosy Museum. There should be someone there who could help. Etienne went to the hotel to register, and Michael and Alice headed toward the *lazarette* that housed the museum. Within minutes they came upon a tiny, old wood structure with a steep A-frame roof that looked no different from many of the other houses in Old Bergen. Inside, a guard directed them to the office of the curator, Nils Kreugstad.

"Yes? Can I be of some assistance?" The curator was a gangly man with a reddish-brown beard and mustache that made him look like a happy, shaggy Irish setter. Half-glasses perched precariously at the end of his thin red nose, and his baggy gray tweed suit looked two sizes too big.

"We need a lot of help." Michael introduced Alice, and then himself.

"Not the Michael Cohen who has written on leprosy and the plague?"

"Yes."

Kreugstad's eyes widened. "I am familiar with your work," he said. "It would be a privilege to assist you." A broad grin swept across the curator's face. "It seems quite appropriate that you are here in Bergen, since Dr. Gerhard Armauer Hansen, who identified the leprae organism in 1873 and whose name is frequently used for the disease, came from this city. He often visited this museum in his later years."

"It's an interesting twist of fate that brings me here." *Fate.* Michael thought of the Indian chief's words in Muniguda about karma and instinctively touched the protective amulet under his shirt.

Kreugstad settled comfortably behind his desk.

"You know about the leprosy epidemic, of course?" Michael asked.

"Of course. It is frightening, a worldwide tragedy. Reporters have been calling me to get information about leprosy. I have heard rumors that the antibiotics are useless, but I dare not believe that." He gazed at them hopefully, but almost at once his expression grew somber. "I see. It must be true, or you wouldn't be here."

"It's true," Michael confirmed.

"How can I help you?"

"I believe the plague organism has a plasmid, a factor that can inhibit the leprosy germ."

"Your theory about leprosy dying out in Europe," Kreugstad said, pounding excitedly on the desk. "I downloaded a copy of your dissertation and have it here in the museum."

"Please keep what we're about to discuss confidential, Mr. Kreugstad. We need a viable plague germ from the fourteenth century — a live germ that co-existed with the leprosy outbreak in Norway."

Sitting back, Kreugstad pulled at his beard. "If you want cold ground in which to find these live germs of yours, Norway is the place, but not Bergen. The temperature is too mild here on the west coast. You must go north and inland, into the mountains or east coast. You need permafrost."

"I know," Michael said. "I was part of the team that found the 1918 flu virus in frozen corpses up in Longyearbyen."

"A major success." The curator nodded enthusiastically.

"Mr. Kreugstad—"

"Please to call me Nils."

"Okay. And please call me Michael. Nils, we have some problems."

"Insurmountable?"

"I don't think so. Alice needs microbiological supplies. We also need shovels, picks and so on. We've got permission to dig." He pulled the forged document from his jacket. "We heard the Longyearbyen equipment is here in Bergen," he continued. "We need it."

"Ha, it's done. I know someone who has access to the new technology that was used in your flu project, like your ground-penetrating radar and core biopsy removal equipment."

"That's great," Alice said. "Also, we'll need diggers."

Nils' face lit up. "I was born in Spitzbergen, or as you call it, Svalbard, and have relatives there. I am certain the people of Svalbard will be more than happy to help you in this work. And my second cousin is the mayor of Longyearbyen, so the people of Longyearbyen will help as well. They are familiar with the dangers of being out in the Arctic Circle this time of year. And I would be honored to join you myself."

Michael grinned. "Are you sure? Even our spring dig was hazardous — bears, freezing weather."

Nils rolled his eyes. "This time of year it will be much worse. And night all the time. Yah, I'm sure. You'll need experienced trekkers, and I'm very good."

Michael grasped and squeezed Alice's hand. "We don't want the press to know what we're doing. They'll only slow us down," he said.

"Only the essential people will know."

Alice asked, "Do you have any documents that locate the exact sites of the fourteenth-century leper colonies on Svalbard?"

"They are usually kept in a church or city hall. I will call Svalbard and check on it."

"We'd also like an account of the pneumonic plague deaths in Svalbard," Michael added.

"A little more difficult, but I think I can get that, too."

"That's all we need for now," Michael said. "I think it's going to be great working with you, Nils."

With that, Nils picked up the phone and while whistling, dialed his cousin.

Huddled in the lobby of the Norge Hotel with Alice and Etienne, a topographic map of Svalbard Island spread before them on the glass coffee table, Michael pointed to the area they had dug for the flu victims.

"We started near the mines to the west of Longyearbyen, without success. Too warm. We had to move east."

"Land looks flat," Etienne observed.

"It was. Easy to travel with snowmobiles."

"What was the weather like?" Etienne asked.

A man in a tight maroon-colored uniform, his wrists extending well beyond the cuff, shouted, "Telephone for Dr. Michael Cohen."

Michael waved the man over and was directed to a phone in a small alcove in the lobby. While gazing idly at the printed scene of a fjord on the wallpaper, Michael was greeted by Anton.

"I've got good news for you," said the chairman of the WHO Executive Board. "We've managed to come up with the equipment you requested for your dig. We'll have six snowmobiles and pack sleds available for you in Longyearbyen."

"Excellent." Apparently they finally understood the importance of the effort.

"We have some other items, like a short-wave radio. Money, too. About twenty-five thousand U.S., to be used at your discretion."

"Where do we get all this?"

"I'm sending three people along to help. They'll meet you at the Longyearbyen airport."

"We'll put everything to good use."

"I'm certain you will."

Michael felt jubilant. He was not going to need any financial help from Sir Hilary. Having the expedition entirely a WHO-funded activity felt pure and right.

"One of the men is from Sweden and speaks English and Norwegian," Anton continued. "He has extensive experience in Arctic weather. Hunted polar bears for pleasure."

Michael's jubilation was short-lived. The WHO had to be desperate to offer this level of assistance after claiming poverty.

chapter thirty-five

Brother Rose refused to think about his health. His breathing was becoming more labored, but he concentrated instead on ministering to the dying. He pushed past the line of patients at the entrance to Pokhara's hospital, and the smell of antiseptic filled his nostrils. He adjusted his mask, walked past a cow and some goats that wandered aimlessly in the lobby, and headed toward the wards, the route he took every day.

Silently, Brother Rose walked down the makeshift aisle past the patients lying in bed, coughing, breathing with difficulty or not breathing at all. The smell of excrement was overwhelming, even by rural Nepalese standards. There were insufficient toilets, and many of the patients, especially those with diarrhea, were too weak to move.

He drew in a labored breath and focused. He had to be strong and do honor to his order. Swatting at the ravaging flies, he approached an emaciated man who was overcome with violent coughing. He grasped the man's upper arm. The man's leprosy had left him with only two withered stumps below his shoulders. Opening his eyes, the patient smiled weakly.

Brother Rose was familiar with the signs of death. When the man vomited, splattering most of the bed, Brother Rose was not surprised and barely repulsed. Laying his calming hand over the man's eyes, he made the sign of the cross and said, *"Per istam sanctam unctionem…"* Touching the man's ears, nostrils, lips, hands, feet and chest, he repeated the anointing words of the Sacrament of the Sick over each.

The man whispered in a raspy voice, "Please give my clothes to my eldest son. He will be needing them for the winter."

Brother Rose nodded reassuringly, even as he realized the man's stained, threadbare garments would be of no further use. He instinctively reached for his amulet. It was gone. He remembered. Michael needed it.

Sitting on the dying man's bed, he looked about the room at the struggling masses, closed his eyes and wept.

When Brother Rose entered the lab, Rowan was sitting in front of the computer poring over information about the historical treatment for leprosy.

"Anything promising?"

"No, Brother, nothing new."

"It's Michael's field. If he didn't know of any other options..."

"I feel so helpless and guilty sitting here in the lab watching the bodies pile up," Rowan moaned.

"There's nothing to feel guilty about."

Rowan winced. "I have to do something. There's always the remote possibility that we're missing something crucial — some treatment like your chaulmoogra oil in India."

"A worthless sham."

A wave of stomach rumblings hit Brother Rose, a common sign in the developing world, but ominous in this setting.

"Maybe I'm being naïve, but I believe that the answer to the leprosy epidemic is in its history," Rowan said. "I can feel it. It's here somewhere, and I shan't quit until I find it."

Brother Rose stumbled into a chair.

"There were reports in Biblical times of leprosy epidemics that were apparently limited," she continued, staring at the screen.

The next warning from his intestines included severe cramping. Brother Rose bent forward, trying to alleviate the pain. Again, he reflexively reached for his missing crucifix.

"What's wrong?" Rowan asked in alarm.

"Something I ate this morning..."

The next wave of abdominal distress doubled Brother Rose up, causing him to crumple to the floor with a groan.

Rowan instinctively tightened her mask, then knelt next to him, pressing her hand on his shoulder.

chapter thirty-six

Glimpses of the cold moon flashed in and out of the partially clouded sky on the hour-and-a-half flight from Bergen to the Island of Svalbard. In the inky polar night, Michael saw a magical palette of pastel colors emanating from the northern horizon; the aurora borealis, the lights generated by solar protons and electrons colliding with the molecules of the earth's atmosphere.

The dancing lights faded as the brightness and glare from Longyearbyen grew near — a city surrounded by utter blackness, a guide in the night. Lost in the darkness were the adjacent Advent fjord and valley, and rocky hills where the local miners spent most of their lives and where Michael's team had initially dug for the flu virus.

Climbing down the exit ladder from the twenty-seater plane, Michael felt instantly numbed by the bitter cold. A minus-sixty-degrees Fahrenheit wind chill welcomed the team into the frigid world of winter in the Arctic Circle, seventy-eight degrees north latitude.

Nils pulled his balaclava over his head and dashed toward the terminal. Michael, Alice and Etienne, clothed in parkas, gloves and boots, quickly followed.

Inside the terminal they were greeted by Per Johnson, the WHO representative Anton had sent. Per's imposing six-foot-four-inch frame towered over his two associates. With his blond hair almost as light as that of an albino, his cold green eyes, square shoulders and strong jaw, the man looked like a block of ice.

"These are my WHO colleagues," Per said, "Jan Hartkopf and Carlo Mangini."

Both men nodded. Per's associates were sooty-haired, burly men, who looked like barroom bouncers.

"I have booked a set of rooms for the team in the Spitzbergen Funken Hotel for the night, and have arranged for the snowmobiles to be supplied for the trip," Per announced.

"Perfect," replied Michael. "It'll save us a lot of time." He adopted his best diplomatic tone. "From this point on, however, I think it best if Alice or I make all the arrangements. I'd appreciate it if you'd clear all of your actions with me."

A look that could crack stone appeared and lingered on Per's face. "I was led to believe that as the WHO representative, I would be in a leadership position."

"That's not the case."

Per took a deep breath. "So be it."

Alice added, "Actually, you'll need to clear your plans with Etienne, Michael, Nils and me. It's a team effort."

A polite smile melted through the frozen face."Of course."

"Tomorrow we meet with the Svalbard governor and my cousin to plan our trip," Nils said. "But no business tonight. It is our way. We go to drink in the Huset. All eleven hundred residents will be there." He laughed heartily. "Especially the miners."

One of Per's aides beamed at the thought. Per glared at him.

"Drink up tonight," Nils said. "It's the last we get. Alcohol is a killer on a trek."

Before entering the stone church, Michael shook the snow from his parka. Etienne, Alice and Per did the same. The building was extremely plain looking, except for its tall, thin steeple and light-colored wooden beams. The windows were made of clear or frosted glass and the altar, except for a large cross, was devoid of religious trappings. It reminded Michael of the Unitarian Church he'd attended in Charlotte, North Carolina during his youth.

Michael took off his gloves and shook hands with the tall, dark-complexioned pastor. "I'm Dr. Cohen. I understand you've been informed about our project and the need for secrecy?"

"Yes, I have. The governor and Mayor Kreugstad explained it all to me."

"You have the books?"

"I will get them."

"If it's this frigid in the church, I hate to think about the weather on the glaciers," Etienne said.

Before Michael could answer, Nils arrived with the governor and his cousin the mayor, who shared the same Irish setter coloring and wiry frame.

"Good to see you again, Dr. Cohen," the governor said with a sober expression. "I hope you scientists don't plan to make a habit of coming here to dig up our ancestors."

"The flu dig made us famous," the mayor interjected. "Tourism has been on the rise ever since—"

"Yes, yes," the governor agreed. "You have the permit?"

He scanned the paper that Michael handed him. "Looks in order. If Oslo thinks it is fine, then—"

"It's an emergency," Alice said.

"Of course, my dear doctor. The leprosy."

The pastor arrived with three dusty parchment tomes and placed them on the table. "These are our church's records from the fourteenth century, the time of the Black Death."

Michael, Alice and Etienne each took a volume and with the translation assistance of Nils, Per, the mayor and the governor, they pored through the yellowed, crumbly-edged pages looking for clues.

While they worked, the pastor prepared hot chocolate.

After a few minutes, Nils broke the silence. "Here is something," he said. "A discussion of the lepers."

"What's it say?" Alice asked.

"The villagers blamed the lepers for the plague. The church organized a group — vigilantes you would call them — to find the leper colony and destroy it."

"A sad moment in our church's history," the pastor remarked.

"It had been done for thousands of years, Reverend," Michael said. "It wasn't anything new."

Nils shrugged. "There's not much else."

"Keep reading," the governor ordered.

The group encircled Nils, drinking their hot chocolate, while he scanned through the pages. "Difficult to read, this old Hoch German-Norwegian mixture. Small print, too. Wait, here's something. I think it says the group returned without any lepers."

"Why?" Alice asked.

"Let's see." Nils mumbled to himself, his finger following each line. "Dead," he pronounced. "All the lepers were dead. They found no one alive."

"Was it the plague?" Per asked.

"Doesn't say," Nils answered.

Alice leaned forward to study the indecipherable text. "Where was the colony?"

"I'm afraid it doesn't say that either. It's a brief note."

"Damn." Frozen lepers from the fourteenth century, dead from the plague, would be perfect. But where were they?

"Are the entries dated?" Alice asked.

"They are."

"Check on when they left and when they returned," Alice requested.

"Four days," Nils said, his head bobbing. "The recordings are four days apart."

"They went on dogsled, right?" Alice continued.

"It was the only way," supplied the governor. "No one would go on foot."

"I would guess travel by dogsled hasn't changed much," Michael prompted, catching Alice's reasoning.

"We probably can go an extra eight or ten miles each day on the newest dogsleds," the mayor said. "At that time one can imagine they could travel ten to twelve miles per hour over the glacier."

"We must also think of the time of year. One can go much further in summer than winter," the governor added.

"Yah," said Nils, clearly pleased with his discovery. "They discuss *Julebord,* so it must have been this time of year."

Per wondered, "The next question is, which direction did they go?"

"West and north is out," mused the governor. "It's the Advent Fjord. South was too populated. The leper colony had to be east or northeast."

"One book I read said there was a colony in Friesland," Michael said.

The governor shook his head. "Unlikely and too far. In two days you cannot get there. The colony we are looking for had to be much closer."

"Sabine Land or Olav Land," suggested the mayor. "Probably next to the Storfjorden Sea. The lepers would have needed to fish to survive."

"Then we are off to the east coast of Sabine Land," Per

concluded.

The governor clapped his hands for attention. "Let's discuss the details over dinner. Tonight, you are all guests at my house."

Michael and his team stood in a cluster outside the governor's white house, a tidy A-frame with a slate tile roof, pale blue trim and dormer windows. Moments after Nils lifted the wrought-iron door-knocker, Michael saw a fluttering at a white lace curtain on the second floor, and within seconds they were admitted.

Immediately he felt enveloped by warmth and the smell of cooking. He admired the classic Norwegian interior as the group shed their parkas. It was a simple but elegant dwelling with light-colored paneled walls and hardwood floors, cozy woolen area rugs in natural tans and ivories and wrought-iron lighting fixtures hanging from the ceiling.

"My cook has prepared a typical regional dinner," the governor announced. "Smoked and pickled salmon, West Bothnian cheese and cloudberry jam. And for the entrée, reindeer steaks or sausages." He led them into a large dining room with a huge, blazing fireplace and took his seat at the head of a long refectory table. "I believe we may have some lingonberries and rowanberries too."

"A feast," Michael said, delighted. "Thank you for the food and your hospitality."

The governor's sober expression didn't change. "You will need it. You will be facing extremely adverse conditions over the next week. Much worse than your spring digging, Dr. Cohen." He turned to the mayor. "Are they prepared for the weather?"

"We have supplied them with the proper clothes. They have a short-wave radio, maps and compasses."

"Bears? Have they been warned?"

"They know to avoid all contact with the polar bears. If one approaches I have told them to try to scare it away immediately." The mayor stood and flailed his arms to demonstrate. "Jump and wave like this. Shout, growl."

"Snublebluss?"

"Nils will set out snublebluss around their campsite. The tripwire warning flares should be all they need."

"I'm not so sure," the governor replied. "Remember last year? The archeology students. We don't want a repeat of that incident."

The mayor smiled reassuringly at Alice's obvious alarm. "We have supplied Nils with signal pistols to scare off the bears... and large-bore rifles if nothing else works."

"They will be in your hands, Nils," the governor said sternly.

"Nils grew up here," the mayor cut in. "He knows his way."

"I can get a guide," the governor persisted.

"Unnecessary, but thank you," mumbled Nils through a mouthful of cheese.

"I also have experience in this type of terrain," Per added.

The governor raised his beer mug and announced, "In that case, a toast to your adventure into the wilderness. The glacier awaits you."

They all raised their glasses and drank.

chapter thirty-seven

Sitting at the side of his bed, Michael pulled on his sealskin waterproof socks, then slipped on his thermal underwear, followed by two layers of woolen turtleneck sweaters and woolen pants. He yanked on his mountain boots, grabbed his hooded parka, and headed out of his room. Once outside, he took a deep breath of the minus-thirty-degree air. His sinuses burned.

At six p.m. the sky was completely dark. Not surprising. On this trip they would see no sunlight.

An omen?

He added a leather cap with an attached headlight, a balaclava and mittens to his ensemble, then crunched over to the seven snowmobiles that were assembled like a herd of sheep in front of the hotel. All had packs on or behind them in sleds, sprinkled with a powdering of snow. He waved to the rest of the team and winked at Alice, who looked like a cross between a veiled harem girl and a toddler in a snowsuit.

"It was a shame to waste most of the day sitting here," Per said irritably.

"We are leaving now so we'll have the moonlight to light the way," Nils answered.

"Hmmpf. I've used the light from the aurora."

"Not nearly as good as the moon."

Per grumbled, then pulled on his face mask.

"I'm glad to see you all dressed so warmly," Nils said cheerfully to the team. "Unfortunately, you will have to change your clothes into scooter suits, goggles, boots and gloves. That will keep you comfortably warm. The forecasters predict good weather for this time of the year. Tonight's wind chill will be minus-eighty-degrees Fahrenheit."

"What's in those packs?" Alice asked.

"While you slept some townspeople loaded them with food and equipment. I have a community tent on my pack sled; the rest of the loads are essentially the same. Everyone has his or her own tent and supplies. If anyone gets lost, they will have a compass, map, shelter and food. You also have radios, what you call walkie talkies, in your vehicle. Make sure they work. We'll have regular radio checks as we travel."

"I also have a short-wave radio," Per chimed in, "and I have the money for supplies." He reached for his pocket.

"When we return you can reimburse us," Nils told Per.

"Do we have the equipment from our dig in Longyearbyen?" Michael asked.

"We have all the dig equipment on my sled. My cousin and I checked it out several times. If we are lucky the sky will be clear and the moonlight will help." Nils frowned slightly. "In the best of circumstances visibility can be a challenge. We'll put the novices toward the back, so you have the greatest number of people to follow. I will lead the way, followed by Jan and Carlo, then Per. Then Alice and Michael. Etienne, you have Arctic experience from your time in Russia. Do you feel secure taking up the rear?"

"*Certainement,*" answered Etienne. "Then I can keep my eye on Michael and Alice."

Laughing, they all mounted their respective snowmobiles.

"I will call you on your receivers every thirty minutes," Nils said. "When I decide we should stop, we will form a circle. We must set up the tents as fast as possible. Even in good times the winter weather is not our friend."

Starting up his vehicle with a roar, Michael adjusted his goggles over his eyes and watched as Nils moved off into the obscurity, followed by the rest.

The lights from the city quickly faded, and only a sliver of light from the snowmobiles illuminated an otherwise black landscape. There could be arctic foxes or a family of polar bears ten feet to the side of the narrow beam of light and Michael would never know it. They drove on, the wind picked up and breathing became more difficult. Michael pressed his gloved hand over the mask that covered his nose.

The uneven and bumpy ice and snow made for a jarring ride. Were they moving too quickly? Michael checked the speedometer, which read a mere twenty miles per hour. He felt as if they were racing. Periodically he checked on Alice and Etienne, who seemed to be holding their own on the powerful machines. They'd each had a lesson while he'd rested.

The droning of the snowmobiles provided a comforting constant in a world devoid of sensory input. Michael's mind wandered as he drove, soon turning to the disasters that could befall them in this barren and frigid place. He trusted in Nils — significantly more than the misanthropic-looking Per and his gang. Where had Anton found those characters? But Nils could drive into the sea and everyone would follow. More likely he could fall into a crevasse and half of the team would follow. Then there would be no guide, no digging equipment and little else. The maps would be useless. They would surely freeze to death trying to find Longyearbyen.

How would he proceed in such a situation? He could follow the western coastline... but in the wintertime the fjord would be frozen. There would be no clear signs to follow. The compass and the stars would help. Michael visualized the northern winter sky. Orion, Sirius and...

The radio sputtered to life, and Nils' voice squawked the third or fourth radio check of the night.

Is it getting colder? Nils had said the wind chill would be minus-eighty-degrees Fahrenheit, but Michael had no idea what that would feel like. The thought of the number sent a chill coursing through his body.

What if a storm hits?

Okay, stop it. Michael decided it wasn't productive to think of all the catastrophes that could befall them. The dying were counting on him. He was going to succeed. His only problem now was to stay in the present, stay focused on the vehicle in front of him. His meditating practice should help to keep his mind from drifting.

Michael fought his wandering thoughts, and a brushstroke of colored lights filled the northern sky, awakening his sluggish mind. The flashing lights and the rise of the glowing moon brightened his blue-white surroundings, and he could see, off to his left, ice caps, the spine dividing the team from the sea. In all directions rose a surreal landscape of ice-covered mountains, irregularly shaped plateaus, undulating mounds and flat plains. Precipitous white walls dotted the horizon. He could see cracks in the permafrost base, as well as caves and pointed masses of ice in the glacier, the seracs. The side of his snowmobile was covered with rime, the coating of frozen water that seemed to form on everything. Only he remained ice-free.

Watching the labyrinth of formations in the shimmering light, Michael veered off the trail. A series of violent bumps were a quick reminder to return to the safety of the caravan. He looked back to see if Etienne had followed him into trouble, but the Frenchman shot him a brief thumbs-up and returned to the hard work of snowmobiling.

Driving on, Michael and the team entered a flat, smooth area that looked like a sparkling white Sahara Desert.

A crackling noise startled him. Michael grabbed the radio receiver that was hooked on the dashboard and clicked it to speak. "Michael here."

"This is Nils. I plan to stop in five minutes. I will slow down, then stop. Form the circle immediately. Comprehend?"

A chorus of grunts answered him.

"Your tents are on the top of the packs on the back of your snowmobiles. If you need help let me or Per's men know. Alice, Jan will show you how to set up yours."

A clicking noise, silence, and Michael was returned to the world of the droning vehicles, flashing yellow and purple sky-lights, and the white terrain.

After the group formed a circle, Michael unpacked his one-man tent. Hindered by his bulky gloves, he was slow in setting it up. He tossed his sleeping blanket inside and was ready to settle in when Nils came clomping by.

"We meet in my tent in five minutes."

Michael put his cap with the light back on and forged through the dimness toward Nils' tent. The crunching and creaking noises under his feet made him wonder if they were camped out on the frozen sea.

The wind had increased, forcing Michael to keep his goggles on in order to see. Spying Nils' large, yellow clamshell-type tent, he zipped open the door flap, bent low and entered. Immediately, his goggles fogged in the heated tent, already warmed by a central heater. He found a spot on the reindeer skin on the floor next to Per. Ice had formed on Per's eyebrows, adding to his frosty mien.

"This weather must remind you of Sweden," Michael asked.

"Mostly bad memories," Per answered, not inviting further discussion.

When Alice and Etienne entered, all were present.

"We traveled six hours. About one hundred and sixty kilometers." Opening a map, Nils pointed. "This places us in Bunsow Land, about two thirds of the way to the coast."

"Why did we stop?" Per asked.

"The driving becomes hypnotic. Someone could doze off. That is serious, even with the walkie talkies." Nils looked at his wristwatch. "It's twelve thirty. We'll eat in our own tents, then sleep until seven. Tomorrow will be another grueling day."

"We won't have any moonlight to help. What will the weather be?" Etienne asked.

Nils shrugged. "It is always the same. Frigid and dark. A small front is coming through. Expect some snow."

Michael got up, gave Alice a brief nuzzle, and headed out to his tent. It was hard to imagine they could find any long-buried bodies in this tundra. The lack of a precise location was obstacle enough, and he found the endless whiteness and blackness, devoid of color except for the intermittent appearance of the aurora, otherworldly and intimidating. He hoped Nils knew his way.

"Wake up," someone shouted in Michael's dream. He opened his eyes and was confronted by a flapping tent, howling winds, and Nils shouting at him above the noise.

Michael stretched and opened the tent flap. "Is it seven already?"

"No. It's four-thirty. But there's a bit of a storm passing through. Thought we might head east and get out of it."

"I'll be ready to go in ten minutes."

Michael grabbed a power bar, sipped some barely defrosted juice out of a plastic container, folded his sleeping bag and left the tent. The snow and wind made the previous day seem like a tropical vacation.

The blasted wind chill must be minus one hundred.

He pulled on his goggles, folded his tent and packed it on his snowmobile, a tedious task in the snow and wailing gale, since he could barely see or feel anything, or maneuver his fingers in the thick mittens. Removing the cover from the vehicle, he hopped in and drove slowly toward the area where Nils' tent had been. The visibility was twenty feet or less, despite his headlights. Nils' voice came through on his receiver. "Everyone sign in."

After hearing from all the team members, Nils announced, "We are going to ride closer to each other — and slower."

Anything else would be suicide.

"We should be out of this within an hour or two, according to the weather report. Follow me."

Michael pulled up close to Alice's snowmobile, exchanged a thumbs-up, and they were off. The snow fell around him, and Michael felt as if he was wrapped in a pristine, womblike cocoon. All remained invisible except for the snow falling in the light of his snowmobile. He found himself wishing for wipers for his goggles. Ignoring all else, Michael concentrated on the rear of Alice's pack sled. He tried to make out any objects on the sled that would facilitate his focus, but the dense snow limited details.

Time moved slowly. It always had when Michael was acutely aware of it, but if Nils was right, they would be out of the storm shortly. If he had a Walkman, some music, it would be easier. But he needed to be able to hear in case Nils called on the radio.

Michael's world constricted to the narrow beam of light, the falling snow and Alice's sled. Life was simple. Stay focused and live; lose focus and die. The caravan droned on.

Was the snow worsening? He could barely make out Alice's pack sled. Maybe he was too far away. He picked up speed, but noticed that he was not getting closer to the sled. Wiping his goggles, Michael squinted.

Alice's sled was not ahead of him.

He grabbed his receiver and shouted, "Nils. Nils."

The only response was a crackling hiss. Could he have been lost for a long time? The walkie talkies only carried for a mile or two. The team couldn't be that far away. "Alice. Do you hear me?"

Nothing.

"Alice, Per, do you read me?"

Faint static greeted his pleas. Then a voice. "This is Etienne. I've lost you. Where did you go?"

"I don't have the vaguest idea. Let me check my compass. I'm going to stop."

Michael halted his vehicle. "I'm facing east-northeast. The reading says…"

The noise in the receiver faded. "Etienne?"

There was no answer.

Blast. What should he do? He couldn't sit still and keep the light on because he would kill the battery, but he needed the light if he wanted to be found. Yet he didn't want to drive just to save the battery if he was going in the wrong direction.

The solution was simple. He would drive slowly in the east-north-easterly direction. Toward the sea.

Starting up his engine, Michael peered into the area illuminated by his headlight. Nils was wrong; the storm was worsening… and he was alone and lost.

chapter thirty-eight

Brother Rose felt terrible when he awakened. Not able to find a comfortable position in bed, he got up. He sat slumped in his room, his head in his hands, when the abdominal spasms hit. Groaning, he rushed into the foul-smelling outhouse and squatted in an attempt to relieve himself. Nothing came. When the excruciating wave of abdominal pain passed, he was able to stand and return to the cabin. The instant he sat down, the next wave of cramps hit. These felt worse than the first, and moaning audibly, Brother Rose rushed to the bathroom again. This time he was able to move his bowels, but the passage only stopped after a long period of time.

What could he have eaten that would do this? He couldn't remember having any uncooked foods. Certainly no unboiled water. He refused to think the worst.

He walked, unsteadily, back to his bed. Another severe gastric pain struck like a boring knife plunging into his stomach. He retched but nothing came. His habit was soaked through with sweat, and his legs trembled.

He rifled through his backpack and found a bottle of Pepto-Bismol. He gulped down the pink liquid. Then he took a deep breath and wiped the perspiration from his brow. He needed help — right now. Reflexively, he reached for the missing amulet, then looked at his watch. Six p.m. Rowan and Koirala should be at dinner.

He mumbled a prayer, then left his cabin and staggered toward the dining tent, but halfway there a seesawing dizziness engulfed him and he fell to his knees. He tried to call out for help, but before he could, his throat closed up, making it impossible for him to speak.

He coughed violently, trying to clear his lungs, as another wave of abdominal pain doubled him up. Groaning, he collapsed flat on the dusty road. Summoning his will, he crawled along, thinking about his friends. He couldn't abandon them. He struggled to lift himself, then managed to totter onward toward the dining tent, looking for help. He was not going to die.

The snowmobile crept along in the moaning wind and pelting snow. Michael followed the wedge of light in front of him. He did not want to fall into a crevasse.

Despite his concerns about the reliability of the compass so close to the magnetic north, the reading held steady. Picking up the communicator, he shouted hopefully, "Anyone there? Etienne, Alice, Per, Nils." Michael realized he might never see his friends again. Never see Alice again. He settled in his seat as a wave of sadness overcame him. Was it going to end so soon? He thought of his loss and of the pain Alice would feel. So little time together and so much time wasted away from the woman he adored.

The headlights flickered. Was the battery going to fail? He sped up and the light brightened. He was going faster, but in what direction? The thought of dying in the tundra invaded his mind, tempting him to succumb to fear, to lose hope. He had to survive. To find a frozen body, a plasmid. *The storm will pass*. But where would he be when that happened? Out on an ice floe, a lost frozen body himself?

There must be a flare in his gear. When the storm abated he would send up a flare. Why the hell hadn't Nils or Per better prepared them for this emergency?

Although he was traveling faster, the snowfall seemed to be lighter. Was he imagining things, or was the storm abating? Slowing the vehicle, he scanned the area in front of him. He could see further. Nils was right. Traveling in the northeasterly direction would take them out of the storm. He picked up speed and drove out of the blizzard.

The sky lightened as the moon darted out of the clouds, allowing Michael to see his surroundings. He was on a vast white plain with a mesa jutting up in the distance. He looked at his watch. He had been lost for almost an hour. He might be able to get to the top of the plateau and survey the environs... even set off a flare. He pushed the accelerator to the floor and bounced toward the formation.

He approached the mesa and saw white objects heading his way. The teasing moonlight drew behind a cloud while Michael approached the icy plateau and moving forms. When the moonlight reappeared, painting the area in a silvery glow, Michael saw three polar bears lumbering toward him.

He hit the brakes. The vehicle skidded to a stop, tottered and tipped over. *Damn*. He slid out of his seat, then pulled on the lower side of the snowmobile. The heavy machine would not right itself.

The animals slowed their pace and approached — sniffing, shuffling, but always moving in his direction. He might scare one animal by flailing his arms. But three? Not likely. He ran to his pack sled, fumbled to open the canvas covering and searched in the cold light for a weapon. There was no large-bore rifle.

The animals were less than a hundred yards away.

He couldn't manipulate his fingers to do fine movements with his scooter gloves on, so he slipped them off, despite Nils' previous warnings. The cold instantly bit at his hands, making them burn. Michael groaned.

The moonlight disappeared and he snapped on his headlamp. Working rapidly, he tossed away supplies, delving deeper into the pack.

The animals were at fifty yards when he found the flare gun. Two extra flares lay next to the pistol. Michael blew on his frozen hands, grabbed the loaded weapon and turned toward the bears.

He fired.

A brilliant pink color shot forth, terminating at the chest of the closest bear. The animal roared and scurried off while the other two retreated a few feet, but remained, their eyes fixated on Michael. Grabbing the spare flare, he loaded the gun and fired again. He hit the second bear in its neck. The animal growled loudly and lumbered off without looking back.

The first wounded bear and the third one wandered in ever-closer circles. Michael reloaded the gun and raced toward them, screaming and wildly waving his arms. The bears hesitated, then ran away.

Exhausted, Michael trudged back to his snowmobile where he pulled on his gloves, unhooked the walkie talkie from its mount, and clamped on his foot spikes. Then he began walking to the plateau, carrying the last flare.

The aurora borealis appeared, bathing the area in a ludicrously tropical orange-red. The distant silhouettes of the mountains looked peaceful and inviting, belying the dangerous nature of the Arctic. Hiking onward, Michael realized that the plateau was further than he'd thought — possibly a mile or more. But as long as the weather held, he would be fine. He surveyed the expanse of the deserted glacier, and a feeling of supreme loneliness overwhelmed him. He clutched his handheld radio and flare gun more firmly as his crampons crunched into the snow.

It was hard to imagine a leper colony existing in this environment.

He wondered how the others were doing. Were they thinking of him? Was Etienne lost out here as well? The expedition party must be close if they had followed Nils' course. They would see Michael's flare in the darkened sky.

At the foot of the rise, he stuck his spikes into the hill and began his climb. Trekking up was not going to be easy.

The roar of a polar bear startled him.

Where the hell did he come from? Turning quickly, Michael saw the animal charging. Instinctively, he fired at the beast, and his last flare ricocheted off the bear's head and rolled away on the ice. The animal raced off. *Success.* But the flare was spent. Michael collapsed onto the snow. There was no longer a reason to climb the plateau.

The snowmobile was out of action, but Michael decided to return to it, set up his tent, eat some food and look for another flare or weapon before any or all of the bears returned. He had no other options.

chapter thirty-nine

Erik felt confident. Despite the initial set of disappointing results, the process was once again on the right path. He snuggled his attaché case on his enormous lap and glanced about Anton's spartan office. The Danish modern chairs and desk looked like a school project his thirteen-year-old son could have completed more tastefully. The spindly pressed-wood chair he sat in threatened to splinter under his weight. The monotonous row of plaques behind the desk were illegible and blended in with the photos of totally forgettable people on Anton's desk.

Anton was a true bureaucrat: colorless, invisible and cowardly, and probably never took a courageous step in his life. A boring cog.

The door swung open.

"Herr Koenig, how good to see you again," Erik said in his most animated and pleasant tone, making no effort to rise.

"Sorry to be late," squeaked the mousy man, "but as you can imagine, things have been quite frenetic here."

Erik pictured veritable whiskers twitching on Anton's rodent nose. "How is the Norwegian expedition coming?"

"The team is out in the tundra."

Erik snorted. "A remarkable endeavor that quite frankly has little chance of success. Finding an ancient leper with the plague out in the Arctic Circle is not a project I would consider sound from a business point of view."

Anton sat behind his desk and folded his hands on top. "This is not a business venture," he answered bluntly.

"Even if they find this hidden treasure, one has to accept the wildest of scientific theories that a viable germ could be obtained and that it will kill the leprosy." Erik gazed at Anton pitiably. "I find the whole effort a waste of resources."

Anton's face collapsed upon itself.

Erik waited a beat, then continued brightly. "I have good news for you. Our vaccine is coming along nicely."

Anton's expression did not change. "I read your preliminary report. No significant protection from the disease with your vaccine."

"That was only our initial run. We're modifying the vaccine using an attenuated form of the new virulent leprae bacilli. We hope to have the final product available for human testing in six months."

"A ridiculously optimistic appraisal," Anton said, waving a weak hand. "There is no way you could have anything before a year, and the human testing will take another year."

"We have top scientists working on it."

"Two years at best, especially if you're embroiled in a costly, time-consuming lawsuit."

"If you mean the frivolous suit by Sir Hilary, he is merely venting a father's pain. He has no basis for his suit, and I believe it will die a natural death as his emotions subside."

Anton looked at his wristwatch, but before he could speak, Erik removed some papers from his case and blurted, "I heard you plan to distribute the Wellcome vaccine. I strongly suggest you distribute ours as well."

Erik laid the papers on Anton's desk. The WHO official ignored them.

Erik tapped the documents with a fat finger. "We compared our results with theirs, and although we did not alter the course of the disease from a statistically significant point of view, we did a little better than their vaccine, if you look at the mortality numbers but not morbidity or rate of spread."

"The previous leprosy didn't kill."

"We are also willing to supply you with our vaccine at half the cost of the Wellcome material."

Anton glanced at the papers, then picked them up.

Erik couldn't resist a soft, "I-told-you-so" grunt. The WHO was going to be especially interested in the Farberg vaccine, and willing to pay even more when the Norwegian adventure failed.

"They're definitely lost," Alice worried to the group gathered in Nils' community tent. "I keep trying, but I haven't been able to raise Michael or Etienne on my communicator for the last two hours."

"It only means they're more than two miles away," Nils said.

"We have to go after them." Alice stood up with her hands on her hips.

"Maybe we can get the specimens and pick them up on the way back," Per said.

"The hell we will," Alice shouted. "Would you want to be left out there — lost?"

Per shrugged. "Nils said a bigger storm is coming. We don't have much time. I thought we might save time by—"

"You thought wrong. We need Michael to find the samples. We need his expertise. We need Etienne. But most of all, I need them, and I'm going back to find them. You and your buddies can go to hell."

Per glared at Alice. "I did not plan to abandon them. They have food and a tent. I simply wondered whether, if we don't need them now, we can go to the colony and—"

Alice was ready to explode. "You don't get it, do you?"

"Per, we cannot leave Michael and Etienne out there alone," Nils intervened. "Alice and I will go back. You and your men can stay here."

Per frowned. "Of course we will go with you. I am not insensitive to your feelings, Dr. Morgan-Wright."

"I'm shocked that you'd even considered leaving them out there."

Per opened his mouth to speak, then said nothing.

"Okay. It is agreed. We all go back," Nils said, unfolding his map. "There's an ice spine to our north, so they can't have gone in that direction. I presume they're behind and south of us in the glacier flatlands. That's where we'll search."

"The storm. When is it coming?" Per asked.

"We're going," Alice snapped, stomping out the door flap. "Now."

They all ran to their snowmobiles. Alice thought about her father. Killed in Africa by bandits. She'd been working in London and not with him on his expedition. She couldn't save her father, but she was not about to lose Michael, the other man in her life. Fate couldn't be that cruel to her.

The five snowmobiles turned to the left and headed southwest. Following Per, Alice scanned the horizon and the moving sky lights. As soon as the storm blew over, she would be fine. The moonlight would help her see.

She should have noticed that Michael's headlight was gone, but she'd been so busy watching Per's pack sled she'd never noticed the difference in the backlighting.

Per. She had never felt comfortable about him, and her latest conversation with him had confirmed his hard-hearted nature.

"I see a snowmobile," Nils shouted over the communicator. "Due south."

Thank God.

Alice strained to see who it was. All she could see was a snowmobile on its side.

"Alice." Michael's voice shouted over the communicator. "Nils."

Nils pulled up to Michael, who was standing next to his vehicle waving his arms over his head. The others followed.

Alice jumped out of her snowmobile and ran to Michael. They hugged clumsily in their bulky scooter outfits, then rolled up their facemasks and kissed wildly, their goggles clacking awkwardly. His cold lips chilled her.

"What happened?" she cried.

"I don't know. One minute you were there, the next I was alone. I must have dozed, because I called and you were out of my radio range."

"Where's Etienne?"

"When the weather cleared I was alone. I couldn't raise him on the radio."

Nils, Per and the two others pulled up. Nils extended his hand. "It's the good Lord's blessing that you are alive."

After they shook hands vigorously, Nils asked, "How did you tip over?"

"I was heading into a group of polar bears, so I turned and stopped — too fast."

"Bears? How did you get them to leave?"

"I shot them with my flares."

"Let's get the snowmobile upright," Per said. "We have to go. Another storm is coming."

All four men pushed the snowmobile upright. Alice called repeatedly on her radio, "Etienne, do you hear me?"

"We must go," Per repeated.

"No way. Etienne is still out there," Alice said.

Michael eyed Per incredulously. "I have to go back for him," he said. "It's my fault he got lost."

"We all go back," Nils ordered.

"Damn you all," Per snapped. "We'll never find this body of yours if we don't move on. My orders are to find—"

"We're going back for Etienne," Alice said flatly.

Nils gestured with one mittened hand. "We split up. Alice, Carlo and I go west; the rest of you go south."

"We will lose each other when the storm hits," Per warned.

"As guide, this is my order. You said you know the Arctic," Nils said. "We keep in touch by radio every five minutes. Let's go."

Alice stared achingly at Michael. She could hardly bear to leave him again.

Michael had been leading Per and Jan for almost an hour when, in the moonlight, he noticed the flatlands widening and spires of ice sticking up like white candles on a cake.

In addition to the loud engine drone, Michael could hear a creaking noise beneath him. Were they out at sea? Suddenly, he spotted a dark object stuck in one of the flatter, broader projections in the ice.

"What's that?" he shouted. He raced toward the object, relieved. He could see it was a snowmobile. Etienne's snowmobile. But no tent and no Etienne.

Michael jumped out of his vehicle, put on his headlamp and crampons, grabbed an ice axe and binoculars and headed onto the mound of ice, gesturing to Per that he was going to climb it.

After ten minutes of climbing with the moonlight fading, Michael reached the top of the ice hill. Resting his hands on his knees to catch his breath, he spotted a flare pistol lying in the snow just past his feet, but no footprints. He lifted his binoculars and searched the ice field. *Where are you, Etienne? You can't have gone far.* He tried to imagine a scenario in which they would find Etienne healthy and well... with little success.

Looking back in the direction he'd come, Michael couldn't see Per or his man, either. *Where the hell did they go?* Returning to his scan of the ice field, Michael caught sight of a dark spot below him.

Unhesitatingly, he jumped off the least steep section of the cliff and slid down the icy, slippery face, twisting and turning like a skier to slow his descent. Falling ever faster, he banged and slammed against the frozen wall of ice until he came to a rest at the foot of the hill.

"Good God," he groaned.

Etienne lay in a heap, his body frozen, blood red ice framing his head. He had fallen and hit his head. Etienne was dead, and it was all Michael's fault.

Michael slumped to the ground next to Etienne's body, his arm resting on the frozen corpse. "I'm so sorry," he whispered. "Go with God, *mon ami*."

Standing up, consumed with grief and self-recriminations, Michael looked around. He was alone. He lifted Etienne's body, balanced it across his back and began to trudge around the hill, heading back to the snowmobiles. The heavy weight of the frozen body slowed his pace, but he wasn't going to leave his friend out on the tundra.

Michael watched the exhaust from his breath as his crampons dug into the creaking ice. The noise under his feet seemed to grow precariously louder with each step. He moved closer to the more solid ground at the base of the mound. After his second step, he heard the sound he'd feared. A crack.

Looking down in horror, Michael saw the ice splitting beneath his feet. *The weight*. He tossed Etienne's body from his back as the solid ground below him gave way like a plummeting elevator.

He dropped into a frozen pit.

Within seconds, Michael was submerged in the freezing cold of the Storfjord Sea.

He floundered in the murky, frigid water, and the ache of the unimaginable cold hit home. Michael looked up, and in the darkness could only see a continuous sheet of ice.

chapter forty

Sir Hilary waved Reimer into the library, a small dimly lit room decorated with thick, eighteenth-century Chinese blue and white area rugs and glass wall cabinets housing elegantly bound leather-covered books and his collection of ornamental votive candles. One wall displayed a large sixteenth-century painting of the crucifixion, once part of an Italian altarpiece.

Leaning forward in his leather wingback chair, Sir Hilary motioned for Reimer to sit opposite his desk. He gripped a fountain pen in his arthritic, deformed hand. His swollen fingers would barely hold the fine object these days; he recalled that he used to take pleasure in writing with it. Nothing gave him much pleasure anymore. He had just returned from a bittersweet ceremony in which he was honored for funding the new wing of the medical school library that had been dedicated in Jennifer's name.

How was he ever going to continue his philanthropic work? The passage of time had not been his ally. He was old. The foundation needed youthful exuberance; it needed Jennifer.

He sneezed, then blew his nose in a fine linen hankie. "I played with my nephews last week and caught this beastly cold," he said to his secretary. "Put me in a foul mood."

"Do you want me to leave?" asked Reimer, who was dressed in black, which made him look more cadaverous than usual.

"No. Please stay."

Sir Hilary's butler silently entered the room. "Excuse me, sir, a Mr. Koenig is on the phone. Do you care to take it?"

Sir Hilary dropped the pen next to two folders, lined them up then picked up the phone.

"As you requested when you generously gave us the money to fund the Norwegian expedition," Anton said, "I'm calling to keep you informed as to the latest developments in that adventure, as well as other relevant leprosy matters."

"Thank you. You know that I have a keen personal interest in the leprosy affair because of... my loss."

"Yes." Anton cleared his throat. "We have decided to fund the Farberg vaccine."

An instant wave of fury washed over Sir Hilary. "Are you mad?"

He regained his composure and continued in a calm, reasonable tone. "Herr Koenig, the Farberg vaccine is a complete and utter waste of your monies. They have inoculated groups of armadillos with this new virulent strain of *leprae,* and their worthless vaccine didn't prevent the growth of the bacilli."

"There are no alternatives besides the Norwegian effort. It's a matter of expediency."

"Rubbish." Sir Hilary picked up the pen and tapped it on the desk. "The Farberg vaccine is ineffective. Useless. What is it with you people? Why don't you face reality?"

After a moment of silence, Anton replied, "They believe they will be able to develop another vaccine using an attenuated form of the new strain. Optimistically, their new vaccine should be ready within a year, more or less, for human trials."

"What rot. Even if they are successful, development of a new vaccine for human use will take years," Sir Hilary said.

"We have no other options."

An unfortunate decision by the WHO that will result in the financial salvation of a company not worthy of assistance, thought Sir Hilary, but he refrained from saying so. Arguing with Anton would be counter-productive. He poured himself sherry from a crystal decanter on his side table, gulped most of it down, then carefully replaced the glass. "What about the Norwegian group?"

"The last I heard from the Svalbard governor was that they were on their way via snowmobile to search for frozen bodies east of Longyearbyen."

Sir Hilary thanked Anton curtly and hung up. *Idiots.* "Morgan-Wright and Cohen," he wondered aloud. "Reimer, do we know if they have made any progress?"

"Per communicated with me today that Cohen and Roche are missing."

"Morgan-Wright?"

"She's still doing well."

Sir Hilary finished off his remaining sherry. "Quite so. Please bring me any news immediately. I want to stay on top of their activities."

The aching in Michael's arms made it difficult for him to keep himself against the rough sheet of ice. His clothes were like weights pulling him down. He began to do a version of his walking meditation, calming his mind, feeling along the thick icy ceiling, searching for an air pocket, no matter how small. *Right hand, left hand, right hand.* Whenever he found pocket, he sucked in the precious oxygen, then dropped away to look for the break in the ice.

He had never visualized himself drowning. He was an expert swimmer and his experience in the frigid San Francisco Bay should help him survive underwater, but for how much longer?

He watched the images that arose in his mind. Alice. The eyes of the wise leper chief in India, boring into him. The eyes of the dying in Pokhara, imploring him. Alice again. *Beautiful, beloved Alice.*

Right hand, left hand. Knocking as he went, then dropping to search. He would not surrender to his exhaustion. This time, when Michael swam back up to the surface for air, he saw a lighted circle on the ice. Struggling toward it, he banged on the ice directly below the spot. The lighted area moved slowly away. Michael followed.

His breath gone, Michael prayed that the hole was near. He could last only a few more seconds before losing consciousness. With his lungs screaming and his arms leaden and burning, he couldn't go on.

The light brightened and a beam penetrated the rippling black water.

The crack.

With his last bit of strength, Michael reached the hole. He grasped the edge of the ice and lifted his face out of the water, gasping for air. But he was unable to move, no longer having the strength to pull himself out.

Jan grasped Michael's hand and yanked. Michael's drenched body emerged from the frigid water into the even more frigid air. Per grabbed Michael's shoulder and the two men pulled him onto the solid ice.

He lay on his back, panting for air, all his strength gone.

"Jan, get the snowmobile. Hurry," Per barked to his associate.

Per kneeled next to Michael. "It was brave of you to try to bring Etienne back, but not wise."

Michael tried to speak, but couldn't.

"We must change your clothes immediately or you'll die from hypothermia."

Michael grunted.

"It's going to get colder before it gets warmer," Per said, pulling off Michael's dripping scooter jacket and cap. Michael began to shiver violently, his teeth clattering uncontrollably.

"Now your shoes, socks and pants." While Per continued to undress Michael, the snowmobile came into sight. "Bring dry clothes and a towel from the pack," Per shouted. "Fast."

"Thanks," Michael managed to stammer.

"Alice says we need you," Per said. "Don't try any more foolishness."

Jan ran over with clothes and a towel. Per rubbed the towel vigorously over Michael's nude, trembling body, then he and Jan dressed him in the dry but cold clothes. After Michael was fully dressed, Per supported him over to Jan's snowmobile.

With effort, Michael climbed in, followed by Per. "Jan, take my snowmobile back," Per yelled.

After driving off, Per radioed Nils. "We found Etienne. He's dead. Michael fell through the ice into the fjord. We're heading back to the base camp with him as fast as possible. We'll see you there."

Michael found his quivering voice. "Poor Etienne," he was able to mumble. "A good man, lost in the sea."

Huddled in the heated tent, Michael drank hot chocolate while Jan worked outside with the gear and Per paced the small space.

"As soon as Nils and the others arrive we must leave," Per insisted. "Another storm is heading our way."

Michael waited until Per turned toward him to make eye contact. "Thanks again, Per."

Per sat next to him and poured some tea. "It's what I'm here for — to help the team."

"Mind if I ask you a personal question?"

"I don't know. Ask."

"Are you a hired professional?"

Per sipped his tea. "What do you mean?"

"You and your friends are definitely not WHO types."

A slight smirk creased Per's face.

"More like bodyguard types," Michael guessed.

"You're an astute observer. I usually work as an executive protector."

"An interesting euphemism. Why would Koenig send someone like you?"

"You're in a dangerous place. You need someone who knows the territory, someone strong."

Michael put down his cup. "An executive protector... have you ever had to kill anyone?"

Per appeared mildly amused. "After I saved your life, you ask me that? Your question seems a bit out of place."

"I've been wondering about you three since you joined our team. I thought this might be a good time to broach the subject of why you're here."

"You're too analytical, my friend."

No wonder he had such a cold way about him. In his profession, emotions are an interference. Michael thought about ways he should deal with this strange, detached man. Given time, he would figure that out.

When Michael leaned forward to get more hot chocolate, his amulet swung away from his partially opened jacket.

"What's that?" Per asked.

"A talisman given to me by a friend, Brother Rose. He insisted I take it when I left Pokhara."

"I noticed it when you were undressed. It's striking. Is it an antique?"

"It's beyond antique; it's ancient. It was given to the Order of St. Lazarus twelve hundred years ago to protect them from disease. Their order has always taken care of lepers. Surprisingly, most of the priests lived to an old age."

"Fascinating."

"I'm not the superstitious type, but I somehow feel safer with this."

Per reached for the pendant and allowed the crucifix to rest on his palm, then turned it over in his hands.

"I received a similar gift once," he said quietly. "Looked something like this one, only much smaller. My uncle, a Lutheran minister, gave it to me. He had worn the cross every day since graduating from seminary school." He stared at the rotating amulet. "Then I wore it every day. It gave me a feeling of hope."

"It must have meant a lot to you."

"My uncle was the only one who cared for me. He believed in me, my abilities. He stood by me. He always thought I would do great things one day."

"Do you still wear it?"

Per frowned. "It was taken from me when I was... hospitalized. They saw it as a potential weapon. When I recovered, no one knew where it was. They never found it. In time, I forgot about it... until now." Per released the crucifix. "But that was a long time ago."

For the first time, Michael felt warmth toward Per. They sat in silence for a few moments, then Michael spoke. "I'm going to find that plasmid and prove my theory."

"I know."

Alice burst into the tent, ran to Michael and hugged him, almost knocking him off his cushion. "What happened?" she cried. "You can't keep torturing me like this. My system can't take it."

"Mine either."

"Your lips are blue."

"So's the rest of me."

She ran her fingers over his frosted face.

"We found Etienne... dead." Michael told her gently, "When I tried to carry him back, I fell through the ice."

"Dear Etienne." Alice slumped, her eyes filling with tears. "He was a beautiful soul. I'm going to miss him. He was like my brother." Alice took a deep breath. "Where is he?"

"In the fjord. We couldn't bring him back. Per and Jan barely saved my life."

Alice smiled gratefully at Per, then turned back to Michael.

Per got up. "I have to speak to Nils."

After he left, Alice sobbed. "Etienne saved my life in Tanzania. He's always been there for me."

Michael squeezed Alice tighter as if to expel her pain with his grip.

Nils popped his head into the tent. "The wind is getting stronger. The storm will be upon us within the hour. There will be no outracing this one."

"What do you want us to do?" Michael asked.

"You remain in the tent. Alice, I need you to help batten down all the supplies. We're staying here. The good news is that Isfjord Radio says after this storm we will have several days of calm."

Alice kissed Michael on his tingly lips and stubbled beard. "We're not going to be separated again," she insisted. "No more dangerous separations. My heart can't handle it. From now on, we travel together."

He watched her leave. Though he no longer felt cold, a chill shook his body. He curled up and dozed off.

The howling wind awoke him. Looking around the tent, he saw all of his colleagues huddled against the tent walls. Alice was sitting close, watching over him.

"How long have I been out?" Michael asked.

"About two hours," she answered.

"What's happening with the storm?"

"It's not as bad as expected," Nils said. "Winds are only… in miles, forty to fifty per hour. They've been more quiet over the last half hour."

"We're going to be fine," Per said. "After the storm, we head out."

When the heavy snow and moaning winds let up, the team took down the tent, cleaned the snow off their vehicles and formed a caravan that headed northeast. Soon the moon rose and in the yellowish light Michael saw a familiar setting: a mountain range to the north, flat lands ahead and seracs, mounds and precipitous ice walls dotting the southern range.

Michael watched the ever-changing show of pink and purple shimmering over the northern horizon. He drove on, and the glacier began to slope imperceptibly downward.

Within an hour, Nils stopped and radioed the group. "We're at the coast. We should look for an inlet or cove — a sheltered area where the lepers could have lived. They would have needed to hunt for seal, walruses and other animals in order to survive the winters."

The snowmobiles slowly made their way north. Michael wondered how anyone could survive these winters. When Nils stopped a second time, he called, "Everyone out. We set up camp here."

Michael put up his tent, supplied it with food, then joined the others.

"First we get our generator going. Then we look for bodies," Nils said.

For once, Per nodded his approval.

Michael connected the ground-penetrating radar device, which looked like a small black vacuum cleaner, to the generator, then scanned the area for bodies buried in the permafrost, five or more feet down. The instrument had worked perfectly on his previous dig on Svalbard, revealing several bodies with the flu. Walking in an ever-expanding circle, he spent the next hour searching for corpses. He found nothing.

"Let me take over," Alice said. Michael agreed and trudged into Nils' tent to warm up.

Per was sitting inside, drinking hot water. "Find anything?"

"Not a damn thing."

"There are only two sheltered coves on this section of the coastline. The other one is several miles north. Nils figures the lepers would have stayed as far south as they could."

"Up here, I don't think it would make much of a difference."

Per shrugged. "Maybe not."

As Michael sipped his tea, Per continuing to stare at him. "Anything wrong?"

Per frowned. "There's a belief, a superstition where I come from, that if you save someone's life you have a responsibility, a duty to protect their soul. To remain their guardian angel forever."

Michael chuckled. "I can use all the help I can get."

There was a rustling at the tent entrance as Nils, Jan and Alice entered.

"Alice has the umbles," Nils said, sitting Alice down and grabbing some hot tea for her.

"What's that?" Per asked.

"Stumble, fumble, mumble and grumble," Nils said. "Mild hypothermia."

Jan added, "I saw her staggering around, so—"

"I'm feeling fine," Alice slurred. "I was thinking of poor Etienne, his wife and two kids. Didn't think about the cold."

"We have Carlo out there now," Nils said. "When it's calm, it's deceptive. The cold sneaks up on you."

"Then we should rotate every thirty minutes," Michael said. "Everyone else should remain in here except for emergencies."

Nils nodded in agreement, melting ice dripping from his shaggy red-brown beard.

"How're you feeling?" Michael asked.

Alice began to shudder uncontrollably.

"Delayed reaction," Nils explained.

"Etienne, my dear friend," Alice repeated.

Michael slid next to Alice and began massaging her hands. After a few minutes she relaxed, resting her head on his shoulder while he caressed her locks.

"Etienne gone..."

Michael kissed her hair.

"Do you know how long we'd been friends?"

Michael remained silent, warming her with his bulk, letting her talk.

"He saved my life."

The team continued the search around the clock, with each taking their turn outside. After the first day they moved the camp a thousand yards to the north. Michael slept for eight hours, then Nils woke him for his rotation. Outside it was high noon and totally dark. Switching on his headlamp, Michael took the radar instrument from Carlo and walked in the opposite direction from the area the team had been scanning.

Nils might be wrong, he thought. The lepers wouldn't stay right on the coast because of tides. They would have settled at least several hundred feet inland. If they'd used igloos, the sonar wouldn't detect the structures even if they'd survived; wooden structures may have deteriorated before being frozen. The best chance of detecting anything would be first to find the large stone structure that usually marked the center of the colony. Even further inland.

Michael walked in a northwesterly direction, swinging the radar apparatus before him. In the obscurity of his surroundings, he marched on, two hundred, then three hundred yards from the camp. When he looked back, the camp had disappeared.

With his crampons crunching into the ice and snow, he pressed on, making bigger circles. He had to spread out farther. It would be easier to find a structure than a single body. It had taken days to find a corpse the last time, even though they knew a precise spot. Now, with vague directions, it might take weeks.

If he were a leper, where would he settle? *A sheltered spot near a cove in the sea.* What area would be sheltered? Over the past six hundred years, formations would have come and gone. Looking for a protective wall made no sense. Even the coastline would have changed. Michael stopped walking and scanned the wasteland around him, a flat white tundra extending to the horizon.

It was going to be impossible to find a body. How could he have thought otherwise? A ridiculous fantasy built on hope.

A shiver spread through his body before he marched on.

chapter forty-one

A stream. The leper colony might be near an inland source of water. No. Sheltered. That's the clue.

The plague had hit in the early spring of 1366. Since the people blamed the lepers for the epidemic, that would mean the lepers were expelled shortly thereafter, probably in the summer or fall. The prevailing winds in this area would have been northwesterly, so the best fishing in the cove would have been on the leeward side of the northern landmass. That should be the starting point of the search.

Michael retraced his steps inland and walked along the coastline until he reached the northern end of the cove. He had little difficulty feeling the change in consistency in his footing as he trod upon the frozen fjord, a lesson learned the hard way. *Too close a call,* he thought with a shudder, remembering the sensation of near-drowning under an Arctic sea.

Marching inland, he felt more confident about the possibility of finding the colony. For the first two hundred yards, the radar remained depressingly silent. Then the first weak blips awakened a fervent hope. Michael ran in all directions, looking for the area of the strongest signal. Finding it, he stopped and listened. A large solid object lay beneath his feet, buried deep in the frozen ground, covered by centuries of ice and snow.

Michael tossed the radar aside, fell to his knees and kissed the snow.

"Okay, let's start digging," Michael shouted. "We'll work in a fifteen-by-fifteen-foot area."

Immediately, all the team members began to shovel the surface snow. Twenty minutes later, when they reached the permafrost, Alice and Nils grabbed electric jackhammers and began the process of breaking up the tundra. Within twenty minutes Alice collapsed, so exhausted she could barely pass the jackhammer on to Jan.

The work continued unabated for almost two hours, with everyone taking turns.

Michael organized the continual removal and dumping of the ice and snow into several piles. Periodically, he cupped his face to breathe, trying to lessen the burning in his sinuses caused by the bitter cold air. The slight wind made the minus-forty-two-degree temperature feel colder still. He hoped no one would get frostbite. The team took turns warming up in Nils' tent to eliminate that possibility, and Alice and Per brought hot tea out to the workers as well.

When the work stopped, six hours later, they had removed barely four feet of the ice. Although Michael couldn't see anything in the tundra, the radar's signal had grown stronger. They were in the right spot. After the site was covered with a tarpaulin and secured with rocks, Michael and the exhausted team dragged themselves back to the tent for hot cider and chocolate.

Michael and Alice reconvened the group at ten o'clock. The weather was clear and lack of wind made the low temperature quite bearable. Michael, however, felt chilled.

The moonlight seemed brighter and the aurora borealis more playful, with pastel colors cavorting in the sky. Maybe it was reflecting the mood of the team, or vice versa. Michael organized the rotation of diggers then he began to work, hoping the exertion would warm him.

He glanced over at Alice, an upper crust British woman scientist, in frozen overalls, shoveling ice. Despite the cold, the fatigue from the long journey, and her ice-caked gloves — she worked on. A rugged adventurer. A dedicated scientist that he loved. He was not going to run away.

After their turns, Michael and Alice marched into the tent. Inside, they nodded to Nils and sat silently for a while, thawing out. Michael reached for Alice's hand and removed her glove. Her skin radiated warmth up through his fingers. *How could such pale skin contain so much heat?* He rubbed her hand, letting her warmth spread into his body. For a brief moment, he shivered.

"I read that people thought the rats somehow caused the plague and buried them in the gravesites," Alice informed Michael. "We should collect any animals — rats, whatever, that are near the bodies. Gather human intestines as well as bones."

"It's cold enough. We should find intestines and rats aplenty." Michael grinned broadly. "Al, you're a rat genius."

"I'll have to get special media for growing the material from rodents." Alice turned to Nils. "I'll give you a list of items. You can get them from the Longyearbyen Clinic pathology lab. They can have it all ready when we return."

"I'll use Per's short-wave to radio back and have one of my cousins get what you need." Nils frowned. "What if you find nothing here?"

"Think positively. The fates owe us," Michael said through chattering teeth, unable to shake the cold.

"Michael, I can't help thinking about that same possibility, of not finding a live germ," Alice admitted.

"We have to find it. Brother Rose, everyone, is counting on us. We have to stop the leprae before the accelerated spread kicks in."

Nils left the tent.

Michael shivered, then clapped his hands against his body. A shuddering gripped his body and wouldn't let go. He rubbed his hands together without effect.

Alice asked, "Are you okay?" She felt his forehead. "You're hot. Feverish."

"Damn this cold weather and my icy swim. I must be getting the flu."

Nils rushed in. "We found something."

Michael and Alice dashed out to the site. The hole was seven feet deep. At the bottom, in the center, was a grouping of stones arranged in a circle.

"It's a religious sign," Michael said, "usually placed at the edge of a village to protect the people."

"Which direction should we dig?" Jan asked.

Scanning the cove and the coastline, Michael pointed northward. "Use the radar and go in that direction. I bet you'll find bodies there. They had crude instruments for digging, so the graves shouldn't be deeper than the stones."

Climbing out of the hole, Nils grabbed the radar and walked off, swinging the instrument before him.

Michael trudged back into the tent, swallowed two aspirins and sat back waiting for more news. His chills relented only after he drank hot tea.

Within the half-hour, Per came into the tent to announce, "We found something — size of a body and at the right depth." Then he quickly disappeared.

His fever tiring him, Michael dozed until Nils returned to awaken him. "We have a body."

Michael hurried out to the site and saw, in one corner of the hole, partially exposed clothing and an arm. The jump into the shallow pit made his knees buckle. His strength was leaving him. He examined the exposed bones. "They're pitted. We've struck gold," he shouted joyfully, looking up at Alice.

"Let's use the ice picks to chip down to the clothes. Be careful," Alice said.

While Jan and Carlo chipped away, Nils tossed Michael a battery-charged hair dryer, which he used to loosen the clothes from the body. Occasionally Michael aimed the dryer at himself to relieve his shivering. It didn't help.

The deceased appeared to be a man in his thirties or forties, wearing layers of hide and fur. The remains of his skin were as dark and leathery as his clothing and clung like a sack to the rib cage beneath. His scalp still held sparse wisps of hair. His eye sockets were empty, but the eyelashes were intact and his cheekbones and teeth protruded in a welcoming grin. As would be expected in a leper colony, he was missing the ends of his fingers and toes.

"Get me the core biopsy remover," Michael shouted. Despite his worsening aches, he was too excited to stop. Alice passed down the instrument, a nine-inch-long hollow cylinder that had circular grooves on its outside, like a screw with a serrated edge on the tip. After driving it into the body, Michael pulled it out, removing successive layers of lung, liver and spleen.

He passed the tissue up to Alice, who bagged the specimens. He smiled to himself when he saw the man's belly protruding with intestinal tissue. In Nils' tent, Alice and Per distributed the tissue specimens into a series of labeled tubes filled with different types of media. Alice also spread tissues onto a variety of culture plates.

"There's a rat here," Jan yelled.

"Dig it out and give it to Alice."

Michael felt his ague growing worse. The damn dip in the fjord must have lowered his resistance. It had to be the flu. The onset was acute, his fever high. He'd have to get one of the new flu pills or inhalants as soon as they got back to town.

When fifty samples had been taken, Michael climbed out of the hole and kissed Alice's cheek but couldn't feel anything — his lips were numb. "I think we got it," he whispered, shaking and perspiring.

Alice took one look at him and frowned. "Are you sure you're okay?"

"I'm coming down with the flu." Turning to Nils, Michael said, "Do you think we can dig out the whole body and take it back?"

"Is it necessary?"

"It'll increase the odds tremendously."

"Then we do it. Considering the temperature, if we leave a coating of ice on the body we should be able to get our friend here back to Longyearbyen in a completely frozen state."

Jan and Carlo jumped back into the hole and began jackhammering around the body.

"See if there are any other bodies or rats in the area. We need all the specimens we can find."

Michael headed for the tent where he tossed down several more aspirins.

Later that night, Michael awoke feeling better — less feverish and sweaty. Everyone else was asleep. They needed it.

What bothered him was the fact that despite four more hours of searching, no more bodies had been found. Why was there only one body? The only conclusion he could reach was that they had found one of the last survivors of the colony. The others must have been buried deeper and further afield. *A lonely death,* Michael reflected.

Anxious about the condition of their only specimen, whom the team had nicknamed Lazarus One, Michael quietly left the community tent and walked over to Nils' pack sled to examine the frozen body and rat that were strapped to the vehicle. The aurora borealis had disappeared, as had the moon; only his headlamp brightened the area.

He gazed at the frozen specimens. The plasmid had to be there.
The sound of crunching snow startled him.

Polar bears.

He shut off his light and crouched next to the vehicle, his instincts
telling him that he shouldn't move. He remained still. *Why didn't the
trip wires go off?* When the noise continued to get closer, Michael
dropped to the ground beside the sled.

The animal approached, stepping almost silently. Michael heard
labored breathing. It sounded like a person exhaling, not a bear
grunting. The noise was less than ten feet away.

Then Michael heard a barely audible whistle. In a few seconds
another whistle came in response from the opposite side of the camp.
He listened as another person approached. Now the two figures were
standing not fifteen feet away. His heart pounded so loudly he was
certain they would hear it.

One of the men said, "He's out here somewhere. He left the tent a
few minutes ago."

Two headlamps flashed on.

It was Carlo and Jan.

"He can't be far," Jan said while the lights scanned the area.

"Why do we have to get him first? The others are easier," Carlo
grunted.

"Those are the orders. He's the key. After we take care of him, the
rest will be easy. They're all asleep."

Michael stifled a gasp. *What the hell?* He saw the glint of Jan's
headlamp reflecting off the object Carlo removed from his pocket, a
long narrow stiletto.

"You hear anything?" Jan whispered.

The two men remained motionless for a couple of minutes — for
Michael, an excruciatingly long period of time.

Finally, Carlo said, "There's nothing here. Let's check his snowmobile."

Michael's leg muscle cramped and a sharp pain shot through his
body like an electric charge. He was familiar with this type of pain,
because it occurred whenever he meditated in the lotus position for a
long time. He had no choice but to remain still. He had no weapon.

The pain in Michael's leg continued to worsen — he had to
stretch it out.

The men moved away, heading back toward the camp. Michael breathed a sigh of relief and stretched out his aching leg. His foot bumped a discarded soup can. The faint noise sounded to Michael like a rocket blasting off.

The two men froze and turned. Whispering to each other, they separated and moved deliberately in Michael's direction. When a second knife appeared in Jan's hand, Michael lowered himself so that he lay flat on the ground, then he slid under the pack sled.

How was he going to survive the attack?

The two men drew closer, until they stood less than seven feet away. A chill gripped Michael's body as Jan and Carlo, knives in hand, started moving toward him, crouched and ready to spring.

Standing in the middle of the deserted street, Vera and her team of four looked down Madison Avenue toward the skyscrapers to the north. Not a car or National Guardsman to be seen. They were alone in the middle of the normally-teeming Garment District, amongst thousands of people, all indoors. She was most concerned about the people they could hear coughing through open windows. They were the ones dying of leprosy, but there was nowhere to send them. The Lord was going to be receiving many this day. Too many.

Heading down the street to the Red Cross van, she passed heaps of uncollected trash littering the sidewalks, and several abandoned cars that had been stripped to skeletons. The scene looked as if everything had been painted with a dirt-laden brush. The entire area smelled foul. The monotonous sameness of the surrounding slum enveloped her — thousands of people stuffed into this prison. She wondered if they felt as trapped as she did.

It was unusually warm for December and the forty-five-degree temperature and high humidity exacerbated the stench and made it difficult for her to breathe. Her mask and gown only aggravated the suffocating feeling. Unhooking her cell phone from her belt, Vera called the newly-established New York City Leprosy Coordinating Center. There was no response.

"What the hell are they up to?" she yelled. *The useless new mayor and his useless committee.* "And the CDC is no better," she grumbled. Her cell phone buzzed.

"Any news?" a co-worker from the Bowery asked.

"Hell, no. We have thirty-five workers and a dozen ambulances and trucks sitting here and no place to take anyone. What the hell do they expect me to do?" She was yelling now. "They tell me to oversee the effort to control the disease and no one is cooperating. I told the new mayor yesterday that the dying need to be taken to a hospital and the dead buried, and so far they've done nothing. Since the mayor died, I've had no responsible city contact. Don't they know every hour is crucial?"

Vera hung up and called the local coordinating center. Again, there was no response.

"Shit." She dialed the CDC Office for Communicable Diseases in Atlanta. "This is Dr. Sarkov. I'm sitting in New York in the middle of the goddamn epidemic and nothing is happening. What's with the hospital situation?"

"Sorry, Doctor, but except for Bellevue and St. Vincent's hospital, which are full, the local Manhattan hospitals refuse to accept any patients with leprosy. They're not equipped to handle this extensive a problem."

"What about a burial site? Central Park is loaded with empty space."

"Your new mayor refuses to let you move the bodies out of their homes. He's worried about spreading the germ. The head administrator at NYU is trying to free up their gym for dying patients. We're working on it."

"One goddamn gym? You got to be kidding."

"It's a start."

"I think you CDC guys need to get your asses up here." Vera took a deep breath. "We also need food."

"I'll check on it."

"And where's Dave?"

"On another assignment."

Vera tromped down the street, going nowhere in particular. She passed an alley and saw an abandoned baby crying, and coughing violently. Vera collapsed to her knees.

chapter forty-two

Michael rolled to the far side of the pack sled, the ice scraping his skin like sandpaper. He gritted his teeth. At the slightest noise he would be dead.

Jan and Carlo now stood less than four feet away.

A light played over the pack sled and snowmobile. "No one's here."

"We'd better split. We've a big area to search and not a helluva lot of time."

With that, the two headlights veered off, heading in opposite directions. Once the lights were out of sight, Michael crawled out from under the vehicle. He had to work fast. Silently dashing to Alice's tent, Michael raced in and roused her.

"We're in big trouble," he whispered. "Carlo and Jan have been ordered to kill us."

Half-asleep, she asked, "Are you sure?"

"I heard them," Michael whispered. "My guess is we have less than two minutes to escape."

He pulled Alice to her feet and beckoned her to make haste.

"Per involved too?" she asked.

"I assume so."

"Why in the world would they want to kill us?"

"Take Nils' snowmobile with the specimens. I'll take Carlo's. It's next to his."

"What about supplies?" Alice asked, pulling on her scooter clothes.

"No time. We gotta get out of here now. Change your walkie talkie to frequency eleven. I'm going for Nils."

Crouching, Michael sped over to the main tent, awakened Nils and told him the bad news.

"Nils, can you radio your cousin to send help?"

"I didn't want to worry anybody, so I didn't tell you that I can't find our short-wave radio."

"Those bastards probably have it."

Nils dressed rapidly, and the two of them slid out of the tent and raced toward the snowmobiles. Alice and Nils jumped onto his vehicle, started the engine and began to move out of camp. As Michael climbed onto Carlo's sled, a hand gripped his shoulder. *Jan.* He twisted away, just as a knife whisked past his neck, tearing his mask and scraping his skin like a pointed fingernail.

Michael yelped as the stinging pain radiated across his cheek. He whacked Jan's forearm, then lunged toward his leg, yanking his foot and causing the burly guard to topple backwards to the ground.

Jan leaped to his feet and they stood facing each other. Michael had to move fast; Carlo and Per would surely arrive soon. He watched Jan swinging the knife, readying himself for the next attack.

Realizing that any aggressive move on his part could bring him in contact with the weapon, Michael backed up against the snowmobile. Jan slowly closed the distance between them. Michael crouched, coiling himself into a striking position. Jan lunged forward, stabbing Michael in the shoulder. Despite the pain, Michael sprang up, grasped Jan's arm and snapped Jan's wrist over his knee, breaking bones.

Jan screamed, and Michael heard the clink of the knife as it fell to the icy ground. Lights appeared thirty yard away. Michael grabbed Jan and rammed his head into the side of the snowmobile. Jan crumpled. Michael jumped into the seat, started the vehicle and sped off into the blackness as pinging noises struck the side of the sled pack. *Gunshots.* They were shooting at him.

He ducked low and drove toward the distant light of Nils' snowmobile. It was going to be a race to Longyearbyen.

Pulling a handkerchief from his pocket, Michael stuffed it into the slit in his scooter jacket to stem the flow of blood in his shoulder.

Nils radioed. "Are you okay?"

"I've been better."

Michael swiped at the bleeding scratch on his face with a gloved hand.

"As if the weather isn't bad enough, we have to worry about assassins. They have guns, Nils."

"Why are they trying to kill us?" Nils asked.

"They must be after Lazarus. But I don't know what the hell they can do with him. Maybe sell him."

"To Farberg? Wellcome?" Alice yelled over Nils' shoulder.

"Who knows?"

Checking his speedometer, Michael asked, "Can't you go any faster? At this rate, they'll catch us in an hour."

"With this weight, this is the fastest I can go," Nils answered. "With me and Alice and the frozen corpse and our supplies—"

"In this clear weather with the aurora lighting up the sky, they'll come at us full throttle. We'll never make it to Longyearbyen."

"If we get close enough, I can call my cousin on the walkie talkie."

There was no way they could get that close. They'd have to fight off Per and the others.

"Do we have any weapons?" Michael asked.

"I have the two large-bore rifles we brought for the bears. A few knives, the flare pistols. That's it."

"Within an hour we'll have to stop. One of us will make a run for it with your sled and the body and the others will have to hold them off."

A gastric pain rammed into Michael's stomach and drove into his intestines, causing him to double over. *What the hell was that? Spoiled food?* The pain subsided rapidly and Michael concentrated once again on driving.

Michael scanned the darkening surroundings. Clouds were forming and the aurora borealis and moonlight were fading. This complicated matters. He had to make a decision. In the dark they would be harder to find, yet, it would be easier for them to get lost, and if caught they would have more trouble defending themselves.

Only forty-five minutes had elapsed. Michael opted for making a stand now. "Nils, look for a place for us to stop."

"It would be best for us to fight it out here in the flatlands. We can see them better."

The sleds slowed to a halt and Michael ran over to the other snowmobile. Nils was unpacking the rifles and flare guns.

"I'll stay and fight," Nils said to Michael.

"Me too," Alice said. "You're the one most needed back at

Longyearbyen."

"No, Alice. Nils and I will hold them off. You take the snowmobile and go."

Alice gaped at the blood on Michael's uniform. "What happened to your shoulder?"

"It's nothing. A gift from Jan."

"You have a fever, you're injured and you're the expert with the plasmid. You go," Alice insisted.

"Don't argue. You're a microbiologist. Read my thesis. I don't think you'll have any trouble once you have the viable yersinia."

"But Michael, I hunted with my father. I'm a good shot." She searched his eyes. "I swore we'd never be separated again. I meant it."

Despite his injured shoulder, Michael enveloped Alice in his arms. A sharp pain radiated down to his fingers, causing him to wince. "Don't worry. We're going to make it. I'm not going to leave you. Get Lazarus to the mayor."

Their numb lips touched. Alice blinked back the tears from behind her goggles then jumped onto the snowmobile and drove off without looking back. Watching her fade into the murkiness, Michael was stricken with fear and longing.

Please protect her. Be safe, Alice, he prayed, not knowing quite to whom or what. He took a deep breath of the frosty air and shivered. He needed more aspirin; his fever was returning.

"Let's turn your snowmobile perpendicular to the trail," Nils said, "and disconnect the pack sled. It'll make the snowmobile faster if we have to make an escape."

They grunted, working quickly.

"You stay behind the snowmobile and I'll stay behind the pack sled," Nils said. He handed Michael a shotgun. "Have you ever fired one of these?"

Michael peered at the clumsy-looking weapon. He shook his head.

"It makes a lot of noise and has a kick," Nils explained. "Not very accurate. Great for bears, not so good for humans."

Michael grabbed some shells.

"We only have fifteen rounds, so we have to use them wisely," Nils cautioned.

Hopefully the others were not better armed, but Michael doubted that likelihood.

In the dimming light they sat, tense and ready. *The longer the wait, the better. Alice needs time.* A second round of cramps knifed its way through Michael's intestines, causing him to moan aloud.

"You okay?" Nils asked.

"Never better."

"They're coming."

Michael heard the droning of snowmobiles. More than one. The moonlight made a sneak attack impossible. Squinting at the glacial field, he saw three enlarging dots in the distance. Per was with them.

"As long as the weather holds, we should be in a good position," Nils hoped.

And as long as the ammunition lasts.

The snowmobiles stopped a hundred yards away, Per and his gang invisible behind the blinding glare of their headlights.

Michael heard several pings ricochet against his vehicle and then a splintering, crashing sound as the headlights of his snowmobile shattered, rendering the machine basically useless for an escape. They could use the headlamps on their hats, but the light would be so dim they'd have to drive too slowly.

The enemy's headlights continued to expose them.

Nils fired, making a gash in the side of the snowmobile closest to them. "If we can damage their engines, we have a chance to run for it."

He fired again, missing everything. "These guns are terrible," he complained.

"Let's hold off firing for a while. Give Alice more time to distance herself."

Michael scanned the surrounding area. Their assailants would probably try to encircle them. Holding the light from his headgear at arm's length, he clicked it on, quickly reviewed the area to the side of them, then clicked it off. No one was there.

"Good idea," Nils said. "We'll take turns doing that at irregular intervals so they don't get a fix on us."

Per and the others were professionals. It was only a matter of time before they got the upper hand. Listening to the howling wind, Michael knew their assailants were getting colder and more uncomfortable in the icy weather. They would attack soon.

With the severe abdominal pains and fever returning, and his medication in Nils' tent, Michael was going to have a difficult time staying alert, but he knew he had to. For Alice's sake.

chapter forty-three

Alice kept her compass fixed on her southwesterly position. If the weather remained clear, and she continued moving in this direction, she should be on the outskirts of town within an hour. She's be safe.

The moonlight continued to flood the plains before her. She could see the now-familiar crest of ice to her right. It signaled that she was on the right track.

When the winds strengthened, pushing her to the south, she turned to the right. She must stay close to the range.

Suddenly, the snowmobile dropped, flipping a startled Alice into the darkness. She hung suspended in a breathless moment of nothingness, then landed face first in the glassy snow and ice.

What the hell happened?

Dazed, with her face burning, she wiped the snow from her goggles and turned quickly, in time to see the snowmobile tilting into a crevasse.

She ran to the gaping crack in the ice and gazed down. The fissure was deep, too deep to recover anything that fell into it.

She had to save the frozen body.

Rushing to the pack sled, she worked on the cables holding the pack sled to the snowmobile. She unscrewed one before she felt her feet sliding toward the snowmobile as it continued to slip into the fissure.

The second cable snapped free. *Only two more.* Her cumbersome gloves hindered her movement. She tore them off and began work on the third cable.

The pack sled with all the specimens continued to slide forward, tilting toward the hole. The third came undone. *Now the last.*

Working frenetically, she remained focused on the cable, despite the weight of the snowmobile pulling her and the pack sled downward into the hole. When the last cable unlocked, the snowmobile, in a headlong noisy crash, disappeared forever into the crack.

Alice breathed a sigh of relief, but only for a moment. Even without the dragging weight, the pack sled continued to obey the laws of gravity and crept over the edge of the chasm. She braced herself at the edge of the crack and tried to push the sled back. The bulky weight merely creaked and screeched as the contents shifted; her trim hundred-twenty pounds could not stop the inexorable slippage into the crevasse.

She changed strategies, grabbed her knife from her jacket and began cutting at the ropes holding the frozen body to the sled. Her hands were numb and bleeding. She could barely feel the knife in her hand as she sliced at the ropes. The shrieking noise told all. The pack sled was going into the cleft.

It was too late to save Lazarus.

The specimens. She was going to save the specimens tied to the body or go into the chasm with it. She sliced and ripped away the plastic covering of the body, exposing several of the treasured specimens. They were stuck, frozen to the corpse.

Hacking at the ice, Alice felt her foot slide into the hole. Half of the pack sled was now angled downward in the chasm, teetering, ready to fall. Alice frantically chopped at the ice, her frozen hands burning and covered with blood. *One piece. If I could save one.*

Screeching, the sled tilted to forty-five degrees, slipping further into the pit as it did. Alice jumped atop the pack to continue her hacking.

She was going down.

Michael flashed his headlamp over the surrounding terrain. A half-hour had elapsed and they'd seen no movement from the assailants. *What are they up to?*

Nils whispered, "They'll be making a move. Watch your flank."

"I didn't see anyone. But we'd better look more often. They'll try to time us and probably move in right after we shine our light."

"I agree. I'll check in a few seconds."

Nils flashed on his headlamp, and as soon as he did a flash of light and noise exploded off to the side.

Nils groaned and fell over. Michael fired at the light, then rushed to Nils, grabbed his rifle and fired a second time at the same spot. This time he heard a howl.

Got one of the bastards.

Quickly loading, he placed the rifle on the ground and slid back to Nils. "You okay?"

"I'm hit on my side. I think it penetrated my chest. I'm having trouble breathing."

"Where are the medical supplies?"

"Forget it. Use my body as a shield."

"No way."

The rumble of a snowmobile engine caught Michael's attention. He lunged for the rifle as one of the snowmobiles drove by, heading south. Michael fired. Nothing. The sled continued on. Someone was going after Alice.

This called for a new strategy. "I'm going on the offensive. Then I can get you back to a hospital and go help Alice."

Nils coughed weakly. "Don't worry about me."

Michael loaded another shell into the rifle, popped up to aim over the pack and fired, breaking the glaring headlight of one of the snowmobiles.

"What are you doing?" Nils mumbled.

Reloading, Michael whispered, "Alice needs my help now. If I'm going to go on the offensive, darkness may be my best ally." He fired at the other headlight and the popping, cracking sound was followed by darkness. Success. They were all in the dark. Now to save Nils and himself.

Michael reached into his shirt, pulled out Brother Rose's amulet, and kissed it. He needed help. He stuffed all the rounds of ammunition into his pocket, shouldered the rifle and heaving Nils in his good arm, crawled in the blackness in the direction of his wounded or dead attacker. His stomach began to rumble ominously.

The next cut from Alice's knife broke free all of the specimens in one frozen lump. She grasped the precious bundle and tossed it to safety. The sled vibrated and started its descent into the ravine, Alice on top of it.

With all of her remaining strength, she leaped. Half of her body landed on solid ground next to the specimens. Her lower torso and feet were left dangling in the open space. She tried to pull herself up, but with her frozen hands the weight of her body was too great. She slid back toward the fissure. With a thunderous noise, the pack sled crashed against the walls of the crevasse on its way down.

In one desperate lunge, she reached for anything solid and found a frozen spike of ice. With her muscles quivering and the icicle slicing into her bloody hand, she pulled herself from the hole. She crawled along the ground until she reached the specimens. They were safe.

Shoving her frozen hands into her jacket pockets, Alice sat panting, trying to think. Her hands began to burn like they were gripping hot fireplace logs. At least she could feel her fingers again. She looked for her gloves, but they were gone, fallen into the crevasse.

Blowing on her fingers, managed to grip her knife and went to work on the specimens. She chopped away the large plastic zipper bag holding the specimen of the rat until it separated from the other pieces, placed it under her arm and with her hands in her pockets she rose and tramped on. Keeping the ridge of ice to her right, she headed in a southeasterly direction, looking for snowmobile tracks.

She had not been aware of the extreme cold while in her sled, but trudging in the snow exposed her to the dangerous elements. Every breath burned her sinuses and chest, and her mouth felt parched, like it was filled with cotton balls. Her forehead ached and despite her goggles, her eyes continued to water, fogging her vision.

She commanded herself to concentrate on the path, the sled marks and the urgency of getting the specimen back. Despite her best efforts, grievous thoughts ran through her mind: Etienne dead, Michael and Nils fighting off Per and his thugs, and hundreds of people dying from leprosy.

When the moon disappeared behind the clouds, she found herself in total darkness. Her headlamp had broken in her fall.

Trying to stay focused on her mission would now be nearly impossible. She repeated over and over to herself that she had to get the rat back to Longyearbyen. Her best estimate was that it would take two hours before she would see the lights from the city.

She marched on, her mind wandering. She caught herself engaging in a long conversation with the medieval rat, who closely resembled her cherished childhood memory of Rat from *The Wind in the Willows*. They were discussing Alice's tumble down the rabbit hole into Wonderland, where she met a swimming mouse who had taken offense at Alice's mention of Dinah, her rat-hunting cat...

This was not a good sign. She needed a new fixation. Counting footsteps. It would take twenty thousand steps to reach Longyearbyen. She would do the counting in increments of one thousand. It was doable.

Time passed slowly and she kept losing count. *Where was the blasted moonlight?*

Her legs felt heavier, but Alice didn't give it much thought until her crampons slipped into a small crack in the ice. Suddenly, she was stuck, her shoe wedged in. She wriggled and pulled, but couldn't get her foot out of the hole. *This is no wonderland,* she thought in fury.

"Damn you," she cried out, then remained motionless for a moment, as if she expected a reply.

With all the energy she could muster, she yanked at the crampon and the shoe broke free from the hole. When she tried to take another step she couldn't. Her leg muscles wouldn't respond and could barely keep her erect. She stood helpless and alone in the black, frozen wasteland. She could go no further.

Alice slumped to the ground. A ten minute rest would solve the muscle problem. She closed her eyes. Just for a few minutes, she promised herself. *What do you say, Mr. Rat?*

She must have dozed; something had startled her. Did she hear something? Amid the wailing noises of the wind, there was another sound. A droning noise. A snowmobile. Someone was coming. Off to the north, she thought she saw a light. Was it real? The light continued to grow brighter and larger.

She should hide. She rose stiffly and plodded fifteen feet off the trail toward the spine of rocks to her right, then slowed and stopped. She could no longer move her feet. She had no choice but to await her fate. Maybe it was Michael.

The gleaming headlight spilled over her and the surrounding tundra. When the snowmobile stopped, a figure climbed out of the sled. The driver pulled a pistol out of his pocket and aimed it at Alice. He lifted his mask.

It was Jan.

chapter forty-four

Michael pulled Nils along the bumpy ice until he reached Carlo's body. Most of Carlo's face had been blown away. He lay sprawled on the ice, the blood trickling off his face making an ever-enlarging red stain in the snow.

Nils whispered, "My lungs feel like his face."

Michael shivered. His fever was getting worse. "You lie here. I'm going to circle around toward their sleds."

"Be careful."

"Here's my knife," Michael said. "Do you want me to go back for the other rifle?"

"Too dangerous. Go ahead. I'll be fine."

A wave of intensely painful abdominal cramps struck Michael and he clutched his lower intestines. He desperately needed a bathroom.

With his breath coming in labored gasps, Michael pulled himself across the tundra, the sharp ice shredding his parka and stabbing at his ribs. In the darkness he could see the outline of the snowmobiles to his right, about fifty yards away.

Bent over, his rifle aimed ahead of him, Michael used the darkness to sneak closer to his enemy. The howling wind scattered the clouds and as the moonlight blinked back on, he saw Per, not twenty yards away, turn and aim a pistol at him.

Michael dove between two ice boulders as he heard the crack of a shot echo in the air. Just as he reached the protection of the iced-over stones, a second crack resounded. Michael slammed into the rock. An excruciating pain nailed his hip and side and continued to pound. He was hit.

He rolled over onto his back, the falling snow brushing his face. He had to get up and run. Per would certainly come to finish him off. He struggled to his knees, woozy from the pain. He tried to walk, but staggered and fell onto the boulder. When he looked down at his torn scooter pants and bleeding leg, he couldn't see any points of entry for the bullet. The side of his leg was abraded and bleeding.

No bullet wounds.

His parka seemed to be intact too. His injuries must have come from the fall. Crouching behind the rock, Michael peered out. No one was in sight. The moon, playing her thoughtless coy dance, slid behind a cloud, leaving him in darkness again.

His hip screaming, Michael stood, and staying low, started to limp away. Before he could retreat five feet, he felt the cold metal of Per's gun barrel pressing against his neck.

"Don't move."

Jan approached cautiously, scouting the surroundings with his headlamp. His injured left hand hung loosely by his side. His right held the gun, which was pointed at Alice's chest.

"Take your damn hands out of your pockets. Slowly," he ordered.

Alice did so, exposing her bare, shredded hands. "I only had them there to keep warm."

"That's not going to be a problem," Jan said. He spotted the specimen of the frozen rat under her arm. "Where's the rest of the stuff? And where's your blasted sled?"

"Back over that mound."

When Jan turned to look, Alice swung the frozen rat, smashing Jan's face. Startled, he stumbled, and the gun slipped from his hand.

She scrambled off into the darkness, away from the beam of the snowmobile. There was no way she could physically stand up to Jan. She could barely walk. She needed to find that small crevasse she had stepped in. Trudging along in the blackness, she retraced her steps back toward the trail, knowing the chance of finding the hole was remote. With the strength in her legs rapidly diminishing, she fell to the ground and crawled along, feeling for the hole.

Cursing, Jan raced back toward his snowmobile.

She needed to find... Alice's hand slipped into the small crack in the ice. *Thank God.* Groping along the ground, she estimated that it was only eight or nine inches wide. *It might work.*

The snowmobile swung around and within seconds Alice was exposed to the ray of light coming from the vehicle. Jan hopped out of the sled, stomped toward her and smacked her across her face. "Now take me to the body, or I'll make your death as painful as I can. Get up." He pushed Alice. "Move, bitch."

Alice rose, sliding her foot along the ground, feeling for the crack. She found it, walked a couple of feet beyond, then stopped. Jan followed, but nothing happened. He had missed the crack.

Alice's mind raced. "I'm sorry. I'm a little confused. The body is back over there."

"One more mistake and I'll rip your tongue out."

Jan stepped back, stumbled, then fell backward, his foot caught in the crack. Alice stomped on his hand with her spiked shoe, ramming it as hard as she could. Jan screamed and Alice yanked the gun out of his wounded hand.

Stepping back, she pointed the gun at him. "I'm going to Longyearbyen." She tramped over to the rat specimen, picked it up and headed to the snowmobile. "I'll get someone to come back for you."

"Freeze," Jan said. "Don't take another step."

He had another gun in his bleeding hand. Alice moved on, doubtful that he had the hand strength to fire the gun accurately. The cracking noise from the gun and the lancing pain in her thigh indicated she had miscalculated. She turned and fired five rapid shots at Jan. All hit the target. He crumpled face down onto the ice.

Her father had taught her well.

Alice took a step forward, then tottered and collapsed to the ground next to the vehicle — and passed out.

Whiteness covered everything, as if God had decided to purify the land. But under the brightness of the glistening snow lay the horrible truth. An unstoppable germ was spreading all over the planet, mutilating and killing those in its path.

Rowan pressed her boots into the clean snow, trying to leave a deep imprint in the smoothness. To leave her mark. Ten, fifteen steps and she reached Brother Rose's cabin. She pushed aside the blanket covering the door and entered, where she saw the immobile body of her friend lying in bed. She took a deep breath and approached.

"Brother, Brother."

He stirred.

Thank God he's still alive.

"Rowan... it's nice of you to visit. Considering the risk and all."

"I brought some hot lentil soup — *daal bhaat* — and tea." She placed the tray on his table, lifted the bowl of soup and sat next to him.

"Open up," she said as she spoon fed him. Most of the liquid dribbled away from his mouth. "How are you feeling?"

"Lousy. My lungs seem okay, but the diarrhea won't let up."

"Any bleeding?"

"A little."

After five spoonfuls, Brother Rose waved off the next. "More will be counterproductive." He lay down again. "How are things going for you?"

"Badly." Was God punishing her?

"The WHO sent us the Wellcome and the Farberg vaccines as a last resort. Farberg's is experimental. Neither works at all, or we were too late when we gave them."

"Too late? Do you think I should get the vaccine?"

"I don't believe so. It takes a long time to rev up the immune system. And even under ideal circumstances, the Wellcome vaccine never worked well. Farberg's material may not even be safe."

Brother Rose inhaled deeply and nodded. "Hear from Michael?"

"Nothing."

"I had a bad dream about him"

"I'll call their home base in Norway. Today." She rested her gloved hand on the Brother's forehead and looked at his closing eyes. He couldn't last much longer.

chapter forty-five

Alice awoke in a bed. A warm, cozy bed. Despite the snug, soft nest, every bone and muscle ached. She'd been dreaming of the hawk, circling protectively, shrieking its high, shrill cry. She inventoried the length of her body; hands wrapped in huge bandages that looked like a giant's mittens, left thigh bandaged, an IV stuck in her left wrist. Chills raced through her body, followed by a shivering spasm.

Where was she?

Her throat felt dry. "Hello?" she croaked.

A nurse rushed in and seeing Alice awake, smiled and ran out. A doctor with a red-brown beard and hearty smile strolled into the room and leaned over her. "Dr. Morgan-Wright, good to see you awake. I'm Dr. Kreugstad. One of Nils' many cousins."

Alice grinned weakly. "What happened? Where's Michael?"

"Some of our guides found you on the glacier. They saw the light of your snowmobile. They brought you here to the mayor's house."

"The specimen?"

"It is safely frozen and on its way to the CDC. As you ordered."

"Ordered? Me?" Alice tried to sit up, but fell back on her pillow.

"You were raving when we got you here, but you said enough for us to figure out the value of the specimen and where it should go. Dr. Epstein at the CDC confirmed what you said."

"Did I say anything else?"

"Yes. About the attack. We have police going to find Michael and Nils. Even the mayor left with the search party. We'll save them and apprehend Per and Carlo."

"How long have I been out?"

"A couple of hours," Dr. Kreugstad answered. "You'll be fine. You have mild hypothermia and your fingers are frostbitten. The bullet went through your thigh."

"My hands are numb."

"We have warmed them in hot water for an hour and then

wrapped them in gauze to protect them and keep them warm."

"What's the prognosis?"

"We don't know just yet," Dr. Kreugstad said. "In the meantime it is important for you to eat. I'll have the nurse bring a hot fish soup."

Alice closed her eyes and pictured Michael fighting for his life.

When the nurse returned with the soup, Alice asked, "What's happening with the leprosy? How far has it spread? I've been out of touch for so long."

"Let me get the English paper and read it to you," Dr. Kreugstad agreed.

He soon returned, shaking his head. "It's not good news about the leprosy. It might be best if I didn't upset you with the details."

"Let me hear about Nepal."

"There's nothing about Nepal, but a section on India." He read aloud, *"Leprosy Epidemic Spreads into India. Eight thousand deaths have been reported in Benares and Calcutta, as panic strikes Northern India. Ninety-six thousand cases reported."*

Alice squeezed her eyes shut. That figure was double the number of cases reported in the previous WHO summary — the one Michael had used to calculate the time until super-spread.

Dr. Kreugstad continued, *"Officials fear the death toll will increase dramatically unless drastic measures are instituted immediately. The Indian government has considered quarantining the two cities and beginning mass treatment with antibiotics. The region has been declared a disaster area and Indian officials have requested help from the Red Cross and the World Health Organization."*

"They refuse to believe that the antibiotics don't work," Alice said. "It's typical of the Indian bureaucracy."

"I guess they're trying to give their people hope."

"Anything on the States?" Alice asked.

"Just a few lines." Kreugstad scanned the paper, then read on, *"More than ninety two thousand cases reported as the president declares a State of Emergency in the Northeast, Southeast and Far West. Federal officials are implementing a twenty-four-hour isolation in fourteen states."*

"Michael's friend, Dr. Sarkov, said San Francisco and a few cities on the east coast were a mess, but not the whole country."

"It seems to be spreading quickly."

"Could I call Pokhara to see how my team is doing? I need to speak with my sister."

"Absolutely. I'll dial her for you."

Alice was able to sit up in bed and had taken some hot soup by the time the call went through. "How are you?" she asked Rowan.

"I'm fine. I've had little exposure. I've barely left the lab since you left."

"How's the good Brother?"

Rowan paused. "He's confined to his cabin. He's a little worse."

"How much worse?"

"Diarrhea, shortness of breath, bad cough."

Alice said a quick, silent prayer. "The villagers?" she asked.

"There's no stopping the spread, even with the total isolation and the Wellcome and Farberg vaccines."

"But we know the Wellcome vaccine doesn't work and the Farberg vaccine is still in the animal testing stage."

"Quite true. But Koenig had the WHO send us a batch and requested that we give both to all the healthy villagers. We started eight days ago."

"Anything else?"

"No."

Alice cleared her throat. "I miss you."

After a moment of silence, Rowan asked, "What did you find? Anything?"

"We have one good specimen. We've shipped it to the CDC lab." She paused. "Etienne died." Alice's voice cracked with emotion. "He got lost and froze on the tundra."

"Oh, Alice, that's terrible. And the others?"

"Michael is still out on the glacier. We had some trouble with the three WHO helpers."

"What sort of trouble?"

"They tried to kill us. One of them is dead. The other two are out there with Michael and our colleague, Nils. The police have gone to find them."

"Good Lord," Rowan said, sounding truly stricken. "And you?"

"I have a little frostbite on my hands." She paused. "Oh, Rowan, what will I do if they kill Michael?"

"Drop your gun," Per said.

If Michael could only swing his rifle around he might have a chance.

"Now," Per snapped.

Michael allowed the gun to fall to the ground.

"After saving your life, having to kill you seems such a turnabout," Per said. "A waste."

"I thought you were supposed to be my protector. You don't have to kill anyone."

"I told you it was just a superstition. Just like that amulet of yours. In my business, if you want to work, you follow orders. And my orders are to kill you."

"Wait! At least let me hold my cross." Preparing to die, Michael reached into his jacket to grasp Brother Rose's crucifix. The sharp edges of the amulet bit into his palm. The moonlight brightened slightly, illuminating the tundra — and a moving figure.

Nils was crawling in their direction, knife in hand. Painfully slowly.

Why hadn't he left a damn gun with Nils? His stupidity was going to cost him his life unless... Michael had to stall.

"It makes no sense. Why would the WHO want us dead?" he asked.

"They don't." Per snorted at Michael's confused look. "I don't work for the WHO. I was simply positioned to be hired by them."

Michael frowned. "I deserve to know who commissioned my death. Was it Farberg?"

Nils had stopped moving. He wasn't going to be able to reach them in time.

"Bittner'll need me and Alice to do the work," Michael went on.

Per cocked his pistol. "My boss doesn't think so. In any case, he wants you dead. Goodbye, Michael."

Nils looked at Michael, a weak smile on his face, then he coughed loudly. Per's face tensed. He spun around and fired several shots into Nils' body. Simultaneously, Michael ripped off his talisman and rammed the sharp edge into Per's neck, aiming for the carotid artery.

Stunned, blood gushing from his injury, Per toppled backward, firing wildly into the air. Michael dropped onto the ice and grabbed his rifle, swung it around and fired point blank into Per's stomach.

Flying shreds of clothes, skin and blood blinded Michael. Spattered with gore, he sat motionless listening to the silence, broken only by the wind and his own raspy breathing. He staggered to his feet and gazed down at Per, who now had blood pouring out of a gaping hole in his midsection as well as his neck. Michael trudged toward Nils.

Per was a good shot. Nils was dead.

Michael washed the amulet in the crystalline snow and secured it in his pocket. Then he dragged Nils' body to their snowmobile and lifted him onto the pack sled. Resting his hand on the cold body, he gave his friend his heartfelt thanks and blessings. He grieved for the toll this journey had taken.

Nils had sacrificed his life for Michael's. He prayed that Alice had not joined the list of casualties.

chapter forty-six

A feverish Michael burst into Alice's room and rushed to her bedside. "Thank God you're alive."

She smiled, extending her bandaged hands for his embrace.

"Everyone's been telling me about the heroine who saved the specimen." Michael kissed her flushed cheek.

"I realized how precious you are to me when the thought of losing you became a reality."

"Now you know how I felt."

Michael brushed her hair away from her forehead. "What's with your hands?"

"At last look, the color was good. I think I'll be fine. And you? Are you all right? How's Nils?"

Michael shook his head. "He's dead. Per killed him."

Alice gasped. "That's dreadful. And Per?"

"I took care of him." Michael kissed her forehead then stroked her hair, holding her close. "Thank God you made it."

"But we lost Nils… and Etienne." Alice fought to hold back the tears.

"A terrible price."

Alice looked down at her bandages.

"Don't worry, if the color is good you'll be fine," Michael said confidently. "Dr. Kreugstad arranged for a specialist on hypothermia to fly up from Oslo. He'll be here this afternoon."

"Please thank him for me." Alice smiled thinly.

Michael gently grasped and kissed each of her huge mittens in turn. Then he frowned. "I still can't imagine who hired Per and his men. He said he didn't work for the WHO."

"It must have been Farberg. Lazarus might have been quite valuable on the open market," Alice said.

Michael shrugged and hugged Alice to his chest. "We'll let the police figure it out," he said. "Right now we have an epidemic to stop."

When severe nausea hit Michael an hour later, he finally had the luxury of being alarmed. Lowered resistance, latent leprae in his body. Could he have survived Per, only to have his worst fear attack him? He had to pray it was the flu.

He felt momentarily better, but during dinner at the mayor's house he had to run off to the bathroom to vomit.

"Sorry about that," he said when he returned to the table. "I'm coming down with the flu. My swim in the fjord…"

Alice asked the mayor for a thermometer, and a maid left the room to get it. After Michael sat down in the chair, he crumpled over and groaned. "Cramps." Taking a deep breath, he lowered his head between his knees. Alice wrapped her bandaged arm around him, and he began to shake.

"It's so cold in here."

Alice helped move Michael closer to the fire, then left to get a quilt. He rubbed his hands together then massaged his body, but the shaking continued. She flopped the quilt over his shoulders.

"I'm sure I have a viremia or bacteremia. I feel lousy."

The matronly housekeeper poured hot tea for him. The maid returned and gave Alice a thermometer. Michael's fever was 103.5 degrees Fahrenheit. The mayor excused himself, and Alice sent the maid for aspirin, which she fed Michael along with a gulp of tea. Then he snuggled back in Alice's arms while the housekeeper added logs to the fire. Despite the added heat, Michael's shivering only worsened. He couldn't get warm.

Two hours later, Michael's temperature was up to 104.3 degrees, despite the aspirin. After he took two more tablets with sips of water, Alice, limping herself from her gunshot wound, helped him back to the guest bedroom. Michael staggered; he could barely feel the floor. Alice covered him in woolen blankets and a quilt, placed cold compresses on his forehead, then sat down at the foot of his bed.

Unable to control his convulsing body, Michael twitched and thrashed, trying to get comfortable. He panted rapidly. *I can't get enough air.*

He removed Brother Rose's amulet from around his neck and clenched it firmly in his fist. *Could this truly be leprosy?* Could his dip in the frigid waters have allowed the inactive germ to grow? *God help me. Don't let me die. Not now. There's Alice... and I've got to finish the plasmid work then...*

If it was leprosy, the disease had to run its course. He knew the sequence of events all too well: the bloody vomitus would come next when the germ infected the bronchi and lungs. Then would come the suffocation and death. He tightened his grip on the crucifix. For the first time since the death of his parents, Michael felt futility. He was at the mercy of whatever he had — a microbe. He wondered dreamily where his parents were and if they would be there to meet him if he died.

The mayor poked his head into the room, startling Michael who thought for a moment Nils had returned.

"My housekeeper has a lukewarm bath ready," the mayor said. "And Dr. Kreugstad will be here soon."

Michael's mind wandered as the maid and the sturdy housekeeper lifted him and carried him to the bathroom. In the moist bathroom he felt someone removing his pajamas. *Alice?* He continued to perspire profusely. He felt as if he were drowning in his own sweat. The kind hands lifted him again and placed him in the water. The coolness against his skin immediately revived him.

"Alice, I'm so sorry."

"There's nothing to feel sorry about," Alice answered.

The housekeeper washed his flushed, perspiring face with a washcloth.

"The water feels good. How's my fever?"

"Not great, but the doctor'll be here in a few minutes and we'll take care of that," Alice said.

Michael retched and coughed violently. There was something blocking his throat. Holding up her bandaged hands helplessly, Alice asked the housekeeper to bring a full glass of water. Even after drinking the whole amount, Michael continued to cough. He dry-heaved once, then coughed violently to clear his lungs.

"Alice, I may not make it," Michael mumbled, half delirious. "You finish the work. You can do the rest without me... I love you."

chapter forty-seven

The foul aroma of the enteric bacteria filled the air. Dave sat in the warm and humid CDC lab in Atlanta, watching his two associates from the Colorado Plague Branch, Division of Vector-Borne Infectious Diseases. One slender, the other obese, the pair reminded him of Laurel and Hardy.

The technicians reverently approached the stand-up freezer and removed the bag holding the rat from Norway. With meticulous precision, they positioned the specimen on a Petri dish top and swabbed it with a sterile, broth-moistened, dacron-tipped applicator stick. Next they swept the newly-contaminated applicator tip across several blood agar plates. They repeated the process with chocolate, Sabouraud's and Lowenstein media. Re-covering the agar plates, Dave set them in the carbon dioxide incubators.

After placing three-millimeter samples of tissue in a sterile broth tube, Dave and six CDC technicians spread parts of the rat specimen over a half-dozen clean glass slides. They air dried the slides, then alternated staining them with the Gram and Giemsa solutions. By noon, they had cultured tissue from the ancient rat. Now it was time to examine the stained material under the microscopes.

Dave paced in agitation, awaiting the results.

A few minutes later, one of the CDC technicians yelled, "Dr. Epstein, I think I've got something."

Looking through the binocular eyepiece, Dave gasped. There it was: a cluster of pink Gram-negative rods that looked for all the world like yersinia. He checked the label; it was the rat intestines.

Excitedly, Dave and the Plague Division experts hurried to examine the other slides from the same specimen.

"I found it on the Giemsa and the stain looks great. I think we've got live yersinia," the portly man said in triumph.

The other shouted, "It's on the one-minute Diffco stain, too. Dark blue and looking good."

"Yes!" Dave punched his fist into the sky. "We've got viable yersinia. Thank you, you wonderful Norwegian *ratus ratus*." He turned to the plague experts. "What's next?"

"We've got to grow it to be certain they're alive," the thin man replied. "The colonies will only be pinpoint at twenty-four hours, so we wait forty-eight. We can start testing it then."

"What will the colonies look like?" Dave asked.

"They're small, usually less than two millimeters, gray or gray-white and mucoid, but the appearance is not pathognomic, so we'll have to stain the colonies and do some chemistries to rule out the other enteric bacteria."

Taking out his checklist, the stout man scanned it and read aloud. "We'll test with the *Y. pestes* fraction 1 antiserum, coagulase and fibrinolysin reagents and the phage testing material. That'll confirm whether it's yersinia or not. We'll get on it as soon as we see some growth on the agar plates."

"Let's take a break then," Dave said. "The sushi and beer's on me."

All smiles, the staff and technicians left the lab. Dave looked behind as he flipped off the light, leaving the six-hundred-fifty-year-old tissue in the warm, moist darkness to incubate.

Michael lay in bed, writhing and turning, his fever still at 104.3 degrees despite the antibiotic injections. The mayor and the doctor stood near the doorway while Alice sat at his bedside, resting his hand on her bandaged hand. All were masked.

"The governor is also quite ill," Dr. Kreugstad said. "He and a few of the others who were with Michael at the governor's house have symptoms similar to Michael's. Are these symptoms typical of your mutant leprosy cases?"

"Some patients did have these symptoms," Alice answered gravely.

"I see. As you might suspect, we are all quite concerned about the possibility that they may all have leprosy — that Michael may be a carrier." Kreugstad remained silent for a few moments. Then he gave the cheerful smile that seemed to run in his family.

"It's also possible that it's not leprosy," he proposed. "It may be an enteric bacteria like shigella, from some spoiled salmon or other food. I'm told Dr. Cohen ate heartily at the governor's banquet. I gave him and the others ciprofloxacin IV and IM with the anti-pyretic and analgesics. If it's shigella we'll know soon enough. They'll get better. If not, it's more likely to be leprosy and we are all in serious trouble."

Alice had eaten the fish and she felt fine.

Michael groaned and they all turned toward him. "Did I hear that it could be shigella?"

"A distinct possibility," Alice answered.

Michael closed his eyes.

Dr. Kreugstad turned to Alice and whispered, "There's nothing more I can do."

On his way out of the room he added, "I'll be by tomorrow. Let's hope for the best."

Michael twisted painfully in bed. Alice rested her head against the back of her chair and gazed out the window at the falling snow.

When Vera began to cough, she wasn't surprised. Given her long, grueling working hours with little sleep and high stress, surrounded by sick people with deadly germs, it was only a matter of time. At least she was back in San Francisco. Dave had finally sent a replacement for her in New York.

She slogged down some cold coffee and left the residents' room, dragging herself to the elevator. If she had leprosy, her only hope was that it would be mild. For that to happen, she needed rest — immediately. Her resistance was zero; she was running on fumes. But how could she abandon the ER team? They needed every able body. As well as the not-very-able.

Vera entered the administrative wing of the hospital, where the pastel-colored rugs and drapes and modern, maple furnishings stood in contrast to the stark battered chairs and beds in the patients' wings. The banal piped-in music and insulated walls made her feel isolated from the chaos of the hospital. She suspected the administrators liked to be separate from the painful realities in the rest of the building. They dealt with numbers, not people.

She walked into the office of the Director of Medical Services, trying to adopt her best no-nonsense sway and noted a quickening of her heartbeat. She wondered if it could be related to the disgust and fear she felt for all the bureaucrats in Russia.

The Director led her to a chair next to his huge oval desk, strewn with patient files. "Dr. Sarkov, what can I do for you?"

"I suspect it would be wise for me to take my vacation time."

He frowned. "It's impossible to change the schedule. It's been worked out for the entire year."

Vera knew bureaucrats. "I'm leaving today for two weeks."

"What?" He shot out of his chair. "You can't leave. Especially now. We're already short-handed because of the staff illnesses and this blasted epidemic."

"I live the situation every day in the ER. I know the problem."

"Good. Then you realize that you can't renege on your commitment." He strutted over to Vera. "And where would you go anyway? No one can leave the city."

"I have to go home and rest."

The Director pointed a finger toward Vera. "Everyone needs rest, but we can't just leave our..." He stopped speaking and moved back several feet. "Are you sick?"

"My cough is getting worse every day. Breathing is getting hard, too. My index finger is numb."

"Leprosy?" he asked in a high-pitched voice.

"Maybe... I think so."

The Director turned and walked to the window. Looking out at the deserted street he mumbled, "Of course you can go. Use your sick days, not vacation time."

Vera headed for the parking lot. The rumbling of her stomach told her that she was doing the right thing. She'd call Michael from her home.

Alice jumped when she felt a hand on her shoulder. It was the mayor.

"What?"

"You've been asleep for almost two hours."

"What's happening?"

A huge smile lit his face. "His fever broke. It's down to a hundred and two and he's drenched, dripping wet."

Alice rushed to Michael, ripped off her mask and pressed her lips against his wet cheek.

Michael smiled weakly. "I'm not in heaven am I?"

Alice stayed indoors the next day to care for Michael, limited by her recently changed but equally large bandages, which allowed for little use of her hands. In the evening, when he got out of bed, Michael still looked pale, wasted and weak. The housekeeper helped Alice dress him, then fed him a little supper.

"I never felt this pampered before," Michael said in a hoarse voice.

Alice led him arm-in-arm to sit before the blaze in the stone fireplace. She stared into the flickering orange glow. The spires of flames looked like hands reaching skyward for help.

"I thought we were going to lose you," she said softly.

"You're not the only one."

"Dr. Kreugstad thinks it was just the flu and food poisoning. Shigella or salmonella. The governor is beginning to feel better too."

"Thank God it was responsive to cipro."

After wiping the perspiration from his face, she kissed his forehead. Then Michael rested his head on her chest.

"Before we face anymore life-threatening situations," she said, "I want you to know that I find you irresistible, and that I worship you."

"I am in heaven."

It was two a.m. when the phone rang.

"Michael? It's Dave Epstein at the CDC. I've got great news. I was positive that you and Alice would want to hear it immediately."

"What?" Michael jumped up in bed.

"Our Infectious Disease Laboratory is loaded with the plague from the Middle Ages. Loaded. It's growing on all the plates."

"My God, you've found live germs," Michael shouted. "That's great. Fucking unbelievable."

"We're going to start the *in vivo* and *in vitro* work tomorrow. My people would love to have your input as soon as possible. Our protocol is so-so. Can you fax us yours?"

"Yeah. Absolutely. I'll have Alice prepare one. Or even better, let me talk to Alice about going to Atlanta. We could fly out tomorrow, be at the CDC in a couple of days."

"Then you can direct the rest of the operation," Dave said. "We have a Guest House across the street. I'll reserve some rooms for you."

"One room will do."

"We did it," Alice shouted when Michael woke her and told her the news. "It's fantastic. You're fantastic. The most problematic part is done. Now we just have to see if the plasmid will kill the leprae bacillis. It's almost cookbook." Alice pointed to her head. "I've the protocol stored here, ready and waiting to go."

"Let's pack."

"This microbiology part is right up my alley. The CDC techs can be my hands." Pulling away, Alice frowned. "But I'm still concerned about everyone in Pokhara."

"The best thing you can do for the people in Pokhara is help the CDC."

Alice nodded. "But the Pokhara project is still my responsibility. I have to check with Rowan about Brother Rose and Koirala."

Michael grinned. "In a couple of weeks we'll return to Pakhara — with a cure."

"Let's call Rowan and Brother Rose with the good news."

Michael dialed, then held the receiver against Alice's ear until she could brace it with her forearm.

"Rowan, I've got great news," Alice blurted. "Michael is completely recovered."

"That's incredible. So few people recover from leprosy."

"It was a flu and a severe enteric gram negative infection," Alice said. "And in case that's not news enough,. the yersinia germ is growing. The bloody six-hundred-year-old yersinia is alive." Alice bounced on the bed as she spoke.

Rowan let out a deep breath. "Thank God. I'll tell the others. They need cheering up."

"How are Koirala and Brother Rose?"

"Koirala is fine." Rowan spoke numbly. "But Brother Rose is

barely hanging on."

"And you, Rowan?"

"I'm okay." Alice's sister resumed her crisp tone. "What are your plans?"

"We're off to the CDC. I hope I can be back in Pokhara within a couple of weeks. With a cure."

There was silence at the other end of the line. Then Rowan said, "Be careful, Alice. Don't trust anyone. Things may not be as they seem."

"What?"

"Just be careful." She hung up.

chapter forty-eight

Michael followed Alice and Dave along the narrow, deserted corridor to the quarantine wing of the CDC. Glad as he was to be back in the States and as pleased as he was with their progress so far, he worried about the upcoming experiments. He knew Alice would be up to the job and all that was expected of her. He had no concerns regarding her competence, only for his theory.

"The new virulent leprae bacillus has to be handled with extreme care," Dave said, "so the sterile environment of the quarantine wing has been made totally available to us. Even the yersinia pestes is dangerous. It's biosafety class three. We need hoods with negative airflow and a filtering system."

Once in the wing, Michael watched through a window as technicians handled the leprosy organisms in an isolation booth, using glove ports. Next, Dave led him to the Microbiology laboratory. There, a dozen technicians sat hard at work swabbing, reading and plating different agar plates or working up molecular models on the computer. The scene was quite a contrast to the lab in Pokhara. This one was brightly lit and all white, save for the gleaming new metallic equipment.

"Impressive," Alice observed.

"Looks like the plague samples are in good hands," Michael added.

Dave nodded with satisfaction. "We have only the best."

"When can I get to the animal facility?" Alice asked. "I'm anxious to start working on the experiment."

"So am I," echoed Michael. "We've got to move fast."

"We have to determine the dosage of plague and leprosy organisms needed to produce moderate disease in the hamsters and mice," Alice explained to the technicians in the equally impressive animal facility. She held up her bandaged mitts and smiled ruefully. "I'll have Dr. Cohen show you the special techniques required to inoculate animals with the virulent leprosy organisms."

Michael and six technicians put on sterile masks, caps, gowns and a double layer of latex gloves. Then Michael helped Alice with her mask, gown and cap.

After he removed one of the hamsters from its cage, Alice instructed Michael on how to hold the animal firmly, find a large ear vein, shave it, then rub the area with a specially-prepared sterilizing and irrigating solution. Once the vein dilated, she had him run a thirty-gauge needle into it and inject 0.2 milliliters of the leprosy bacillus that was incubating in broth.

Michael applied pressure to the injection site for thirty seconds with a dry cotton swab, then discarded the swab in the contamination container and placed the syringe and needle in a hydrogen peroxide-alcohol solution for sterilization.

Replacing the hamster in its cage, Michael, with Alice's help, directed the technicians until all the animals were inoculated.

The race had begun.

Sir Hilary finished his after-dinner chilled desert wine, then regarded his somber secretary. "What's the legal situation with Farberg?"

Reimer sat at the glass dinner table, eyeing the array of colorful, health-defying desserts spread before Sir Hilary. He waited until the butler left the dining room before he answered. "Our lawyers met with their people."

Sir Hilary walked over to the bar and picked up the bottle of Chateau Y'quem.

"They want to come to terms with the Wilson Foundation for a mere two million," Reimer said, drumming his fingers on his thighs. "And they want us to keep the settlement a secret."

"That is not acceptable." Sir Hilary banged the sherry glass on the table. "It's an insult to my daughter."

He pushed away the tray of desserts, knocking over several in the process. "They'll make a great deal of money with their vaccine the WHO so shockingly approved for distribution."

"I'll have your lawyers refuse the offer."

Sir Hilary narrowed his eyes. "There is something strange and unhealthy about the relationship between Bittner and Koenig." He poured himself more wine. "I wonder what those two are up to?"

Reimer's fingers went into overdrive. "Cohen is at the CDC. We'll know his results within the week."

In the early evening darkness outside Brother Rose's cabin, Rowan tripped on a rock, and as she stumbled, her hands flailing, a powerful hand appeared from the shadows and steadied her. In the fading light, she faced a huge man, over six feet tall and surely close to three hundred pounds.

"Thank you," Rowan said, her mouth dropping.

"Dr. Rowan Morgan-Wright?" asked the stern-faced giant.

"Yes?"

"I'd like to speak to you about an important private matter," he said in a distinctly teutonic accent.

"Are you new here?" she asked.

"Just arrived."

"From the WHO?"

"I have a message for you."

Brother Rose called out from his hut. Rowan couldn't hear what he was saying.

"Could we speak in the lab where it's lighter?" The man gestured toward the laboratory.

Lighter? Rowan felt a chill run along her spine. "First I have to see to Brother Rose."

The man grabbed Rowan's arm, pulling her away from Brother Rose's cabin. His other hand removed a long, pointed knife from his jacket. "Move on or this instrument will find its way around your dainty little throat, ripping out your vocal cords in the process."

A light was on in the laboratory, the door open. The man tossed Rowan against the lab bench, then placed the knife against her neck. "I've got a few questions. And if you give me the right answers, this will all be over, painlessly. Are there any records kept of your telephone conversations?"

"I think there are," Rowan answered, her voice coming in a high squeak.

The man twisted the knife against her skin. "Where are they?"

"I don't know," Rowan mumbled, too frozen to move. "All my conversations have been recorded."

The man glared at Rowan, his eyes narrowed to slits. "Why don't I believe you?"

"Stop."

The man spun as Koirala charged. Rowan pulled away, shrieking as her assailant thrust the knife at Koirala. The handsome Indian dodged, but not quickly enough. The blade bit into Koirala's arm.

Koirala grunted, then swung a half-full Pyrex container of boiling water at the goliath stranger. It shattered on the side of the man's head. The attacker tottered back toward the wall screaming, then fell to the floor, dazed. Koirala and Rowan dashed out of the lab.

"Run," she panted. "Get help. Hurry."

Koirala looked at her with unspoken questions etched on his face. *Who was that guy? Why would someone attack you? What's going on?* Then he hurried off.

Rowan ran into the darkness, knowing perfectly well why this assassin had appeared. Trusting her associates had almost been a fatal mistake and not one she was going to repeat.

Early the next morning, with the team gathered around Michael, Dave yelled, "Look at the culture plates."

Michael opened the first plate and found the yersinia growing as a continuous sheet all over the agar surface. No leprae colonies were present. Opening plate after plate, he saw no leprae.

Michael ran to the microscopes and peered into the eyepiece of the first one. There were plague organisms all over the slides taken from the culture plates in every high-powered field — and no leprosy.

"The leprosy germs didn't grow," Michael shouted. "It works."

Alice, beaming, let out a yell.

"There is absolutely no leprae anywhere." Michael hooted. "The wonderful, beautiful plague and its plasmid killed the leprae. Thank God." Michael lifted Alice in the air, then let her fall against his chest. He pressed his lips against hers.

Dave whooped it up. "This is as fucking good as it gets."

"So the yersinia definitely kills the leprae," Michael shouted. It was as if he still didn't believe it. "We'll be able to stop the epidemic."

Alice held up her bandaged hands. "Two caveats," she warned. "We have to test it against the new strain of leprae *in vitro,* and we have to see if the *in vivo* experiment works, too."

"It should, shouldn't it?"

"We can't be completely sure yet. There may be a competitive inhibition involved on the plates. That *in vitro* phenomenon wouldn't translate to the human situation," Alice said. "Remember, the leprae don't grow well anyway, even on this special media."

The triumphant cheers in the room faded.

Alice quickly added, "Don't get depressed. The plasmid should work against the more virulent strain, too, and usually the *in vivo* results will mirror the *in vitro* results."

"What's the quickest way of determining which it is?" Dave asked.

"Unfortunately, there is no quick way. All we can do is wait on the animal work. That will definitely give us the answer."

"Damn." Michael punched his fist with his hand. "More waiting. We don't have time to wait."

"Only a few days more," Alice said. "If it's the plasmid killing the leprosy, then the animals won't get leprosy. If it's only an *in vitro* or culture plate phenomenon, then most or all of the animals will get the disease."

Michael threw the paper with the lab results onto the bench. If this didn't work, he'd be devastated. The whole world would be devastated.

Although there wasn't any news, Michael called Vera to report on their progress and to get and update on what was happening in San Francisco.

"Mission General Hospital," a voice said.

"Can you page Dr. Sarkov?"

After a few moments a squeaky voice said, "Six B. Nurse Fleming."

"I'm trying to reach Dr. Sarkov."

"I'm sorry, she's not available. Who's calling?"

"I'm Dr. Cohen. A close friend."

"She's very sick, Doctor. Critical. She's in intensive care with Hansen's disease…"

Michael let the receiver fall from his hand. *Not Vera*.

chapter forty-nine

Several days after the plasmid-protected mice and hamsters had been inoculated with the *M. Leprae,* Alice ordered the technicians to begin killing the animals. It was time to start testing their tissue for the presence of live leprosy organisms.

Since these technicians hadn't worked with this bacillus before, Alice instructed the group. "Remember, this is a double-blind experiment with an extremely virulent leprae organism. You gave half of the animals the placebo treatment. They'll serve as controls and they'll have the deadly leprosy. So be careful in handling all of the animals. Wear your gowns, masks and double gloves at all times. If you cut through the gloves, check for bleeding. If you cut yourself, you must sterilize and cauterize the spot immediately."

Michael added, "Hopefully, we'll see a major difference."

Alice could sense everyone's anxiety over handling the leprae. "We don't have to tell you how critical our success might be to the world. I congratulate you on being part of such important but dangerous work.

"The safe technique for sacrificing these animals is similar to your routine one. There are only a few, but important, differences. Dr. Cohen is going to take care of the first few animals."

Alice instructed Michael to inject Nembutal into the ear vein of a hamster, dab the slight bleeding with an alcohol sponge, then gently remove the sleeping animal from its cage. Laying it on a long stainless steel table that had several holes in it to catch runoff blood and other bodily fluids, Michael then injected it with another, lethal dose of Nembutal solution. The animal soon expired due to chemically induced respiratory paralysis.

Turning the animal over, Michael incised the stomach with a number eleven blade on a Bard Parker handle. When the expected greenish liquid flowed out of the abdomen, he used a small pipette connected to a rubber suction ball to collect one milliliter of the fluid, which he released into a small vial labeled with a code number.

Next, Michael meticulously removed pieces of dark maroon liver and brick-colored spleen from the animal's body, storing each piece in its own small vial. After snipping off skin and muscle tissue, he crushed the animal's skull with rongeurs, then separated the bony plates and removed brain tissue.

After disposing of the animal in a contaminated materials bin, Michael took the vials with the hamster samples to the adjoining lab where he cultured the tissues and examined the specimens grossly under the dissecting microscope. Lastly, he fixed the tissue in formalin.

"Later, a different tech will imbed, slice and stain this tissue, then label it with a code," Alice told the team. "A third tech will examine it under the high-power microscope. This way none of you will know whether the specimens you are examining came from the infected group or the control group." She looked around. "Any questions?"

The expressions of apprehension had turned to eagerness.

"Okay, then. Let's go."

Michael hung his coat on an old-fashioned brass rack, then went to wash his hands in the chipped, white porcelain basin in the half bathroom of the foyer of the CDC guesthouse. He emerged to escort Alice into the tawny-colored dining room filled with mismatched worn chairs, threadbare brown throw rugs and a long dark wooden dining table. The other guests — visiting dignitaries and on-loan technicians —, a dozen people in all, were already eating supper. None spoke. The tension was nearly unbearable. The *in vivo* experiments had to work.

At the buffet, Michael filled his plate, then Alice's, with a whitefish and pasta that resembled wallpaper paste. They, too, ate in silence, Michael's mind filled with thoughts of the consequences of a failed experiment.

After dinner, Michael sat with Alice on their bed. Her right bandage had been removed and she continually flexed and relaxed the splotchy, red and white hand.

"It feels good," she said. "I was lucky. No impairment. But my left hand still burns. The doctor says that bandage stays on for another week."

"This waiting for the lab results is hell."

"We did everything right," Alice said.

Michael massaged Alice's right hand. She closed her eyes and wrapped her arms around him.

For the first time all day, Michael felt certainty, a sensation as unglamorous and matter-of-fact as the gaze of the leper chieftain in India, peaceful and resolute.

"I can feel it, Al," he said softly. "I don't know how I know, but I know it's going to work."

chapter fifty

Sitting at a table outside a small straw tea hut on top of a hill in Nagarkot, Nepal, Rowan stared numbly at the eastern range of the Himalayas. She drank her hot tea with yak milk, as the colorful Buddhist prayer flags strung from the teahouse flapped in the strong breeze like saluting soldiers. Normally, the noise and the wind would have bothered her. Not today. She had other things on her mind.

If she could only go back to that pivotal meeting. She tortured herself with the thought of how easy it would have been to simply walk away. If she had only said no. But his offer had been so generous. All she had to do was tell him Michael and Alice's plans. It had seemed harmless at the time.

Rowan looked at the green and yellow terraced fields leading up the hill and marveled at the beauty of her surroundings. An empty beauty at the moment, filled with desperation and regret.

Off in the distance, she could make out a small black dot winding its way up the hill like an ant searching for food. The dot eventually became recognizable as a car. Rowan felt as if two hands were pressing on her chest. The arrival of that car would bring her closer to finality. There would be no escaping her destiny.

"*Chiyaa?* Ma'am, want more tea?" the waiter asked.

"Yes, please. I am expecting a guest. Could you please prepare another pot for him?"

The waiter bowed and left.

Rowan watched her freedom slipping away as the taxi drew closer. Scanning the horizon once more, she mused that this would be a good place for this phase of her story to end.

The taxi pulled up to the hut and she couldn't help but smile when she saw Brother Rose. His miraculous recovery was one of the few joys in her life. He hobbled over on his crutches, clearly still recovering from his leprosy. His damaged legs dragged behind him.

"Rowan," he said, opening his arms and accepting her with his embrace. After a few moments, they sat down and balanced themselves on the fragile, misshapen wooden chairs.

"I heard about your turnabout. It's wonderful," Rowan said.

Brother Rose grinned. "The doctors think that my twenty-six years of working with people with leprosy built up my immunity."

"How are you now?"

"I only lost one finger." Brother Rose held up his right hand and exposed the withered remains of his index finger. "And, of course, my feet have limited function. But some of that may come back. I'm feeling stronger. And you?"

"No signs of the disease."

Brother Rose's laugh lines creased with concern. "I was worried when you suddenly left. Then I received your fax saying you needed to meet with me. And in such a desolate spot."

"I'm sorry to have brought you all the way out here, but I had to get away from Pokhara and I wanted to speak to someone. I thought it best that it be you."

"I'm honored," Brother Rose said. "You've become a dear friend. What's troubling you?"

"Have you heard about Michael?"

"Yes, it's wonderful. In good health and his discovery seems to be working. The veil is lifting." Brother Rose used his left hand to position his teacup in his right. "I needed to learn a new technique without that right index finger," he noted jovially. "I'm better with the handle-less cups."

"Have you heard anything else?" Rowan asked.

"Like what?"

"Who the people were who tried to kill Alice and Michael?"

"No."

"One of their collaborators was a person at our camp."

Brother Rose stared at Rowan, his eyes widening. "What are you telling me?"

Rowan cleared her voice. "Brother, I gave them information about Alice and Michael's activities."

"You?" Brother Rose crossed himself. "Rowan, why?"

Rowan shook her head miserably, tears forming in her eyes. "I don't think you'll be able to understand. No one will."

"Try me."

Rowan looked at the bright flags snapping in the wind. "All of our lives Alice has always come out on top, and I have always been the loser. I thought she had finally lost something she wanted when things didn't work out with Michael." She paused. "And I'd had feelings for him, you see. I guess I thought maybe he would turn from her anger toward me... But she's always so perfect, so beautiful you know, and she won his heart again. So when the trachoma project failed, I was happy and when I discovered that amiomycin caused the epidemic. And while I was aghast at the tragic illness and deaths that resulted, I was delighted that it was Alice's fault."

Brother Rose remained silent.

"I know it sounds horrid, but I wanted Alice to experience the feeling of failure and appreciate how I've suffered, you see? When the opportunity to help take Alice down came, it seemed God-sent. They offered me a lab — my own facility to do research. What I always wanted."

Brother Rose shook his head. "Not God-sent."

Rowan sobbed and turned away from Brother Rose. She couldn't face him, or maybe anyone, ever again.

"And you agreed to their plan?" Brother Rose prompted.

"Those awful people betrayed me," Rowan wailed, "I knew nothing about the plan to kill Alice and Michael. I thought they only wanted information on what Alice and Michael were doing. I thought they were going to make it public that Alice was the cause of the epidemic and that she and Michael were wasting valuable time and resources searching for ancient germs."

The waiter brought another pot of tea, left it on the edge of the slanted table, further enhancing its precarious tilt and left. Rowan slowly stirred her tea as she collected herself, then sip by sip she drank it all down. "Now they want me silenced," she concluded.

"The attack in the lab."

She nodded.

"Could Alice and Michael still be in danger?"

"I don't know." She fell silent as Brother Rose waited for her to resume. "Brother, what should I do?" she asked finally.

Brother Rose gazed heavenward for a moment, then met her eyes. "This is a mess, Rowan, but you can still put things in order. You have to turn yourself in and tell all you know. It's the honorable thing to do, the only thing to do."

"Honorable." Rowan sighed, her eyes tearing again. "These last few month... it's been difficult living with myself. Indeed, my whole life has been difficult."

Brother Rose grasped her hand in his.

Rowan continued, "There's nothing for me now. My career will be ruined and Alice, the only person who loves me, will shun me."

"That's not true. God also loves you and so do I. What you thought and did were terrible, but—"

"Please, Brother, don't be too harsh with me," Rowan begged. "I called you because I had to talk to someone. A friend. It means a great deal to me that you came. I need your help." She grasped his hand, her head bowed. "Please..."

A pained expression formed on Brother Rose's face. "You can ask God for forgiveness. For the damage you've done to yourself and the others in your life. He will never refuse."

Rowan looked into his eyes, tears running down her cheeks.

"I'm with you," he continued. "It's okay. I'll pray for you and we'll go to the police together. It's the only path. And you'll have to warn Alice and Michael."

Rowan cried. For the lonely, insecure childhood she'd been unable to leave behind.

Dave's call came on Michael's rented cell phone as he and Alice sat over breakfast in the CDC guesthouse.

"You and Alice better come to the lab," he shouted. "Now."

They rushed up the street just as a car swerved around the corner heading in their direction. Michael pulled Alice back as the car raced by them down the street.

"Drivers here are worse than Berkeley."

When they entered the lab, the techs erupted in cheers.

"What the hell's going on?" Michael asked.

Dave's grin nearly bisected his face. "It's absolutely amazing. All the treated hamsters are as healthy as you and me. They never got leprosy. It's almost too good to believe."

Michael stood still and speechless, a lump forming in his throat. There were no words for the feeling of relief that coursed through his body.

"All the leprae organisms taken from the treated animals are dead," one of the CDC technicians said. "The plague killed the virulent leprae. You were absolutely right about that plasmid."

"Yes!" Michael shouted, poking a clenched fist in the air. Alice gave a delighted whoop and wrapped her arms around him.

"I never dreamed it would work so well," Dave gushed, his words coming in a tumble."We also put tens of millions of the new strain of leprae on agar plates and the plague gobbled them up. More food for the good old yersinia."

Dave produced a bottle of Veuve Clicquot, clearly chilled and stored for the occasion. "Champagne, anyone?"

Michael planted a half dozen kisses on Alice's face and she returned the gesture. Then they turned to shake everyone's hand.

Dave raised both his hands in the air to quiet the group. "This is a historic moment. I'm honored to be here and to have Dr. Cohen and Dr. Morgan-Wright as my colleagues."

The technicians erupted in cheers. When they quieted down, Michael turned to them. "This has got to be the greatest moment of my life. Thank you all for the work you've done. It's really been a team effort." He grinned. "And to think, just four months ago, I was sitting in a coffee house in San Francisco feeling unappreciated."

Everyone laughed. Dave passed out plastic cups. Bottles of champagne appeared as if from nowhere.

"Remember, there's still lab work to be done to perfect the treatment and eliminate any chance of people getting the plague," Michael called out. "Isolating and purifying the plasmid will take time and there are a lot of sick people out there. We still have no time to waste."

"Remember to give the animals a shot of penicillin. We don't want them dying from the plague," Alice said. "And I'll get to work on the protocol."

"In the meantime, the yersinia can be shipped with the penicillin," Michael said. "This germ is going to save millions of lives. We can all be proud of that."

"Here's to my favorite rodent," Alice said. "The Norwegian *ratus ratus*."

The technicians cheered yet again. Dave held up his cup and cried out, "To the Norwegian rat. Let's all get drunk." With that, he started filling glasses with champagne.

Michael could scarcely believe it all. The world was saved from a rampaging disease, a horror that would have more than rivaled the Black Plague of the Middle Ages, and the savior was none other than the very same Black Plague, as though the germ itself had somehow fought its way through time in a quest to redeem itself.

Redemption and grace. Mysteries Michael could scarcely fathom. He'd have to take up the questions with Brother Rose the next time they spoke.

chapter fifty-one

Michael and Alice clasped hands in the lounge area of the guest-house, waiting for the pickup car. Sir Hilary was in Atlanta for a business meeting at the CDC and had asked to see them. *He's probably trying to get a piece of the plasmid business,* Michael thought.

The black limousine turned the corner and parked in front of the guesthouse. He and Alice started down the steps, and the back door of the car swung open.

"Dr. Morgan-Wright, there's a phone call for you. It's your sister," called the guesthouse clerk.

Michael raised an eyebrow. "Want to take it?"

Alice hopped into the car. "Tell her I'll phone her back in an hour," Alice called in response. "That way I'll be able to fill her in on this meeting," she said to Michael.

Reimer was sitting in the front passenger seat. "Good to see you both. Sir Hilary congratulates you on your success. Please settle back. It's only a ten-minute drive to our meeting with him in Buckhead. He wants to toast your accomplishments and make an offer."

Merging onto I-75 Northwest, the limousine picked up speed to seventy miles per hour and at the Buckhead offramp, veered to the right and abruptly exited. Michael and Alice eyed each other in slightly alarmed amusement. The chauffeur drove as if he needed to lose a tailing car, swerving around corners, looking back periodically in the mirrors and running a couple of red lights. All the while, Reimer's fingers roamed on the dashboard.

"Must've been a New York cabbie once," Michael whispered to Alice.

She grinned. "Or he freelanced driving getaway cars for bank robbers."

A few minutes later, they pulled into the driveway of an elegant, ivy-covered Georgian-style mansion. Reimer got out of the car and ushered Michael and Alice out, then waved the driver on to the livery stables at the rear of the house.

Walking up the driveway toward the imposing front door, Michael inhaled the fragrant aroma of the freshly mowed lawn.

"Follow me," a sullen Reimer ordered, pointing with a languid bony hand. He led them through an ornate living room featuring high ceilings criss-crossed with dark wooden beams, elaborate wall trimmings, stained glass windows and Louis XIVth furniture.

Despite the elegant French furniture, the house, shadowed by huge willow trees and Spanish oaks, felt gloomy and smelled musty, as if it hadn't been aired out for a long time.

They entered the den. The oak-paneled room was even darker than the living room, with windows that faced the north. The parquet hardwood floor was bare, adding to the cold claustrophobic feeling.

"This is one gloomy…" Michael stopped talking. In front of him, waiting grim-faced at an antique desk, sat Sir Hilary, a revolver resting neatly by his folded hands.

"What's going on?" Michael asked, pushing Alice behind him.

"It's obvious, isn't it?" Sir Hilary answered. He straightened his tie, then moved his hands back to the revolver.

"So it was you," Michael spit out. "Per and his thugs were working for you. The near miss by the car yesterday—"

"Brilliant Ph.D. deductions," Sir Hilary said. "After those misses, I've decided it might be best for me to do this in person. If you want something done right… In addition, I get an opportunity to personally experience the moment."

"For God's sake, why?" Michael asked.

"You really don't see, do you? Your callousness astonishes me." Sir Hilary rolled the gun over in his hand. "I owe it to my daughter to avenge her needless and horrible death. You two were instrumental in causing her illness then allowing her to die."

Michael held up his hands in an appeasing gesture. "Your enemy is nature, bacterial resistance, the leprae bacilli, not us."

Sir Hilary's face remained rigid. "And Farberg will suffer where it hurts them most: in the financial market."

"At least let Alice go. She loved Jennifer. She would never have hurt her."

"Her amiomycin study killed my daughter, my foundation, my

future. Please, have a seat." Sir Hilary waved his gun, motioning them to two wooden chairs in front of the desk.

Michael looked around to see Reimer blocking the door to the den. Reimer removed a gun from his jacket holster.

"This is so pointless," Alice said, stepping forward.

"It was my daughter's death that was pointless," snapped Sir Hilary. "There aren't any Wilsons left."

"You don't bring back your daughter by killing us," Alice continued. "The Jennifer I knew would find your actions deplorable. She was a kind, forgiving person who never thought ill of anyone and would never—"

"Don't you dare lecture me about my daughter," roared Sir Hilary, rising to his feet. "This discussion is over. It's time for closure."

He picked up the gun in his gnarled, vein-ridden hand and left the desk. He walked behind Alice and pressed the pistol against the back of her head.

"Any last words? Ladies first."

Trembling, Alice remained mute. Michael grasped her hand and squeezed it. Sir Hilary and Reimer released the safeties on their guns.

Sir Hilary spoke to Michael. "How about you? Any last words?"

Michael felt Reimer's gun prodding his left temple. His mind raced.

"It's senseless for you to kill us," he said. "Let's end the deaths. The leprae is the enemy, not us. We can work together—"

"Oh, my dear fellow, don't be tedious. I know that the germ is also an enemy," said Sir Hilary.

Michael looked up at Reimer, whose eyes remained fixed on him. "Then surely—"

Sir Hilary interrupted. "By the way, your time is up."

"I'd like a few moments to pray before you—" Michael said.

"An agnostic developing religion?" Sir Hilary said. "Very well. You have exactly thirty seconds."

Michael felt Alice's trembling worsen.

He removed Brother Rose's crucifix from his neck and held it in his hand. It had gotten him this far. He'd only removed the amulet twice before... during the karate training in London and with Per.

"Your time has expired," Sir Hilary said. "Now it's time for you to die."

He and Alice were not going to die. Michael motioned with his hand. In the momentary silence of the room, Alice turned and stuffed her bandaged hand against Sir Hilary's gun. He fired point blank into the wad of cotton. Alice shrieked like an enraged samurai. With her other hand, she smacked him in the face, knocking him backward onto the floor.

Reimer pivoted to fire at Alice. Michael tossed the amulet in Reimer's face, hitting him in the eye, distracting him momentarily. Before he could get off a shot, Michael swung the side of his hand into the wrist of Reimer's spidery gun hand. Reimer howled and fired off target. Michael grabbed for the gun and twisted Reimer's wrist violently backward. At the telltale cracking of bones, the weapon dropped free. Michael delivered two direct karate blows to Reimer's head. The secretary collapsed to the floor, face down.

Sir Hilary, however, regained his balance and took aim. Alice, her bandaged hand now bleeding profusely, dove for him. She yanked the older man's legs out from under him. He fired wildly. Several shots lodged in the ceiling as he tumbled backward against the wall. When he slid to the floor, the wind knocked out of him, the revolver dangled from his gnarled hand.

Panting, Sir Hilary glared at Michael.

Everyone in the room remained motionless for an instant. Sir Hilary, with a burst of energetic fury, raised the gun and fumbled to regain his hold with his deformed, arthritic fingers.

Michael leaped toward him, grasping his arm. They struggled for the gun, then Sir Hilary spun the weapon around, placing it in his own mouth. "I shall join my dearest—"

Horrified, Michael flinched and cried, "No. Don't!"

With his eyes closed, Sir Hilary fired his weapon and spattered his brains over the wall.

chapter fifty-two

Michael parked his jeep in North Beach and accompanied Alice into the Caffé Trieste. The crowd cheered when they entered. Michael and Alice waved, despite their embarrassment. When the commotion subsided, they sat down at a small table and ordered orange juice and buttered, toasted bagels.

Vera limped into the café wearing one of her trademark silk shirts, which no longer strained across her bosom. *She's lost weight,* Michael thought. The disease and the stress had taken their toll.

She spotted Michael, grabbed him and kissed him several times on his lips. Then she winked. "Don't worry, Mickey, I'm not infectious anymore."

"It's great to see you," Michael said. "You look wonderful."

"Much better than last week." Vera's voice cracked. "And only because of you. The plasmid saved my life." Her eyes filled with tears and she kissed him again.

"I'm glad I'm not the jealous type," Alice said lightly.

Vera turned. "Alice, I've heard so many wonderful things about you. Mickey adores you, and that means so do I." Vera reached for Alice and pulled her into a group bear hug.

Michael grinned as Vera released them. Alice looked a bit stunned, but pleased.

"Thank you both. Thank you so much," Vera said in a gush. "I had to stop in to say hello, but I'm on call at the ER. Can you believe it? One day out of bed and the next day my boss sends me back to the dungeon. I'll call you both tonight. I want to hear the whole story. Every detail."

Michael laughed. "You will."

epilogue

MARCH 2005
JERUSALEM

Brother Rose was enjoying his mandatory recuperative stay at the Jerusalem monastery with a rare nap in the cloister garden when the dinner bell awoke him. He limped over to his cell to wash his hands. The first thing he noticed was an envelope that had been slid under his door. Opening it, he read the message:

As it is written in the Tao: The hard and stiff will be broken. The soft and the supple will prevail.

Peace, Michael and Alice

With tears running down his face, he hurried out of his room.

In the dank anteroom waited a beaming Michael and Alice. Brother Rose hobbled forward and embraced Alice, then Michael. The tears continued to flow. He couldn't speak.

Michael removed the crucifix and placed it reverently around Brother Rose's neck.

"This is a magnificent gift," Michael said. "It's more than lived up to its legendary past. It protected us, as well as all of humankind. Thank you. I return it with the greatest appreciation."

Outside, the hot desert breeze wafted across the vast Upper Sinai wadi, then swept up into the hills surrounding the old stone monastery atop the mount. Brother Rose, Michael and Alice sat in silence and enjoyed the winds for the way they provided relief from the relentless valley heat.

Redemption and grace, thought Michael.

It was the year of our Lord 2005 and the Black Plague had saved civilization.

Gil Smolin, M.D. is a Clinical Professor and Research
Ophthalmologist at the University of California Medical School,
San Francisco. The author of seven textbooks and over two
hundred research articles, he has lectured worldwide and serves
as co-editor of *International Ophthalmology Clinics* and as a
reviewer for many ophthalmology magazines. Dr. Smolin has
worked for many years in the developing world and received a
humanitarian award for his service. He is one of the founders and
a board member of a public charity devoted to offering medical
assistance to the needy in other countries. He served as a consultant to the New Hope Leprosy Hospital in Muniguda, Orissa,
India,where he treated and observed those with leprosy.

Enjoy these books available from Ad Lib Books, LLC

Fiction Books	Price	Quantity	Total
Reign of the Rat *by Gil Smolin*	12.99		
A Matter of Time *by Julie Mears Henry*	10.99		
The Spring Habit *by David Hanson*	11.99		
Kings Row *by Henry Bellamann* published by Jay Miles Karr for the author's estate	21.95		
Landlady *by Erica Stux* published by Winston-Derek Publishers, Inc.	12.95		
Non-Fiction Books			
Adolf Hitler *by Leonard and Renate Heston* Published by Baypoint Press	24.95		
Poetry Books			
Three Faces of Autumn *by Charles Guenther* published by The Mid-America Press	40.00		
The Longest Breath *by Greg Field* published by The Mid-America Press	10.00		
From Ink and Sandalwood *by Cecile Franking* published by The Mid-America Press	10.00		
Telling of Bees *by Ronald W. McReynolds* published by The Mid-America Press	10.00		
Dreaming the Bronze Girl *by Serena Hearne* published by The Mid-America Press	10.00		
Red Silk *by Maryfrances Wagner* published by The Mid-America Press	10.00		
Promises in the Dust *by Bill Bauer* published by BkMk Press	10.00		
Last Lambs: Poems of Vietnam *by Bill Bauer* published by BkMk Press	11.95		

SHIPPING
Number of Books	S&H
One Book . . . . $2.00 USD
Two Books . . . . $3.00 USD
Three Books . . . . $3.50 USD
Four Books . . . . $4.00 USD
Add .50 for each additional book

Subtotal:_____

Shipping: _____

Total:_____

Your shipping information:

Name:_____

Address:_____

City:_____ State:_____ Zip:_____

Make checks payable to Ad Lib Books.
Return this form with payment to:
Order Department, Ad Lib Books, LLC,
217 E. Foxwood Dr., Raymore, MO 64083